W. James Chan earned a degree in Creative Writing at the University of Wollongong. He currently resides in Sydney, Australia.

Blackcloak is his first novel.

"As if David Lynch rewrote the works of George R R Martin."

KIRKUS

"An eminently readable novel...no less than thoroughly absorbing."

San Francisco Book Review

"Reads like poetry from its very first line... a book that demands your attention... the urge to read it through again with discovered knowledge is overwhelming."

Self-Publishing Review

"A hell of a start to an unusual dark fantasy series that deftly combines psychology, magic, and philosophy into a disturbing character study."

Indie Reader

THE BLOODY TAPESTRY OF KAEF'RE

BLACKCLOAK
A MAN OF HIS SWORD

W. JAMES CHAN

Table of Contents

First published May 2015
This edition published by JSS Press, June 2025.

Published in Australia

ISBN 978-1-7640270-1-4

No generative AI tools were used at any stage in the production of this work.

The First Commandment:
There is no God without The Night.

Prologue

Viestrada Forest
Highmoon
882 A.R.

This is how I begin his song.

There is blood on a leaf. The leaf has edges that curl like a tongue, seeking moisture from above. It has lips over which the blood cannot spill. The leaf might lick the rain, but for now it is blood that has pooled in the lush chalice. As small as it may be, this deposit of life is great enough to milk the moon and to hold its light within a shiny bubble. This is mysticism in minutiae, a miracle of the basest order. It eludes artists and their entangled oils. Poets and their unreasonable rhyme fail to capture this infinite, infinitesimal truth.

There is blood on a leaf.

A momentary gust warps the moon's reflection; it bends and swims. The blood is resilient, however, sliding within the waxy-gripped leaf.

"We must hurry. The scent weakens." An ethereal whisper in the distance – but even faraway thunder is loud *somewhere.*

I cannot clarify for you the significance of that sibilant language – only interpret it. A person could no more explain the texture of eternity or the flavour of immortality. Free from the prison of definition, those few words would bypass mere hearing and impress myriad meanings onto an unready mind. A mortal brain would collapse under the spontaneity of it all. But let me share with you what you can never hear. Each hiss, each growl is as sinister as a shadowed glade, as deep as a dark mountain spring and as powerful as the roaring black waterfalls. This is nature's most magnificent savagery given an obsidian voice: the tongue of the Nobles, ghastly masters of my world – Kaef're.

A rustling replaces the wind, not tossing the leaf but shoving it, a solitary disturbance of furry passage. The blood slips again, rolling to the upturned edge of the leaf. It clings for a moment, hangs like a dead pendulum, then falls, seeping into the passing pelt.

"I smell something else, Milady. Feline, perhaps. The scent has diminished. He's gone." Eyes of wide ebony question the Lady.

"He's not gone, Sa'Hres'z," she replies. "Perhaps your hunger for cat has made you dull."

Her callous words are a glacier melting under the warmth of the intimate insult. You might regard her majestic poise and label the Lady a queen, as some dreaded hunt-mistress leading her wild band – but she is of neither legend nor fireside tale. Some wonders are too great, too terrible for even your imagination and fear. Some things you should not know, and so you do not, not even in vague myth or dream.

At least, not yet.

"*Fha*! Milady mocks me? I would not stoop to that, even were my throat as dry as dust." Sa'Hres'z is a Talon, her elite vanguard. He is permitted such effrontery. The other four Talons still bristle at his rebuke. "The cat's smell is too strong now. I detect nothing else!"

"A withering on the kitty," the Lady dismisses, willowy fingers flicking through the dim air. "There is blood on the breeze. Find it."

A cat has brushed against the leaf.

A host of gashes streak the beast's flank. The drop of blood from the leaf meshes with the prowler's coat, attacking the rank secretion of the cat's own. But the conquest is not complete. Were the foul intruder any more than a drop, it would kill the cat with one lonely moment of exhilarating augmentation. Like most creatures of my world, a cat is not designed to bear strength of that magnitude.

Let us give this battle-weary stalker a name, something worthy of his part in this tale. We shall call this cat Longstride the Feral. I imagine Longstride is old, but veteran rather than sedentary; he has lived through worse than this, or so he might tell the kittens if he survives. Longstride, being no ordinary cat, has a history of hunting snakes, foxes and even young wolves. His greatest achievement, though, is he once feasted on a lost two-legged thing fat with soft, nourishing flesh.

And for all this prowess, a little unwelcome blood may bring an end to the legend of Longstride the Feral.

"It moves. Both scents move!" the Talon announces, but the Lady has already broken into a run. Undergrowth bends and flows around her. She plunges past trees, between ferns and into verdant, luscious darkness. Her cohorts, pale and quick, hurry through the heady residue of her imperious but ephemeral presence. The Talons leap, bound and cavort into the dense foliage.

There is rhythm to this gleeful dash, but their cries are silent; the flitting chaos of displaced greenery is enough to drown out laboured breath, should the Nobles even be so exerted. They say nothing. Hunting is their purpose, as dictated by the fullness of the moon. Understanding this is song enough for them: a hymn appreciated only by those who prey with hands reaching forth, paying homage to The Hunt with the timeless offering of stolen life.

They are like fools chasing a poisoned arrow and its sweet promise.

As Longstride the Feral yowls and charges, gnarled twigs and scratching thicket hinder his speed, tearing the wounds wider and offering even easier access for the foul blood into yielding crevasses.

This draws to mind a claw shredding starless gauze:

The hunting party closes on its target. They duck and swoop beneath branches, over branches and sometimes through branches; slicing, flickering silver. Their formation suggests military control, with the Lady taking point, the Talons her wings and tail. The weaving deliberately obscures their number, should anyone dare to estimate the power of the Night's Own.

But one has dared.

He knows how they hunt, thus he knows how to hunt them. He understands the means by which they cut through all distractions to focus on their game, and thus he understands how to distract them. It is his blood that they track even now, and it was he who left it on that leaf. It was his blade that raked the side of the cat; his hands placed that cat near the leaf, near the blood. He is the one the hunters seek, and he is the one who seeks them. In this, prey and predator are one and the same, and shall remain so until they meet.

Then: disaster, as a ritual becomes routine.

The hunters continue to slash soundlessly towards the cat – the only trace of the enemy. The decay of a tight formation reflects their enthusiasm. One Talon streaks around another and that one slides between two more: black ribbons in the wind, curling and flapping but never once stopping, never lagging.

But the Lady hesitates.

One of them *is* moving slower. He who led is not yet lost to the mad song of the hunt and, for one unfortunate moment, pulls back to second-guess his predatory impetus.

She whose dread power once earned her the unique title of Mindwarp stops to look, but it is too late.

I imagine a jagged diamond falling into a lake of oil.

He rushes towards the silhouettes of the complacent night. The lone Talon, although behind the others, is still too intent on chasing a hint of the enemy to realise that the enemy is right beside him.

Poor woman. All she can do is watch. Helplessness is a dirty but belated visitor amidst her formerly exclusive gathering of pristine certainty.

All she can do is watch.

One trained to kill, the other with an instinct to hunt.

Sword and Talon.

The sudden intruder pounces from behind the Noble's back-tracking senses. What was a mere whiff of the prey is now an explosion of immediacy. There is a flutter of fabric; a tenebrous distortion of limbs; two figures thrash into the primal concept of one.

A discordant, lonely crack. The writhing knot unravels. One shadow crumples, the other springs away.

The Lady just stares, for she has now witnessed the death of a Talon, he who once tracked and slew an entire pack of Wolves alone. Talons do not fall, not to mere humans! But surely she remembers: *this enemy is no mere human.*

"Stop!" Is she calling to the figure or her remaining companions? She frowns, and this, too, is a new configuration for her calm composure. Her brow is slick with dark sweat and strands of clammy white hair. She *is* afraid, and that fear fuels her voice again: "Talons! Turn about! The enemy is here!"

I know she does not care if they hear her. Something else is driving her, something more important than the Hunt. It is unlikely that the prey-turned-predator will retain a direct course, but the Lady strikes off after him as best she can. In passing the twisted remains of the slaughtered Talon, she speaks his name.

"Ran'za."

For his quick judgment, The Lady gave Ran'za the privilege of command. Against her slight, he was not the one to settle for cat-flesh. Her most perceptive of warriors has, just this once, fallen behind, and now he will never catch up again.

Ran'za's head rests against his back, as if his neck has been crushed to jelly rather than just snapped. I see something in the Lady's eyes, almost pity, for she has known Ran'za since his birth and taught him much. But then she moves on, aware that even this pause has given the enemy ample time.

Elsewhere, we find three Nobles declaring war on Longstride the Feral.

Mundane sight has confirmed that the enemy is not here, but the scent of his blood is still strong enough to fool them, to make them believe they are attacking more than just a cat. Longstride, eldritch killer of mice, who once took down a young boy lost to these lost woods, does not live long enough to die from the inevitable blood poisoning.

The trio bury themselves in the dire business of dividing the cat into palatable portions. But then one looks up, his lips thick with gore – and even his grey cheeks seem to lose their colour.

He sees.

Fear arrives the moment it exists.

The enemy does not approach the feasting foe; he is simply there, driving a silent sword through the grinning one's face. This time there is no need for subterfuge. The black-cloaked horror scrapes the blade across Noble flesh, severs Noble muscle and cleaves fresh chasms into Noble throats.

The Lady hears the screams around her just as the aroma of death punches into her gut. She knows then what she suspected: the enemy is not easily tracked. She has been proud to ignore the only indication of his presence – the speckle of blood mingled with feline redolence. That is too obvious a trap. Or is she the one trapped? The howls mix and then terminate without even an echo. Three more Talons are lost and she speaks their names as well.

"Inahs'z. De'Hrex. Fana'Hrez."

They have hunted together for countless years, perfecting the extraction of sweet agony from ripe, mortal prey. Now they would practice their craft in Heaven Below.

She falls to her knees and keens a reedy wail – a mother's graveside lament. The smell of rich Noble blood crushes her like a shroud laced with ground glass.

All is lost, all but her. They have been stalking this foe for what feels like so many months, watching his movements and circling the signs, closing, always closing. First, there had been a murder of humans, humans devoted to the Night as was their duty. Blood Peddlers. Then this tool of death found his way towards Noble sanctuaries and brought death to them as well. He gained a name, or perhaps made one for himself – Blackcloak the Scourge. Most consider him a thoughtless storm, spinning here or there, killing aimlessly. The Lady is not convinced, for she has noticed patterns in his chaos. Suspicion was enough to see her descend from a distant home, to see for herself. If everything is as she feels, then perhaps this can be stopped. If she is wrong, there are worse ways of returning to God's heart than falling to one's foe – than chasing a hope, catching the truth and facing a nightmare.

She finds him when the reek of murdered cat and Noble are all but overwhelming.

There is blood on a leaf. There is blood on the ground. There is blood everywhere she looks.

A starving dog has slaughtered the overfed pride.

The enemy is crouched over a mess of bones, fur, a liver, maybe a heart. Meat. Pale hands, washed in vermilion, work the remains of the cat, scooping the sorry slop together like a child fixing a broken toy.

Severe lips that have uttered naught this night now attempt a worthy eulogy.

He looks up at the sound of her approach: a muting of crushed leaves. Midnight slurs curl over his round cheeks, flow from elongated eyes. This is not what she expected.

"I really didn't want it to be this way," he says in what the Lady finds to be an inferior, crude tongue, and yet her shudder is not one of revulsion. "Wish I could have done it without killing the cat. It did nothing wrong, nothing but cross my path when I needed it." He gestures at the mutilation of her three companions. "I had to, or it would've been meaningless. An unfair exchange, even if it's not finished."

"So you are the Scourge," she replies, appearing to listen but always looking, sniffing, thinking. "The one trained to hunt We Who Hunt, the herdling who fancies himself one of us. You upset the way things ought to be." She takes the opportunity to work her own way, but his mind is closed to her. By now, anyone else – Noble or otherwise – would have been willing to answer her unspoken questions. She has known only a few whose minds refused entry, and each of those was somehow related. Her theories harden into a foundation of belief.

The Scourge does not respond.

She notices the elegant sword on the ground, a thought away from his left hand. It is a good instrument, should one wish to move with speed and accuracy. Most men of this region wield crude, cumbersome monstrosities – claymores or morning stars, axes or hammers. This is a foreign creation, designed to ignore the particulars of foreign armour, to penetrate layers of lacquered plate. Furious heat swirls about the honed edge; traces of sharp light play over the ripple-marked steel.

He is the Scourge; that is his sword.

Contemplation gives way to a half-word from her mutinous lips, some inarticulate seed of concession. The sound evokes a cant of her counterpart's cowl. She takes one step toward him, but is interrupted before completing another.

There is a hideous shriek from above them both. The last Talon, who neither lagged nor surrendered to the Hunt, dives from the depth of an oversight. His surgical weapon points like a skeletal accusation, erring neither left nor right. The Scourge snatches up his own blade and attempts to duck, to whirl, to knock aside the determined needle. He swings too early, swiping nothing but air – air which shall soon be full of unnaturally cold metal.

Grief and uncertainty have made the Lady weak, but this new possibility, unforeseen and drastic, is beyond petty mourning. She flies forth, determined to intervene. She is still and always shall be too late to save him. To save anyone.

A good thing, then, that the Scourge has learned to save himself.

An eruption of light and heat halts her charge, drives her back, pinches her vision for just a second. The Talon's attack meets the manifest energy now surrounding the Scourge with an incredulous chime. The forest vibrates a sympathetic hum. The blade, loosed from surprised fingers by the impact, spins into the night, which swallows the deadly shard as easily as it consumes daylight. Tendrils radiate from the sparkling sphere to entwine about the Talon's arms and legs, pinning him to the air. The Talon blinks a few times, looking quite dumbfounded as he hangs in brilliant stasis just above his intended prey.

A sword must obey its nature.

The Scourge lifts his gently curved weapon and eases its tip into the last Talon's stomach. The impotent Noble spasms, mouth gaping wider than any human jaw as it tries to inhale the night whole. The blast of his final breath slams into the Scourge's hood, blows it back. The Lady searches her enemy's face for any sign of emotion and finds only a vacuous stare. He looks bored or tired.

The Scourge slides his sword from the suspended Noble and, without stopping, impales the creature again, this time through the groin. Pale and pitiful limbs, sprouting from sundered garb, twitch like the legs of a helpless beetle. These two stabs were simply practice. The Scourge becomes a fury of thrusts; even the potent Mindwarp would have to concentrate to see individual movements. The mechanical efficiency with which the Scourge dispatches her cohort seems to transfix her.

Her Talon does not even get a chance to bleed.

But two seconds later the Scourge steps back, the light begins to fail and the Noble bursts in a lively fountain. The Scourge moved this quickly: his cloak is dry when he turns away. Behind him, the last vestiges of illumination fade and the Talon falls to the ground with a sickening splash. Whatever is left of him lands in whatever came out of him.

The final Talon's grisly demise earns a whisper, a prayer from the Lady:

"Erotas'z en fhia'rez, Sa'hre. Vahm en."

Sa'Hres'z stood in lower favour than the others until now – because he was always one to hesitate before moving. The Lady appears to fortify herself against the irony, returning her attention to the Scourge, to whom she has lost every member of her personal guard.

His existence, no matter how twisted, is a straight line. That is what she is thinking, unaware that she once appraised another with those very words. The Lady stares at the blank expression and sees even more resemblance to one whom she knew but cannot remember in any real detail. Association teases the shadow of memory.

The Scourge's face then melts into hurt and confusion. He still wants to kill her. The intent rises in his deserted eyes as the blood evaporates from the tempered sword. He blames her for what he is, and how right he would be. But something restrains him from completing the work.

He sheathes the sword, hissing it home to a satisfied click behind his left shoulder. Then his pained mask turns her way and we see – recognition! Faint, fleeting but absolutely *there*.

Her thoughtful joy is thoughtless terror.

He bows to her, a modicum of trust breaking eye contact, and says: "Now it is finished."

The Scourge steps forward, avoiding the massacred Nobles with an unconscious but subtle sidestep. She mirrors this, and there are certain similarities, genetic reflections. Mortal blood is said to have a memory of its own, habits and idiosyncrasies linking even those who are not traceably related at all. The blood shared by Lady and Scourge intensifies this notion, such that each is the answer to the other's question. Every movement brings them closer to the unyielding plane of merciless self-description.

Then the Scourge pauses. Umbilical contraction binds the Lady's subconscious mimicry – she stops as well. He leans towards her, onyx eyes lolling star-ward. His knees buckle and this unbound slayer of Nobles, of the Night's Own, slumps forward and down, disconnected from any sort of life. The Lady flies forth to catch him and is perhaps amazed at how limp the wiry shadow has become, how absent.

But then Dhiana surprises me at last, and looks directly my way. Can she *see* us? A moment, only a moment of scrutiny, before she hefts her heavy trophy and stalks deeper into the forest.

History always happens now; it demands a witness.

If the Lady is the Mindwarp, manipulating the past and future through memories, then I change and improve the present through your dreams. I am the one who takes reality and hides just enough of it to make my own truth. Some call me Nightsong, some address me as Chantal, and perhaps they are both right. Many have tried to guess my name, but only I know who I really am.

You shall call me Vachaelle.

I have to admit, he handled himself rather well. Did not even blink those lovely dark eyes of his. Still, I have let him go again. Maybe I never really had him. *Oh, my sweet Half! If you cannot control yourself, am I not a fool to think I can do the same? Will you come back to me this time?*

I do not know.

With this admission, I shall withdraw. I do know now why Dhiana did not use her full power as the Mindwarp to dispose of him. I understand why she pursued us both for so long.

That shall suffice.

Things are on course once more. We just need to figure out which course, and then determine how best to sever it.

The dreamer thinks: I'm dreaming again, aren't I?

"Now that you have him, Dhiana, what do you propose?" asks a male voice in the void. "No doubt...Vachaelle has done her damage." The pause twists her name into an ugly, hated string of unwelcome sound.

Him? Who is he talking about? Me? And who is that?

He knows her, knows her name! Her real name.

"She's not my equal, Arius. She is not Jaydemyr." The Lady! He tries to turn towards her voice; it's as close to home as his errant soul can recognise. But he can't move, not even in his own mind. Their voices remain behind him, around him, but never before him. "And you know what I plan. I will make him remember, just as I made him, made everyone forget."

"Jaydemyr." What does it mean? The male delivers it like acid, like a mouthful of bitterness. "You say that name as if—"

"As if it is *not* a Clan dragged down by treachery and deceit? As if it weren't anathema in the eyes of the Night? Maybe it isn't, Arius. This, too, we will see when we remember." How can she know these things, if she can't remember? The Scourge understands nothing. He listens.

"Remember what?" The male is cynical, but there is a taint of awe in his tone.

"Everything. Long ago, I took only that much, for his sake, for ours. I cannot guarantee this is what really happened – it is just what he remembers."

"You're implying that she might have influenced him."

"I do not doubt she has afflicted him with everything her Dreamsong can conjure. Despite that, there is not a single door in his mind I can't access, Arius. Ultimately, however, he decides where those doors lead. Her 'influence' over this decision is the unknown."

"What isn't unknown?" He waxes despondent.

"We have him now. *That* isn't unknown."

"And *who* will he be? A child? A teenager? In whose voice will he narrate his own supposed life?"

"Whichever voice and age he chooses. Don't worry, my Champion. He won't start babbling like a baby. This is recollection, not regression. Quiet now. It's about to begin."

She pauses, and when she speaks again, her voice is louder. It is directed at him.

"You will now remember and you will tell us. Take us where you have been. Show us everything."

Everything. When I remember nothing, where do I start?

And then the dreamer answers himself, grasping the first link in the chain of remembrance and not letting go. He does not wonder, at first, why he can do this now and never before – why he is remembering things he didn't even notice at the time. The Mindwarp is, as she herself affirmed, peerless in her ability.

He tells his story to the darkness and it listens. If it asks, he answers. But with the first response, it is clear that not even Dhiana can keep the Dreamer in one voice, one tense. The darkness hears the child who was, the man who is and the saviour who will be.

"I remember the first time I will see her," he begins – little more than a disembodied voice and an accumulation of self-enhancing memories, "because it is my birthday. I returned to the village, and she will be waiting for me..."

I. Dog-Ears

Swimming Carp

873 A.R.

Chapter 1: *Rin*
DREAMS

There I was, seventeen years old and sitting under a tree looking down at a village I barely recognised. I was thinking about a childhood spent languishing in its unrelenting grit. My name was Wong Shah-Long, or Shah-Long to my friends – not that I had any. The only person who called me 'Shah-Long' in Swimming Carp was me. The village gave me another name, which made sense since they didn't really know me. Their name for me was what they saw and only that, even though they made me that way. Nothing strange about that.

But I *should* have considered it strange, because *I* was strange. In so many ways. And I know now the most important way, the reason for all the other problems, was the vision. Other people had different dreams from night to night, but I saw the same thing, night to night, month to month, year to year. I knew this was strange because the other children of Swimming Carp sometimes talked about their dreams after school. I used to hide behind the big tree in the courtyard and eavesdrop, knowing they'd ignore me until someone (not me) had the grand idea to beat someone else (me) up. I tried to put that off as long as possible, but it was never long enough.

"When I grow up, I'm gonna be a dancer," I heard Wu Jen-Wah say one day. I think I liked her but now I look back, she was just a nasal and petulant eight-year-old. She prattled on, "I'm gonna be the best dancer ever and move to the city and live with Lord Ayakawa and everyone will love me!"

I took a peek and saw that she *was* dancing, wobbling circles on the spot, dirt smearing her tattered skirt. One of the boys around Jen, who probably liked her, then snorted, "Love you? Not with a nose like yours!"

I winced, knowing a storm cloud when I saw one. Sure enough, the boy standing next to him, who definitely liked Jen-Wah, elbowed the first kid in the face and quipped, "Still looks better than yours!"

"Chang!" Jen squealed, and I was entirely too young and too ignorant to see the delight in her eyes. "Jaku didn't deserve that, did you, Jaku?"

She moved to check on Jaku and his bloodied nose, but he shoved her aside and launched himself at Chang.

I imagine that's how a conversation about dreams ended in Swimming Carp – with someone punching it in the face. I crept away before the brawl broke out for real.

As I had anytime I could get away with it, I wandered around the fields and forests surrounding Swimming Carp that afternoon. What Jen-Wah had said wouldn't go away. My dream was not like that at all. It was not about ambitions or desires. It wasn't about anything really. It wasn't even about me, or so I thought.

This dream always came at night, when the moon glazed over the sleeping village, over Chūnko, over the entire Mifūné Empire, over the whole drowsy world. Although *I* wasn't really asleep, when I'd 'wake up' I'd think about the remnants of the vision – a jumble of ideas, sounds and images. Staring at the ceiling, I'd listen to Father's discordant snoring as I pieced together what I could remember. There was more, though I don't know how I knew. This is how I'd describe my dream if anyone asked:

Moon of blood. Moon of snow. White falls through black. Screams and laughter. I don't understand what they're saying. Then I see a red shape glowing in the sky. I do not recognise it but I know it is a sign I must fear: two uneven lines, like the frame of a kite. I know that once I see it, I will be torn away. I always see it. I hear metal crashing against metal. Reverberation. Silence.

I knew better than to ask my father about it directly, but one time I did sort of hint that I was seeing something weird in my sleep.

"Tsk! Dreams? You waste my time with dreams?" thundered Father in response, adding a slap to the back of my head to make sure I got the message. "Here I am, Village Elder, stuck with a good-for-nothing bastard like you. Stop asking about…Just stop asking! Things are the way they are; always have been, always will be. You're just a grub, boy, and grubs gotta work hard. Respect yer elders, respect Miss Master at school, and respect that this is all yer ever gonna be. Those are just the Ways of Life. Life, not dreams!"

Life, according to Father and everyone else in Swimming Carp, was simple: serve Lord Ayakawa by being happy and hard-working. As Miss Master said: "Ayakawa-sama is the Daimyo of Chūnko. He rules from the faraway capital, Kaifeng. Ayakawa-sama is part of the Tsukamoto clan, which you know rules the Mifūné Empire. And the most glorious of all is Emperor Tsukamoto, whose voice is heard by God and Heaven Below. So you see, boys and girls, you really are small and worthless in a much bigger world."

Now that I say it, even in her voice it's kind of complicated. Miss Master must have known this too, because she'd end every lecture with a snap of her teaching-rod (over my knuckles, usually) and yell, 'Obedience!' and although it didn't make much sense to me, the others must have gotten the message, because they never bothered her for an explanation.

It didn't end there – the Emperor Tsukamoto was himself subordinate to the will of God, expressed through Her spirits on Kaef're: the Night's Own. We knew nothing about these holy beings other than what Miss Master taught:

"Fear the Nobles! Good children, heed the Night and Her Own! You don't *ever* want to meet an avenging spirit of God. Those Of The Night can take any of you, if they find you unworthy of life! *When the moon shines round, be asleep, safe and sound.* She takes not the good dreamers." Then she'd yell the first word again – "Fear!"

Obedience, fear. Of the two, obedience was the best I could manage. I wasn't really afraid of anything, which is funny and sad since I had lots of reasons to be afraid. Maybe that's why the villagers said I was 'slow'. They *were* afraid and that's why they were obedient. What I felt wasn't fear but certainty. There's probably a quote in the Book that puts it better, but I was considered too 'slow' to read it properly, let alone understand it.

Miss Master was careful not to teach the 'slow' kid very much. I didn't know this at the time, but some part of me saw enough to want more, and 'more' wasn't allowed. Whenever I made the mistake of speaking my mind, Miss Master would pull on my ears and correct me. This happened a lot more when I was younger – I had a habit of asking the wrong questions. Took me far too long to realise the questions weren't the wrong ones. They were just wrong *because* they were questions in the first place. So I stopped asking her as well, but it was too late.

Miss Master had 'corrected' me so much that my ears were pulled out of shape. Even now, their pointiness serves as a reminder of the name they gave me, the name I accepted. When the children of Swimming Carp had nothing else to do, they would get together, corner me and call me that name, throwing rocks and making faces. Sometimes they'd do more. Maybe they were hoping I would bite back, but I never did. That strange boy, obedient but not afraid, would say nothing and just wait for it to end. After a while, I couldn't even blame the children. They were, after all, just obeying another of Miss Master's lessons: 'Fighting is bad, but sometimes you have to. Sometimes, children, you will have a good reason, and then it will be a good fight.'

They always had a good reason.

"Hey Dog-Ears! Been eating your own shit again, Dog-Ears?"
In the courtyard.
After school.
My twelfth birthday.
Just like any other day.
Jaku lead the group. Closed the circle. Landed the first punch.
"That'll teach him! Do it again, Jaku!"
Doubled over from the punch, I staggered to the jagged ground.
They gathered around me.
"Why are you so stupid?"
"It's your fault Miss Master makes us stay back!"
"Why are we punished for *his* idiocy? Same shit, every Eph'ing day!"
They might have been doing God's work, but that didn't stop them from blaspheming. Invoking the name of Ephriem, The First, was far worse than ordinary foul language, and somehow subdued the torment, but then another voice filled the silence, as another voice always did.

"Let's just kill him, Jaku. It's what the Night would want."

This last suggestion held more authority than the bitter cries of the other kids. Jen was no longer quite so clumsy, but still petulant and nasal. She and Jaku had been 'together' ever since he'd made fun of her nose and then left Chang a broken wreck. The girl always knew exactly what to say to guide Jaku's fists.

"You're right, Jen. We should do as God wishes."

I was on my hands and knees, blood drooling from my swollen jaw, but didn't dare to raise my eyes. I felt something hot and savage clawing at the back of my eyes, a need to visit searing white pain upon every single person there. As Jaku glared down at me, I wanted to make fun of his crooked nose, broken by someone who dared to defy him. But it hadn't been me, would never be me.

"Someday, we will. I'm done. Do what you want to the prick."

He swiped spittle from his chin, took Jen by the hand, and the two of them stepped back to watch. One by one, the other students of Miss Master advanced upon me, eager to do their little bit of good against the wicked 'Dog-Ears', Wong Shah-Long.

I limped home, bleeding and bruised, eyes puffy, ears ringing, head aching – and Father was waiting, because that's what Elders do while everyone else works.

"Only the strongest survive in the world," he asserted before showing me what 'real strength' feels like, as if the kids hadn't already done that. I didn't resist, of course, and Father was too proud to say, 'hit me back!' I suppose he felt his fists were encouragement enough.

Maybe I thought I could— that was my attempted response to Father's insistence I fight the kids, to defend myself. But before I could say what I 'thought', he continued as though I'd only said one word.

"Maybe what? *Think* your way out of it? And while you were busy thinking, they hit you! Stop thinking and *do something!* What use are your thoughts when you're supposed to be doing your work? Do you think you can just 'think' food onto the table? You idiot, you…Dog-Ears!"

Still cursing, he made me sweep the house for the third time that day and then sent me to bed without any food at all. His last words to me were snide: if I were hungry, I could just 'think' some food up to fill my belly. But that's not what I thought about.

My father didn't love me. No one loved me; no one wanted to be around me. Most of my childhood, I tried to figure out who to blame. Them? Me? I'd tried acting different ways, but the result was always the same. They wouldn't change and I apparently couldn't. Before too long, however, the need to blame anything had dwindled to nothing more than a churning in my stomach, and that was probably just hunger.

That night, the vision of blood, snow and loss woke me for the last time and merged with other, more indulgent fancies I'd concocted for when I would not go back to sleep. The resulting experience was the only gift I got for my twelfth birthday, but it was a good one.

When I first woke up, it was like I didn't know anything, and had to slowly register reality in small, basic facts. Heart pounding: echoes of dream and trauma. Dark: must be night-time. Wet: swimming in sweat and swallowed screams. After these came together, I knew where and who I was, and that nothing had changed.

I struggled to sit up on the naked wood, supporting myself with my left hand. Light from the window overhead fell on the bruises decorating my pasty skin. Most of the houses in Swimming Carp had no windows at all. During the day, people should be outside and taking advantage of the light; that is to say, *working*. And at night, well, the night is for The Night's Own, for the good people to sleep. Dream. Good people have no use for light during those hours. Being the Elder, Wong Chu-Deng had cause to stay up later than the other villagers. So his house, our house, largest in all Swimming Carp, had a single window for ventilation, and it was directly overhead from where Father told me to sleep. And they expected me to sleep? Northern Chūnko weather is not a pleasant thing at night: extremely cold in winter, noisy from the insects in summer and *always* too bright. There was a shutter, but even when it was closed, thin shafts of light pierced the gaps. If it rained, those gaps proved even less of a comfort.

I clambered onto my knees, wearing only a pair of grubby shorts. The bed creaked with each shift in weight. I eased the thin shutter up and outwards, noticing briefly my stubby fingers, then propped the shutter open to reveal the world. I gripped the glassless stone, leaned out the window, and pressed my chest against the sill. Not long ago, this feat was impossible with kneeling – I had to stand on the bed, which wasn't so smart, considering how fragile it was. Dreamers rarely bother with what's smart, and though I was a workhorse during the day, at night, in the forbidden hours when everyone could sleep, everyone but me, I awakened and became a dreaming butterfly.

Strange as ever, I turned Father's attempt to torture me into something else. After all, what do prisoners yearn for if not a window through which they can look and pretend that what is inside is actually out?

The moon overhead was a splinter of curved bone. Where the deep red slash of my vision was eerie and threatening, the milk of this gentle smile comforted me. I now know why: my mother must have looked up at the same moon and thought about me too. Maybe she still did, somewhere. Father never spoke about her, and I never asked. Not about that. This didn't stop me from thinking and conjuring questions, if only for and of myself. Did she love me? Was she beautiful? Her voice – was it everything that Father's could never be? These questions, of course, all carried an assumption of "yes": that was how I structured them; less questions than hopeful suggestions. Yes and yes and yes. That's all I wanted to hear.

Thoughts of mother and moon drifted away as I continued to gaze at the open world. It was mid-spring. The deafening chirrup of insects had yet to reach a painful peak, and the weather was neither chilly nor humid. The violent torrents of summer were just a memory destined for distant recurrence. But here were soggy squares of grey – rice paddies with knee-deep slush and there, endless rows of newly-sowed grain. How could such a wonderful scene of freedom not spurn a twelve-year-old back into his fantasy? This was not that baffling vision of blood and snow that felt like it belonged to someone else. This was my fantasy, a dream I made and built upon and cherished. It was everything and it was anything.

If I could do anything, I would become a famous scholar, known for knowing everything. I wouldn't have to ask anyone any questions ever again. No one called me 'Dog-Ears', and all the world revered the Great Scholar's wisdom and goodness. A beautiful lady loved me – she had gorgeous silky black hair that reached her waist and eyes like dark honey. She was nothing like Wu Jen-Wah. As I taught the world about all the good things of life, she stood by my side, supportive in silence. I held great banquets, arguing good-naturedly with so many friends about the smallest of subjects and the greatest of matters. Clusters of children danced and laughed around us all. They called me 'Father', and her, 'Mother'. They were happy. They had real parents.

This was my fantasy and until now, now that I've turned out nothing like the Great Scholar Wong Shah-Long, I've not revealed it to anyone. I'd ask that you forgive the naiveté of it, but I won't, since I happen to embrace my naiveté whenever possible. It's better than the alternative.

The fantasy always ended the same, until that last time, when the fantasy I chose chose a different conclusion to the same old story. Lulled by the peace of the night, I must have closed my eyes, and what started as looking out one window turned into falling through another.

This is how my fantasy ended.

The world is white and soft, like the mother moon. It goes on forever, because I want it to.

"It is time for me to say goodbye everyone," I always say.

"No! We cannot live without you, great one!" They always reply.

I shake my head in venerable sorrow, in gentle disagreement. I am the Great Scholar Shah-Long, shuffling from person to person and caressing their tearful faces. There is a special message for each of them, a private and personal gift. I go down the line of gathered friends, a line so long that my wrinkled eyes cannot see the end. They are known to me, one and all, from the oldest of sages to the newly-born heirs to this wonderful world. It is a world I have made possible. There are no Night's Own here, no Lords ruling from afar. No more puppets who were masters of puppets themselves. Long ago, some old fool who called herself Miss Master preached that 'God' and Her Night's Own were the final power. I have now learned and taught otherwise. A greater power came with that knowledge, unique to the once-oppressed people of the world: the power of true faith. All is made one with that faith, and all have come to bid their founder farewell.

This is as it always has been. I feel that. It is RIGHT. It is supposed to end here. Happily Ever After.

But it doesn't, not this time and never again.

"What about me?"

This comes from behind. Are not all the people of the world assembled before me? Who, then, could it be? But I know. I know that voice. That harsh, how-dare-you bark of disbelief. He does not belong here, in my world. So I ignore him. Pretend he isn't there. It's my dream, so he is *not there*.

I try to move further down the line. Next is a young boy. His head is bowed, so I cannot see his face but I know I don't know him, that he is new to my world as well. Still, the Great Scholar's wrinkled hand rests upon the boy's head, and a blessing eases from my suppressed unease.

When it is over, he steps back. My hand falls limp as the boy looks up. The face that stares back at me is my own from long ago: round, ruddy, insolent. Now I can make out the odd shape of his ears. Bruises and welts cover his cheeks and neck; there are so many, not even a Great Scholar like me can count them all. His lips bend into a mocking grimace. Is this how I had appeared to everyone else back then, back in Swimming Carp?

"Dog-Ears! Dog-Ears! Stupid, weak Dog-Ears!" the boy spits, his own ears growing until they resemble massive leaves. I stumble back, lose my footing. Then I am on one knee, weary joints cracking at the strain. Everyone around me begins to follow the boy's lead, cursing and pressing towards me.

The world is no longer white. It is not even black. It might as well not be there.

"What about me?"

The person behind me is tugging at the hem of my robes again. I half-turn at the insistence, but it is then that I notice the crowd has fallen silent.

I return my attention to them, barely able to stand, and see first that boy who is me and yet is not.

He is holding a sword.

A weapon. Here? Words can cut and thrust and parry just as effectively as steel. My world has no use for killing tools, for things that exist just to hurt people.

And yet—

I find myself reaching for the sword; it…*she* is art, beautiful, slender, beckoning me with crooked allure, and the boy gives her up as soon as my fingers curl around the handle, wrought in black and blue like an elegant bruise. This feels right. I stand up straight. Terrible and perfect. Shah-Long, the Great Scholar who has never harmed anyone, now holds a sword of irrefutable sharpness.

I think: she has a name.

"What about me!?"

That voice breaks the rapture for a third and final time. At last, whoever is behind me manages to turn me around, and I come face-to-face with the source of all my childhood torment. Wong Chu-Deng has not aged at all. He still has that flat nose, the blemishes on each cheek that might be moles. This is the face of all my fears, but he is the one who is afraid. I almost have enough time to appreciate the terror and affliction twisting his expression before it seeps away like muddy water spilling over a dam. With drained deliberation, the Elder peers down at himself and then begins to tremble. I have no clue why until I remember the sword.

She…it is buried in Wong Chu-Deng's stomach.

I try to let go, to say that I didn't mean it, didn't want to kill my own father, but it's beyond me. Can't release this unholy thing of murder.

Invisible cords bind fitting fist to fitting hilt. My mouth won't move because if it does I'm going to scream so hard my throat would be set aflame. Worst of all, deep down, there is incredible peace and satisfaction. Like finding the sudden words to end a long-incomplete sentence. This sense of oneness, an understanding that the answer was there all that time. So very simple.

I had meant it. I did want to kill Father. Blame the Elder for pulling me around though I did, I had taken the opportunity and thrust the sword. Now, with his death, Wong Chu-Deng had released his despotic hold upon my soul, a grip I'd so long ignored, but not even a Great Scholar escapes his past by pretending it didn't happen.

"Shah-Long…Shah-Long…Shah-Long…" The crowd began to chant and make bizarre motions with their hands. Strained, determined, I wrenched saturated weapon from desiccated corpse. All around me, I saw people. My people, but not. People transformed. Long-time friends sprouted slick wings from stalwart spines; others were wolves in the shapes of men, slobbering and clawing the air; but most of those I loved had grown tall and spindly, their sun-leathered skin now sullen and grey.

Stunned into silence, I could neither fully acknowledge the crowd nor look at my father's body. I laid the weapon down so that it divided me from the chaotic assembly. Everything, especially the sword, was suddenly so heavy. I bent my head, as my younger self had done, and wept, as he had not. The tears that dripped to the ground were hot and painful. And they were red. Brighter and richer than blood, which can also be black or blue. Flat and shiny tears.

The wicked crowd continued to chant. This was the day I was supposed to die, to ascend into legend and immortality. The passing of a Great Scholar, a good person…but good persons did not murder their fathers. Not even if their father was a bad man. A very bad man. Still a man, and I killed him. Nothing could excuse that.

"There is no excuse needed."

I'd never heard this voice before and yet knew it. I felt her hand upon my head, and beheld the bearer of that voice. We were both hesitant, curious. It was she who had stood by me, with her unrivalled hair and gentle eyes, and, at the same time, it wasn't. The colour of her hair reminded me now of fresh wheat, giving way to a capricious breeze. Eyes that once were brown had become twin shards of bleak intensity. Even her voice had gained an edge of subtle anger.

Had it been Mother at my side all along, comforting and helping me, nurturing and loving?

The woman shook her head and glided back, removing her hand. The absence of her reassuring touch prompted a desire to beg: come back! But I knew she hadn't truly left me. Spreading her arms wide, she craned her neck and gazed upward. Her back arched, imbued with a force that wrenched her body into the air.

"It is time to reclaim what is ours, Charan." Her voice hardened with that command. Where it had been feathery and forgiving, now it was sharp, demanding. She was speaking to the sky itself; had I heard her correctly? Shah-Ran? It sounded a little like my name, Shah-Long, but that's all: like my name, not my name itself.

Perhaps she had been speaking to someone else. When I did not react, she lowered her gaze, letting it fasten upon me. Her face had changed appearance again. Golden hair faded into grey…no, silver. Almost white. Like the moon at its most majestic, when it seemed the least real. And her eyes! Devoid of all colour, they were two oval stones of solid darkness, elongated and exotic, swept back under severe angles of browless bone. Her skin was almost transparent. Was this what the Night's Own looked like? I had not thought about those dread masters since I left Swimming Carp and made my own world. I would have panicked were I not certain this was Mother.

"Destiny calls you, my son. It is time to answer him!"

And with that came the final change, and it was much more than just the face and hair. Her body gained a certain amount of muscle here, a little more bulk there. When it was done, she seemed to be around forty years old, and male. This new face was rounder, resembling far more my own, yet retained that innately inhuman distortion of before.

The man-being strode forward until its heavy shadow covered me. That which was once my mother knelt to take in his left hand the accursed thing that started it all. The warrior raised the sword in a grim salute. Some of the blood flew free of the steel to warm my face. Sudden thoughts of snow and darkness threatened to blur the moment. I stared at the man-thing as it stared at the sword. It…he turned towards the gibbering crowd. As one, they fell to their knees just as I had done. My entire world, as real as any other, surrendered to that sword-wielding monstrosity.

Or to the sword itself.

"You have always reflected upon things, my son." Anger and compassion both were absent in the baritone declaration. His voice was incorruptible and magnificent, like a stubborn statue defying even the assault of time. My mind circled his statement and replayed it over and again. He knew me, because I was reflecting on this as well.

Then came the three revelations.

First: there was a sword in my world – and it was my sword.

Second: my mother had been with me all that time, and she permitted me to use that sword – but she did not hold the sword now. She was not the one who came before me, as a wielder of the sword.

Third: He was. He was—

"Father."

Whoever I had cut down before had not been my father. He was no one.

Father nodded once, turned his back to me and marched into the distorted ranks. The steadiness of his gait was full of ill-intent. I knew my Father's wish then. I tried to stand, to stop the unavoidable. Just before reaching the first of the genuflecting congregation, he looked back at me and spoke again.

"Reflect, then, on this, for what I start is but a reflection of what you must finish."

Then he turned away and raised the sword once more. Before intellect could protest, instinct hissed: that's my sword. I should be wielding her, even though the beasts were once my friends and family. No. Not 'even though' – *because*. Because of that, because of my love for them, I would set them free from what they had become, as I did so long ago. Emboldened by intuition, I rose, prepared to take back that which was mine.

Then the sword fell, pulled by a gravity against which no true warrior makes war.

Anarchy should not be this clear:

Just before the first kill, I cried and looked away, hearing then the dull rip of flesh forced apart. I could not move. The fifth saw me bite back a million curses upon this fatherly figure who was both more terrifying and powerful than Wong Chu-Deng had ever been. I still could not move. After the tenth, I realised there was an absence of screams. I started to move. By the twentieth, nineteen corpses marked my wake. I closed distance with the monster who should have been me. To interrupt the thirtieth fatal swing, I reached out and seized his wrist as Father pulled back for yet another attack. The unique weapon fell from his suddenly empty left hand into mine in another surrender to primordial gravity.

It was a mistake, the Great Scholar in me cried, to meet one violent action with another.

But now the sword had returned to me. Mine. She was neither heavy nor unwelcome. Strong and tall, I rounded upon her previous bearer, forgetting what he'd said about reflections. I knew only that he had murdered those who were dear to me. He had killed my world. Action preceded thought and sent the vindictive edge through a path of deliberate evisceration. I knew precisely how to do it and, with that curious, fleeting omni-essence of dreams, knew also that I now looked just like him.

The sword froze in that tiny, miraculous space between homicidal intent and horrified regret. The halt was too quick, too clean. Had I been the one to stop, or was there more to the sudden frown upon Father's face?

The figure shimmered and then was gone, leaving me alone with my dead. In my hand, the sword that made me feel dirty and divine seemed to hum in exultation. Determined to end it there and then, I hauled the weapon back and hurled her…it away with the last vestige of my strength. It sailed, end over end, and then, like Father, was gone. There were no more weapons in my world, and all would be well.

I searched here and there for survivors. Surely he could not have killed my entire world! And he did not. Soon enough, I found myself staring into black eyes and leering faces peering their hunger at me. Mouths that were too long and too wide moved up and down with fetid impulses. The horde was ready to fall upon me, but something held them back. I knew it was not fear, because they were creatures of fear. They were nonetheless obedient.

Then I felt it, an even darker source of hatred radiating behind the writhing masses. Behind, and within. As the presence approached, even those grisly masks could not resist a semblance of dread. Upon emerging from the ranks, this representation of complete maleficence seemed to laugh at me, but I saw neither face nor mouth. It was just a vague tower of untethered contempt. But then it had arms: thorned convolutions of ebon flesh, crackling with an energy that promised spasms of agony. The abomination pointed straight down. Endless eyes snaked away from their liege to focus and narrow upon me.

The grim lord spoke, and his voice was a whisper of malice, a howl of rage.

"Xenides-ra Kas'Daen fha hremor'kha, kien'dre! Sax en sa'ha'khra dah'resz!"

More than gibberish: though I could not understand, it was a language. I perceived syllables and words, but that might just have my imagination. The overall intention of what he'd said burnt itself into my brain, and one word from the torrid condemnation stood out:

Sa'ha'khra.

I knew what that meant.

"Faithwar." The ground quaked at my breathless comprehension. Flashes of world-spanning slaughter invaded my vision, staying just long enough to elicit a single scream. I was the war: I ended every life, I felt every death. I was the cause and the consequence, the question and the answer and the awful serenity that always follows it all.

Then the word was gone; in its wake, I knew the world was still at war, a war that would never end as long as I resisted it.

Pulled by taut strings of terror, I backed off as the minions advanced, their spidery fingers reaching forth to rend flesh and spirit both. I raised my hands in a vain warding gesture and then *she* was in my left fist, radiant with smug immediacy. The vivid orange aura of the weapon cast a contrastingly baleful shroud around me. I felt revitalised. My fingers, arms, heart – they were no longer those of Wong Shah-Long, the Great Scholar. Every part of my everything had become the finely tuned elements of a warrior. A killer. Me. I had become me. My father. He had been right. This was what must be done. It was time to answer.

As if from a thick mist, I heard his laughter, and it was an approval, a command. His ultimate consent. Father wasn't frowning now.

The opaque figure moved aside; he was my father, he was the thing that killed my father. One and the same: I would become this as well. The massive circle of monstrosities closed in, but I knew what had to be done. My fists radiated the same charred lightning that had enshrouded the fell lord, my father, my father's bane. I was all of these, and it was a simple matter. The sword, in my hand, grew warm with anticipation and understanding: she would join me.

I began to smile.

And then laugh.

And then roar…

"Shut up! Damn it, Dog-Ears, go back to sleep!"

Eyes snapped open. I was floating on a soaked sheet; my veins boiled through freezing skin. I could not unclench my teeth. White-knuckled hands refused to open. They seemed to believe they still gripped that awesome, heinous weapon. I realised then that I must have been laughing in reality as well as in the dream. Laughing so loud it had awoken…Father. With a held breath I waited for the heavy snoring from the bedroom to resume. I was safe for tonight, but there would be words in the morning. Words and fists.

I wrapped myself in the sodden sheet and tried to sleep. The fleeting memory of the true dream *the world has faded to white* began to mingle with the vision *moon of blood moon of snow* in some disfigured courtship of ecstasy *moon* and abomination *cross*. There would be no sleep as long as I thought about *what* had happened. So I dwelt on *how* what had happened made me feel, the conflicting emotions that had come with murdering Wong Chu-Deng, with seeing my imaginary friends turn to monsters, meeting my possible real family and then killing a whole bunch of people who weren't people anymore. My only solace was that I knew I hadn't come up with all that myself, because if I had, what the villagers did to me was the least of what I deserved. Just when I started to wonder if I were really *that* messed up, I succumbed to a long-overdue slumber. I even slept in the next morning, a new event to which Father responded with a bucket of cold water and a kick out the door.

That was the end of the vision, of my fantasy, and of my childhood. The real tragedy is that as bad as it was, with its harrowing symbols and the eventual shattering of my most private world, I would come to miss it soon enough.

Chapter 2: *Pyo*
MESSAGES

The real nightmare could begin only after I suffered and outgrew the imaginary one. With their inner turmoil and premature maturity, my teenage years were in many ways too typical to bother recounting, although not for the typical reasons. That is true. I can work with that.

Of the many things that confused me as I grew towards adulthood, the most frequent was the mere fact that I was still around. I'd learned about the Blood Peddlers by then, of course. On Lord Ayakawa's behalf, they'd steal into the village once every month or two, always at night, and the next morning there'd be a few people missing. No one said a thing, no matter whom the Night claimed. A handful of lives a year was a fair price for the peace and prosperity God allowed us to enjoy. Even I, the village idiot, knew that. When the Peddlers came, and when they took the old, the sick, and the socially misaligned, you kept your eyes away and head down.

Yet they never took me, even though I was clearly 'socially misaligned' and showed no signs of improving.

But I tried. Following Elder Wong Chu-Deng's lead, the villagers were happy to order Dog-Ears to do whatever needed doing, whatever they felt was beneath them. Instead of hiding, I embraced everything they could throw at me. I swept neglected floors, scrubbed massive clay pots, fed fat animals and then, when it was time, slaughtered them for feasts and banquets. On top of that, I wasn't seeing the vision anymore, and I wasn't pretending to sleep as I created and enjoyed a secret world better than this one. Now I could sleep like everyone else. I was one of them. I was good, finally.

So why wasn't anyone treating me differently?

In the absence of an answer, I had only more questions. Was it my fault? What had I done? And even if I found out, would I be able to stop? Would I *want* to?

I was being punished for *something*. Father was angry because of me, and no teenager reacts well to unexplained parental antipathy. So I began to rebel in my own little ways, mostly nothing more than sneaking into the school library and reading whatever scrolls interested me, which was almost anything. History. Philosophy. Legends. Myths. Shopping lists. Anything. The part of me that still held onto the fantasy, that would hold a sword again, knew it needed *everything* at its command. And it knew that nothing would be offered. It had to be taken.

Years of being battered and pushed around had made clear to me that mental enrichment wasn't enough. Ironically, Father himself enabled my physical improvement when, upon noticing I was growing into my lankiness (or beyond Miss Master's educational control), he took me out of school to make me work the fields until my body begged for a moment's rest. I didn't listen to it. In fact, I exerted myself twice as hard as anyone else, happily swinging a heavy scythe for hours. The other villagers grumbled about stupid Dog-Ears not knowing when to stop but since I was doing what was asked of me, they couldn't really complain. I revelled in this completely sanctioned means of empowerment. My arms grew strong with the repetition and my hands became callused and familiar with the once-painful haft. With each swipe, something dormant within me remembered the fantasy and what it had been like to use a sword. This sensation added extra effort to the next swing, and then the next. And when I was alone at home, I would take up my broom and toy with it, whirling it through the air with clumsiness and ineptitude, quite often smacking myself almost as effectively as everyone else. I was no killer and the broom was no sword. I understood that, which is why I knew I'd need something more.

As well as hair in unexpected places and urges at unexpected times, puberty is also when one receives their Talent, a special gift from God that made life a little easier. These were usually limited elemental control, healing the sick or being able to help plants grow, but I'd read about other Talents, more dangerous and much rarer due to being a high priority for Blood Peddling. Outlandish things like calling lightning from a clear sky, moving faster than other people or even, and this one was just a rumour, being able to read others' minds. Thankfully, most of the teenagers in Swimming Carp found their Talents to be either *Gaifu*, healing, or *Dao-chi*, simple manipulation of rocks, soil and the ground. Both were useful in the various roles a villager fills with exemplary mediocrity. A few channelled *Feng-chi*, which was always a good thing as they could do things like summon a small breeze or fan a fire. We even had a *Shui-sha*, and she was treasured above them all for her ability to make water for growth and sustenance.

Of course I didn't get a Talent when the other kids did. Miss Master had made clear that I would never be found in God's grace. No matter how hard I worked. In the wrong hands, a Talent could be incredibly dangerous, and there were no more wrong hands in Swimming Carp than mine.

Having been taken out of school, I was alone more than ever, and in solitude alone could I be angry. Angry at everything. Even a harmless little tree bore the full focus of my fury – why didn't I have a Talent? Wasn't everyone hating me enough? Wouldn't a Talent give me a chance to show them I'm not useless, not stupid?

Did *God* really have to add Her weight to my burden of failure?

And then, maybe answering that last blasphemous thought, the stripling burst into flame.

Of the Talents known to the villagers, *Huo-chi* was the least appreciated. There wasn't much a good villager could do with fire, and although it was tempting, I would *never* dare use even this Talent to hurt someone. Miss Master taught that anyone caught doing that would be punished instantly by the Night. This had yet to be tested, but no one, including me, wanted to find out whether or not she was lying.

No one expected me to go through anything like puberty, especially not the revelation of a Talent. And although I went to lengths to ensure their lack of expectations was met, I secretly gloated about my Talent. God finally approved of me. She saw that I was being tormented and gave me a weapon to fight back, even if it was forbidden and I never would. As far from the village as I could get, I practiced my 'sword' skills, augmented now with *Huo-chi*, until it was certain I could defend myself.

At these times, I felt I was becoming Shah-Long, the warrior-scholar: thoughtful but ferocious when provoked.

Or so I told myself when contemplating what I was really doing. No one could question my unspoken intentions, and that alone seemed to make it all the more necessary to justify them, if only to myself. Things were still *strange,* and to make them normal, I wanted to use my fire. Now when the village kids gathered around me, mocking my ears, my height, my damned stupidity, I didn't just close my eyes and take it. I looked at them, derelict tears distorting their faces until my tormentors resembled those once-people I'd slain in my dream. My fantasy was, in its complete form, one of killing, and now I had real targets. Right there. Just waiting.

But there was something I could not say, because it would have been giving in, which would have been *real* submission: Go away! Leave me alone! Disappear! And if you don't...

I will kill you all.

These were not the thoughts of a noble warrior-scholar. Sometimes, I'd look down at the village from the entrance path, sitting under that tree, and feel overwhelming shame. They wanted *me* to disappear, drove me out of their midst just far enough to be out of the way, but never so far as to be out of reach. I refused to feel the same way. I was not like them!

No, I wasn't like them. I was different. *I was worse.* They might not have known what they're doing to me. To them, it was just the way it was. I, however, was not ignorant to what suffering I wished upon them.

Was it really just their antagonism pushing me away, or was this gnawing suspicion that the worst person in the village really was me driving me even further into a solitary life?

Something like an answer came when I was fourteen. Father told me to bear a package to a nearby village. Coincidentally, I'd been thinking about running away, or maybe there was no coincidence to the timing at all. Anyone else, someone not so slow, would have tried it by then. Once it was clear I wasn't going to do it for myself, *he* told me to run away, and added that if I didn't run back he'd skin me alive and feed the leftovers to the dogs.

Figuring this was just another test, I came and went as ordered. The other villages were smaller than Swimming Carp and the people there paid me little heed. Still, out of some odd fit of shame, I made a habit out of wearing a hooded cloak that failed to hide my face but succeeded in hiding my ears. It was black and dark and I liked the mystery of it. When I returned from an errand run swathed in cool shadow, Father said nothing other than, "don't wear that in the house." I was also glad to find out that it served well as a deterrent for unwanted attention, even from the likes of Jen and Jaku, who were too busy trying to rule the other kids to notice I'd found my escape and still chose not to take it permanently. Not yet.

Now that I had seen a world beyond Swimming Carp and knew that the road leading *into* the village also led *out,* I clutched the belief that someday I might be allowed to leave this drudgery and torment. I now knew that it would probably involve dealing with Father first. And I could. I could kill my father, Wong Chu-Deng, if I had to. Only if I had to.

And *there* was the root of it, the basest thought that sustained me through my teenage years. As with most pubescent philosophies, it was fundamentally flawed. I had the words right, but not the order. Not the tone. "I can kill you, if I have to" is arrogant and complacent, two things no one would ever accuse Dog-Ears of being, but that is what I'd become nonetheless. What should have been my focus, my drive, was much more uncertain, a sentence that would never let me rest: "If I have to, can I kill you?"

Despite all my efforts at subverting Swimming Carp's ordeals, they'd still managed to take from me the one thing that really mattered: the ability to ask a simple question of myself.

And clinging to that sort of unproven belief is how you turn five whole years of farm work, errand running, fire starting and stick-swinging into almost nothing.

When something finally changed, everything changed.

Just before my seventeenth birthday, Father sent me to Bitter Lotus village with a private message for its Elder. This was exciting, since Bitter Lotus was at least a few days away from Swimming Carp. I set out immediately, kept out of sight as much as possible and completed the trip on time and in one piece.

After crossing under the entrance-gate, I sought Elder Leung Guan-Pi's house, quietly proud of my safe arrival.

"You're early."

Although it wasn't really a question or an accusation or even my fault, I answered with an apology for the uneventful journey. The squat, fleshy man, who was more opulently dressed than anyone I'd ever seen, just grunted and led me into his home, which was easily larger than Father's. I saw *three* windows, two of them allowing light into the main room. The Elder stared at me as I stared at his amazing clothing and his amazing abode, until I remembered why I was there. He coughed throatily as I handed over the tightly-wound scroll. The Elder frowned as he unfurled it and began to read. Not long after, he looked up and the way the Elder's eyes lingered on me made me want to squirm.

Embarrassed and anxious, I asked if I should wait outside.

"You should stay right here, boy. Haven't you read this?"

Had he expected me to invade his privacy? I just shook my head, knowing if I said something, I'd say too much.

He clicked his tongue, thrusting the message my way. I looked at it, and then back at the Elder, and then at the note again.

"Read it, Wong Shah-Long."

I forced the text to eye level so that I could read the note and, more importantly, hide my very confused expression. The first few words made me gasp and it wasn't until the end of the short message that I let out an explosive gust: part sigh, part silent what-the-Eph.

I stammered. I stuttered. I managed a few words.

Was this true? Or a joke?

"Elders are not inclined to joke, young man."

But he was smiling now, and I'd learned that an Elder's smile usually represents a threat.

I begged his forgiveness and asked if this normally happened when a person turned seventeen years old.

"Ah, so it's your birthday as well? Soon? Close enough. Another reason to celebrate. Come, let us drink!"

Avoiding his attempts to hook my arm as inoffensively as possible, I asked what was supposed to happen next.

"Well, you and I talk for a little bit more. Get to know each other. But this has all been arranged, give or take. You stay here, of course. Take one of the rooms upstairs. You'll find much more appropriate clothing up there too. Get you out of those…rags."

A *room*? All to myself? I'm fairly sure that's when I finally started to smile as well. As usual, I latched onto the wrong fact, missed the key word.

"I take it that's to your liking. Good, good. And how about wine – is that to your liking too?"

There was no way Father would ever let me touch alcohol (I was slow and stupid enough) but I nodded anyway, and the Elder hobbled over to a large table. Sloshing scarlet liquid into a pair of shallow porcelain bowls was clearly an effort for this Elder: not quite *all* of it splashed onto the opulent table.

"Well and good, then. Come, sit, boy. Boy? No, oh no. Man. You are indeed a fine young man!"

Guffawing, the Elder raised one of the bowls in invitation. I approached and sat on a stool as I examined the table's details. Sinuous dragons curled around the wooden edges, clutching orbs of painted gold in their polished claws. I was unable to draw my eyes away from the beautiful workmanship. Father's table back in Swimming Carp, although larger than this, was crude, practical. This one looked more like a work of art than something you'd eat at.

"Don't talk much, do you? Drink up, it'll help."

The old man, now positively jovial, took a great slurp, rivulets dribbling from each side of his mouth. I focused on this unintentionally – no, *against* my intentions. The dripping wine could have been the tears of a dream, bleeding, seeping from the wounds made by a sword – *my* sword—

"Eh? Something wrong? Boy? Oh, there I go again! I'm sorry. Man. You are a man. Did I mention that? You're going to be a fine young man."

That was the second time he'd said that, and I was trying very hard not to think about why. Feeling his scrutiny, I tried a sip, careful not to let any slip down *my* chin. Although the wine was both sour and bitter, the warmth it brought to my belly encouraged a deeper draught. The taste wasn't so bad that second time. In fact, maybe with another it'd be almost pleasant…

My first experience with getting drunk was unsurprisingly hazy. I'd like to say I don't remember most of it, and I am sure I normally can't, but now I can tell you exactly what happened, although I'm not sure I want to.

Two bowls of wine taught my tongue how to bend around things I'd not dared talk about in the past. The Elder proved an excellent listener to all my woes, prompting me with thumps on the table and earnest grumbles of "Damn right!" and "That's just not fair!" and "Well, that's all in the past now." Never mind that he kept doing it as I was mid-sentence. It was still the nicest thing anyone had ever done for me.

A few more servings later and Elder Leung Guan-Pi, who insisted that I call him *Goong* – 'Gramps' – began to sing. His crooning moved me, first emotionally and then actually. I'd never danced before but it's enough to say I never had any right to make fun of Wu Jen-Wah in that regard.

Two servings further had 'Gramps' and 'Dog-Ears' slopped over that wonderful, amazing, I-could-just-sleep-right-here-it's-that-comfortable table. By that point I wasn't sure if I was blinking slowly or slipping in and out of sleep quickly.

"You know," The old man slurred, "I feel like I known you forv…foreverer, Dog-Ears, 'n thassa damn long time. But somethin's botherin' me."

After missing a few times, I managed to prop my head upon one of my hands (not sure which one – fairly sure it was mine) and almost look at him and ask what, but it was probably more like 'wassat?'

"Long time but still you haven't taken your hood off at all since coming into my home house here."

Beneath a fuzzy quilt of intoxication, I remembered telling him the name I'd been given but not why. Unwilling to ruin whatever was happening, I fumbled for a less incriminating but still honest response. One word came to mind. Strange. So I said that.

"Eh? Ever' one's a stranger 'n th' world, boy."

Nono, that's not what I meant. What I meant was what was under my hood made me strange.

"Your head?"

He narrowed his eyebrows in a vain attempt to concentrate. I threw that cowled head back and forth in violent denial. As soon as I opened my mouth, however, there was a bubbling urgency in my stomach. Wine that had warmed and soothed now curled and soured. Falling off the stool, I half dashed, half crawled out of the house and into the night-lit street outside.

As soon as he arrived, Gramps must have been shocked to see his great new friend 'Dog-Ears' bent over at the waist, making a fine mess of the street. After my gurgling subsided, I heard Gramps laugh, pause, choke a bit and then lose control of his own stomach.

"Urgh!" He coughed a few times, hacked and spat and it sounded like he was dying. I thought of fruit and poison for only a second, and then it was gone. Some weird memory, maybe.

"Ah, I feel a bit better. You okay?"

I responded by retching a second time.

Of course, no one had ever told me about what happens when you drink too much wine. My mouth and throat felt like what I imagine they'd feel like after a hearty meal of raw chilli covered in chilli sauce chased by a nice mug of chilli juice. I gasped for breath, reached out for something to lean on and was glad to find the wall was close enough to fall against. Without thinking, I pulled the hood away in the hopes it'd help me breathe more fresh night air.

"Hey, what's wrong with your ears?" I heard him almost yell from across the street. "Your ears are a funny shape!"

Obeying a sudden burst of grumpiness, I shoved off the wall and stalked past Gramps back into the house, mumbling about how everyone called me strange and weird and made fun of me. Maybe he felt a bit ashamed: he followed me with sincere if sloppy apologies. I almost made it back to the table when my legs buckled. I collapsed in a heap on the floor. I just wanted to sleep there forever, or at least a damn long time. Just as I was about to go, I felt his shaky hand on my shoulder.

"You're one hell of a son-to-be, Dog-Ears…Dog-ears. Ha-ha, ha. I get it now!"

And that was the beginning of my wonderful new life as a 'fine young man.'

Happy seventeenth birthday, Dog-Ears.

I soon learned about hangovers as well. As Elder Leung's son-in-law, I would have to get used to them. The man drank as much as Father didn't; the reason for this would be very apparent before my time in Bitter Lotus was done.

The note was short and to the point. Elder Wong Chu-Deng had found me, his son, worthy of being married to the honourable Elder Leung Guan-Pi's daughter, Plump Treat. Should Elder Leung require any funds for the ceremonies, Elder Wong Chu-Deng would be all-too-happy to provide. As a result of the union, Bitter Lotus was entitled to even more of Swimming Carp's resources than before. Trade would flourish between the two towns and everyone would prosper.

As usual, Elder Wong's idea of 'everyone' had no room for me.

Of Leung's five daughters, Plump Treat was the only one yet to be married off. One morning, perhaps a week after my arrival, the old man and I were seated once more in the living room, seedy and humbled after another night's 'couple of drinks'. My dark hood, which I retained despite the gaudy new clothes that marked me as one of The Most Important People In The Village, was firmly in place and the matter of my ears forgotten in a wine-soaked haze. Fighting through a debilitating headache, I asked Elder Leung, who was no longer 'Gramps' but 'Father', if I could meet my betrothed.

"Of course. Just give the word and I'll have her summoned."

But I had just given the word, hadn't I?

"Eh? Oh, so you did. So you want to meet her now? Sure you don't want a drink first?" Elder Leung muttered something under his breath after that but, in my determination, I missed it altogether.

One of many errors that day.

I declined the offer with as much control as I could muster. No, I did not want a drink!

"Are you certain? I mean, it's still early in the morning." Yeah, right. The faint light outside the window told me that Highsun had long passed and night was not so far away.

I was begging him now, and 'now' didn't seem like it would last much longer, at least for that day.

"She could be busy, but if you really insist…"

I did.

Elder Leung waddled over to another window and leaned out a fair way.

"Would one of you lazy bastards fetch my GORGEOUS and BELOVED daughter?"

A week ago, I wouldn't have laughed to myself at an Elder acting this way. And I definitely wouldn't have so much as twitched my lips at the responses from outside.

"Do it yourself, you old pisshead!"

"Maybe if you didn't drink so much she wouldn't avoid you, Guan-Pi!"

Had anyone, anyone at all, spoken to Elder Wong Chu-Deng in that tone, they'd have been tied up and left outside 'by mistake' come the next full moon.

But Elder Leung just yelled back out the window:

"Damn insolent *lay loh moh pok gai…*" his bluster trailed off in a senseless string of insults. "Ah well. What can you expect?"

Before Elder Leung could meander towards the table and its ever-present bottle of wine, I leapt to my feet, placing myself between 'Father' and his precious booze. I folded my arms and spoke with what I hoped was a commanding tone.

No more drinking, no more excuses. If I had to march into Plump Treat's house right damned now to see her, I would. Damnit!

"But—"

But *what?* She was the reason I was there – had he forgotten?

"Well no, but, are you sure? I mean, why don't we just…" Was he actually nervous?

I screamed: NOW!

With that, I spun on my heel and strode towards the door. Just before opening it, I paused with my hand tense around the handle, thought for a bit and asked, deflated, where she lived.

Not the most well-executed Dramatic And Final Exit.

"Go out, cross the street, four doors down. Look for an extra wide entrance."

And then Elder Leung laughed yet again, mumbling into his cup.

I nodded my head, yanked the door open and left the house.

I should have asked myself why the entrance to Plump Treat's home was 'extra wide'. When I knocked on her door, I heard a muffled, "Coming!" and then, after a time that suggested she had quite some distance to travel, a more distinct, "Who is it?"

Who indeed. Did she know? I figured it best just to say my name and go from there.

Just as I drew breath to speak, the door flew open, almost knocking me backwards. The biggest person I'd ever seen crammed itself into the frame. There is no kind way to put this: Plump Treat was like a pig with pigtails in a sleeveless pink dress.

"Hello there! Oh, I am so happy to meet you at last!"

Before I could do anything, this living mountain had found a way to sweep me into a breath-crushing embrace. I blamed the headache for dulling my reflexes, and I blamed her idea of a hug for sharpening the headache.

Can't breathe let go! I might not have said that, but definitely felt it.

She released me with her father's chortle and I stumbled backwards. The woman bowed her head and shuffled back from the entrance. "I am terribly sorry if I hurt you, my dearly-betrothed Dog-Ears. Please, come in."

Stunned by her shift from gusto to humility, I followed her into the poorly lit but tidy enough room. If I hadn't been so put off, I'd have noticed her use of that less-than-friendly nickname.

"Take a seat, Shah-Long."

The massive woman crashed into a lounge probably made for three people. Trying extremely hard to not stare at her, I shrugged and sat on the floor a good distance away from this woman who was to be my wife.

"You came alone. I assume Father was indisposed. He is too quick to bury his despair in a bowl of wine. It appears you have tried to do the same."

She pronounced every word clearly, as though afraid they wouldn't make any sense any other way. This precision and her soft voice seemed mismatched for her slovenly appearance, but I realised that even thinking that let alone judging her was hypocritical of me.

Again, she spoke before I had a chance to think of something less offensive to say, something about the wedding perhaps.

"I have known about this coming wedding for quite some time. Unlike my father, I am aware of why it has been arranged. He thinks it is just convenient to get me off his hands, with you being the son of an influential Elder thrown into the bargain."

Is that what I now was? Not Dog-Ears. Not the bastard. No. The son of an influential Elder. I'd been warming to the idea of marrying into Elder Leung's family and never having to return to Swimming Carp. But when she put it that way, it was starting to look like I was trading one cage for another. Drinking to the point of illness would replace the beatings; the constant scorn of Bitter Lotus for having to marry and take care of Plump Treat might be no better than how Swimming Carp had treated me.

I *swear* I didn't say any of that, but still her expression softened into pity, though whether for herself or me I could not tell.

"Am I that much of a burden? Probably. It is of no matter. I act as I feel, as I truly might be inside. And you, Shah-Long. Does your Pyrotic — sorry, wrong word. Does your *Huo-sha* soul affect your appearance?"

How? What? I choked back so many confused responses, settling on simply admitting I didn't know. Feeling that was inadequate, I added a maybe, then a yes, but also a suggestion that there were other things as well.

"Such as the torture Swimming Carp puts you through daily? Or the lonely life you lead? Hm, this is possible. I myself appear bloated and sluggish because this is what we have become. Not only Bitter Lotus, but this entire region. Maybe all of Kaef're. It is no good, really."

There was a question she had been setting up, right from the start. It was a trap and I had no choice but to step into it.

I asked her how she knew so much.

Her frown was like a rusty mouth of spikes snapping shut around my stupid foot.

"You mean, how could a fat sow like me possibly know anything?" Sudden crude language contrasted her pronunciation like a cleaver wrapped in silk. "Well, you have your ways and so do I. Your talent is fire; mine is minds."

I stared.

She laughed. If the frown was the trap closing, that laugh was the almost unnecessary venom coating the teeth.

I wanted to ask her what she was, and it was then I realised that in all the scrolls I'd read, there *was* no name for this Talent, only descriptions. It was truly that rare.

"It is called Maliscience. A foreign word, yes. And you know why Maliscience is rare, do you not?"

I didn't notice her query because it was just the shadow of something gargantuan obstructing the light. This woman could read minds. My. Mind. Years of physical punishment, abuse, torment, and yet I'd never felt so helpless, so worthless. She'd already begun to respond to even that before I could change my mind. Ha, *change* my mind. For all I knew, she could do that too. I shook my head, wondering for the first time if there was any point at all. To anything. To me.

"Oh, my betrothed, you are far from pointless. It is amusing though. Just about everybody I have read feels that, in some way, they are destined for greatness. Despite all evidence to the contrary, people always cling to their dreams."

Dreams? I didn't dream much. Damn, she caught that too.

"Well, not anymore, hm?"

Oh, Eph me. None of the legends or myths said anything about reading memories. So not only could this woman (my future wife!) 'hear' what I was thinking, she could actually know everything I'd ever thought?

Ever?

"Not quite," she said, and then wagged a fleshy finger at me. "And watch the profanity please. Ephriem ill-deserves your abuse. Yes, even in thoughts."

I ground my teeth to resist a frustrated howl. If she could just read it all, past and present, what was the use in saying or even thinking anything?

"Your mind is not an open box, Shah-Long. No one's is. Most people give me vertigo when I try to pry beyond whatever is on their mind in the moment. People literally do not know what they are thinking most of the time. Imagine trying to get through a maze of rooms where every door is mislabelled. Not even that is quite right. Still, if that is how it is, let us say your doors have much more honest signs. They invite exploration. Would you let me?"

Now she asked? I remember wondering: why can't she just take what she wants? What does she want? What DO you want? Are you reading this? What else can you see in here? What can't I see in my own mind?

"That is the key, Shah-Long. Let me dig around and see if I can drag up what you do not know you know. Do you want to know?"

She fell silent, eyes humble upon folded hands. Something about this pose struck me as familiar, comforting. Had I seen my mother in such a stance? I was immediately drawn to obey, not out of fear but the only emotion stronger than fear. Yet I'd just met this woman. I *knew* she was cheating, but what was the point? There was really only one answer I could give, wasn't there?

"Yes?" Was she answering my thought, or confirming something else? I just nodded. "Yes, okay. Here we go."

As her expression lost its brief uncertainty, I thought: she knew everything, and not only did she know everything, she could know more, and *more* with each passing second. I considered the nature of the web I was suddenly drawn into, because she'd known who I was, which meant she'd read her father and maybe even my father which meant it was all about me—

"Stop that! It is making it harder when you cloud your surface with blatant thoughts. And do not get too cocky. This is not just for you. Look. Try to empty your mind. Meditate or something."

I'd read about meditation, an exercise of the mind focusing on nothing at all. Although sceptical about the idea of thinking about not thinking, I closed my eyes and concentrated on the concept of nothingness. From the very first not-thought, I was feeling that I was failing at not-thinking. Every time my mind neared that empty state, my thoughts began to wander. Throwing her arms in the air, Plump Treat's voice cut through the insufficient void.

"Shah-Long, you are making this impossible! There is no help for it. I'll guide you through it, step by step."

It was then that she dropped the precise enunciation.

"Close your eyes. Again. That's right. Now, take a deep breath through your nose. Hold that breath, and then exhale through your mouth. Do it again, and again. In through the nose, out the mouth. Any sounds you happen to hear should flow in one ear, and out the other. You should listen only to my voice. Now, I want you to visualise your body, sitting there. Pretend you're outside your body, watching it. See that body as transparent; there's nothing to it. You are a shell."

I know now that she meant it as metaphor, but Dog-Ears didn't exactly do those. Where others might simply imagine, I became.

"A shell, waiting to be filled. Imagine a thick mist, rising from the ground and through your body. It fills your legs, your waist, your arms, your chest. Then the mist gathers upwards, until all of it rests in your head. Breathe in, deep through the nose, hold it, and feel that mist grow in your head as you do so. Exhale, and the mist shrinks. Repeat this, over and again. Relax. You are totally relaxed."

Yes. For the first time in my life, there were no questions. Not of myself, not about others. I'd emptied myself of even myself, and the feeling was utter serenity.

But not even that could last, because that was just preparation. Plump Treat's task was never to calm me or reassure me that everything was alright. If my mind was that maze she'd talked about, then all she'd done was clear the clutter in the entrance room. She chose her first door, and then another, and another, and each time she was more brutal, more insistent.

Much of it was a revelation at the time, but it's nothing you don't know about me already. My name might not have been Shah-Long, I saw strange visions and dreams, oh, and yes, deep down, I wanted to kill everyone. Though I knew these things, hearing myself say them just once and in such a dead voice negated years of explanation and forced self-placation. I can be candid about it now, but there were tears soon enough as I related what the villagers did to me and how my Father treated me. My fears, my desires, my hatred: she had access to them all.

It should have ended there, with the total disassembly of my concept of self. That, however, was just half-way, like reaching the middle of a labyrinth. This is what she taught me that day: once you strip away all the known layers, a previously unseen core reveals itself, something that is more than just your 'self' – it's your history, all the events leading up to who and what you are right now and maybe even your future. I didn't believe in a pre-destined course; I still don't, *unless* you examine the past and future as one thread, predating *and* outliving your body. Your place upon this thread? Take into account exactly what you want and what you're willing to do to achieve it. If you don't, you'll just be a knot in the line. Accept that Fate is just a game of narrowing your options down to one ultimate goal and you are free to be special upon that thread, like a shiny, unique bead.

Did she say all that, or did I know it?

She might have continued:

"Beads make the necklace. Knots ruin it. Some beads work well together; others clash and repel. But this is essential, just as it is that you become a bead and accept the conflict: let it define you, empower you and ruin you."

I don't know if I took much of that in at the time. I was too busy being a shell, a paradox (as usual): an empty reservoir. But there was no reservation here, no hesitation or regret – those were cast away as part of the now peeled skin.

It ended, for me, with a whisper, a crucial moment that demanded an answer. A return to the uncertainty of a question, but one loaded with a determination that was anything but uncertain.

For my ambition, to become a unique bead upon the thread of eternity: what will I take, and what will I sacrifice?

Everything was darker when I opened my eyes; the shadows of the room were much longer and deeper than before. It felt as if I'd only closed them for a second, yet hours had passed. Seated on the floor, cross-legged, I was at ease but alert, like after a good night's sleep. The oversized Plump Treat sat in her oversized chair, her face flaccid: mouth loose, eyes almost closed, chin pressed against a mound of flab. The resemblance to her drunken father was more than passing.

What did she find? Not sure why I asked that – one look at her said more than enough: *something she wasn't supposed to find.*

"Moon. Tears. Cross…" She moaned, and my immediate thought was surprisingly indignant: *she stole my vision!* But then I softened: *and it's done something bad to her.*

"Charan!"

This cry lacked neither clarity nor intensity, and I almost fell over backwards.

That name again: was it real or did she pluck it from my fantasy? Perhaps this was the problem with being able to read memories as well as thoughts.

Either way, she got what she wanted – and, it seemed, what she definitely *didn't* want.

Then, quiet as a sigh, she started to move. One of her hands snaked in crevices of complicated fabric. It squirmed there, as though trying to burrow and hide, until it emerged with something in its fangless mouth. I thought it might have been a brush. Plump Treat began to run the instrument over her naked arm, fervent but focused. I saw dark lines marking the passage of the brush, which I then knew wasn't a brush at all.

It was a little knife.

I sprang off the floor, the meditation lending me rare explosive energy. Trickles of blood crept down her forearm. Plump Treat continued to score her flesh with dedicated precision. Upon nearing her, I was surprised yet again: the wounds were neither deep nor random. I looked at her face, but there was nobody home.

With one last decisive cut, it was done; Plump Treat passed out. The little knife fell from her hand and into mine. I stared at her grisly work, knowing I'd find something deliberate and all the more horrifying for it.

To see what she'd done, I had to wipe the blood away from each cut. I memorised the design; there was no time to examine the image now. It seemed familiar but was also unique in its intricacy. Blood continued to well from the wounds and, suddenly guilty about my priorities, I tried to use her knife to cut a makeshift bandage from my shirt, but for some reason it only poked holes in the fabric. After a few attempts at sawing the cloth, I gave up and just ripped strips of the stuff and bound her blood-slick arm.

I checked one last time to make sure she was actually breathing and then crept out, worried that if she woke up before I left, she'd say or do something even more unnerving. Something that might break not only her, but both of us.

"Oh?" This was Elder Leung's reaction to my slightly bloodied, ragged return. "Tried to warn you."

Stalking towards the stairs, I didn't even bother looking at him.

After my brief visit to Plump Treat's house, she had not been seen or heard from for days. Her few visitors reported no responses upon knocking on her door. I explained some of it to Elder Leung, who didn't care other than the fact that this might have upset his son-to-be. Forcing a casual attitude towards the matter, I reassured 'Father' that all would be fine. Each day, however, I waited for him to fall into his mid-afternoon drunken slumber to go check on her.

She was physically fine; her arm was healing well. A pity her gifted mind wasn't so quick to recover.

I asked her if she was alright; she just continued to stare at nothing. No, not nothing. Something, something I could not see. She didn't say anything, not even that name, which was a small reassurance. I was still dubious as to how she had come upon it. It was, after all, not from the visions but from my own supposedly self-made True Dream Gone Horribly Wrong…or Horribly Right.

Afterwards, I would return to Elder Leung's house, sit in my room upstairs, alone, and stare at the sketch I'd made of the unnerving image. There was a crescent moon, and inside its curve, that sacrilegious cross-shape, and a handful of sharp symbols around both. It looked like writing, if writing could be scratched out by a restless rat. And, contrasting those angles, there was a single, beautifully round tear underneath the moon – or was it just a drop of blood? Something told me the entire image had a name, but I was wrong about that too.

Eventually, I'd just fold the sketch and, in a strange reversal of what Plump Treat had done with the knife, tuck it somewhere safe and return to the farce that was my presence in Bitter Lotus, saying nothing about anything.

Two weeks after the incident, Elder Leung himself had been forced to investigate his estranged daughter's condition. Without paying too much attention, he pronounced her insane and thus unfit for marriage.

"If she can do that to herself," he concluded, "I fear what she might do to you."

The cancellation should have relieved me, but it was my fault. I was guilty; why wasn't I being punished? I had unwittingly done this to the poor woman, this martyr who was the first to ever truly understand me. And for what? What theft could possibly be worth a person's sanity? A name spoken and an image revealed. Tiny clues in the impossibly large puzzle of whoever I was.

As Vachaelle would say, 'big fuckin' deal'.

With the wedding no longer an issue, my place in Bitter Lotus was equally nullified. Like or not, I had to go back to Swimming Carp, and not just because I had no reason to be here. I harboured vague plans to show the image to Father, because it was clear to me that if it came from my history, he was the person most likely to know anything about it.

It was time to leave, but I couldn't quite bring myself to call it 'going home.'

"Are you certain, boy?" Elder Leung wasn't exactly eager to change my mind; I was no longer worthy of being called a 'man', apparently. "I have no more daughters to give, but I could use you around the village."

Knowing that I was done being 'used', I made it clear: I had to be elsewhere. I was sorry I could not come to call him 'Father'.

"As I am, my boy. But I like you, and wouldn't want to see you suffer being wedded to that good-for-nothing lump."

His relentless spite for the woman I'd ruined reminded me of my 'real' father and how the bastard was always ready with an insult just for me. I bit back an angry contradiction and nodded, as if to agree with Elder Leung's questionable benevolence.

"Well, I guess that's it then." He trailed off, paying more attention to his cup of wine than me. "Here's a final toast to you, my son, even if you're not really."

Not even a month had passed, and now I was heading back to Swimming Carp, dressed in the same 'rags' I'd worn upon leaving it. If not for the foreboding image given by Plump Treat's sacrifice (sacrifice? She wasn't willing, and she wasn't mine to give over, was she? *I let her in*), the whole thing had been a waste. Still, that's a stupid way to think. If not for this or that. It's entirely possible my only reason to go to Bitter Lotus, from a fateful-bigger-picture-cosmic-proportions kind of level, was to meet Plump Treat, learn a bit about myself, destroy her in thanks and then move on. Could I be that selfish? She'd said that everyone she'd read, everyone, felt that they had some greater destiny, and then she'd scorned the idea…but if that were true of me as well, then there really was no point to what had happened to her, to what I'd received.

I *had* to have a destiny, but not once did I dare imagine it was going to be a good one.

Chapter 3: *Toh*
WINDOWS

"This isn't the village I remember," I said to myself.

I was taking shelter from Dyingsun's heat beneath that one large tree beside the path, toying with Plump Treat's deceptively little knife and the idea of not walking down into Swimming Carp. The trip back had given me time to think – although the return journey felt a lot quicker than when I left. By the time I reached the familiar crest looking down at the houses and streets, I'd decided exactly what would happen.

What was *supposed* to happen. What I'd like to tell you happened: I returned to Swimming Carp, armed with Plump Treat's tragic clue, and confronted Father, demanding to know what he knew. I backed the Elder into a corner, towering over him as he himself had towered over me, shouting and belittling. When shouting wasn't enough, I beat him so thoroughly that fountains of blood spurted from his pulpy mouth, his smashed nose. His arms and legs were mashed bean paste and rice. All he could do was wail and beg me to stop, speech mushy from swollen lips and missing teeth. And I did not stop.

Whoever it was that had swung that dream-sword and *did not want to stop* danced through this ideal, this one last fantasy to remind me why I'd come back. Destiny. Life. My life.

"This is my life," I said. "It can begin here; it can end at any moment, too."

I normally didn't talk to myself all that much – too much risk if anyone were to catch me. Something told me that wasn't going to happen here. I was well and truly alone.

"But it can't end here until it begins here."

So I stood, put away the knife and began the long descent down the dusty track linking Swimming Carp to the rest of the world. I noticed how empty the road was, but if that meant no one picking on me or giving me dirty looks, I wasn't about to wonder why.

I really should have.

It was almost dusk when I entered the village proper, and had seen precisely zero people. The unnatural deadness stretched down the main street of the village like a grey shadow. I had to accept then: something had happened; I should be careful. I crept from building to building, glancing into open doorways and the windows of each store. Every house and shop: deserted.

And yet, for all this play at being cautious, I know now that I *was* talking to myself the whole time, as though trying to rationalise the irrational. Or maybe hoping someone, just outside of my vision, would respond.

"No, more than deserted. The village is dead. But not even death compares to this stillness; death follows life, is a part *of* life. Death ends life; life evolves into death. This isn't death. Swimming Carp has been pulled away from the world and set aside. Why? I'm taking this too deep, aren't I? Set aside, like an unfinished project, an incomplete meal, and maybe whoever set it aside has forgotten about it? Should I even be here?"

There wasn't an answer for that, but it did give me an idea of where to go next.

I came to the Common Hall, shivering despite the summer sunset. Unlike most other buildings of Swimming Carp, the Hall had neither ceiling nor entrance door. The gateway, in stark opposition to the crude houses around it, radiated grandeur. The wooden sign dominating it displayed intricate carvings of gilded fish flanking the village's name, itself painted a gaudy gold. A thick post of smooth wood, lacquered in bold red, stood at each side of the entrance. Various blessings and declarations of wealth were etched into the pillars.

"This was everything Swimming Carp thought it was," I said, letting my fingers dip into grooves of the characters. I read some of them aloud: "Fortune. Happiness. Friendship. Unity."

I pondered these for a moment, then concluded:

"What a load of shit."

I don't think I'd said that word out loud before, not even when I was alone. Where the inexplicable absence of the villagers failed, a simple word succeeded: I felt liberated. What punishments had they promised if I said this or did that? Whatever they were, it hadn't happened. I unclenched my fist, determined not to hurt myself in response to those who'd gone to such lengths to hurt me. "Yeah, *Eph* the lot of them."

Still no thunderous retribution from God for breaking one of Her great rules. Maybe Swimming Carp really had been forsaken by even Heaven Below.

I slid around the pillar to examine the meeting area itself. Newfound freedom or not, things were *wrong* in their lifelessness: no chatter of villagers, or clamour of earthenware pots; absent the hectic patter of bare feet over a chalky, unswept floor. Unattended tables and benches, rough and practical, dotted the room. And, of course, there was the centrepiece of the Common Hall: the Slaughter Pit.

I could tell you all about that horrible little hole well before I saw it that day. That pit and I, we'd spent a lot of time together. It was almost square in shape, easily wider than an average man's height, and just as deep. I didn't have to get any closer to it to see the bloodstains covering its coarse walls and the splinters of bone littering the ochre floor. During my time in The Pit, I had learned a thing or two about joints, muscle and how to slit an animal's throat quickly, mercifully. The villagers had, I suppose, always enjoyed the idea of making me prepare the very meat I'd never be allowed to taste.

And not once did they consider that I might turn this knowledge against them.

"They were just shit-eating animals themselves," I grunted, still enjoying the taste of forbidden language. "And now they're all gone."

Not hiding, not gathered somewhere. One way or another: gone. But the villagers were stubborn. Nothing less than an army rampaging down the streets could convince a family to walk away.

If Swimming Carp had been forsaken, did this mean the villagers themselves had somehow angered the Night? Maybe their treatment of me! No. That was too fantastic a thought, and...

"I'm done with fantasies."

So the reality, then: in less than a month, every single inhabitant of my home village appeared to have *dis*appeared, leaving the place looking like no one had lived there for years. There wasn't any sign of conflict, of invasion. No bodies, not even any blood or broken windows. And it happened while I wasn't there. Was I sent away on purpose? Did Plump Treat's influence extend this far? Had she summoned me and then arranged for the village's fate? That made little sense, but there wasn't a lot to go by. What, precisely, did I *know* about Swimming Carp? Outside of Father's house, the school, the Common Hall? The fields? All in all, almost nothing.

And, as I mused about all this, 'outside of Father's house' is precisely where I found myself. Upon seeing the closed door, I knew that's where I should have gone straight away. Why would Father close the door if he's not planning on coming back? He might have been inside, alive or dead, but after seeing no signs of life around the village, I suspected otherwise.

Still, I wanted to look inside, and knew the perfect way to do it.

When I first became aware of my true dream's significance, I had been leaning against the wall and looking *out* the window. The second revelation was granted by sneaking around it, inching the shutter open from one side and looking *in*.

My bed was gone. In the pallet's place was a pile of clothes, layer upon layer of vibrant fabric. It might have been women's clothing or laundry. Before looking elsewhere, I sighed. Although my bed was gone, that soft, inviting rainbow might have been more comfortable.

The fire was lit and just bright enough for me to take in further details of the room.

As with the rest of Swimming Carp, there were no signs of forced entry or theft. Father's rough-hewn table was intact. His beloved chess set, a militant array representing the closest thing to an army the village had ever seen, was ready for play.

Past the table was Father's kitchen. A brick bench just over half a man's height and topped with a wide wooden counter separated it from the living room. If he were in a better-than-terrible mood, Father would prepare some of the more exquisite dishes known to Swimming Carp. I envisioned him labouring at the elongated bench with his cleaver, a freshly-plucked chicken and his focused temper. The broad blade of the cleaver rises, pauses, and then streaks down to thud against the chicken's flesh. Up again it goes, this time encrusted with shattered chips of bone and slivers of glutinous meat, and then down for another hack. It seemed so savage, so reckless, but the end result was always a carefully arranged dish defying scrutiny and demanding immediate consumption.

That image was so real, so immediate, I could smell the herbs and taste the onions. I closed my eyes, breathed in and heard a thud far more real than Father's chopping. Louder than it should have been, closer than even the memories.

Someone *was* in there. I immediately thought it was Father. After all, this was his place and the door was closed. Then there was a moan, coming from somewhere inside but beside me, out of my view. Maybe they were hurt? It was that sort of groan, a low and tired croak accompanying an almost contented breath. As crazy as this seemed, I thought that the person could be content that they were still alive.

I had a second thought: Father could be drunk. He didn't drink as far as I knew, but that didn't seem very far anymore. Which meant that everything I knew could be wrong and that meant I didn't know anything at all…

Before I could continue this dismal chain of thought, there was another moan and then a husky laugh. It sounded like a woman.

A woman, in Father's house, my *home*, moaning and laughing.

So Elder Wong Chu-Deng gets rid of his bothersome bastard and cosies up with some slut? As much as I despised him, and as little sense as this made, I found the notion that he needed to discard me, just for the sake of a woman, nauseating.

"That feel good?" asked a distinctly male voice. "Hmm. How about this?"

Now *that* could have been his voice. And if it was Father in there, and he was with a woman, couldn't it be Mother? *Shouldn't* it be?

Still, I'd never heard the man sound quite so passionate, so lustful. The woman made another noise: a childish giggle. He was apparently tickling her, although the laugh itself contained something more carnal. I wasn't exactly an expert on the matter, but something in that little laugh made my gut wrench. What little I knew about sex came from listening to the boisterous kids of the village. Instead of boasting about how strong they were, the boys would now claim that they had charmed this girl or that and they were 'doing it' as much as they'd wanted. And whatever they'd meant by that, I had a feeling it was going on just out of my sight.

Neither man nor woman spoke for several minutes, although the moaning and erratic laughter did punctuate my espionage with disturbing levity.

"It should be safe for you to go out soon," she said at last.

"Not yet, though. Don't tell me you're done already?" he replied.

Were they done 'doing'? Half of me hoped they were, and the other half tried not to feel cheated. Be it about swords, secrets or sex, my craving for knowledge was the only real weapon I possessed; as with all weapons, inept hands were bound to have trouble working out which end was which. The irony of knowing what I know now, of course, is that I had to learn it to realise I'd rather *not* know it.

"I have to know," I whispered.

I crouched once more, spidering beneath the window. Then I straightened again and, just as careful as before, eased the shutter open from the other side. What I saw in my impatience caught my breath; somehow, I almost choked on air.

The truth's a scary thing when you've been building yourself up for a lie and *knew* it was a lie.

I saw the woman from behind; her shoulder blades seemed to penetrate the slick skin of her sweating back. She *was* naked, but only from the waist up. The rest of her was almost hidden by a thin skirt the colour of pumpkin flesh. Almost hidden. The smooth curvature of her buttocks squashed against the bare floor but retained their firmness. Her arms were spread out, a little behind herself with the hands palms down, supporting the extended posture. Her head was tilted back and long, reckless hair tumbled down her back like slimy noodles.

Long, reckless hair the colour of wheat, of honey, like nothing I'd seen outside of a dream. Everyone in Swimming Carp had black hair. There wasn't even a word in Chūnko-go for this colour.

If this was my mother, then she was not from my world. I would not have recognised her even if we walked right past each other.

But then frantic emotion drowned this lone rebel of logic. If this was my mother, someone was violating her. I forgot that the couple had been mutual in their activity, that it had been the woman who laughed first. The tightening in my throat eased itself and my breath hissed out with a sibilant rage.

Only the second wave of immature reasoning kept me from screaming. The woman, my mother, was with a man. My father? Although I could not see who was ravishing the woman, I was willing to believe. Father *was* making love to Mother. Another deep breath consumed my shame before the weight of it could push me to the ground. I was ashamed, yes, but relieved as well. If one man was supposed to touch my mother, it should be Father. I had no business interfering.

Reassured, I started to lower the shutter and then turn away but caught a glimpse of the man's face. I stared, struggling to see my father in this stranger's features. They were gaunt and shiny, wet and leery. Father's eyes always seemed hard and unforgiving; these glowered, dark with hunger as they surveyed the woman's slim body. Despite the angle of view and poor lighting, there were certain discrepancies. In fact, compared to Father's face, there was no match at all.

This wasn't who I'd been expecting.

I was wrong; I was right. Someone *was* molesting my mother. I felt the enormity of the situation sink in as I sank to my haunches and stared at the village. My eyes became dry and painful but refused to blink. Swimming Carp looked almost flat, like a painting or picture. Nothing moved, nothing breathed – it had always been this way, would always be this way. Was I right about that, at least? If so, I had to admit this to myself: without its people, this was not my home. All of my careful training, self-discipline and resistance to Swimming Carp's stranglehold had amounted to this realisation. Without someone to yell at me, I was just a set of deformed ears listening as people ignored me. If no one looked at me, maybe I just didn't exist. Filling a hole with rotting meat and garbage is still better than leaving it empty. Empty, I was just a shell, an egg with all hopes of birth sucked right out before the first cracks could form. But I remembered. And memories are not nothing. *We* are nothing without our memories. And I had memories. Thanks to the very people who treated me like rotting meat, like garbage, it was impossible for me to be nothing! It wouldn't end here. I was ready to see what came next.

So I blinked.

Oblivious to the possible danger around, behind and awaiting me, I stood up and walked around to the front of the house. I knew I was going to say something, but what? To whom? Not other people – they were obviously gone. Not even to myself: I no longer had a clear idea who that was. Still, something had to be declared. My feelings. My faith. This is what I *wanted* to say:

I will not let this defeat me. Whatever malevolent force attempts to control my future, the future of these people, of Swimming Carp, I will never permit it to succeed. It has taken so many lives, for whatever purpose, but it will not have mine. Swimming Carp might be dead, but its lessons live on in my heart. Father, you hated me but in that hatred you taught me so much. I will not bow to this cruelty that eclipses even your deliberate injustice. I…will…not.

Inadequate and clumsy, yes, because sometimes it's true: words just can't describe how you feel. That's why the really big changes in the world never go like that. Before people have time to frame their speeches, to rehearse and plan, and probably say far too much; before they even understand that History is about to tap them on the shoulder and whisper, 'I can *seeee* you'; and before thinking they should straighten their clothes or neaten their hair, people change the world with but a single word.

"No."

That was when it happened.

As though it were no less substantial than the only window to my home, I opened the Window in my mind and looked through. I saw something beyond colour, beyond all the senses – boundless awareness, immediate and unrestrained perception. The anarchy then bent towards a single point: nothing was irrelevant and everything made sense.

I know there are two people in the building. One is female. One is male. Both are occupied. One is not my father. The other could be my mother. This is not likely. I know this house. I can navigate it with my eyes closed. I know its details. These people have not been here as long as I have. They do not know this house. The front door is closed but they probably didn't lock it. The village is empty. There is a broom resting against the wall beside the door. I can use this.

I considered all of these facts in less time than it takes to draw a breath. Than it takes to blink. It didn't strike me as strange, although I'd never been able to think this way in the past, and now wondered why I'd never at least tried. It was like I'd been walking around a lake in the dark when there was a well-lit bridge right in front of me, all that time. Everything was new, enriched. Reborn. Dwelling on this newfound clarity revealed that I already knew so much. I'd just never known it.

Not easy to 'use your head' when you've never really understood what's in it.

Chapter 4: *Sha*
CONFRONTATION

Most people burn bridges behind them; I have a habit of burning mine while I'm still halfway across.

My feet were silent upon the stone steps. I eased the door open – unlocked, as I had known. The fading twilight couldn't carry my shadow across the threshold. I couldn't see the couple through the doorway, which meant that I might also be hidden. The erotic sounds continued – the two of them wouldn't be looking anyway. Entering the house, I swiped the broomstick from its resting place beside the door. Not a sword, but better than a knife. It would suffice.

Then I saw them, across the room past the table, twisting on the floor near the far wall. I judged the distance between myself and the two to be twenty footsteps. Plenty of room.

"What are you doing here?" I asked.

The woman squealed, grabbed the discarded clothing scattered about the floor and hastened to dress, like a lazy warrior who'd slept in and was late for battle but still didn't want to get out of bed. The man growled and rose to his feet; his litheness belied an ungainly height. The woman obscured my view of him from the waist down, so I focused on what I could see. With the awakened acuity, I noted instantly: the man's torso was developed but not overly muscular; his arms were gangly; and his skin was almost the colour of ash. Even though the fire's light failed to reveal his face, I saw a mouth wide open, lips pulled back into a snarl.

"What are *you* doing here, Half?" he asked, twisting my own question back at me. Before I could answer, the beast turned his attention to the simpering girl at his feet. "I thought you said you'd take care of him?"

She crawled onto her knees and tried to climb his thighs.

"I did! I made sure of it, I promise. I did not lie to you, my love! I would not lie to you."

Did she look at me during this tearful tirade? A fleeting acknowledgment, no more.

Or was it a smile?

While the two were diverted, I stole a few steps to improve my view. The woman beseeching 'her love' appeared to be barely twenty years old. I was horrified that I'd ever mistaken this whimpering waste for my mother. The woman's hair, which had seemed so radiant before, now looked dirty, flecked with flat patches of brown and even a few streaks of grey.

I returned my attention to the man. Although his flesh was pale, it wasn't quite the milky translucence of my fantasy's final horrors. And as wicked as his grimace might have been, it was still just a mouth, not some gaping maw full of fangs. His short hair was black and clammy. Contrary to these signs of normalness, the ears sticking out from his triangular face were not round, but pointed. As the dearly departed of Swimming Carp would have put it, they were *strange*.

Another burst of lightning flashed in my newly-opened eyes; another stream of thought tore through my mind.

He's tall, like me. His ears are strange, like mine. My ears might not be the result of being pulled too much. He could be related to me. Wong Chu-Deng might not be my father. This man could tell me more about myself. If I can subdue him or avert this fight, we could talk. The girl is still crying but has moved out of the way. Two more seconds and he will be in range. Four more seconds and it will be too late to move. If I take another step forward, that time difference becomes one and a half seconds and three seconds. The table is beside us. I can use this.

Setting the makeshift weapon before myself, bristle-end closest to my body, I called across the expanse dividing me and the imposing giant.

"Can we just talk? No need to make this a fight."

"Are you serious?" he answered, and while I expected the disdain, that hint of genuine query caught me off-guard. *Was* I serious? "It's more than a little late for just talk. Time to end this." The large man cocked back an equally enormous right fist and crushed the gap between us with a few surprisingly quick steps.

Before I could think about his reply, even with heightened power of reasoning, those few precious seconds were gone forever.

The Window closed as spontaneously, as inexplicably, as it had opened, sealing the light of intellect and its shadow of intuition beyond my touch; it left me in the darkness of animal instinct.

There was nothing to do other than repeat what I'd practiced so much: a diagonal cut from behind the right shoulder. I'd hammered at many a tree this way, hours upon hours. I had the movement down, didn't even need to think about what to do with my hands, arms, legs, feet. For a moment, there was hope that I might actually hit the advancing behemoth.

Unfortunately, he wasn't a tree. As the broom sailed towards him, the giant lowered his body with unanticipated swiftness – in fact, it seemed he'd known from the start how I'd attack. The broom *did* hit him, and because it was a broom, it did nothing. I had just enough time to look down as the man drove his fist up into my chin.

My face was no stranger to the hard kiss of knuckles; the punch still knocked me clear across the room. Father's table interrupted my flight and the landing scattered the chess pieces to the floor – they sounded like hailstones. I lay there, legs dangling off the edge of the table and arms spread-eagled, trying to figure out which way the room was supposed to spin.

"Hua-Shi!" The woman wailed. *Wa-Shi?* "Just kill him and be done with it!"

"Why? You were beginning to bore me anyway."

Pain muffled their voices and my thoughts. My jaw was a separate entity rejecting the rest of me – some limp, uninvited excess. Raising my head brought on a spasm of nausea, but I had to shake it off, or be pulverised. Hua-Shi was bearing down on me like a rockslide.

Still gripping the broom, I fell off the table and landed in a clumsy crouch. I heard a sharp, splintering crack – that was the end of Elder Chu-Deng's table. The monster just ploughed through the wood as though it were a paper screen.

Hua-Shi, surrounded by debris and dust, turned towards me. I straightened my knees into something resembling a ready stance. Our eyes met like blades on a battlefield. I'd hoped to find a little fury in Hua-

Shi's expression, or some sign of emotional imbalance. He seemed only slightly bothered that his new toy had dared to retreat; his calm gaze never wavered from my nervous stare.

I had to blink.

That was when he rushed at me again, a tangle of muscle and power clotting my vision. Hua-Shi raised his arm: a knuckle-headed hammer, ready to pound a rebellious nail. I understood only one thing: if I didn't move, the impact would turn me into the messiest part of the floor.

I moved, trying to stab at him with the broom. I was overextended, off-balance and had taken my eyes off the enemy: all the classic mistakes of an amateur bound for a life-time career with zero wins, one loss.

Something very heavy thumped against my back and sent me sprawling. I rolled over, raising the broom as if *it* could block whatever came next.

Have you ever seen a tortoise on its back? It wobbles and wriggles but can't do a thing. That was me, except this tortoise had a foot-sized meteor streaking toward it.

I abandoned hopes of using the broom and skittered to the side. Dog-Ears avoided yet another gruesome death.

That his savage stomp didn't squash me seemed to confuse Hua-Shi, who winced and grumbled. Maybe he sprained his ankle. It gave me time to stand back up, regain a flimsy guard.

He growled again, turned and unleashed a reckless left punch. The blind swing lashed around like a chain. I waited, heart threatening to push through my chest. Couldn't move too early, or he'd adapt. Move too late and it would all be over. The *moment*, then, was—

Now.

I slid to my left and back. Just in case this wasn't enough, I leaned into it – and still felt the air ripple across my cheek.

Hua-Shi followed through with a quick right. I shuffled back again, this time to my right. He had not anticipated such an obvious repetition: I could see it in the way he paused.

I kept backing away but knew I couldn't keep it up. The wall was not far behind me and I didn't want to be pressed against it. Another second passed, and Hua-Shi came at me with his final assault: one fist was head-high, the other barrelled towards my gut – a double-fisted lunge, a certain killing blow.

For once, I didn't even have time to hesitate. I dove to the right, aiming to roll just past Hua-Shi. I tucked my head into my chest, curled into a ball and hoped I didn't break my neck. My spine bumped over stone, grinding vertebra; my knuckles, tight around the stick, crunched against the floor. Careful not to pitch into another tumble, I slammed the broom down and spun around in a crouch, hoping to see the cost of Hua-Shi's committed dash.

Although he had managed to stop before running into the wall, Hua-Shi was a little out of sorts. I stood, prepared to take any sort of advantage at his hesitation, but then another, unforeseen development in the conflict held me immobile.

"I have him, my love! Can I kill him for you? Please?"

The girl! I'd forgotten all about her. Now, *somehow*, she was behind me, both arms firm around my chest. I tried to wriggle free, swinging the broom side-to-side for leverage, but she wouldn't have any of it. For all her beseeching and theatrics, she was *strong*. Perhaps she was fuelled by the chance to redeem herself to Hua-Shi. Resigned to her feral embrace, I sucked at my lower lip. It was bleeding; must have bitten it when Hua-Shi first hit me. Again, I've lost count of how many times I've had my face bashed bloody, but never before had I experienced this: the taste tingled my tongue and tempted my teeth.

"Let the little bastard go. He's mine." Hua-Shi sounded spiteful but his swagger had returned. Stamping her foot in indignation, the girl released me and then pushed me away with one smooth motion.

"I just wanted to help."

For some reason, I glanced back at her. The girl had flopped to her knees and began to sob.

She reminded me of a wilting orchid.

I stumbled to a halt and created as much distance between myself and Hua-Shi as possible. Bringing the much-abused broom before myself, I returned my attention to my enemy and noticed a soft aura tracing his silhouette. At first, I took it to be something magical. Hua-Shi was like no one I'd ever seen — this meant he could have been a Night's Own himself. But if an Incarnation of God's Will was going to kill a nobody like me, it wouldn't deign to be so intimate. One look from a Night's Own could stop a man's heart, taught Miss Master. Those chosen by God were above petty fighting. Very few people taken by the Night would ever know how they died. No pain, no suffering. *Everyone* knew that.

Like most things *everyone* knew, it wasn't true.

Hua-Shi lowered his fists at last, tired of his punching style. This switch in attitude gave me just enough time to figure out why that thin outline of light enshrouded Hua-Shi. He wasn't holy after all.

The fire-pit was behind him.

Fire! Only a moron, a stupid, shit-eating Dog-Ears, could have forgotten. Like a fool with a death-wish, I had rushed into the room, relying on nothing but a *broom*. No wonder Hua-Shi didn't take me seriously.

I continued to pull on the blood leaking from my cut lip. Something moved in my veins, returning life to heavy limbs and battered joints.

Holding the broom with my left hand, I caressed the coarse fan of bristles with the other, and called upon that which none knew about, none but me and poor Plump Treat. Small whips of flame caught hold of the hairs and melted them together in my fingers' wake.

Hua-Shi was watching, inert but on the verge of another attack. He didn't appear surprised at my Talent or especially impressed that I had chosen to play with Fire. He threw his bony shoulders back and thrust fists against hips – mocking, inviting. A taunt I chose not to reward.

I couldn't risk closing my eyes to concentrate but tried to release a more potent surge of *Huo-chi* anyway. I stared at Hua-Shi's face, looked past it and noticed, once more, his pointed ears. *Strange* ears. Like mine, and until then, I'd thought of them as a disadvantage. Bringing the lessons of Swimming Carp full circle, I widened my eyes but began to *listen*. And with that decision to trust a different sense, the rush of perfect perception filled my mind. The Window opened one last time.

I hear the girl crying to the side. I hear Hua-Shi's breathing quick but not heavy. I hear my own breathing ragged and uneven. I hear sweat sliding down my skin. I hear the fire. It is a soft whisper of heat, spitting tiny sparks into the air. I hear smoke wafting and curling above the fire. I hear the fire. It wants to burn brighter, to become that which it was created to do. The sparks are its incandescent birth, the smoke its heavy passage. I hear the Fire; its song is in my heart too.

Then my thoughts fell into a straight line again. I listened more, and what I heard aligned with what I saw. The fire behind Hua-Shi was within me. Voracious flames feasted on the wood; soft snapping replaced my erratic, helpless heartbeat. Its pulse quickened; the magnitude of the envisioned flames grew. They consumed more and more of my sanity — after seventeen years of self-imposed discipline, stubborn defiance and incomplete Dreaming, I had more than enough to burn. My Fire, in turn, was ravenous in grateful savagery.

I can't tell you why I did what I did next. It wouldn't make sense to anyone and yet it was *right*.

I grabbed the bubbling bristles. The tender flesh of my palm softened with the heat, but there was no pain. Hua-Shi started laughing as he watched me burn my own hand. I squeezed, crushed the mass of hair like a raw egg, and released the anxious Fire that had been gathering in the cauldron of my stomach. Hua-Shi stopped laughing. He narrowed his eyes and took a step forward, perhaps to see that which I already knew: my hand was closed into a fist. This was impossible; Hua-Shi's own large hand could not have enveloped such a thick wedge of hair. And yet it had happened, and when the orange glow faded I saw the bristles were gone. Not melted, not concealed. Just gone.

The broom had become a stick, and I knew what to do with sticks. Or so I thought. As Hua-Shi watched, his smile waxing incredulous, I held the stick in front of me, left hand keeping it level with the ground, right hand travelling the length, palm not quite touching the rough wood. It was as though I were drawing the real sword from within the broom, a weapon of air-searing flame. But whatever I expected to happen, didn't: the splintered wood glowed, caught alight and then fell apart in a mist of ash. I lowered my now-empty hands.

Although he might have been confused, Hua-Shi was done with my little show. Limbering up his legs with quick shakes, he bounded towards me. Between one step and another, I saw something else, or rather imagined I'd seen it. Maybe I was just predicting how it was going to end for me, Fire or no.

Hua-Shi's next move would be to deliver a brutal heel kick to my chest. His foot, upon contact, would somehow not only smash the bones beneath but part skin and penetrate muscle as well. If this Fire was anything less than a miracle, and Hua-Shi managed to land such a kick, that was how I would die: impaled on the end of his too-quick, too-strong leg.

Why in Heaven Below had I destroyed my only weapon?

Hua-Shi roared as he jumped off the floor. His bellow would have made mountains shiver. One leg became stiff as it spun through an arc of impossible speed. I knew what he was doing. I knew what it was called. My whisper named it.

"Kuraiden-geki."

Dark Thunder Shock Attack. Silly name, serious problem. This was even worse than what I'd anticipated. Unhindered, that devastating kick was designed to knock my head clean off. At the very least, it would have broken my neck. I knew and again I didn't know *how* I knew.

I'd wished for a way to test my Fire and my broom…well, my *blade* skills, and here it was, in one neat package.

And I was suddenly unsure if I were prepared to pass that test.

Now I was afforded scrambled thoughts about defence, about the futility of arms and hands as shields. I raised them anyway. Something winked in me, and tendrils of warm light slid up those arms and enveloped my shoulders, my neck. The sensation was one of safety, of being guarded by an impregnable barrier. The feeling also held a hint of affection. The Fire *wanted* to protect me. It would not tolerate any harm dealt to me, its vessel.

Somehow, between one second and the next, I knew that everything would be fine.

Hua-Shi's kick neared its apex; his foot slammed into the nimbus of light encasing me.

And stopped. It just hung there – a half-thought confused by its own spontaneity.

I looked at it for a while.

Time didn't slow down or become clearer. Rather, I felt altered, tampered with. *Accelerated.* I could do anything before the rest of the world even had a chance to know it. Was this just another effect of the Fire, or a delusion, a deception? I could have spent a long time pondering this if the displacement from everyone else's reality had lasted. How was such an obvious paradox possible – how could I have been locked in stasis one moment, one eternal and immovable moment, and then a part of that other, rejected, reality the next? Could eternity last only a second or two?

I had time to see one last thing clearly, and I was meant to see it: the girl scrambling towards the door. I thought about sending something lethal her way. Sure, she'd tried to help Hua-Shi in the fight, but that was forgivable. Impersonating my mother, however, was a sin beyond reckoning, even if she had no idea she'd been doing it. That's no excuse! My impulse and the Fire grappled in that instant. One wanted to erase her, the other was occupied with more pertinent matters, such as the seven-foot-tall bastard about to kill me. The struggle ended in a stalemate; the girl left the scene unscathed.

The same cannot be said of the two caught within the infernal maelstrom that used to be, an age ago, my home.

Time resumed. The glow surrounding me took form and coiled about Hua-Shi's foot like a snake slithering around a dead branch. The impetus of the kick met a stronger opposing force. The serpent made of flame twisted the foot around and shoved it straight back. I watched, impassive, as the lash pulled his body around, set it ablaze and then dashed it straight down. Hua-Shi's collision with the floor dislodged fist-sized chunks of stone. He smouldered. He hissed.

He did not move.

Having performed its task, the Fire flickered and fell away like flayed skin. I remember two very clear feelings: ecstasy at the Fire's fulfilment of purpose; and then amputation at its unwelcome departure. The Window, which had still only opened to a tiny crack at most, began to shut.

And yet it closed so quickly I thought I heard it slam.

The Fire, gone. The Window, shut. Leaving me. Empty.

As it turned out, I was anything but, because I then reacted as any villager of Swimming Carp would have in the same situation. I doubled over and vomited a river of blood-stained acid. My cut lip burned as the juice burst over the open wound. Dizzy, disorientated and exhausted, I fell to my knees, retching in misery. Shameless tears simmered and overflowed. At that moment, I wished I'd lost, that I'd died. That Hua-Shi would get back up and finish me off.

Wary that he might just do that, I sucked up both my remaining courage and dangling drool then stood as best I could. I looked at the crater created by Hua-Shi's fall. Rubble littered the edges like little islands, crowding the coast of a stony sea. When I took a few unsteady steps towards the hole, I was both disconcerted and relieved to see it empty. My enemy had survived and made good his escape. Disintegrating brooms is one thing. I never presumed to think killing someone as clearly powerful and experienced as Hua-Shi would be as simple.

The remnants of the struggle were all around, from the scattered chess pieces and the broken table to that yawning fissure marking my dubious victory. The dwelling was made foreign by this conflict, a violence much more tangible than whatever Father had inflicted upon me over the years. I never wanted to live in that house, but it had been 'home' to Dog-Ears; right now, I actively wanted to leave.

Night, however, had truly set in. Leaving the relative safety of four walls and a door could be a mistake I might not have a chance to regret. I made my way around the wide hole and headed for the front door. A tingle of reassurance tickled my restlessness – the door itself was intact. I closed it, slammed the long wooden bar home with a flat thump and then leant against it. My mind had been a straightforward lance before; now it was a sack of grain. Thinking was a heavy, tiring exercise.

Idle and very banal thoughts held sway. For example, I was thankful I wasn't itchy, because my hands, arms, even my shoulders, would have refused to respond to the call. They were chained in manacles of tight weariness, if that even makes sense. Tight weariness, slack-jawed tension: both applied. I knew that something could happen to interrupt the respite. This knowledge, coupled with an inability to react, made me paranoid yet numb and hopeless. I couldn't remember when I'd ever felt so miserable. With my sorry upbringing, that's saying something.

The duel with Hua-Shi was the most important period of my adolescent life. It was the first time I, Dog-Ears of Swimming Carp…no, Shah-Long of Chūnko, faced a lethal opponent and discovered, in myself, the means to not only survive but also overcome. It was the first time I channelled Fire without a tranquil environment to inhibit my distractible nature. It was, finally, the first time I had wished for the peace found only in death, despite seventeen years of relentless abuse.

The fight only took five minutes. Five minutes for Dog-Ears to lose three little virginities. Sure, I eventually got better at it and started to last longer, but when they say 'it doesn't hurt so much the next time', they're God-damned lying.

Chapter 5: *Kai*
LESSONS

I did not dream that night.

When I woke, the room held no surprises, just a faint scent of vomit and the brutal evidence of Hua-Shi's defeat. He had not returned last night to really finish the fight. Perhaps he was as exhausted and worn out as me, but I doubted that. Hua-Shi was a seasoned brawler. If not for the Fire, it would have been my broken corpse occupying the heart of that crater.

A strained grunt put me on my feet. The repetitive work of the fields and around Swimming Carp was different to the five-minute clash against Hua-Shi. Muscles long unused cramped in stiff protest as I limped across the room.

I collapsed at last beneath the window, right near the pile of cloth I saw last night. Upon inspection, it became clear this was not typical villager apparel. Colours strong and brilliant overlapped one another with playful chaos, highlighted by strips of selective sunlight. I lifted a layer of azure silk, only to find it sliding over my palm like heavy water.

Mother would have honoured such splendid clothing.

But it had *not* been my mother! Disgusted, I flung away what little fabric remained in my grasp and ground my teeth. How dare that harlot even consider herself worthy of this? A spiteful tic pulled at my lips.

Wandering the interior for a few minutes, I considered taking a memento of my few pleasant times as Elder Wong Chu-Deng's ward, but every item from this house carried with it unwanted weight. If I were to leave Swimming Carp under my own terms, it would have to be without baggage. I closed my eyes, trying to recall all the times Father had mistreated me. I concentrated on these events, letting them affect me one last time, and then deposited them in this corner or that of the now ruined house.

Father's home was now crowded with invisible spirits forced to play out their vindictive dramas over and again. When I finally opened the door leading outside, I knew that I had cleansed myself of all anger, terror and acrimony towards Father. There was still fear, but it was a vague thing, no longer that constant dread that made me flinch just thinking about his voice. I feared Wong Chu-Deng as I would fear any other man. His influence over me had shrivelled and died in the Fire last night.

I stepped over the threshold and closed the door to the house, to Father…no, to Wong Chu-Deng, and his malice, behind me forever.

Clad only in tattered clothing and a determination to walk onward, I once again passed the squat buildings of Swimming Carp. Instead of heading straight for the road out, I decided to take a hazardous but crucial roundabout tour. This was the first morning I'd *ever* experienced a Swimming Carp without the jeering villagers and their abuse. It felt like the first morning I'd ever been in that village.

Shielding my eyes with an upraised hand, I reckoned the time to be somewhere between late Bladesun and early Morningsun. This gave me a few hours until Highsun, which was more than enough time to peruse Swimming Carp one last time. There was little pleasure in the exercise, yet I couldn't deny a certain pang of sentimentality as I passed the various houses and workplaces. All were quiet but for the soft draft that did not disturb the dusty floors and walls.

I felt sentimental because I didn't know any better, didn't realise that the stinging desire for the old Ways of Life was just a cold fear of the unknown. Each time I looked down the road towards the exit of Swimming Carp, I knew it was to be the last time. And I just wasn't ready. I'd always had somewhere to go when I went, and something to do when I got there. This message to be delivered, that mess to be cleaned. Take this, bring that. Go there, do this, come back here. Simple tasks comfortable in their predictability. Now the infinite possibilities of an unknowable, unplanned future smothered me. What if I went 'there' and I didn't know what to do? What if there was *nothing* I could do there? Wherever it was, maybe I didn't even belong 'there.'

Did I belong to Swimming Carp after all? If so, it was time to declare my independence, but not by just pulling away. I had to look the village in its ugliest of faces and say it, and that face was one place, the one place where everything I'd wanted to learn was everything I'd been told I never could.

I went back to school.

When I reached the main hall, I almost tugged at the thick rope hanging beside the door. I always arrived early to school, having completed my Bladesun chores before anyone else, and each morning I rang the bell so that Miss Master would let me in. The old witch lived there, and there were worse places to call home. Still, she knew what treasures lay within and invariably kept the door locked until the other students arrived.

With a smirk, I drew my hand back from the rope, opting to push the door open instead.

It gave without resistance.

The classroom was precise and organised. Miss Master demanded total conformity from her students, right down to the layout of the desks and chairs. Upon each desk were a few sheets of rice paper, a pot of ink and a writing brush. No desk deviated from another – they were lined up with a strict structure by which military ranks would have been shamed. Eight by four. Thirty-two places awaited just as many zealous students. With my presence, thirty-one. Passing the desks with my eyes fixed straight ahead, I came to stop at the front row. Here, isolated, was the 'idiot's chair', right near Miss Master's own but facing the entire class. I dragged the crude seat back and sat. The tiny stool held my weight too well.

"Dog-Ears! Answer the question!"

Miss Master's demand was an iron rod rammed down my spine. I knew the room was empty. I knew *all* of Swimming Carp was empty, yet for me, this room was anything but dead. In my memories, that for which Swimming Carp stood and endured could all be traced back to Miss Master and her teachings.

As I had done eleven years ago, and many times afterwards, I failed to answer the question.

"Deepest apologies, Master. I am stupid and did not understand it. Please repeat it, Master."

Miss Master knew it wasn't sarcasm. She drew in an exasperated breath and asked me once again.

"Which hour comes between Fallingsun and Dyingsun?"

Not a hard question. Any six year old knew the answer. Miss Master hobbled down the aisle past me, her pointing stick held like a commanding baton. She was out of sight but not forgotten. I bunched up my face before mumbling,

"I think it's Lowsun, Master."

"And what makes you *think* that, Dog-Ears?"

Miss Master's query tagged itself onto the end of my cautious answer like a dragging anchor. She was daring me to admit that I thought altogether too much. This would be confessing a sin against God. There were two simple choices: I could remain silent, be dubbed an idiot and get punished for it; or I could explain my reasoning, be dubbed a *stubborn* idiot, and still get punished for it. Before I could make up my mind as to how I would call down God's wrath, the horrid crow did it for me.

"Too busy *thinking* to tell me, Dog-Ears? Don't bother answering. You are correct. It is Lowsun. Can someone else, someone who *knows* rather than *thinks*, recite the hours?"

Before me, thirty-one hands shot up. I could almost feel Miss Master's smile as she declared that, as a whole, the class would recite the hours, starting from Highmoon. The fervour with which the kids announced the hours actually made me shudder. I listened with a pang of envy as the class droned out the hours. I could never find anything in which I believed so strongly that I would recite it and not question it.

There is never a question in the classroom chant.

"Highmoon. Lethalmoon. Lazymoon. Lowmoon. Bladesun. Morningsun. Nighsun. Highsun. Aftersun. Lazysun. Eyesun. Fallingsun. Lowsun. Dyingsun. Awakenmoon. Risingmoon. Fullmoon. Eyemoon. Nighmoon."

"And then Highmoon again. Good, class. Can anyone tell me why we use 'Sun' in some hours and 'Moon' in others?"

Even I raised my hand with that one but my time was past, at least until Miss Master wanted to make another example of me. Someone else answered, regurgitating Miss Master's own writing.

"The hours with 'Sun' in the name are when people are permitted to be awake." I doubt the snot understood the word 'permitted'. "When there's 'Moon' in the name of the hours, people should sleep as The Night's Own cleanse Kaef're of evil in the Divine darkness of God."

"Well said, Jaku," Miss Master cooed. "But if we are supposed to be asleep during the 'Moon' hours, why do we even have names for them?"

"I don't know, Master." And how *miserable* that little boy sounded!

"I will tell you. There are some very bad people who *are* awake during the Moon hours. These people want to hurt you. They are *bad* people, so we must know the hours they are out. No one in this class is going to become a bad person who is awake at Night. Isn't that right?"

The class chorused that they would never be bad people. Afraid that my silence would reveal my guilt, I joined the answer, just *very softly*. I couldn't help it if I didn't want to sleep, didn't want to see that awful vision of blood and snow.

"*Very* bad people. But they are not the only reason we have names for the Moon hours. Long ago, people were truly good. They believed in God and had no sin, as we do. These very lucky and faithful, these *good* people were allowed to walk at night, to be with the Night's Own. If we're all *very* good people, someday we too will be allowed to walk at night. That would be nice, wouldn't it, class?"

When the class answered this time, my lips refused to move. Even my *strange* ears did not hear Miss Master's serpentine approach. Her left hand clamped onto my ear. Her fingers dug in, pulled.

"What about you, Dog-Ears? Are you a bad little boy? A *very* bad boy who is awake at Night?"

"No, Master, I'm a good boy. I swear!" I tried to stand to reduce the pain, but she anticipated that and let go, shoving me back down with her other hand.

When she was that close, I did believe one thing: only God could grant an old woman so much force. Her wrath was *holy*.

"I'm not sure I believe you, Dog-Ears. Maybe the Night is watching you, every night, and seeing your evil ways. The moon never blinks, little Dog-Ears. Remember that, boy. The Night knows your name."

She bared her yellow teeth at me in a grossly misplaced attempt at a grin and then pulled her talons from my shoulder. The class continued after Miss Master moved away from me, but I did not accompany it. Now that I had been punished, it was alright to go back to musing and contemplation. Why would an all-powerful being, God, need agents, the Night's Own? If She was so powerful, couldn't She just make things happen? Why was She so angry with us, we Her people who toiled day after day to glorify Her?

What would it take to make God happy with us, if our entire lives of servitude weren't enough?

With unanswered queries like that, I took the first unconscious steps towards understanding the visions and the fantasy, which would not be corrupted for another six years yet.

Somewhere in my head, a crescent, a cross and a single tear began to orbit each other.

I blinked, and the recollection of a six-year-old questioning the very fabric of society returned to the recesses. I wondered, sitting there in that idiot's chair, if I'd have to relive all the lessons of Swimming Carp. What good would it do, really? Everything was different now, and here I was trying to focus on what would never be again. No. I had been a fool to return – should have just left Swimming Carp without this laughable stumble down memory lane.

Nostalgia is for those who have *good* memories – otherwise, we call the memories 'scars'.

One more thing to do before I left. I reached for the desk, for the shelf under it, and pulled out what I knew would be there: the Book, bound in black, the red *f* representing the Flail of Afraen Who Was Ephriem on the cover. There were many scrolls and texts in Swimming Carp's library, but as everyone knows there is only one 'book' in the world: The *AkraVahm*. I lifted the weight of it with due reverence. Nine hundred or so pages of history laced with lectures and teachings, epic stories and personal parables. The words themselves were simple enough – even a twelve year old could understand most of them. What they meant and implied, however, was different for everyone.

Despite my issues with the text's messages, the enduring nature of the Book had been the catalyst for my scholarly aspirations. Thoughts come and go, but writing them down is acknowledging not all thoughts should stay gone.

I opened The Book to the first page. There, in my own conscientious, simple handwriting, was the question Miss Master had asked over and again. Thick and solid, the characters seemed bold, but few questions are ever that confident. A question like the one I'd written wasn't really meant to be answered anyway. It existed to compel people to face themselves and examine their own beliefs and opinions. Well, that's the effect it had on me. Doubt the other teenagers of Swimming Carp saw it as much beyond another set of do's and don'ts to commit to memory. A person can make anything deep and seemingly philosophical with enough probing – maybe even a story about a village idiot who wasn't really but sure acted like one. But the question: was there nothing more to it? So I asked myself one last time, just as Miss Master had done during that other lifetime. When Swimming Carp was its people and their spite, and Dog-Ears seemed to be the cause of it all.

"What is the Twelve?"

Because I didn't want to give her the wrong answer, I reached for the Book on my desk. I knew exactly where to look: *Vahm*, Volume Five, Chapter Seven. It was by some miracle alone that I pulled my hand back before the snap of her pointing stick could break my fingers.

"You should *know* by now. Answer."

I screwed up my face in concentration at the question. Six years of study had passed and I was still making that pinched expression, that façade of thoughtfulness.

"Uh…One. There…uh…There is…No God Without The Night. Two…er. Oh yeah. I remember now."

"He remembers now. How fortunate for us."

It was poor humour even by the dehydrated standards of Miss Master. No one made a sound. I *knew* what she wanted to hear. I just couldn't say it.

"Two. Those Who Dwell in The Night Are Of God And Are Closest Unto Her. Three is…um…"

"Stop. You are incorrect. Hold your hands out, Dog-Ears, palms up."

Well, that lasted longer than usual.

She didn't need to tell me how to do it, because I was 'incorrect' just about every day. Miss Master flicked her wrist thrice. With each stroke, a severe crack cut off an airy whistle. Any other student would have cried out. The rap of cane upon *my* knuckles had long since lost any educational value. It hurt, certainly, but showing any sort of emotion just gave the kids something else to pick on. I remained as blank-faced as possible.

"Sit, Dog-Ears."

I sat.

Using the rod for its original purpose, Miss Master pointed at a student farther back in the room.

"Wu Jen-Wah," she coaxed, "be so kind as to clear the air of this fool's rambling and tell us all. What is the Twelve?"

The girl stood and gave the room a beatific smile. She checked her hair, completely aware of the rapt attention, but the delicate bun was well-tied. Sure, she couldn't dance but that didn't stop her from slaving over her appearance.

"The Twelve *is* the set of guiding principles by which we all live, as dictated by Afraen Who Was Ephriem."

Three blood-welling strikes of Miss Master's cane couldn't break my silence, but what Jen said made me groan to myself. The emphasis she put on the word 'is' made clear my mistake. Miss Master had tricked me. No, I'd let her. They were right; I was an Ephing idiot.

"Precisely so. It is gratifying to know *some* people actually listen when I ask a question. Now, while you're standing, tell me, what *are* the Twelve?"

Wu Jen-Wah, basking in the moment, took a dramatic breath and rattled off all Twelve Commandments in a sharp, arrogant tone.

THE TWELVE COMMANDMENTS

1. God is The Night. There is no God without The Night. Revere and fear The Night and Her Own.

2. Closest to God are Those Who Dwell in the Night. Hearken unto Them, cower from Their wrath and exult in Their benevolence. Those Not of the Night are distanced from God and are not to be worshipped or honoured.

3. The name of God is sacred. Do not invoke the Name of God and Of The Night for any purpose other than praise and worship.

4. Sleep at Night. Do not work while the Moon shines. You may work under the sun for the glory of God, but The Night is for rest, for God and Her Own. The Night is sacred.

5. Honour the way of your parents before yourself. Emulate their lives and perpetuate their beliefs for they are closer to Heaven and to God.

6. Do not kill without the Night's blessing. Life is Given by The Night and only The Night may take it away.

7. Propagate. It is your duty to create children who will serve God and The Night.

8. Do not reach for anything you cannot hold. Ambition is the seed of discontent.

9. Do not hold anything you cannot keep. Blessed are they who know their limits.

10. Do not lie or spread falsehoods to further your own station. The truth is sacred.

11. Do not ask questions if you don't know the answer. Curiosity is a sin beyond Salvation. Thought is the seed of rebellion. The Night provides all you need to know.

12. The word of the Night's Own is holy. They are closest to God and know Her Name and Will. Their command overrides all.

How I hated her right then. Hated, and pitied.

Just as a good fisherman knows when to give a little and when to tug the line, Miss Master waited for the Twelve to sink in before aborting the silence with her cackling lecture.

"Excellent. We know these Twelve and will know them forever. But there are meanings and distinctions within them that are less than clear. Take, for example, Commandment Six, which teaches us that killing others is wrong. If Lord Ayakawa commanded you right now to kill the person next to you, would any of you hesitate?"

No one raised a hand. Friends were good, companionship longed for, but the word of the great Daimyo was second only to a command from the Night's Own. As if disappointed, Miss Master continued, lowering her voice to an almost conspiratorial level.

"What if it were your parents you were told to kill? Does this not contradict Commandment Five?"

She was baiting them and apparently only I saw it. Again, no one said anything. Miss Master's words had them enthralled. I was bored.

"Hmph. You will answer these questions when the time comes, perhaps. The reason I wish to discuss the Twelve today is simple. You must remember them all the time. When working in the fields, when hunting for dinner, when playing, when eating, even when sleeping. The Night knows your name and It knows your guilt. We are guilty from birth, and the only way we can hope for salvation is in being perfect servants of the Night and Its Own. Your own reckoning will come, someday. At this time, you must submit to the fear totally. Accept that every breath you draw is one more step towards the last. Treasure it, and do not waste it. Live a good life and you will be rewarded."

Nothing I hadn't heard before. I could see Miss Master as she paced up and down the aisles, but mostly just stared straight ahead and rubbed my swollen knuckles.

"Do. Not. Forget. Now, open The Book to *Vahm* Volume Five and read to yourselves silently. Put your hand up if you have any questions."

Yeah, not likely.

The Book is divided into two uneven parts. The first part, called 'The Light', *Akra* in the Holy Speech, is significantly longer than the second. It deals with Kaef're in its most primal time: the age of fallible Man. In the thirty-four Volumes that comprise The Light, Man ruled the world with greed; Man was ruled by greed. Man did not worship God, did not adhere to Her teachings. Rather, they marvelled at their own magnificence and domination. Some even worshipped He Who Shines, the immortal enemy of God. Although immensely powerful, Men were hindered from truly becoming great by their own wars and self-destruction. *Akra* is full of murder, blasphemy and treachery. Nations with names no one remembers rose and fell, queens of great desert kingdoms were seduced by emperors from across the sea. Weapons that could tear down entire walls rumbled over corpse-laden fields and a great, corrupt church dedicated to He Who Shines fell into ultimate ruin.

I found myself wondering if the wisdom of The Light couldn't be turned to better purposes. This, of course, contradicted the core message of *Akra*: If power corrupts, then the virtuous deny themselves any power at all.

Miss Master favoured the second part, 'The Night', thirteen Volumes of *Vahm*, as teaching material. Where *Akra* preached the virtue of impotency, *Vahm* explained the conditions and rewards of such powerless existence – and the punishment awaiting those who seek tainted power.

Volumes One through Four of *Vahm* detail God's creation of the Night's Own, Her perfect agents. Those who served Her faithfully during the *Akra* epochs were taken into Her breast and taught the ways of God. Sent to Kaef're to guide the squabbling Men, they are spirits of flesh, of both love and hate. The First among them, Afraen, led the Night's Own against the rebellious armies of Man, who were under the sway of He Who Shines. Afraen brought order from the chaos. There was much bloodshed, *more* tales of treachery and murder and entire pages of parables ranging from simple to simply baffling. The first four Volumes ended with Afraen being controlled by the Forces of Light – he was then known as Ephriem, a General in the Shining Legions. Lord Tangariel, most foul Angel of He Who Shines, planned on exposing Ephriem and then hanging him for all to see. I knew what was coming – everyone did, but still we read it and re-read it, reminding ourselves that Afraen died for us all, and that we in turn had to live *good and obedient* lives for His sake.

Volume Five was about the Twelve. Ephriem, with the help of his troubled consort Adael, escaped the Forces of Light and was once more Afraen, reunited with his bonded-mate Lady Shynsa, 'The Ragemother'. Together, they conquered the last evil army of Men and Angels in the Battle of Ocharaya. This decisive clash saw Afraen Angelflay become the First Overlord of Kaef're. Governing bodies were formed and linked to the great order of God; cities were built and realms were divided among the Night's Own. Those Men who submitted without violence were given ranks and domains. In short, the birth of Kaef'ran society. Eighty pages later, the Night's Own withdrew and allowed Man to govern itself in accordance with Afraen's legacy: the Twelve.

Nice ending, but Volume Six shows what happens when Men are left to their own devices. We turn once more to He Who Shines. Lord Tangariel has his revenge: he captures Afraen then tortures him to death. The Holy Afraen's corpse is left to hang from the gates of Ruslym, unholy stronghold of He Who Shines. Men rejoice, Men lament. A whip is curled around His neck like a noose: Afraen's holy icon, the Flail. That curved *f* on the front of The Book. Afraen disappears in a flash of light two weeks after his death: God's first sign of holy retribution against He Who Shines. Men rejoice, Men lament.

Volume Seven begins with Afraen's return from Heaven Below as the Messiah. His judgment makes sure The Light will not shine ever again. This, then, is the core message of the *Vahm*: Only power granted by the Night is without corruption.

When I finally closed The Book, I realised that everyone was looking at me and Miss Master was standing over my desk.

"Did you hear me, Dog-Ears?"

"No, Miss Master."

I waited for the inevitable violent retribution, but she only sighed and said, "the class will be staying back until Lowsun because *someone* couldn't answer me when asked. Next time, *someone* might do better, for the sake of their friends."

That was when I knew the inevitable violent retribution wouldn't be coming from her, and I had a whole hour to anticipate what Jaku, Jen-Wah and my other 'friends' had planned.

With no feigned contrition, I opened The Book and tried to lose myself in it once again. It didn't work, and every sound I heard I imagined as one student or another turning to glare at me. I cringed. I winced. I waited.

I sat there for a little longer, adjusting to the present. It was roughly Fallingsun – the room was darker than in memory. Darker, and quieter, without the fanatical presence of Miss Master and her students. The tranquillity tempted me to move further into the school's depths, plumbing the library for all sorts of forbidden texts. There simply had to be secret material somewhere, some hidden key that would unlock the chest that contained all the answers. But the more I thought about it, the more I could accept that no response but my own would satisfy me.

Since that day, the class studied the Twelve only to pick at them, to discover loopholes and exceptions-to-the-rule. Of course, Miss Master hadn't said that was the purpose of the exercises. But if the way they treated me was any indication, the pupils of Swimming Carp were *very* good at employing the Twelve to their own ends.

There are, I've decided, two outcomes when you're exposed to daily abuse. You can snap and become as your tormentors: if inflicting pain makes them happy, it could do the same for you. By being a bully, you can stop others from hurting you back, sometimes before they even hurt you first.

The first outcome, then, is a beast created by beasts. A beast that creates more beasts.

The other outcome is noble, proud and typically short-lived. You can escape the thorns of cruelty by believing that no one should suffer as you have.

The second outcome is a human who transcends, and comes to command, the beasts.

I'd like to think I'm on that second path, that I'm an arbitrary zealot. What did you mean by that term, Vachaelle? That I have my own Commandments? What would they be without their opposition of the Twelve? Did I owe everything I believed in to the things I didn't want to?

I stood up and walked out, with the *AkraVahm* in my right hand. I'd retrieved what I came for, and left everything else behind.

I was still incomplete, though. Half. My left hand remained empty, waiting for something else.

Chapter 6: *Jin*
HAVEN

A departure is always instant – no matter how long you take before that first step.

After spending time reliving the horror of my youth, I turned my back upon seventeen enslaved years and left. The manacles, however, were not gone: absence of concern merely made them loose. Just as I had tucked the *AkraVahm* in the folds of my simple apparel, I allotted the lessons of Swimming Carp a quiet but accessible fold of my mind.

The irony is that I neither read The Book nor thought of the village much at all after that.

Even though I lingered in Swimming Carp, the actual leave-taking was nothing more than a decision and a step forward. I made my way up the path, bearing neither sword nor pole-arm – the 'armoury' of Swimming Carp had turned out to be useless. Those rusty relics would've had trouble cutting through jook. My clothes were shredded, my skin was abraded after the fight (was it only a night ago?), and it hurt to remain upright and inert for so long. My sole comfort came in the black travelling cloak, which had somehow survived the ordeal.

Unarmed and wretched, swathed in thick umbrage and trying to conceive of a life beyond Swimming Carp – that was me: poised, uncertain, terrified.

Then one foot followed the other.

That's all it took.

Despite being Swimming Carp's most accomplished messenger, it wasn't long before I found myself lost. Within days my usual landmarks gave way to alien formations of rock and branch. Roads converged and split and I did not know their names. In the sunlit hours, I tried to move in a straight line. Each night, as I made camp, I remembered less and less of the brawl with Hua-Shi, and would have thought this strange had I noticed. I guess it's only fitting that someone so lost within himself would get equally lost in the 'real' world too. I had no destination, after all – but how can you get lost if you don't know where you're going?

"I should return to Bitter Lotus," I proclaimed to the darkness, which might have responded had a campfire not kept it at bay. I prodded the uncertain little blaze with a gnarled stick. Cinders danced free from the crumbling wood upon which the fire dined. "I should return to Bitter Lotus, but will I?"

I continued to stab at the helpless embers with growing ire. I frowned, feeling hungry and sour and sulky – my mood probably reflected the fire's flaring answer to the poking. In hindsight, I should have been a *lot* hungrier.

"And if I don't go to Bitter Lotus," I continued musing, "just what *should* I do? I can't turn back. If returning to Swimming Carp was going back, wouldn't a second visit to Bitter Lotus be the same?"

Perhaps accepting that I was lost further encouraged that tendency to talk to myself. Lost and truly alone, without even the hope that people might return at any moment, as may have happened in the abandoned village. But as alone as I might have felt, I was really anything but by myself. And I wasn't really lost, either. This did not become apparent until I got there, even if it wasn't where I meant to go.

"Huh, that wasn't there last time," I said to myself, regarding the dilapidated building beside the empty road.

I took time to study the place, or maybe just used that as an excuse not to get any closer. The ground floor looked like it was being squashed by the overhanging tier above it. In the dim radiance of Dyingsun, each edge of the establishment seemed to blur and blend, erasing the definition between wall and shadow. Even the name invited the end with a smile.

" 'The House Of Joyful Leave-Taking,' " I read from the large wooden board dangling from above the entrance. I moved closer if only to seek a better reason to move away. Repulsion is too often little more than compulsion in denial.

And then I saw it, painted over the entrance: an open hand, white and cupped upwards, with a drop of red blood falling into its palm. It was a familiar symbol I'd never seen before.

I asked myself, "Where's the other one?"

Why couldn't there be just one?

Movement around the building caught my eye. Since leaving the village, I didn't remember seeing anyone during the day and certainly no one approached me at night. The moon was barely half-full last time I checked, which I had to admit was probably before everything went to Hell Above. Perhaps these people were busy for other reasons, but they wasted no time getting indoors.

I looked away from the House, away from the sinking sun. Searching. Just to make sure.

A distant, chalky but certainly full moon crept up from the horizon above the tree line.

Now I had my justification to get inside.

Dusk before a Hunt reinforces the reality behind the abstraction of hourly time-keeping. It divides not just light and dark, as any twilight will, but the more basic safe and anything-but. You thought you had all the time in the world until then, but when the sun's almost gone, so is your idea of *now*. And 'after' will only happen if you are not out there on those brightest of nights.

Standing right in front of the House, I tried to look deeper into the engulfing gloom. There were no real doors leading in – just a set of roughly equidistant columns supporting the second floor. My eyes traced the deterioration in the ceiling until they hit a solid blackness. It was almost a wall, a clean cut-off. The light just wouldn't let me look very far past the entrance.

Other senses only intensified the despondency. The place creaked dangerously. The air even tasted dead. There was a reek of submerged waste from within, a distinct odour of condensed sweat. Dank remnants of desperation and distress. I tried to hold my breath.

"Hey!"

Shock shattered the introspection and I gusted out a blast of suspended air. The first voice I'd heard since leaving the village that wasn't one of mine rooted my feet. I looked around for the source, although I knew where it had come from.

"You!" came a crotchety grumble from within. "Whatcha think yer doin', boy? Either get in here or get lost." His voice was muffled; perhaps he was crouching behind a shelf or a counter. The speaker might have been fifteen steps away, he might have been five hundred steps away. He might have been right in front of me. "Eh, by the looks of you, it might well be good that you come in and get comfy. It's crowded, though. Wouldn't go hoping fer a table to yerself."

Crowded? I couldn't see or hear a thing, but there *had* been people entering before.

Wrenching a fistful of black cloth, I pulled my cloak even tighter about myself. The evening heat was almost stifling, but I felt strangely exposed. My life had been one of silently observing others, of being unseen when unneeded. Now I was the one being watched, and I had no idea by whom.

Nonetheless, I shuffled towards the imagined counter, into the unimagined darkness. I waved my free hand through the air, as if I were trying to part a thick curtain. "Hello?" I asked, knowing it was a waste. If they could see me, they certainly didn't need to hear me.

"I dunno what yer playin' at, boy," responded the same age-hardened voice. "Quit foolin' around."

This was my first time in a real inn; people made provisions for a messenger from Swimming Carp, from the *extremely* important Elder Wong Chu-Deng. I was playing this by ear, albeit strange ones.

"I...I'm not...I don't...help?"

A meaty slap of flesh against wood answered me before the old man said anything else. A palm being placed against the counter? Another step and I couldn't even see my own hands. I touched my nose with an unseen finger: it felt like it belonged to someone else.

"Just come a bit closer, boy."

And 'a bit closer' seemed to be all that was left anyway.

"That's the way. Nice and easy. Now reach out, just a little to the left," coerced the elderly man. His bark seemed to have softened; perhaps he'd realised I wasn't just fooling around. I groped, waved and swept my hand about, all with painful deliberation. Bare knuckles collided with a dry, rigid surface – a door or a wall, perhaps? I rapped the back of my hand a few times. Wood.

"*Your* left, boy. My right." I dragged my hand to my left, and felt something. Something cold. Smooth. Glass.

"Definitely a stranger, ain't ya? Then again, even a stranger would know about *lighting the lantern*."

I repeated those three words with breath but not voice.

"Now grab the handle and lift it – simple, eh?"

I slid my fingers up and around the curve, but my palm wanted to stick to the glass.

"Why is this so difficult?" I asked as I took hold of what I figured to be the handle.

"I don't make the rules. In fact, you have it easy."

"Easy," I muttered.

"I tol'ja to relax, boy. You're almost safe now."

Almost?

A retort rose from my throat but not even my mouth was big enough to spit it out.

Instead I just bent my elbow. Tilted my wrist. Lifted my fingers.

I lit the lantern.

There wasn't even time to blink, to cower. The Lantern was lit; the world was a solid white revelation. Took a while to adjust my eyes to the shift. It was almost a waste of energy: I couldn't see any more with the light on than I could with it off. Not when it's that bright.

Where is the Rose this time?

What?

Squinting wasn't enough, had to draw my left hand up, covering my eyes. I don't *think* I took a step back and I know I didn't fall over.

It was close, though.

"You can put it down now, friend." The old man's voice was now quite amiable, as if we were just old pals, as if I weren't still cringing and wishing my eyelids were much, much thicker. And did he say 'friend'? The light set me off-balance, yet one word outshone even that. Then I realised both events were linked. It made sense.

I lowered the lantern, pulled my hand away. The light remained. All I could see were the slats of brightness between my stiff fingers.

Yet I *heard* something.

"—hard to believe. Do you really think he—" A male voice, soft but not whispered – just distant.

"*I* believe it. Did you see his face? It was all—" Female this time.

More and more half-conversations became apparent. Louder. Jumbled. Single voices blended and became a distorted din. I quaked beneath the pounding wave of noise but turned towards it.

"Boy?" the old man's voice behind me penetrated the confusion. I pulled my hand away from my eyes, peeling pinkie from nose, but not before closing them.

"You really were raised in the dark, weren't you, son?" He sounded amused. Determined to *see,* I fought through the seething illumination. First I peeked with one eye and then, since I wasn't struck blind, let the other one join it.

And I saw.

The House of Joyful Leave-Taking was more than crowded; it was abuzz with people. I imagine if Elder Wong Chu-Deng had allowed actual merriment in the Common Hall, it would have looked and sounded like this. Every table was occupied, and those that couldn't get a seat seemed to mill about. If I concentrated, I could hear one voice from the many, asking for a refill or recalling a tale from afar, but what they were saying wasn't what made me smile. It was the fact that not a single one of them was looking at me. Maybe they hadn't noticed my ignorant entrance, or maybe they'd gone through the same and understood. Either way, I didn't matter to them and it felt...good.

"If you have anything to hand over," the old man said, "just place it on the desk. Here." Where? I turned around to see what he was talking about, but saw him instead.

What a curious creature he was. A complicated network of wrinkles defined the wizened face and crowned a posture that was tired but firm and resilient. His limbs grew from a hunched-over trunk and torso. To contrast these geriatric signs, russet pebbles embedded within the man's saggy cheeks darted about, here and there, up and down, possessed of an almost child-like energy and intensity.

"Pleased to meet you, young man. My name is Zhang."

"I'm Dog—Shah-Long."

Those frightfully quick eyes appraised me and I felt like I was being picked apart. Zhang's attention gave me the distinct impression the old man was learning something about me. Seeing more than I wanted to reveal.

"Dog Shah-Long?" His lips twitched.

"Shah-Long. Just Shah-Long."

He nodded, satisfied. His eyes went elsewhere, and so, thankfully, did mine. The counter he manned wasn't much different from him. The scrubbed stains in the age-darkened wood spoke of an ingrained history of defiance. There were neither jugs nor glasses on its orderly surface. I wasn't sure as to its purpose until I saw the shelves behind both it and the old man, upon which rested a neat arrangement of things sharp, edged, spiky, blunt. Deadly.

"I've never seen anything like that, Zhang-sinsan." It felt right to call him that: Mr. Zhang. If he really was the keeper of that intriguing place, respect was not misplaced.

"If you didn't know about lighting the lantern," Zhang replied as he shuffled off, towards one of the tables clustered throughout the room, "then that doesn't surprise me at all."

I looked around just in time to catch his smile – then it floated away, just as he did with the final words.

"You're in a Haven now."

Chapter 7: *Retsu*
HAPPY

Haven.

Before anything else, I knew that word and that it was a *good* word. I wanted to ask what it meant, of course, but the dizzying crowd had swallowed Mr. Zhang.

"So, I am in a Haven," I whispered. Once more I found myself appraising the dormant arsenal upon the shelves. There could be no mistaking the collection dominating the wall in front of me, behind and above the counter. Axes, bows, clubs, polearms…and, of course, swords. I'd only ever seen one sword in my life, and even then it had only been in a dream. There was no real reason to think any of these weapons would bear any resemblance to 'my' sword, but I couldn't help looking anyway. And who knows? Had she not distracted me when she did, I might have seen the one thing that would have changed everything. But she did, and so I didn't. And what happened, happened.

If only she hadn't come up to me and said:

"Excuse me, sir!"

There was a young girl behind me, pulling at my cloak. That, too, reminded me of something that might have been real, but surely I turned just out of politeness. She was eleven, maybe twelve years old, and there was something familiar about her lively poise and quick, amber eyes. Her round face was as open and bright as her eyes, although her tight-lipped smile was more bemused than anything. There'd been plenty of girls in the village, but not one of them were like this. I had no idea what to say, how to act, so when she did, I was extremely grateful.

"Do you have anything to hand over?"

Huh? Wait. Something Zhang-sinsan had said. In reference to the weapons? I just stared at her.

"Well, it doesn't look like it, but I thought I'd ask anyway." A playful, buoyant gait carried the girl to the other side of the desk. Her red and white dress flapped around her, clearly too big. She straddled the rickety stool behind the counter – made it seem an easy manoeuvre even though the seat was as high as her elbows.

"I might have something," I replied, not wanting to make any more mistakes. I was carrying nothing more threatening than Plump Treat's knife. Practically no weapon at all; I kept it in my backpack rather than at my hip or in my boot. I loosened my sore left shoulder, easing what I took to be the weight of the travelling pack. After sinking to my haunches, I rummaged through the contents for the knife. It wasn't hard to find – the bag was far from full. So why was my shoulder sore? What weight did it remember?

"That?" She peered at what I'd placed before her, then shook her head. "You can keep that. It's just a little knife."

Had someone else said that to me before? *Hold still. This won't hurt. You trusted me.* Was it Plump Treat? No. A different dream. A dream with flowers. Orchid, blossom and lily?

"Sir? Are you alright?"

I blinked again, and there she was. No dream or flower, not this one.

"No need to call me that," I replied – a reflexive response. "What's your name?"

I have come to appreciate those three simple little words. 'What's your name?' is the last question answered by a stranger. What it really means is 'I want to know you.'

"Me?" asked the girl, pointing a dirt-smudged finger at her own nose for emphasis. "I'm Happy!"

"I guess I'm happy too?"

"No, no!" she shook her head, two black pigtails whipping through the air. "I am Happy, you are?"

Happy swung her finger to indicate it was my turn.

"I'm Shah-Long." I lowered my head by instinct alone, not quite bowing.

"I'm Happy, Mr. Shah-Long! Happy Apple!"

"Uhm, hello. So, why don't you need to take it?"

"It? Oh! The knife." She poked at the sad little instrument. "It's too small!"

"Too small for what?" The answering question seemed to surprise her. Happy's mouth worked through a few possible answers before selecting one.

"Well it's just too small. Don't you know the rules?"

"I'm new here!" I was an intruder in the realm of Defensive Indignation, but seemed to know some of the secret ways in. "I know *some* rules. Like the Twelve." Weren't they *the* Rules?

"They're not the rules, they're the Commandments, silly!" Before I could ask her what the difference was, she went on. "They're important too, but not as important as the rules. Which are all about how people should behave in a Haven. Do you know what a Haven is?"

"It's where people can go to feel safe at night," I answered, piecing together a mix of village hearsay and common sense.

"Right! When the moon shines round—"

"They can come here and sleep, safe and sound." As much as I loathed the little rhyme, it was reassuring to see that it didn't belong to Swimming Carp alone. That something I'd learned there really did matter outside of the village.

"Right again! And one of the rules is that you don't have to give up weapons with blades shorter than your hand." To elaborate, Happy lifted her left hand and showed me her palm, fingers straight. With her other hand, she tapped the tip of her middle finger and then the crease of her left wrist. "See? Your knife is way shorter than even my hand!"

"But even a little knife can be used to hurt someone, Happy." Hadn't it been?

"Why would they? That's not what little knives are for."

Of course the knife wasn't for that, and anyone who thought it might be would be considered *strange*. I reclaimed the small weapon, hoping that my blush was lost in the shadows of my hood.

"Why do people give up their weapons anyway?"

"Don't you – oh. It's another rule. Want me to tell you all the rules?" Happy kicked her bare feet in the air.

"Will it take long?" I wanted to explore this Haven for myself. It teemed with life, with lives, and I wanted to learn about them all.

Happy's grin took on ephemeral qualities, a sudden pout creeping into downcast view. I perceived an error in my simple enquiry. Or, as

Vachaelle would put it in her delightful, outlandish crudity, I *'fucked up big time'*.

"I guess you don't want to hear them all then." Her gaze edged towards the floor and lost a little of its light.

"I didn't say that!" I didn't know then that what I'd said wasn't even relevant; it was what *she heard* that mattered.

"It's okay. You're a grown-up, probably really busy and—"

"I'm not a grown-up, Happy."

"—have lots of other things to do so I'll— wait, you're not? How old are you?"

"Seventeen. I think. Why, how old are *you*?"

"Nine. Almost ten," she added. I'd been a few years off, and at her age, that made a huge difference.

"Aren't you a little young to be collecting weapons and talking to hooded strangers at the bar?" I asked, not quite knowing how I knew what age was appropriate for such behaviour, and completely forgetting that I'd been trying to convince her she could trust me, that I wasn't like the 'grown-ups'.

"Oh, I get it. You *do* think I'm just a kid."

Well that went well.

"Happy." I raised my voice, careful to be heard but trying not to sound angry.

"Yes, Mr. Shah-Long?"

"Call me Dog-Ears."

Happy giggled but still refused to look my way. I just smiled as well.

"Why do people call you Dog-Ears?"

"Can you keep a secret, Happy?"

"Dunno," she mumbled, now not only shifting her gaze about but fidgeting as well. "Never been given one."

"How would you know if no one told you it was a secret?" Something about this conversation, about that too-quick, too-sharp reply, made me sick to the gut. I just wanted to get her to open up again, but this method of interrogation wasn't mine. Worse still, I had a feeling I'd picked it up by being on the other end of it.

"Maybe if they did," she said after some pensive silence, "it wouldn't be a secret anymore anyway."

"Well, it's your choice, Happy. But you really are smart." From cajoling logic to outright flattery and appeal to pride – where was this coming from? "I'm sure lots of people have told you that. Smart people can keep secrets."

"Nope. No one's told me that before. Ever." I might have been making progress again. A twitch of lips that was not a giggle: there lay the irrepressible rebirth of a smile.

"You are. Please. I trust you. I really do. I want to hear all the rules. I want you to tell them to me."

"Okay. But you haven't told me why you are called Dog-Ears."

"I can do more than tell you. Look at me." *Please?*

Inquisitive eyes flashed back upwards. "What am I looking for, Dog-Ears?"

"Yes." I raised my left hand, as she had done when demonstrating the first of the rules. Four hooked fingers guided the hem of the hood away from my cheek, back until the knuckles touched my left ear.

"That's my secret, Happy. That's why I am called Dog-Ears."

She seemed surprised, which didn't surprise me, but then fearful. She glanced around to see if anyone else saw, which told me that my secret would be best kept as such. Whatever these ears might have meant in the village, they had other significance out here. Especially if I shared them with brutes like Hua-Shi.

"Really big secret, Dog-Ears. But if it is a secret, how did people know to call you that in the first place?"

Hmm. Good question. I replaced the heavy cowl's hem before answering.

"Some people did know about my ears, but they're gone now." There was no better way to put it. I didn't want to lie, and yet didn't really know what happened. At this point, it didn't really seem to matter. "They made fun of my ears. I don't want anyone knowing about them now. Except you, 'coz I trust you."

Happy nodded, her solemn mood showing that she also knew what it was to be teased. "I won't tell anyone."

"I know you won't. Because you're smart."

"Yep, I'm smart." Happy nodded again, then looked past my shoulders, past my edgy nerves. "You don't have to worry about them, Dog-Ears. They're grown-ups. They don't pay attention to us kids."

"So I can walk around without my hood on then?" I was teasing, and I had no idea I knew how to tease until I did.

She replied most seriously, "I wouldn't go that far."

Then she smiled and I smiled too. There had been a battle and I had won, with relatively few casualties.

"You were going to tell me the rules." I leaned on the counter, one elbow perched on the corner.

"Oh. Well, you know about the weapons. That's for everyone's safety. Only Grandad is allowed to take the weapons from the rack." *Grandad.* This explained her presence in the Haven and the similarity of her disposition – like sharp lightning. "And he's too old to do anything but mumble and grumble. What else. Oh. Did he tell you about the lantern? I guess he did, since you're here."

"In a way," I said, trying to forget the ordeal Zhang had put me through. "But I want *you* to tell me about it."

"Coz I'm smart?" Now it was her turn to tease.

"Your butt is smart!" Wait – what?

"Smarter than yours, Dog-face!"

I winced, waiting for what would come next. What always came next.

What came next was a light slap on the arm. "Hey. What's wrong? I was just kidding. I'm sorry." She lowered her voice, leaned back and muttered to herself, "I'm such an Eph'ing idiot sometimes."

No, Happy, you really weren't.

"I'm…I'm okay. That was my fault. I just…I'm used to people starting fights after saying things like that."

"Fights aren't allowed in here. Oh!" She brightened. "That's another rule. And it's got to do with the lantern, sort of."

"Go on." And I resolved to shut *my* idiot mouth this time.

"Okay. Grandad has run this place for most of his life. My father was supposed to take over, but he's dead, so he can't. Mother's dead too." She imparted these facts with cold detachment; I felt a twitch in my eyes, even though I didn't exactly have much attachment to *my* mother or father – whoever they were. "I'll probably be the next owner, if I don't die too. So Grandad teaches me things. The lantern is *magical.* It can't be lit by normal fire, doesn't need oil. Someone gave it to Grandad after he saved his life. Grandad, that is. Saved the stranger."

She appeared flustered. I nodded: *I understand.*

"Grandad was just doing his job. He says this is why no one, no matter how bad they are, should be turned away from our Haven. The lantern is our way of knowing that no one here is one of Them."

Them. I've heard a multitude of euphemisms, nicknames and titles for the Night's Own since then, but none rival the sheer eeriness of *Them.*

"Grandad is a very important person! I will be too, someday. He can't save everyone, but he, well, we can save lots of people. He says the lantern won't light for, y'know, Them. I've never seen it not light, so I guess They haven't come here. Well, not yet.

"Once it's lit, the lantern that is, our Haven looks like it really is. All part of the magic, Grandad says. Which is why I'm not allowed to touch the lantern, but that's okay. It's really important. I might break it. That would be bad, 'coz then They would find us, find our place."

Part of me knew that this made sense, despite over a decade of being taught otherwise. I nodded once more. But I also remembered getting my ears pulled for being too smart; that part screamed inside, begging permission to ask so many questions of this sudden font of reality – or was it *sur*reality? I drew a deep breath, held it and then eased the air out with careful slowness.

"You 'kay, Dog-Ears? I said something stupid again, didn't I?"

"No, Happy. This is just a lot for me to take in. So the lantern is magical. You light it just by lifting it. Before it's lit, the Haven looks run-down and deserted. The Haven, your Grandad's place…it's a place for people to stay at night, when the Nigh— when *They* are out, so I guess when the moon is full. Oh, and They can't light the lantern, so They will never find this place?"

"That's what I said, yes."

She was only slightly impatient. I got the impression that I was meant to know at least some of this already, but she'd seen my ears and knew I wasn't like everyone else around here. It was time to see just how far my ignorance went.

"Happy, when I was young…well, I still am, but when I was younger, I was taught that to be taken by the Night was a blessing. It's a sin to want to die, yes, and it's our duty to fear and flee the Night, but when we are taken, it's only what we deserve, as people born in sin, right? That's what the Book teaches."

"What?! No. That's *awful*, Dog-Ears. Why would we deserve that? People who think like *that* deserve what they get. Besides, which book are you talking about?"

Holy. Shit.

"There's more than one book?" I knew it. I knew it. I *knew* it.

"Well, of course. I mean, you're talking about the Book of Truth, right? Only clerics and priests call it 'the' book. Sorry, Dog-Ears. Did you really think there was just one book in the whole world?"

"That's what I was taught, Happy. That only the word of God was worthy of a book."

"Just one book. Shyn's Tits, someone really wanted you kept in the dark."

Now that I knew she wasn't going to hurt me, I found her frequent cursing endearing. It was distinctly opposed to Miss Master's hypocritical piety, she who punished even a hint of blasphemy but preached the finer points of justified cruelty. And now that I knew Miss Master had been lying about the existence of other books, it was that much easier to rally against anything she'd represented.

"If it makes you feel any better, Happy, I think she's dead now. I think they all are. I think the Night took them."

I mustn't have sounded very sad about this, because she skipped right over any sort of consolation in her response.

"Didn't they have a Haven? Grandad says They do horrible things to people who don't find a Haven when the moon is big and round. He used to make me go upstairs when people come, but I looked anyway. Lots of blood, Dog-Ears. It smelled awful, the screams were so loud and I remember I was sick the first time I saw all that. But I don't get sick anymore. It has to be done."

The apparent severance of Happy's brief childhood evoked in me a sense of sorrow, but possibly not empathy. I never really had a childhood to lose, and now I was starting to realise that maybe I was better off for it.

"Don't worry, though. A few of the people working for the Haven are good at making pain go away, at stopping blood from coming out of cuts and things."

"They're Healers, you mean?"

"That's right. Oh, that's another rule! Anyone who can Heal who comes to the Haven must help Grandad with anyone else who might need it. That doesn't usually happen until, well, later than now. It hasn't been night for very long."

"What's stopping them from entering here anyway?" I didn't want to know. I had to know.

"More magic I guess. Not like we have any doors to close."

So at least that much hadn't been an illusion.

"Hm. Are there any more rules?"

"Sure. We were talking about fighting before, right? Just because someone hands their weapon over to us doesn't mean they can't cause trouble. Wait, you *do* know about chi, right? About talents?"

"Doesn't everyone?" Again, I was too sharp, too snappy.

"Hey, not fair. You said you don't know the rules, so I'm not gonna assume you know anything. Anyway, that stuff isn't allowed in here either. I'm sure people still use it to do little things but most don't risk breaking the rules. Just not worth it."

"So, what happens to people who break a rule?"

"They get asked to leave."

Again, I didn't want to know and I had to know.

"What if they refuse to leave?"

"They leave anyway. And they're not allowed back in, ever. It's not as if they try to come back in, not for very long." She shrugged.

"What if they don't know the rules, Happy?" As I did not, and I really didn't want to leave! "Isn't that a bit unfair?"

"I suppose, but you're the first person I've ever met who doesn't. And we get people from aaaall over, and they know the Haven's rules. We've had Hunters from the West, monks from Kaifeng, even a few Halves. But you'd know all about those, I'm sure." She winked at me and instinct told me to nod, just once.

Still: Hunters, monks...*Halves?* Why did that last one resonate so strongly?

Something else caught my attention before I could hold onto that one, however.

"Kaifeng? The Capital? Isn't it far away from here?"

"Huh? No. Maybe a day or two down the road. We go there to get supplies. There's a Haven there I really like. It's called the Benevolent Hand and there's this one lady who works there, she— Eph's Bleedin' Flail, I'm rambling again, aren't I? Shut up, Happy. That's what Grandad says. He's right. Besides, this isn't the rules. We really should get back to those."

"You've been to Kaifeng?" I asked after she tapered off, and then, because even I knew that was a stupid question after this point, I added, "What about a village called Bitter Lotus? Heard of that? Is it nearby as well?"

Recognition burst across Happy's face.

"Oh yes! That's not *too* far from here. In fact, we have someone from there tonight." Happy scowled. "Grandad said I have to be nice to her, even if she is——"

"Is she big?" I interrupted with a confused mix of hope and fear. I only knew one 'her' from Bitter Lotus. But what would Plump Treat be doing here? Had she regained her sanity? Hope, fear and now anxiety of possible salvation. It was my fault she did what she did to herself. If she *were* here, I knew I'd do anything to fix that.

"Huh? No, not really. Why? You know her?" There was a cautious, thin edge to her query.

"Don't think so, no. Hey, Happy." I tried to sound casual, and probably failed spectacularly. "Since we're talking about places and people you know, how about Swimming Carp? It's another village. You might have heard of its elder, Wong Chu-Deng."

She didn't answer immediately, and the knit to her brow told me all I needed to know.

"There's Elder Fong but his village isn't called that. And there's Five Carp village, but, no, sorry."

"How about abandoned villages in the area?"

"I've heard about a couple. Grandad says they're haunted. Now and then people mention they're sometimes used as hideouts for gangs. Why do you ask?"

"Eh, it doesn't matter." I knew then that as much as I liked Happy, as much as I trusted her, and as much as I wanted to know what she knew, she wasn't the person who could help me.

I also had an idea who, and that Happy didn't like her very much.

"More rules, then?" Happy asked, peering at me. She didn't let me answer. "You really do know the most important ones. There's a good rule, though, and if you break it, you won't be asked to leave. You'll just get funny looks. The rule is, don't pay for any food or drink."

Pay? Money? *Shit.*

"Why not?" I asked.

"Not sure. Maybe it's so that people who can't pay don't feel bad. All are welcome here." She giggled.

All are welcome here. I'd heard that before, but not in Swimming Carp, and not in dreams. Something made me look down at my hand, at my knuckles. Memory of a sharp, brief pain.

"Dog-Ears?"

I shook off whatever it was. All are welcome here. Even me. Okay. Good. Because…

"I have to be honest with you, Happy." *I have* to be honest with you: implies that if I had my way, I'd lie. "I'm not even carrying any money."

Confessing this to the Havenkeeper's grand-daughter wasn't an intelligent thing to do. Contrary to her claims, she may well have relied upon the goodwill of generous patrons.

"Were you robbed? People say there are lots of thieves on the roads these days, especially our road, since it's so busy and we're so close to the Capital. I hope you weren't robbed! I heard there was a big fight about a week ago, people were even killed. Did you see that? At least you weren't hurt, were you?"

"No, not robbed. Not hurt." Too many questions! What thieves? Fight? I hadn't seen anyone or anything. "…I just travel light."

"You're lucky you haven't been attacked, especially if all you have is that knife. You really should think about getting something a bit more effective if you're going to wander these parts, Dog-Ears."

"A sword," I said before I could think of saying anything. "I'm going to get a sword."

"Hey, good choice! Grandad won't let me have one but maybe one day. Not like I want to be stuck in this Eph'ing Haven forever," she said, somewhat contradicting what she'd said earlier about her fate as the next owner of the House of Joyful Leave-Taking. "Even if we're doing a good thing here. So Grandad says."

"Not everyone can be a hero," I commiserated, knowing full-well that my own fantasy had always been about precisely that. "At least, not in that way. Besides, beating people up isn't always heroic. Sometimes it's nothing more than just abuse."

"Yeah. Oh!" She perked up, and I was glad for the change. "Last rule. Don't abuse the staff."

"Why would I?"

"I'm sure you never would, Dog-Ears. But some people. They do things they're not supposed to, bad things to the waitresses and stuff." Something clouded her face, threatening to wash away her smile again.

"Like what?" This was one of those times when I really should have known better than to ask a child for elaboration.

"Y'know, touching them the wrong way. Doing things that aren't right."

Now she was definitely upset.

"To you?" I asked immediately, and who I am now could kick who I was for being so *dense*.

"No. Not really."

And just as I'd discovered how to lie, I knew, right then, that I was hearing one.

"Not *really*?"

"It's fine."

"No." Not fine. I tried so hard not to see what she was trying just as hard not to show me, but all I could hear was a voice in my head telling me *ifI'dbeenthereIwouldhave*. Over and again. Would have *what*?

She said something and I didn't hear what. I would have, but…

I was already doing something else.

It was there again: that living, swirling serpent of hot strength lurking just under the skin. Its hissing promises of searing empowerment kissed my apprehension a very warm farewell. There were no boundaries in that fresh realm, no definitions of the word 'impossible'. Clad within that flame's shroud, I was a beast of infinite capacity.

If I'd been there, I would have. I would have had to. Had to—

"Stop it, Dog-Ears! No!"

Her cry failed to rouse me from the encasement of Fire.

"*Huo-sha!*" A new voice carved a curse into the opaque air, scratching the surface without coming close to the core.

"No, no, he's okay now, aren't you, Mr. Shah-Long?" A vigorous shake accompanied Happy's desperate insistence.

"I saw the *chi* about him, brat." The shaking stopped, succeeded by a short, sharp yelp – Happy?! "You know the rules."

"He is better now, I promise." I heard tears in her cracked voice then – real or not, they extinguished the embers of the fading Fire. "He is."

"That's enough out of you!"

Now, if the Fire had receded completely, how was I able to raise my hand just in time to stop the man from slapping Happy across the room? With the cowl drawn, I certainly couldn't see the assailant, and there hadn't been any sensation of premonition. I just lifted my hand and caught the wrist because it felt like the right thing to do. I had been there, so I did.

"What the—"

"Please do not punish Happy Apple for my mistake." There was no request in my statement. I dug my fingers into his wrist for emphasis. There were over twenty nerve endings within my hand-turned-claw – I knew this and did not know *how* I knew what 'nerve ending' meant. A far more enlightened, callous soul was force-feeding me this information.

"Happy! Boy!" Havenkeeper Zhang's voice broke the triangle. The static moment passed, but I did not let go. "You're not causing trouble for our guests, are you?"

"Zhang-sinsan! Your grand-daughter was giving excuses for this *Huo-sha—*"

"Would you like to take this outside?" Havenkeeper Zhang cut the man's shrill complaints straight down the middle. "Tonight, of all nights?"

"Bu-but the rule! That idiot in the black cloak used Fire in a Haven!"

"Jealous, Wu Ming?" Armed with any number of occupational weapons, Havenkeeper Zhang was merciless in his baiting. Wu Ming: 'Nameless'. Was that really his name, or was this just another taunt?

"No! Not me." Surprisingly, he sounded quite sincere. I guess even thugs understand that being able to wield Fire isn't all fun and games. "But he better not do it again. I wasn't the only one to see!"

"See what? Happy Apple!" Havenkeeper Zhang barked at the girl. She had, with typical clarity of wit, moved away from me and resumed her place behind the weapons-counter. "Did you see anything?"

"Nope!"

Sneering at 'Wu Ming', Zhang sent his avian gaze towards the small but growing audience. "Did any of you see anything?"

A voiceless chorus of shaking heads, averted gazes and embarrassed coughs failed to meet Zhang's challenge. The onlookers each found sudden interest in their mugs, the floor, walls…anything other than that which they had clearly *not* seen.

"There. That's settled then. I am sure the young man will *not* do anything." There was an implicit 'again'. I was bewildered at the uncalled-for defence. What could I do beyond nod in agreement? Oh, and let the man's wrist go.

"Sorry." I tried to release my grip. My fingers seemed transfixed about the meaty joint. In that tiny, tense forever, there was a chance I would not be able to let go.

Then the world caught up. I unwound my fingers and lowered my hand. I didn't care what became of Wu Ming's own.

"Yeah, me too." This time, he didn't sound quite so convincing.

"Wu Ming."

"Yes, Havenkeeper Zhang-sinsan?"

"Go have another drink." *Play elsewhere.* "And keep your hands to yourself." *Play elsewhere and play* **nicely.**

"Yes, Zhang-sinsan."

I watched his retreat. Instead of seeing a hulking beast to match that voice, I caught a glimpse of haggard, bent-over figure in a brown robe, hooded and villainous, pushing its way back into the amiable throng. What of 'Wu Ming' then? Nothing more, other than that he was the first person to call me 'Blackcloak'. It remains my preferred label, thanks not in some small part to my habit of wearing one ever since.

"I want you to know that if I hadn't been certain of your ignorance," Havenkeeper Zhang noted, patting my arm with uncharacteristic but not unwelcome friendliness, "I'd have tossed you out myself. Then again, perhaps my little Happy Apple has told you some of that already? The rules and how things work around here?"

"Some, yes." I refused to admit whether or not I knew of the non-*Chi* decree. "I do promise that it won't happen again."

"You can't promise that."

"But Grandad! He promised and I—"

Havenkeeper Zhang raised one hand, palm outwards, slow and gentle. It was more than enough to send Happy into a frowning mire of stewing silence.

"You can't speak for this one. Neither can he himself. Do you remember what I taught you about *Huo-sha*? They're unpredictable, especially if they're untrained. This boy is no exception. Rather, he *is* the exception, which is even worse. I'd say he doesn't even understand much of his Talent yet."

"But he's way older than me, Grandad, and even I know what I can do, well, some of it."

"You have a teacher, Happy Apple. This boy doesn't." Zhang was neither angry nor impatient with her. I thought then, with a pleasant flutter: *she is in very good hands.*

"Then can't you be his teacher as well, Grandad?"

I smiled at her persistence. So simple, so easy. But I knew he couldn't be my teacher. Not yet.

"No dear, only he can teach himself. Although—"

"Although what, Grandad?"

I raised my eyes then, and was not surprised to see that Happy's own eyes had alighted upon Zhang's wrinkled face.

"No, I've said enough. Happy! You have work to do! Say goodbye to your new friend and be about your duties!" All business now, Havenkeeper Zhang was once again the cranky old man I'd met an hour or two ago.

Happy sent an excited wave goodbye my way then scampered off. I wish I had waved back.

"Thank you."

"Hmph. There's another reason I didn't turn you out just now."

"Yes?"

"Someone *has* vouched for you, and her credibility is a little more solid than mine, yours or my Happy Apple's."

Her? The female from Bitter Lotus? Was she watching all that? Or a different female?

"I figured Happy would have told you. That is why I sent the cheeky little mouse your way in the first place. Hm. She probably got a bit sidetracked. She'll talk all night and not get to the point, if you let her."

"Maybe the point *is* to talk all night?"

"I can see why she likes you, boy," Zhang replied, not altogether harshly.

"Shah-Long, Havenkeeper."

"Shah-Long? Oh, right. Your name. She mentioned knowing that as well," Zhang muttered. "The woman, that is."

"This woman. Can you tell me where she is? What she looks like?"

"She's upstairs. Insisted on a private room, and because she is what she is, I gave her one. Regarding her appearance, she said you'd recognise her hair."

"Her hair?" Did I need to ask? Really?

"Yes, it's—" And then Havenkeeper Zhang said a word that, although apparently spoken in Chūnko-go, I did not understand. "Well, it means gold, or maybe yellow? Sometimes even a pale brown, is blonde."

Definitely not Plump Treat then.

I edged away from Havenkeeper Zhang, glancing towards the stairs at the back of the room, and then broke into a run.

"Wait, boy." I barely heard this as I tore across the room. It was not until I was halfway up the stairs that I paused and looked back.

Somehow, the old man had kept pace, but looked a little worse for wear. I trudged back down the stairs obligingly.

"What is it?"

"She knows your name," he said with a solemnity beyond my ability to comprehend. "She knows every name."

"So? I gotta go, Zhang-sinsan. Gotta…do something."

"I suppose you do." It was the first time the Havenkeeper displayed a capacity for resignation.

I was off. This 'blonde haired' woman would answer all my questions, one way or another.

What I didn't figure on was her answering my questions one way *and* the other, and then in some ways I'd really have preferred to never have learned.

Chapter 8: *Zai*
QUESTIONS

In order to fall, I had to rise.

I took the stairs two per stride then three per leap, almost bounding upwards on all fours. After clearing the steps, I began my search for 'her' in earnest. I raced down the hallway, sliding screens aside, each time answered by gasps, cries of dismay and anger. Door after door surrendered to my reckless frustration. When I did not see the shock of anticipated blonde hair, I turned away from each room and their offended occupants.

"What's with all the noise?" a female voice asked from my right, towards the end of the hallway, and the few rooms I'd not yet checked. I knew that voice. It was sleepy and annoyed, slurred and yet somehow deliberate in its timing. "I asked, quite clearly, for a quiet room and—"

"You!" was all I could cry before whirling about and staring at the woman slumped against the wall.

"Who?" she asked, her puzzled expression flushed and puffy.

At least this time she was dressed, and very poorly at that: a tattered hooded red cape over a dirt-smudged smock which might have once been white but now was off-yellow with age. Her hair was barely visible, but what I could see was definitely 'blonde'. She seemed shorter, more fragile; I forgot, then, that she had restrained me effortlessly. Was this truly the usurper, the *whore*, whom I'd mistaken for my mother and then condemned for failing to meet that standard?

"Is something wrong?" she asked. I began to laugh, caustic and sharp. "Okay. A person laughs like that," the young woman decided with a wrinkled nose — as if I were the one intoxicated, "when someone laughs like that, there has got to be something wrong."

She moved toward me, bumping along the wooden wall for support, humming some disjointed melody under her breath.

"Do you—" I began, then cut the question off.

"Do I what?" There was neither insult nor impatience in the girl's prompting — just amusement. By then, she was halfway down the hall; feet, legs and body moved in vaguely the same direction.

"—Know me?" It sounded crippled and brittle, but what else could I say?

"Oh. Looks like I am not the only one to have been drinking tonight, hm?" The ripe blush gained a smile, and that sloppy curve tried too hard to appear wry. It may have worked, had the door upon which she supported herself not been cast aside, causing her to tumble to the floor.

A portly, middle aged man dressed in a gown and little else thrust his face across the threshold, and then looked down.

"For Eph's sake, woman, watch—" he started to bluster.

"Watch your blasphemous tongue!" she cut him off, and he blustered no more.

I almost looked down at her too, but what happened to him transfixed my attention.

The man drew in a tight wheeze, a gasp lacking strength — fuel for a scream that would not come. The flesh of his swarthy face lost all colour, his muscles seemed to sag all at once and his eyes threatened to swell beyond his eyelids. A dark stain spread between and then down his legs. Violent volume had come so swiftly to the man only seconds ago. Now he whispered.

"Forgive."

I swiped my attention back to the girl, expecting something *bad*. The poor bastard had just pissed himself in terror. Was she the very monster I'd been pursuing after all?

She certainly didn't look like one. There was a hint of fear, a denial on her face. That was exactly how I'd felt after the Fire fled, that dread, and the desperate need to not revel in the afterglow of overkill.

Until now, I've never recalled those few seconds as anything more than scared girl smell of pee dead man. Things just seem to have hung there.

Then the man toppled backwards. For one of his girth, the lack of sound upon impact was just as eerie as his last word.

The young woman crawled over to the prone fellow – now she wasn't repentant, but somehow *eager*.

"Uh-oh." She probed the flab, tentative fingers poking sweaty bulges with obvious distaste. "Whoops."

The man did not stir at her touch. I knew he was dead. I should have done something, *anything*. All I could do was stare.

"No help for it now," she sighed, closing the door with odd gentleness. "Only one thing to do, really. You know what that is?"

I didn't answer, even though her eyes, those muddy depressions made murky once more, lanced straight at me, or through me.

"Well?" After rising, she rested her hands upon slim hips and tapped a foot. Drawn by the inanity of the stance, I was able to forget that she'd just killed a man with barely a look – and such a maligned, guilty look at that!

"Uh." I was frightened that the wrong answer would switch her 'harmless' madness into 'deadly' madness. A guess would have been as bad as silence. "I'm sorry, but I don't know."

"No? Well, you will soon enough. But if not, what kind of *kind* are you then, hm?" I had no idea what *kind* meant, or even if the foreign grunt was a word at all. Then she giggled, which made me shudder even more than anything else. I had no reason to question her mental and emotional stability – she clearly had neither, but I was also aware of my own failing balance.

Said Ephriem, Who Was Afraen: 'Cast first thy mud at he whose slate be clean, so that the truth be known – no slate remains clean.' And she was throwing her insanity around like a toddler in a puddle.

The girl sauntered back down the hall. Her gait was direct and upright, as if all the effects of drunkenness had seeped out of her body and into her mind. She was still snickering even after sliding back the door and entering her room. After a moment, she ducked her head back out and looked at me again.

"Well, you have found me. Coming in or what?"

Once inside, I forgot to ask just what that 'one thing to do' was.

In fact, I forgot a lot of things.

"Close the door behind you, please." She inserted that almost-request between mouthfuls from her porcelain cup. I did as she asked, a little louder than I expected.

"Have a seat." The woman, having removed the cape before taking her own place on the floor, looked even less imposing now. She pointed at the low-set table with her cup, not spilling a drop despite its fullness. "Well, have a floor anyway. Yep, the floor is all yours." This was chased by another unsteady giggle.

I sagged to the floor as bid, missing the square cushion altogether.

"Hood off, *kind.*" I gained the impression that the odd word was a form of address, from a superior or elder. *Well, at least she isn't using my name—*

The Night Knows My Name!

She scrutinised my exposed face for one critical second, shrugged and continued.

"Better. Tell me your name."

She wanted to know me?

"I've been told you already know it," I replied.

"I want to know if *you* know it, *kind.*"

No, she wanted to know if *I* knew me. Of course.

"My name is Wong Shah-Long."

"Pleased to meet you, Wong Shah-Long." She did not pause at the response, gave no indication that I'd said or done anything wrong. "You may call me Fa Shai-Yeh. With that out of the way, you have questions, I am sure."

I could have exploded into manic laughter then, joined her in bouncing between chaotic coldness and easy congeniality. It would probably have been one of the sanest things to do.

"I'll ask you again," I said. My face, now revealed, felt tight and stern. Probably looked constipated. "Do you know me? Were you not at my house with Hua-Shi? *What were you doing there?*"

Her answer was just a smile at first – a knowing, smug arc around which she drew a sip.

"I think you *know* what I was doing there, Shah-Long." Shai-Yeh was mocking me and I couldn't help feeling that I deserved it. "And just because you lived there does not mean it was your house. Would you care to rephrase the question, or ask another? I've no time for idle queries, though I shall *try* not to limit your requests."

"How generous of you." Add 'sarcastic' to the list of things I didn't know about myself. I winced, but the flare of attitude seemed to amuse Shai-Yeh. She widened her chestnut eyes and then laughed: a sultry chuckle that demolished the remaining vestiges of the crazed girl from before.

"You have no idea, *kind*. Ask."

"Who are you?"

Her mirth waned at this.

"I told you who I am. Rephrase your question! Think, *kind*!"

After Zhang's test, I had endured enough examinations for my liking, and disliking, which was more accurate. I was, however, helpless to do anything else: she had the answers, so it was I who had to provide the questions.

"Did you kill that man in the hallway?"

"He killed himself," she snapped. "It's not a pertinent matter, *kind*."

A man dies just by looking at a drunk girl and she states it is not pertinent. If she was telling the truth, then just how terrible must the pertinent matters have been?

"Why did you try to kill me at my…at the house?"

The amused smile reclaimed its arrogant place upon her lips.

"I didn't. Hua-Shi did." Shai-Yeh paused, stalking through a series of dark expressions suitable to her opinion. "He is a simple creature. His way is bullying simple people. I am bitterly disappointed in him, in you both, but at least you seem to have learned something from the experience."

So she does know me, or of me?

A few other considerations tugged me away from that tangent of her knowing of me — notably, Shai-Yeh used present tense in reference to Hua-Shi. He is alive, then. I knew my Fire was strong, but I'd never really held any conviction in the chance of Hua-Shi being dead, not with the body missing. Also, Shai-Yeh's explanation of the event contradicted how she'd acted at the time. Was she deluded? Misremembering? No. Even though she'd acted like a helpless, scorned lover, she'd proven immensely strong and walked away from the encounter in better shape than either Hua-Shi or myself. So she'd been acting, and might still be.

"Good. You're thinking now. Make the questions count, *kind*."

Kiend're?

"What does that mean?" I asked, although I felt as if I'd been about to ask something entirely different.

"What? Be specific!" Her amiability cowered behind the easier expression of strict command. Shai-Yeh poured herself another cup. She offered me nothing. Maybe I was meant to take.

"That word. *Kind.* If it is even a word at all."

"It is, and it means 'child', very simply. There are other meanings, but they're not so easily translated into your language." Shai-Yeh was getting bored. Her disinterest struck me as extremely dangerous.

"So there *are* other ways of speaking?"

"Of course there are other languages! Don't ask questions when you know the answer!"

That triggered another memory, one hammered into me from a very young age. The rasp of Miss Master reiterating the Twelve invaded the moment: 'Do not ask questions if you don't know the answer!'

This woman, this dreaded solution, advocated the absolute opposite of what I had struggled to understand for over a decade. By default, I agreed with her, and this feeling of association, bordering on kinship, set its sweet claws deep into my squirming sense of distrust. She could have killed me – of this, I was certain. For some reason she did not, and perhaps it was related to our like-mindedness?

There is seduction of the flesh, of the mind and of the soul. Different levels for different people, and somehow, Shai-Yeh knew the straight line to my damnation. I *was* special. I began to believe it then.

"That is not what Miss Master taught. What you just said contradicts the Commandments, Shai-Yeh."

"Think, then ask. Now is not the time for half-doing things."

But there was no need to think on that one.

"You encourage me to be inquisitive when everything else I remember was about keeping me in the dark."

"Continue." Shai-Yeh reclined, cup in hand.

"You were with Hua-Shi in the village after everyone was gone. What happened to them?"

"Why do you care, Shah-Long? All they ever did was torture you, bring you pain, suffering and abuse. Aren't you glad they are gone?" Her tone was light. Given more experience, I'd have noted that it was too light. I dashed onward, feeling the first few glimmers of something that resembled understanding, that twinkle of light through the Window.

"It is not that simple, Shai-Yeh. They are all I have known. I did not love them, of course, but it was something like that."

"How do you know? Have you ever loved and *known* it was love? No one does, *kind.* There's always a doubt."

"This was more than a doubt. I didn't love them and I didn't hate them. Not really. I didn't think I needed them, but now they are gone. Elder Wong, my father—"

"You know better than that!" Shai-Yeh sundered my dwindling conviction with that abrasive interjection. I knew precisely what she meant.

"And how do you know that, Shai-Yeh?" I tried to sound cunning, but just came across as stunned and somewhat awe-struck. Her involvement had just been revealed as far deeper than I'd assumed, and perhaps wished.

"The same way you know it, *kind*. Because it is the truth. The villagers are gone. That life is gone, and good riddance, wouldn't you say? The villagers are gone, Shah-Long," she repeated, "and that means they no longer matter. It's a big world, *kind*, and you're now a part of it."

Mention of the villagers reminded me of something else.

"In the village, you said something about safety. 'It should be safe for you to go out soon', you said that to Hua-Shi, after. After. Why safe? What threat was there for Hua-Shi?"

"Why, you, of course."

I immediately wanted to disagree, because of course I didn't believe, but I had a feeling she really did.

"You say that as if you knew I was coming. No, as if you knew what would happen when I came. Not even I knew that, so, again, how could you?"

"People always think they know more about themselves than might anyone else. Very few achieve that, and those that do become very, very powerful entities. Or insane." Another giggle.

"A noise." She tilted her head at this, but I knew what I meant. "There was a noise. It sounded like the window being closed, or the shutter dropped."

"If nothing else, you're astute. Then again, I was certain to make it loud. Wouldn't have done for you to remain inert, even if you did succeed in something no one else has."

"And what's that?"

"Still here, aren't you? Thought I said not to ask stupid questions."

"Fine. You watched, then. Made a play at running off in tears, when all you were doing was getting a better vantage point. What if Hua-Shi had killed me?"

Shai-Yeh snorted. "Then I'd not be here talking to you, and you'd be dead."

Too many vague, twistable questions begged to be asked, to be sated. I fell silent and intended to remain that way until Shai-Yeh played her next move.

Which she did.

"But he didn't kill you, and you didn't kill him. That particular tale is not yet over. Hua-Shi is still going to be a thorn in your side." She stopped for a moment, gauging my reaction to this news. Of course he wasn't dead. She'd already said that. So she continued: "He wants more than revenge now." Now? "And he doesn't realise that kicking your head in a few times won't suffice."

"So no one knows what happened, right?" That sparked *another* question. "What about the other villages? Are they the same? Bitter Lotus? Hap— The Havenkeeper's grand-daughter said you were from there, but I never saw you."

"Slow down, for your sake, *kind*. Pick a thread and unravel it, or you'll make the knot even worse."

Again, Shai-Yeh's familiarity with me showed her precisely how to guide the conversation along her desired course. My queries about Bitter Lotus were far from stupid; the answer would have saved me quite a bit of trouble. Still, Shai-Yeh aimed to teach, and I learned. One way or the other.

"Why are my ears pointed? Like Hua-Shi's."

"You were both born with ears like that. I can't tell you *why*, any more than you can tell me why people have two eyes and not three."

"Other people don't have pointy ears!" I didn't want to seem indignant, but couldn't let this one go.

"And other people have blonde hair, or green eyes, or are tall, or short. Do you understand yet? Your physical nature, while rare, is not the important matter here. We can deal with that later. Hua-Shi is the problem. Focus."

And we would. Later.

"Is he seeking me even now?" It seemed arrogant to ask this, as if I were someone worth seeking in the first place. As if I were hiding. As if I could hide.

"He does not need to. After the dissolution of Swimming Carp, there weren't many places you could go. I am certain he knows you're here right now, in fact." I found that word both fascinating and frightening:

dissolution. It was a cold term, one of calm assessment and detached observation. "But you're safe here. This *is* a Haven."

"Haven from what?" I knew, but only in a very vague sense, the Night came with dangers of its Own. Perhaps Shai-Yeh could enlighten me on the subject.

"Angry gang leaders, in your case. And yes, Hua-Shi does have a posse, but they're nothing now. You're straying again, Shah-Long."

"If you're so determined to keep me in line and on course, Shai-Yeh, why don't you just tell me what you want me to know and keep the rest to yourself?" Her invitation to explore and question was turning out to be just another way to control me, to tell me what to do.

"You've been hand-fed all your life, Shah-Long," Shai-Yeh admonished, softer than I'd expected and almost compassionate. "It's time to prove yourself worthy of all the knowledge the world can offer."

"That's not my real name, is it?"

"Of course not. Wong Chu-Deng is not your father; Swimming Carp is not your home. *None of that* is yours, do you see? Treat it that way, if you can. It won't be easy, since it's all you remember right now."

"There is more to remember?"

"A great deal more. And more to forget, which is just as important. Here, look at your hands." Shai-Yeh shifted her weight so that she no longer seemed so slovenly, coming to kneel behind the table almost formally. "What do you see?"

They looked exactly the same as usual. The knuckles were pronounced without being knobbly, the fingers slender but not effeminate. I ran my eyes over the creases about the palms. Nothing. Then I noticed a clear intersection of indented skin, replicated perfectly on both left and right palms. Could that be what she meant?

"There's something odd about my palms I never saw before, Shai-Yeh."

"Is that so?" she prompted.

"Yes. A triangle-like shape in the wrinkles."

Yet again, I was almost too engrossed to see — she balked from this triumphant observation, eyes suffering a very quick but intense storm. There I sat, gazing at my hands as though seeing them for the first time, and she rocked back, recoiling from me as if I were some rampant project, a harmless egg hatched into a fiery apparition of wing and tooth.

"No!" And her objection was as haggard as she appeared. I frowned at its severity — and my own idiocy. I'd been wrong again. Shai-Yeh inhaled, held her breath with steady forcefulness, and then released, pushing all her tension and telltale tightness out. I envied the way she could do that. "No, Shah-Long. Not that. You are just seeing things."

And so was she, by the look of her curdled face.

"Think while you look. What should your hands be?"

"I don't know! Is there something wrong with my hands?"

"Where are the scars, Shah-Long? Did not Miss Master use her cane to hit your hands? Every time you got it wrong, every time you got it right, every time *you spoke,* did not Miss Master punish stupid little Dog-Ears?" And how vicious she sounded now, pouring more hatred and disgust into her voice than seemed at her command. She sounded just like Miss Master. I cowered, whimpering. She didn't move any closer, but whatever Shai-Yeh was now towered over me, ice crackling in her tone and scorching her gaze. "So what are you going to do about it?"

How could she know about even this? Didn't matter. Not there, not then.

Fear churned into rage, and that rage was a welcome heat in my gut. It had fed upon both its bearer and his intent, had served and would serve again. That the current enemy was looming over me merely presented a larger target. What little remained of Wong Shah-Long, trapped within the swollen mirror of flame and destructive intent, begged against what had to happen next.

"No," I groaned, doubled over as though this might contain the fire. "I won't break the rules. Not again."

The pressure grew unbearable. I tried to imagine Happy Apple's face, wrought in disappointment at my failure. And then Havenkeeper Zhang ordering me outside, expelling me from the safety of the Haven to face whatever They were.

But whatever I was becoming scoffed at this, knowing it could just burn anything or anyone. Even 'Them'. I felt the room grow warm. Very warm. My eyes began to water, as though full of tears but I knew that wasn't it.

"That's the way. Let it out, *kind.*"

And with that, it was all gone. The room was again merely warm; my thoughts returned to their usual tepid trepidation.

She looked disappointed.

"Miss Master never called me that, Shai-Yeh," I breathed. "I think you just saved your own life. Or, no. You knew what you were doing, didn't you?" My throat was stripped raw and I sounded as if I'd been shouting for hours on end. "Still testing me."

"Don't look at it that way, Shah-Long." She was calm now, perhaps realising that invoking Miss Master wouldn't work again. "But I think you did miss what I was trying to say. My fault, of course. Why are your hands not ruined with scars from Miss Master's stick?"

"Someone Healed them? I'm sure I had scars before."

"Are you? How often did you check? Maybe you just took the idea for granted, just as you accepted the punishment without question?"

"Why would I check? You get hit enough, wounds and scars are guaranteed."

"Well, I cannot Heal, Shah-Long." Shai-Yeh wiggled her fingers, as if tickling something. Small bubbles of water coalesced between them, and then popped into fine vapour. "Hydrotheurgy's my thing."

Another foreign word, but I wouldn't let it distract me.

"Someone else Healed them?" I could see where she was trying to drive my mind and refused to be herded, now of all times.

"Why would they need to, *if* there were no scars in the first place?" Impatience saw Shai-Yeh make yet another mistake – she took the initiative. "And no, you are not particularly resilient, so do not consider that. Just how far back do you remember?"

"I remember a few things from when I was six years old. Then it's a blur until, I don't know, twelve? I remember everything from then on, though most of it gets repetitive. I try not to think about it."

"Life is diverse, Shah-Long. You have learned that recently, I would bet. So why is yours so repetitive? And why can you not remember much before twelve years of age?"

"I don't know." I was getting sick of saying those words.

"Good." And Shai-Yeh sounded sincere in that, perhaps even pleased. "Then it is not time for you to remember. Can you accept that?" Again, her tone suited the words: she was giving me a choice to disagree.

"Yes." I accepted the possibility that further enlightenment, even more memories, could lead into just more confusion. "What should I ask next?"

"There is a very good question, if a bit lazy." Shai-Yeh acted as though she were in control once more. "Whatever you want. But now you understand that the answers rarely match the question."

"Then why should I ask?"

"Because the answers teach you what questions you either should have asked or should ask next. Eliminate them as you go along, and sooner or later, you'll get somewhere. And I am being far too helpful here! A good thing I like you, *kind*."

"How do you know me?" I asked.

"You have earned a straight answer, I guess." She sighed, a theatrical elaboration wasted on her current audience. "I have known *of* you, Wong Shah-Long, for all your life, oh-so-short as that may well be. I know your name, your origin and even some of your future, should you live to see it through. Of course, should you not, my sources of premonition will be rather upset, not to mention embarrassed."

Still too many factors. I tried to envisage the situation as a tapestry, as prompted by her previous words. It was an incomplete image, of course, but there were details, inconsistencies, frayed threads. *Pick one and PICK at it, Dog-Ears!* – I commanded myself with Miss Master's sandpaper snarl.

"What is my real name?" I'd avoided that one, simply because I already had a name. What did it matter what others called me? Would a change of name change who I was? Was I a butterfly who responded only to 'grub'? I doubted it.

Note the past-tense.

"It will mean nothing to you right now, but you are of a family, a clan, known as Jaydemyr."

I could barely understand it; the syllables were beyond my native language. All the same, I knew it; something new that felt ancient and absolutely right. Instinctively I reached under my cloak for something, thinking about a moon and a cross, but found only The Book, hard and quiet. I just withdrew my hand and made a fist of it, knuckles pressed into my thigh.

"Jei-di-mi-yah?" Familiar or not, I couldn't repeat it, not with my current understanding of pronunciation, no matter how hard I tried. And I tried very hard.

Shai-Yeh snickered. "Close enough. Do you feel better knowing that?"

"No."

"Of course you don't. The name means nothing, as I said. It could be anything, but it is not. You are Jaydemyr, and in time, will learn how significant that is. Why you were taken, brought up as you were. I will not tell you these things yet. You understand why."

"They'd mean nothing as well," I muttered, and Shai-Yeh nodded, her grave mouth tempting the notion of a smile. "But you will help me learn them? I do not think I could do it alone."

"I would not bother with all this if I did not intend to take you further. You do not trust me, and that is good. I could be lying about everything, just as anyone else might and will. I doubt you even trust yourself some of the time, and that is also good – never smart to trust strangers."

"So you will help me," I pressed, not taking that bait. "Or will you just try to control me?"

"Ah, now you are starting to understand. Control *is* assistance. Accept my control and you will be helped."

"Or *you* will be helped."

"I will not claim altruism, Shah-Long. I have a motive and I have my own desires. You have seen that I will go to quite some length to achieve them. All you need to do is play your part."

I frowned. "Like a pawn?"

"Do you think you are anything else?"

"Do you think *you* are anything else, Shai-Yeh?"

I almost broke into a grin at her flinch. Now *this* was a thread I could really pick at, really unravel.

"You do not know, Shah-Long. You cannot."

"Again, do *you* know? I accept that I could be a pawn, for now at least, but you act like—" I stopped, because I'd been about to say 'a shah' – The most precious (and yet most restricted) piece in Elder Wong's favourite game. Part of my not-real name. I had to substitute that quickly, before I lost momentum! "—Like a princess, when you're probably just another pawn, as is the person above you, and on and on—"

"I serve no one!" She fought the desire to clench her fists; gripping her thighs was just as bad, and yet that is what she did. "I answer to nothing short of the grace of God Herself."

"And yet you fear me, Shai-Yeh." Who was saying this? Not Wong Shah-Long, not Dog-Ears. Not *me*. "You've tried to coerce me into a stance of meek confusion,"—the gap between strands stretched, faster and faster, and I knew more and more, but as soon as the knowledge came, it was tapped and then gone—"Using Hua-Shi to test my Fire, perhaps even sacrificing the entire village just to see how I'd react. It seems arrogant to even think it, but you fear me. I could have unleashed more, just now, had I not remembered that Happy didn't want me to use my Fire. Not here, anyway. So, is your fear of me justified? It's crazy but," the third time I stated it, it was with unchained wonder: "you *fear* me."

"Not likely, *kind.*"

"Oh but you do!" Wonder became comfortable in my heart; pleasure made it redundant. "The way you use that word, that word for 'child', it's supposed to humble me, put me in my place! And why would you need to try and push me down if I weren't capable of rising above you?"

"Enough!" she barked, forcing frigidity into her voice, a cold and superior tone that did not reach her expression. "I want you to understand that I can destroy you, could have destroyed you at any time. The whole journey here, when you, idiot that you have become, made yourself a target for those who pursue you, I protected you. I have been doing it most of your life, in fact. And this, this tantrum is my only thanks?" I hesitated; it was all she needed, and she failed to see that. "Peace, *kind.* I mean you no harm and possibly some good."

She would have been better served just being silent. Just as swiftly as it had pacified me earlier, the word '*kind*' drove me back onto the offensive. I was not a child! Not *her* child, that was for damned sure! "Protected me from what? I've been beaten, tortured and ordered for every day I can remember, and if you *have* protected me, it wasn't out of care or affection. That motivation: it was fear, wasn't it? Destroy me, then, you sorry bitch! Do it!"

Shai-Yeh laughed, but I knew it was as deliberate and false as her words. "Too good a fate for you, Jaydemyr. I do not like you enough to give you that." But she wanted to! I could smell how much she ached to end me: a pungent stench of crusty old honey.

"You can't!" Pieces came together, collided, shifted, and when all attempts at mergence failed, the edges melted until teeth locked and cogs began to grind. "There have been predictions made about me, you've gone to all this effort, and now you reinforce knowledge of my fate by claiming death would be too good, too easy. It doesn't matter what you say, Shai-Yeh — I know the truth now. You can't kill me. I can say whatever I wish, and you can't kill me. You can't walk from me, because you have a part to play as well, or you wouldn't have bothered 'with all this'. You know things I want to know, need to know. We're stuck with each other now, aren't we? Damned, bound, joined."

And that removed the rest of her control, stripped her of all resistance to reflex. Suddenly, she had as little to lose as I, her quarry.

Shai-Yeh howled, words of guttural discordance desecrating the air.

The aural explosion permeated my unintentional armour, shattered that too-knowledgeable sanctuary. Shockwaves of decimating fallout rolled through the debris. I'd understood those feral words, had known their meaning without having heard them before, at least not outside of a dream, and yet I could not contain what they really meant, could not have made them finite with even an infinite reserve of words. As with the wisdom extracted from the Window, understanding came, was used, and went back to whatever limitless, incomprehensible well from which it had burst. I tried to chase it, to plunge into that space where everything was revealed, but every thought ran into the same block. A single image, one I remembered only as a smear of dusky blood. Now it blazed, burned into my sight like a sun at which I'd stared too long.

That moon and cross symbol didn't *have* a name. It *was* a name. Jaydemyr. Moreover: those scrawled characters around it were family. I couldn't read them. Not yet. But I knew. Father's name on the left; Mother's on the right. And mine at the top.

And mine I *could* read.

At last, I answered words that Wong Shah-Long could never understand, and I did it in a language Wong Shah-Long could never pronounce. And the moment I did, the image faded.

"But you didn't 'stop me', and now you can't. Ask me again, Fa Shai-Yeh." As I listened to these strange sounds I was producing, I noted that 'Fa Shai-Yeh' was pronounced differently. It was more like: *"Vachaelle. I know your name. Now ask me mine!"*

You wanted to know me, Chaelle? You wanted me to know myself? Time to make it happen.

"What is your name?" she asked, reverting to Chūnko-go in some weak attempt at luring Shah-Long, Dog-Ears, back into play.

"My name is not Wong Shah-Long," I said, refusing to be drawn back into Chūnko-go. *"My name is not Dog-Ears. I will not answer to* kind *or* boy. *My name is that which my father gave to me, and it is as this name that I shall complete his work. My name is Charan Jaydemyr."*

If, when I said those two words, there was meant to be any thunder, any sort of dramatic shift in the basic workings of the world, it manifested only in the woman's baring of teeth and her recoil.

"You are going to help me become who I am," I said to her. *"And then, I'm going to kill you for it."* The Window opened and granted me one last morsel of information. This woman had been in my dreams all along. She had been standing behind me, encouraging every rebellious twitch, whispering grand ambition into my strange ears. She had been standing next to me as I wielded that dreadfully proper sword as had my father before me. Finally, she was standing in front of me, and was as They: just another beast to kill, some unbidden guest, a parasite, to which I had to bring the remedy, the cleansing. And to do that, I had to become…A scourge.

Now I knew who I was, and where she fit, her place. I put her in it.

"I promise you: I will end you, Chaelle, and you'll be so grateful."

My calm, almost relaxed response sang to the storm. Beyond control now, she sprang onto the table, poised, both hands clawing at the pliant surface, one foot pressed against the table's edge. Her teeth were still bare and her eyes hardened towards immediate murder. Blonde hair flared askew, released from a façade of gravity by the freedom found in succumbing to the darkest of intentions. Malevolent and grotesque, this was the face of Vachaelle's heart.

Death slid between seconds. Now that I knew what must be known, the Window slammed shut, leaving me *(Charan?)* abandoned and alone. At any other time, I would have frozen, the rush of lost understanding striking me dumb. Now that I had begun to embrace this true nature, starting with just a name, a new option presented itself. I snatched for it, even as its vile thorns pressed against the delicate film of my dying naiveté.

Seduction is never a one-sided affair.

"Then again," I mused, falling into the local dialect once more but acting *nothing* like Wong Shah-Long, like Dog-Ears, "I could be wrong."

I quirked a manic smile, knowing that my own demise was a very real likelihood in the form of the woman-thing reared upon the table. I knew that I'd called it down upon myself. She paused, saying nothing. The pronounced tendons of her hands sank back into dormancy. The livid fury in her glare melted to a bearable distrust.

"In fact," I rattled on, all but glib now, "I'm way off the mark. You hold all the pieces, Mistress Shai-Yeh. I've no idea what came over me, but I'm really sorry." Charan…*I* recalled enough of the village life to strip this apology of all sarcasm. I was also careful which of her names to use. "Don't hurt me…and, hey, could you get off the table now…please?"

She withdrew, albeit with great wariness.

"There we go. No need to be so upset. Just a stupid villager with a big mouth, right? You can deal with me, just as you did all the other pathetic people of Swimming Carp. And they deserved it! Maybe I do too. I'm all yours, Mistress Shai-Yeh. Do as you will."

I lowered my head in submission then fell into a kowtow, prostrating myself after shuffling away from the table upon which my fate had balanced like a coiled viper.

"You offer what is not yours to give, *kind*." Vachaelle's voice reflected her resignation, her exhaustion. There wasn't even a shade of the otherworldly roar, words I'd not wanted to understand, but the resonance still rocked my fleeting stability. I would not let her see this. "We will serve each other, you and I. The test is done."

"And did I pass?" I snorted, noting her usage of the denigrating appellation; let the woman have what little comforts she needed to restore an illusion of superiority. "Are you satisfied?"

"No. You did not pass, and you did not fail." She was back to riddles, but her condescending smile remained absent.

"I survived."

"Yes."

"My reward?" Life itself had been earned, ransomed with a currency beyond tangible worth. Any further bestowment would be at her behest alone.

"The only thing you desire, of course."

"Answers."

"More," she replied instantly.

"Questions that lead to answers?"

"Oh, more, *kind*, much more." Shai-Yeh indulged in elongated syllables: a queen spider circling her ensnared meal, fangs glistening with a venom she no longer needs to use, but likely will anyway.

"Then I do not know what I want."

"Pity the one who does, *kind*."

"Why?"

Her corruption closed distance, biting my dwindling innocence so gently, almost lovingly.

"Because you will do anything to get it."

I sighed, feeling the foul intrusion eating away at my laughable ideals. My eyes: I wanted them closed again, wanted to see no more; ears, *strange* as they were, sought eternal silence. I longed to be the same person who'd entered this Haven only hours ago: Dog-Ears, who found wonder in lighting a lantern and a friend in just chatting with a little girl. But now I'd broken her rules, and surrendered to someone else's. Now *I* was someone else.

And if one must succumb, let it be willingly and utterly.

"Will you teach me, Shai-Yeh?" After all, I figured, what was there left to lose?

"Everything," she replied.

"More."

"As you so desire."

"I will not be led."

"You will lead and I will follow." But something sizzled in her subservience. I understood it. A 'follower' always plays more of a role than mere servant. If we rise, it is with these 'underlings' beneath us, pushing, supporting, maybe just waiting to catch us if we fall, or to step aside, look down and laugh as above and below swap places.

"We're going to Kaifeng." I threw this one at her with far more deftness than either of us expected. The name arose from my memory, a sweet but somehow aching recollection of the young girl downstairs who had so captivated me. Or somewhere deeper still, perhaps.

Shai-Yeh's reaction was even more obvious. She looked *scared* and I saw this – loved it – just before she smothered her rampant horror with an insufficient question.

"How did you? So you remember that much, obviously. Yes, we are close enough to the Capital. Be warned: you, Dog-Ears, have never seen anything like it. I will try to educate you on the way, but if you insist. You are the leader." It was feigned humility; Shai-Yeh was guiding me still. Her expression waxed shrewd. I ignored it.

"Dog-Ears is not my name. Neither is Shah-Long."

"Then shall I call you Char Ah—"

"Char," I said, cutting her off. I had no idea why, but there was no way I was letting her finish.

"As you wish."

"Good. You're going to teach me, about Elders and villages and dreams. About many things. About anything I want. Is this acceptable?"

I wasn't sure why the statement arrived as a question – it felt wrong. Wasn't I the one holding the sword now?

She said: "Yes."

I rose and turned, revelling in this newfound self-control, in control over other selves. "And so, what would you ask of me?" I returned to the soft void of the cloak's hood. Every movement, from the fabric's replacement to the quiescent footfalls upon insulated weave, felt compact, purposeful – nothing was excess.

"Nothing you have not given already, my lord." And there it was, appending the demure purr as fluidly as wetness follows rain. I didn't even notice it at first. For all my apparent ascension, I was still making mistakes all over the place. But I didn't know, and you know what is said about the impotence of what one doesn't know. What a hopeful lie.

She continued, "Your ignorance, innocence and complacency. Give me those and I will provide you with everything you need."

I paused before reaching for the paper-stretched slats of the door.

"You are not my mother." But you *can* tell me what to do.

"What a silly thing to say, my lord. Look at me – barely a few years older than you! Now you really are acting like a *kind!*"

"Yet you call me lord as readily as you call me 'child'." I *was* joking then, glad to realise Vachaelle could not have been my mother.

"Call it pre-emptive optimism. Let us go."

I couldn't reply to that. There had been my questions, and the answers, while irrelevant (or sometimes even deterrent), satiated just enough of my appetite to let me know that my hunger for knowledge might never be content again. Windows are for viewing – for glimpsing what lies beyond – but I had to *go* beyond, and for that, a mere window would not suffice.

Chapter 9: *Zen*
PHOENIX

You can walk through the same door only once.

Behind me, Chaelle slid the screen to a close.

"Should we do something about the man who die—" Rethink that one, Char – no more questions. "You should deal with the man you killed, Shai-Yeh. I don't want either of us getting in trouble for it."

"I told you, Char. He is not pertinent." A flutter of scarlet: that scruffy red cape of hers. She sidled around me, towards the end of the hall, towards the stairs. Very slight body contact; enough to quicken my breath and stiffen my spine. Not a reaction Dog-Ears would ever have made.

"Yes, but he's *dead,* Shai-Yeh. People will notice." Then I realised something more important. "I noticed and didn't care. Why?" I tracked her slithery progress. "No, forget it. I don't care why. Will this be the same for everyone else?"

"More or less. We will be gone by the time anyone finds him." She paused before descending, balance maintained only through a rigid left arm and a hand curled about the length of an unimpressive wooden railing. "I suppose we could dispose of him. Would you like to spend more time with a dead fat man who probably shit his pants, my lord?" Her delivery was dulcet, the words drenched in crass disillusionment.

I got the message. She busted my proverbial cherry of command so quick I barely had time to yelp. Lesson almost learned: if you can't be smarter than those you lead, at least be smart enough to know it. I say 'almost', because it would take a few more lashings of Chaelle's gentle, unyielding cynicism to penetrate Shah-Long's numb but necessary walls.

"I don't like leaving things behind, Shai-Yeh. Loose ends bother me." I placed no question marks within the enunciation, but 'can I?' and 'may I?' still lurked behind each word. My twisted mentor shook her head – *I cannot believe you sometimes!* – and traipsed down a few steps.

"He is dead," she said with a clear push towards finality. "And there is nothing you can do about it. Gone, see you, hope things are better there than they are here, et cetera. Look, if you want to pray for him, go for it. Cremate him for all I care. Whatever you feel necessary, do. *He is not important.*"

Could I? Was this new me able to control even the Fire? I turned, looked at the door behind which I knew his incriminating corpse waited to be found.

"Are you serious, Shai-Yeh?"

"I am," she said, a few steps down already. "He does not matter."

And I'd already broken that particular rule. Not like I could be asked to leave the Haven twice.

He was still there when I opened the door. How anyone else hadn't found him first, or for that matter noticed the ruckus Chaelle and I had raised in her room, will never be answered, not after what happened, but I was thankful for it nonetheless.

I closed the door, knelt beside him. Thought about moving him. Tried. Too heavy. It'd have to be done here.

How? The last time I'd tried to deliberately use the Fire, it had taken over and left me nothing but a spectator as it dominated whatever threatened me. This time I might accidentally set fire to the entire Haven, which was a *lot* of wood and paper. More importantly, it was full of people who deserved nothing more than a good night's rest. And me. And Happy Apple.

But then there'd been the Fire's containment when Chaelle had tried to goad me into using it. Surely that took control? Now was the time to find out.

I touched the body's arm, neck. Cold and pliant. Where to start? Would the clothing burn first? Should I pull it away? Just tear back the lapel, place your hands above his chest, and let it flow. Think disintegration, not incineration. Dust and ashes. Straight line to nothingness.

"Just *how* stupid are you?" she asked from above – and behind me. I didn't look, just kept trying to channel enough Fire into the corpse to immolate it, and not so much that it'd spread to anything else just as flammable. Anything else. It was like trying to top up an already full cup.

Erring on the side of caution is still erring. I was barely heating the skin, wavelets of warmth blurring the tiny space between my fingers and the man's torso.

"Shit," she muttered. "Look out, idiot."

That was all the warning she gave before leaning over my shoulder and pouring her liquor over the man.

Fwoosh!

"What are you—" I asked, ripping my hands away just in time. "Are you crazy? He's on fire!"

"I thought that was your big plan!" she shot back, grabbing my cloak and wrenching me away from the sudden conflagration.

"Not like this. Eph me," I swore, and then winced as she hit the back of my head.

"Char! I expect better from you. Sigh," she said, as though simply 'sighing' wouldn't have been enough. "Well, crap. This *is* what had to be done, but you've figured it out a bit late. Ugh. Okay. Stand back."

I was already pressed against the wall, shying from the flames and the stench.

Vachaelle stood and made a gesture that looked as though she were scattering a handful of grain. Instead of seeds, though, there was a gush of water, and not a drop of it missed the burning body. Steam filled the room with a loud hiss. Just as I started to breathe it in, the girl held her hands out, knuckles down. The vapid air spiralled into two cyclones, each swirling into her waiting palms. The air cooled and cleared, and she clapped her hands together.

The man's body was still there, now just blackened. At least the smell wasn't so bad.

"Yeah, that really helped," I said.

"Would not have been a problem if you had *just left him* like I said. Moron. Damn, wasted my drink too." As annoyed as she'd been the first time she'd encountered the man, Chaelle kept muttering as she left the room.

"But you said—" No. I wouldn't whine. Not anymore. "Fine."

"Close the door behind you," she said from the hallway. And when I did, she'd already started down the steps. And no one seemed to have noticed. No one knew about this man's demise. About what we had done. But we had done it, and I knew.

I wish I'd at least learned his name – years later, caught in solitude between slayings, writhing within a personal oubliette of recalcitrant sin, I sometimes found myself apologising to 'the dead man in the Haven.' I pray Az'hraeth of The Burning Gates welcomed the poor bastard with a better name than that.

I trudged down the stairs with a hope that motivated many of my more infamous deeds between then and now: *When I die, let it not be in nameless obscurity.*

Testament to the unquiet fatalist in me – I couldn't bring myself to replace the 'when' with 'if', not even in harmless thought.

The common room of the Haven seemed to have shrivelled since my last visit. I know: it was my insight that had grown, because rooms generally don't change size. Still, I think it's fairer to explain the shift from this perspective: the room had shrunk; my world was now smaller because I felt larger.

There was artifice everywhere I looked: the true genius of human invention. The patrons' laughter was thin and strained. Their smiles were like fresh wounds, flaps of skin peeled back to reveal the red suffering and raw bone just underneath. They drank not because they were thirsty, but because you can't scream with a throatful of beer. Cheerful conversation struggled to muffle the terrified thoughts, the facts: you're in a Haven because the moon is full and you'd be dead if you weren't.

"Pathetic, are they not?" Chaelle whispered. She had waited for me at the bottom of the stairs. She craned her neck and stood on the balls of her feet. Occasionally, she would jump, resembling an eager child at her first public execution, trying to see over the overgrown heads. I wondered then if all villains, all lowlifes and bringers of woe, are just children and monsters, one trapped within the flesh of the other. If so, which would be the more fearsome? I resolved to examine my two very fine examples of the scale's extremities, Hua-Shi and Shai-Yeh, when time and place permitted.

A mirror would have done the job.

"They're just doing their best, Shai-Yeh," I lied. "They think this is what life is about, maybe."

"Do you *know* otherwise, Char?" She anticipated an answer. I could almost see the wreckage in her mental wake as she tore through the conversation at a pace determined to challenge me. It wasn't right to leave her talking to herself, and so I tried to keep up. Hey, it's as good an excuse as any, and as she would come to teach me: an excuse is, at best, a decent reason for doing an indecent thing.

"Of course not, but if you say they're pathetic, then surely there's something to life they're not getting." I mulled over my own answer, upset with the disparity between Them and Us. Or Me. Naturally, it had been that way well before this recent change, before Charan interrupted Shah-Long's virtuoso solo performance of 'O Woe, Thou Art I – in Me Minor'. Between Me and Them: just one big game of leapfrog, like the kids from that village used to play before they discovered more interesting ways of jumping each other. With Chaelle's help, I'd gone and straddled the lot of them, but the division remained. Strange as I was, and am, there will always be longing for association, socialisation. I *know* I'm brilliant, but sometimes, even I tire of my own company. I wouldn't have minded being one of Them, if it meant I could still be Me.

Whoever the hell 'I' is. Don't ask me; I'd just met the guy.

"Where's this going, Shai-Yeh?"

She was still moving about, trying to spot something from within the hive, that bloated collective not readily defined as human. No single human can make a sound quite like that manifold susurrus (great word that, though it only exists in Ziegerian-Common. Spoken, it is perfectly onomatopoeic and sounds *almost* like my ancestral tongue).

"Nowhere, really," she said. "That is the point. Someone should put the lot of them out of the world's misery."

"Then why don't you?" I couldn't muster enough horror at her flippant remarks about genocide, but something told me if she really wanted it done, she'd do it herself.

Chaelle stopped her frenetic scanning of the room and dropped the mien of a wide-eyed child in her shiny red hood. Those eyes, in their sudden narrowing, hinted that I might have just made a big mistake.

Which I had.

She waggled her finger at me. "You should know better than to answer a question with another question, my lord."

"But you didn't ask a question at all!"

"Yes I did! Quite a few, in fact. You just did not hear them, did not *get* them." It must have been *so* obvious to her, judging by her patronising tone. Shai-Yeh swivelled her fine nail around, pinning the patronage with one swift stab. "There are a million questions, and just as many answers. Would you want to be the one who has to spend forever watching over them, trying to sort them out, just for the sake of your supposed benevolence? As if that would help any of them in the slightest. But we're not just watching, you and I. We're here with them. We listen. We answer. We care."

"I don't know enough about these people to care much at all," I replied, feigning disinterest in what seemed like a great deal of projection. Chaelle favoured me with another of her looks: critical, cynical and quizzical all at once. Then she turned away and moved into the mess of people. I tugged the hood even harder and slid my left thumb under the sack's shoulder strap. Embracing my wariest of modes, I followed – was led.

"Ow! Grrr! Watch it, kid!" I stopped. Probably another mistake, but when you plant your elbow in someone's face, it's not exactly polite to keep moving. That and I expected something else to happen – his words were a warning. I tried to bow an apology, but there was only space for a half-bent nod. This didn't seem to satisfy the fellow, who then had three friends standing behind him. Big friends, too. They reminded me of the brutish kids from the place where I grew up. Whatsisname Village. Didn't matter.

"Sorry!" I tried to bow again, all the while shuffling back.

"Oh, bother." Thus came the cavalry, trotting past the ruffian whose face didn't like my elbow. The three henchmen seemed a bit taken aback, but their leader glared down at Chaelle as she approached, scolding me without even taking the thugs into account: "I told you to keep up! Come *on*." She latched one wiry hand about my arm, tugging me away from what was quickly looking like a fight. I didn't move at first. Perhaps there is a base rebel in me, someone who will stand still if you say 'move!' or jump if you say 'duck!' Chaelle yanked a bit harder and I gave. We both stumbled a few steps. I didn't see what happened, simply because I was too busy trying to regain my balance.

But I did hear.

"A Priestess of The Liquid Night!"

Such *sinister* words! Both Dog-Ears and Charan found the words 'Liquid Night' nauseating, though neither the foolish villager nor the fledgling lord had a clue why.

"What? Never seen a girl with blonde hair before? Eh?" Chaelle gave the crowd a cheeky grin, taunting them with her unique and very false sparkle. The people around us withdrew together at the sight of her exposed hair. Her hood must have come off when she tripped. Thinking this, I wonder if what came next wasn't my fault after all. Then again, given what little I knew even then, wasn't it *all* my fault?

"Move! Out of the way, the lot of you." Ah, the voice of reason! Havenkeeper Zhang nudged his way through the thick forest of fear and flesh, an old bear sweeping aside troublesome reeds.

Happy came after him. She looked smaller than I remembered, even as she peeked around her formidable guardian, who now stood between Chaelle and the incensed patrons. The little girl rose up and poked her tongue out, tugging on her right cheek to give the 'Priestess' a fine Red Eye taunt. This defiance, to a woman who had killed a man with only a look, was that of an angry man poised on a high cliff, railing against God with a curse and a solitary middle finger, daring Her to do Her worst.

Chaelle responded with a wintry glare that seemed to hold back even more hatred than it conveyed.

"This wasn't part of the deal, Priestess," Zhang said. His accusatory tone, and the word 'deal', proved he was no longer the one in control.

As it turned out, neither was Chaelle.

"Grandad, where's Mr. Shah-Long?" Happy tugged on Zhang's sleeve, although she had more attention than just his when she spoke. The crowd shared an indignant stare at the precocious girl. Only one person did not seem to be bothered by her, and that's simply because she was looking right at him and asking where he was.

"Gone," Zhang replied before I could vouch for my own unquestionable presence. What in *Hell Above* did that mean? Gone?

"Gone where?"

"I'm right here, Happy." No wave, no cute little tickling of the air.

"I guess he left without saying goodbye." As though she hadn't heard me. Then she began to look around – up, down, behind. Where is Shah-Long? Where is Dog-Ears? Are you on the ceiling? Are you on the floor? Are you hiding behind that scary man in the black cloak?

"I think I saw him go upstairs," said Havenkeeper Zhang, now glaring at me. It was all the girl needed – she dashed off with an excited yelp. The ring of ruffians, an apparent Priestess and Yours Truly, being one very bewildered twit, watched her leave in complete silence. Without raising a fist, without raising even her voice, Happy kept a very violent situation in stasis – but she took the odd restraint with her.

"Take him and leave, Your Holiness!" Havenkeeper Zhang seemed weak then. It was as if Happy had taken his resolve with her as well.

Vachaelle laughed in his face.

"You speak of deals, Havenkeeper," she replied, "but it was you who broke the contract."

"C-contract?" Zhang extracted a rag to mop his forehead. "What are you talking about? I just do my job, just do what I'm told. You never— I didn't expect this to happen!" Then he seemed to remember that everyone was watching him. Zhang drew himself up and stated, "I am a faithful servant of Lord Ayakawa and of the Night. I am not subordinate to you, Priestess."

In front of me, Chaelle's shoulders tensed; I felt a sudden chill in the air. This wasn't going to be pleasant.

"Right here, right now, Havenkeeper," she hissed through clenched teeth, "you are more than subordinate to me. Your life depends on how you answer the next few questions. Were you or were you not instructed to deliver him to me unscathed?"

"Does he look scathed to you, Priestess?"

"His little chat with that girl-thing did far more damage than you can imagine."

"I was busy, and I knew she'd keep him out of trouble."

"She *is* trouble, Havenkeeper." A none-too-shrouded implication. Chaelle leaned forward as though examining a gaping wound seeping from a dying animal. I imagined her thrusting her fingers into the fissure and widening it even as her eyes widened with fascination and glee. *Ooh, look what I can do!* "And we really do not need any more trouble, do we? Next question: how are you going to appease us for this error? How, I should ask, will you encourage me to forget her name?"

"I did what you asked, Priestess. Without question. Now, please, leave us in peace!"

Whoops. Definitely the wrong answer.

Chaelle raised her hands. A pulsating bubble of water coalesced from the air around her small, frail fingers. I'd never seen liquid look so hard. Destruction stared back at me as I gazed into the sphere; the shifting surface rippled with an evolving threat scribed in a language dedicated only to defining devastation. So much for the 'no Elementalism' rule of the place; there were no guards rushing to enforce it, no righteous loudmouths like Wu Ming. One more indignant word from Zhang and Chaelle would snap – Haven or not, Zhang's house provided safety for no one now.

I had to take control.

"Shai-Yeh," I said, careful to use her name rather than any title. I also waited until she acknowledged my voice, until she looked at me. She could not ignore this. "Can you afford to destroy this Haven?"

This prompted a hateful look from Zhang. He really should have known that I was trying to help him.

"I can level it in an instant. I am a Priestess of the Liquid Night!"

Like that meant anything to me.

"Yeah, and if you *do* level the place, Shai-Yeh, to whom will you answer?" It was as gentle a reminder of her own subordination as I could conjure. "And will they understand that you destroyed a Haven because of a little misunderstanding with the Havenkeeper?"

"Little? He disobeyed my orders." Chaelle's teeth were no longer clamped together, but frozen condemnation yet dwelt within that statement.

"And haven't you disobeyed *your* orders, Shai-Yeh?" I pressed. "But you get the job done, just as Havenkeeper Zhang does. I am here, unscathed, and willing to go with you. Let it go."

She turned to face me. Her hands were not alone in their watery augmentation. Once-sparkling eyes were awash with fury, clouded with tiny clusters of fog.

Behind her, Zhang began to back away. Was he finally getting the hint?

"They are just people, my lord." And yes, Zhang's glare intensified as she called me that. "The world is full of them, and they kill each other off every day, every night. No one will miss them, and anyone who dares to consider defying us, defying *me*, will need only think of Zhang's ruination and *re*consider their stance." She wasn't quite pleading with me, but there was a request for permission. It was all I had, and so I took it and *ran like hell.*

"No. That is not our place. We are not Of The Night, Shai-Yeh, even if you are some sort of priestess. This isn't your choice to make. Harm even one of these people and I'll walk away from you." I guess I could have threatened suicide, but there wasn't much of a threat there — at least some nefarious aspect of Chaelle *wanted* me gone. Stating that I would walk from her, however, could not be easily refuted, because the only way she could deal with 'insubordination' like that was through violent retribution, and she knew that wouldn't work with me, not after all the physical punishment 'Dog-Ears' went through.

"You of all people should know that you can not obstruct justice, Charan-*ra*." The energetic ebbing within her eyes calmed somewhat, and her hands were naked once again, but I felt as though the waters receded only to accumulate a greater surge. "The villagers got what they deserved, did not they?"

"They weren't real!" I finally admitted. Finally.

By now, Zhang had stepped away from us without quitting the scene altogether. I saw someone talking to him hurriedly, and both occasionally glanced at the two of us. Fa Shai-Yeh was too busy 'teaching' me to notice.

"They were as real as Wong Shah-Long," she said. "As Dog-Ears. As Plump Treat."

No. She wouldn't get away with changing the subject. Not even with *that* teasing revelation.

"Don't do this, Fa Shai-Yeh. Please."

"They have seen far too much anyway, heard too much." She raised her voice to almost a shout, against all her apparent apprehension. Her eyes conveyed the cackle she didn't quite permit herself to express as she declared, "You are, after all, the heir to Jaydemyr."

I didn't understand what she'd done, not until those who heard turned and stared at me. Their expressions weren't precisely damning, but they weren't admiring either. Whatever their reaction, it was to the name.

"Listen to me!" Chaelle said to the crowd. Granted her dumbstruck audience, the priestess launched into a full litany. "Beneath this cloak is no man. A beast has slipped under your gaze and into your Haven. A murderer. A Rose – they who still defy the rule of the Overclan! I am a Holy Priestess, anointed by God and the Lord Afraen Who Was Ephriem to seek the foes of the Night! And I have found him! The enemy is among you!"

Beast? Enemy? Murderer? Rose! Wha—

"She is right!" Zhang burst out, pointing at her, pointing at me. "The enemy is here! *They* are the enemy. Tell them," he said to the listless man with whom he'd been holding quiet conference. Not that I needed to be told.

"Rules have been broken!" he yelled, and everyone listened. "He wields fire, and I found someone upstairs, killed! BURNED to death!"

Shai-Yeh looked as surprised as I didn't feel. But then she whispered in my ear, "Told you we should have just left him."

This only encouraged the Havenkeeper's fury.

"The lantern has been broken!" Zhang was almost jumping up and down. I looked at the desk, at the now-dark but still intact lantern. What did he mean? Just as I was about to look away, I saw the shelves behind the desk. Weapons. Dozens of weapons. Just waiting.

Unfortunately, some of the patrons had the same idea, and did more than merely look.

Their eyes asked, and the Havenkeeper answered.

"To arms! Women and children, upstairs. We must defend the Haven!"

Defend? They were the ones on the offensive! Or is there something innately offensive about me?

"They are going to kill you, my lord," the 'Holy Priestess' whispered, "simply because of what and who you are."

"And what in Hell Above is that?" Hadn't I asked this before? Hadn't the answer been clear enough? I was and am Charan Jaydemyr, but what did it *mean*? Chaelle took my name and wielded it as readily as any of the other swords there that night. She *did* know what it meant, and she knew what it meant to other people. "*Who* am I?"

"If we live, I will tell you a nice story and maybe even sing you a lullaby but now can I PLEASE take care of this as I originally intended?"

Only she could be simultaneously so sweet and savage. I didn't understand why she'd revealed who I was or why she so desperately wanted to wreak havoc upon the Haven. I *did* understand that this was part of the deal: she'd defy me only after I gave permission, and she knew I always would.

So I nodded my head, short and sharp.

"Do what you must."

"Thanks!"

"Try not to—"

But she was pulling away, pulled away.

"—Kill everyone." I finished with a whisper.

And she *stopped*, turned around to wink at me, and then she truly was gone.

Having been given my 'permission', Vachaelle launched into her task. Her deep red cloak became a rolling barrel of bloodied water, a wave that churned and built but never quite broke. She rode that surging crest, feet touching the floor only as a bird's talons might scratch the surface of a lake. I tracked her as best I could but saw little more than a fist here, a tumbling blast of *Shui-chi* there. Knives thudded into sudden barriers of ice then fell to the floor in a puddle as the walls melted; simple splatters sharpened into lethal daggers themselves. Tables and chairs became just so much wood and iron. Frigid bitterness invaded the room but soon gave way to fluidity. Shai-Yeh was a rock, a dragon's tail – rigid and smooth, unstoppable and ever-shifting.

And me: nailed to the fulcrum of this icy tempest, aware that one step in any direction would suck me out of the eye and into the grinding madness right along with everything else.

Her laughter permeated the chaos with transparent glee. The jubilant storm chortled even as she pounced another patron from behind. Gripping his head, she placed her other hand against his gibbering lips, smothering a surprised mouth. The frantic man tried to bring his own hands to bear but he'd have had better luck wrestling a waterfall. Chaelle squealed as thin jets spurted from between her fingers and over her knuckles: overflow from a throat designed for mere mouthfuls at a time. The man's nostrils dilated like eyes too full of terror then gushed – a fountainhead's first sneeze after winter. Out his nose, then eyes and even ears came the bloody torrent. I waited for his head to explode, but he was dead before that could happen. The man's body fell to the ground like a soggy towel. She sprang away from a clutter of confused blades, some of which not only missed her but stuck into the bloated victim, puncturing his shiny skin to release gouts of watery gore.

Chaelle left but a slight splash behind her. It was only then that I noticed the floor was dry – the *Shui-sha* wasted not a drop, even though she manifested a flood. There is, she would teach me later, moisture and liquid in all things; the natural state of most living things is liquid. That was her argument for the supremacy of *Shui-chi*, of Hydrotheurgy, over the other elemental forces.

In light of how thoroughly she demolished the House of Joyful Leave-Taking, I am not inclined to disagree.

But on the matter of elemental forces, I was too flustered to wonder what I now ask: why didn't the patrons use their own Talents? The answer is simple and very sad. Havenkeeper Zhang had authorised the usage of weapons; he never said anything about elemental ability. So the Haven patrons died rather than break a rule of that Haven – even though their choice meant that soon, there would be no Haven left, never mind its rules.

To face a potent Elementalist and priestess without resorting to an equal show of power? It's either unerring courage or, far more likely, fanatical obedience. What had they been taught? Probably the same shit Miss Master had rammed down Dog-Ears' throat: that to use one's Talent to harm another was against God's law. And that's what differentiated me from them: I'd always known that the Fire I wield is a knife. It's not enough to own a knife; you have to realise it *is* a knife. If someone had told the patrons that night: 'that's not a spoon – it's a knife. No! It's a *sword*, and it's yours to wield!' – who can say if either Shai-Yeh or myself would have survived?

I expected a few to try to escape but I saw no one run outside. Even this agony, this guarantee of death, was preferable to trespassing the Night. A Haven from the Night's Own is still a Haven, right down to the last table and chair.

There didn't seem to be many of those left.

The furious twister flung someone towards me. His legs and feet were a blur, sketching a horrible caricature of running on air. I'd have caught him had his unwilling charge not been preceded by a sword. If he'd dropped it, I might not have become involved. Oh, that's just bullshit. Mention of my forgotten family name had *caused* all of this, and afterwards, Vachaelle wasn't going to let me forget it.

What I did next confused the hell out of me at the time, and I'm sure the man about to run his sword through me felt no better about it.

I closed my eyes and embraced the fatality.

There, I saw the straight edge piercing my chest, cracking brittle bone. Breaking a weak, useless heart. I held my breath and felt the steel cleave my lungs. The sword went straight through me, clean and smooth, as easily as a disapproving glare crosses an empty room.

I died before the weapon struck – whatever came after could only be rebirth. When I realised death was not to be mine quite yet, I opened my eyes not in a hesitant peek or squinting uncertainty but wide and hard, and things came into focus much faster than expected.

The sword was still coming, and it was still just as quick, but I knew I was quicker. So much quicker. I could have ducked or jumped over it. Hell, I could have grabbed the damn thing and melted it. These were all possibilities and I knew this as well. And there was a chance of remaining still and letting it run right through me – I was not so impervious, and I knew *that* most of all.

"Time to dance, Charan!" I heard her say as though from afar. "You know the way!"

Well, she seemed to having fun. Good for her.

My sarcasm can't bury the unfortunate truth: I *did* know the way.

Far more competent hands had delivered this style of attack to me before. I looked down at my own hands then, my palms, and saw beyond the strange triangular arrangement, saw precisely that which Chaelle had noted: there were no scars from Miss Master's cane. Of course not. That hadn't happened. My hands were not scarred, even if my memories are. But what is a scar? Just a confirmation of survival, a reminder of adversity faced and overcome. It is a sign of healing.

Of learning, and of remembering.

Thrust-Avoid-Counter.

Go.

I stepped forward and left, twisting so that the sword grazed past my stomach. Unscarred hands pursued very different courses, with the right slapping down upon the flat of the blade while the left crossed over, swinging a hard backfist.

Wouldn't that have been enough? Some part of me didn't think so — the crash of knuckles burst into florescent life. I watched with delight and dismay as whoever I was drove a fireball into the man's chest. The molten comet collided with his sternum, and he flew back as though yanked by some elastic intolerance.

His burning body cut a smooth path through the fringes of the frothing whirlpool. I think I ran, but there was an essence of flight, of acceleration that drew upon *other* sources because the situation called for it. Even now, I can't tell you how I caught up to the man. There was no definable process, no clear steps. This is just what happened: I was here; I needed and wanted to be *there*. So I went, and there I was.

One thing I do recall with unnatural sharpness, however, is that he lost hold of the sword mid-air. By then, I was after him, my enemy in the moment, attached at a visceral, sacred level. And because of this bond, I knew he'd dropped the blade before I saw it, right before I took it from the air myself. My fingers knew the configuration of being wrapped around a hilt. Knew and loved.

That was when Charan Jaydemyr truly woke up and reclaimed his dominion over Wong Shah-Long's remains. He, no, I knew the sword was a *Liuyedao*, that this meant 'willow leaf sabre' — a piss-poor excuse for a weapon. I had no inclination to run my hand along its weak spine.

Much like Shah-Long himself, it would serve only as a proxy until the real thing could be reclaimed. This sword might have had a name but I didn't care to learn it.

The man hit the wall with an unimpressive thud and started to fall. Perhaps Chaelle's manipulation of water and of ice had encased our little world in stagnation, freezing the action into a living gallery. That was it – I was in a picture but the world *was* moving, just at the slowest possible rate. The flames eating my enemy's clothing should have coiled and slithered. But they stood still, ostensibly tangible and bearable. The watery warp of heat radiating from the orange chaos was just a smear on the pane of a Window I'd almost forgotten along with everything else Wong Shah-Long thought he knew.

When I'd first opened the Window, it had been with one sense at a time, albeit in astonishing clarity. Now, they all worked together: I tasted the carnage and I smelled the screams. I could hear the curling cloth and see the air whining. Where before I had glimpsed the infinite, now I knew how to access it at will, and even use it. The Window had become a Door, and I'd gone through it. I didn't take what was needed – it came to me willingly, openly. And when I was done, the Door would remain, receptive to touch and compliant with a wish for flame and potency. The worry of my power being unpredictable was no longer the problem after that night. What greater power can there be than being able to control *when* you lose control? And with it came the last realisation, the balancing weakness, before I shied away from the anarchy of endless understanding: it's so much harder regain control *after* you've made that choice.

Before me, I saw neither arms nor legs; the enemy didn't have a 'head'. There were just targets, and I considered countless ways to assault them. This was not about murder or inflicting pain. I held a sword and a sword should do only one thing. It was my place, my duty to guide it to that end. Here – a blade. There – the enemy. Bring them together. Accept that this is what should be done. Find the unfettered pleasure in a function fulfilled.

Just as the euphoria peaked, something gave and time resumed. Down the man went, clothing alight and body blistering like boiling fat. Scattered and splattered. I followed him, cutting and slicing. Once he hit the floor, I discarded the sword; it was not mine, and thus it was supremely inadequate for what I had to do next.

I straddled whatever was left of the enemy and continued to disassemble it.

"Wow, nice work."

At the sound of her voice, unwelcome in this paradise of unleashed everything, I shrank into myself, grateful for the limits once more, but still haunted by the ecstasy of elegant, efficient mutilation.

I looked up and into the manic gaze of Vachaelle. She was mincing behind a coil of cold cruelty, fingers guiding several tendrils with a mix of relish and ease. Her disturbingly dry grin dipped towards whatever I'd been doing. "But I think he is done, Charan."

I glanced down as well, and saw, for the first time, the extent of my desecration.

It was nothing short of an utter dissemination of a human being, a machinated process of removing organs, of snapping annoying bones in the way and of sealing leaky veins that interrupted my 'work'. Each action had made sense then, but now that all the pieces came together, or perhaps were taken apart and made into a completely different whole, I learned what I'd *really* been doing.

I smiled back at her – weak, drained and absent. I didn't have time to register any other feelings, because a rush of sickness took over. Dog-Ears howled and keened. I felt his disgust twist my guts and welcomed the sensation; maybe something in me was human after all. Charan, almost sympathetically, held Dog-Ears' hair back as I vomited for the last time. Despite all the hours I remembered spending in the Slaughter Pit, *now* I really was a butcher. I used to compare the villagers to animals, but there will always be a difference between killing an animal and killing a person. Human blood has a different smell, some sickly-sweet redolence rich with the unique ability to blush, imagine and lie. It makes me queasy even now, although it is often the only smell I identify.

For both our sakes, this was the last time I let Dog-Ears see my handiwork.

"There, there," Vachaelle said, stroking the top of my hooded head in some grotesque attempt at providing comfort. "Let it all out, Charan. It is for the best."

"Don't touch me," I growled once I could, and I knew I'd never use any language but this one when talking to her again.

"Fine. Here." She replied in the same tongue and knelt beside me, placing her hands near my mouth. They filled with water. "Your breath stinks."

"It's not my breath that's fouling this place up." I refused to drink from her cup.

"Foul? But it is so beautiful."

Reluctantly, I stood and took the scene in. Every vicious detail.

"What have you done, Chaelle?" Against all my horror of her, I meant to ask something else, something far more egocentric.

"What have I done? Well," she breathed, skipping around a haphazard ellipse of body parts, "this one seems to have a ruptured torso. You can see from the lacerations that—"

It was just too much. Couldn't breathe. Had to get out. I dashed for the exit, skidding and careening through the blood signifying Vachaelle's power. I might have heard her protest, perhaps annoyed that I wasn't listening to the answer for which I *had* asked, but it didn't matter. Fresh air mattered. Darkness mattered. The smell of dirt and sky and leaves – *they* mattered, they were real. This madness, this complete unreality, did not matter. It was not allowed to matter!

Just as I rushed for the pillared threshold, my right foot caught on something. I pulled instinctively, prepared to rip and kick, but whatever it was would not give.

Havenkeeper Zhang's left hand was tight around my ankle; his lips quivered and spewed scarlet bubbles as he tried to talk. I didn't want to look at the rest of his body, because I had a feeling there wasn't much of it.

"Zhang-sinsan, don't. Just relax." I switched back to Chūnko-go by reflex. His fingers uncurled at last as he seemed to hear me, understand me. I knelt beside him, continuing, "I'm so sorry." Really? Like saying that'd help now. I groped for something to say that might help. Might be good. Something to salvage from all this. "I…I can find Happy. Yes! I'll take care of her."

Who would believe this, only seconds after I'd torn a stranger apart, after I permitted Shai-Yeh to obliterate this Haven? It was a lie, but *I* had to believe it. Happy was, yet again, the pivot for my survival.

"Gone," he finally managed to say. "Told her to run. Good girl. She knew it was time. I knew she'd do this."

Now that he could talk, I could ask.

"What was the deal, Zhang-sinsan?" If he knew, then now was the time. "What did the Priestess ask you to do? What could possibly be worth this?"

I knew better than to name her; his eyes widened at the title.

"Name," he mumbled, closing his eyes. "She asked me to change the name. Said if I did, she'd be safe. No Peddlers. But no good."

Change *the* name. Of?

"Oh, *Eph me*," I swore. It had been there the whole time, and in my ignorance, I'd read it wrong. Maybe just differently. But still *very* wrong. I repeated the first words I'd said upon seeing the Haven, but this time I pronounced the name correctly. "The House of Happy's Departure. You changed the name of your Haven. Why?"

Zhang's face smoothed over then, as though my revelation was a statement, a confirmation. "She's gone. Yes. Good girl."

He hadn't heard my questions, or ignored them.

Zhang opened his eyes one last time and looked up at mine. For some reason, I expected him to say something about them, but because 'Why?' hadn't been the right question, he gave a different answer.

"Shah-Long, don't let the Night. Don't forget who you are." Here he stopped again, and I thought it a good time to leave, or so the unbidden tears crawling down my cheeks seemed to say. But then: "West, seek the Swords. Heir to Jaydemyr."

The last syllable to my true name came with tidal finality: a long, drawn out, voiceless sound.

"Zhang-sinsan? Zhang-sinsan!" I bent over him, shook him, gritted teeth willing him to answer. But he didn't. I pounded the floor with an impulsive fist, the gesture and the pain both seeming familiar. I wanted to deface Zhang, he who had betrayed me. I didn't kill the man upstairs! Why hadn't the Havenkeeper simply let us leave? He'd known what a Priestess could do, and still he challenged her will. Stupid old fool. The people he was supposed to protect had died because of him!

I howled and raised raw knuckles, but as I was about to pummel Zhang's corpse, she said: "Dog-Ears, please don't." Her voice was so soft my heart gave a single lurch of guilt. Shame smothered thoughtless rage. I lowered my hand; fist melted into unsteady fingers and shaky palm.

"He's gone, Dog-Ears." Happy sounded sad, relieved and frightened all at once. I stared at the body but felt her hold my shoulders from behind. A desire to remain stoic yielded to her tentative touch.

"Cry," I said, "as much as you want to."

Even as she rested her face against my back and wept, silent and deep, I wanted to do the same. But what *I* wanted wasn't the issue. For her, I remained upright in wordless commiseration.

Happy spoke through her tears.

"She'll be back soon, and you have to go with her. Grandad said so."

"Where is she?"

"Upstairs, finishing things, well, finishing, you know. I have to go too. Grandad had friends and I have to go to them. Tell them what happened here. I'm sorry, Dog-Ears. I have to tell them about you and her, but I don't think you're a bad person. Okay? Be a good person. Don't be a bad grown-up, okay?!"

There was a threat of renewed sobbing in the request, although she'd pushed away from my back and sounded distant, dwindling.

"I promise, Happy. I won't forget you."

I meant that and I never did. She came close once more, this time brushing her lips against the side of my hood. Happy whispered,

"You'll have to forget me, but if you can't, keep that to yourself! I have to get away, just like Grandpa said. It's okay, I won't forget you either, but I'm going to try. Goodbye, Dog-Ears."

I looked then, only to catch sight of her sprightly image charging out the front, into the night. There were horrors out there, but she'd somehow survived the horror in here. I could only wish and believe *They* wouldn't find little Happy Apple, even if that meant Zhang's, well, her friends now, coming after us for what we'd done. No, especially because.

My wistful smile disintegrated. She was upstairs. Finishing. The Priestess wouldn't stop until everyone was dead. Because that had been my implicit order. Time to issue a new one. I wrenched myself to my feet, and called out in that language Charan found so familiar:

"VACHAELLE?!"

Halfway up the stairs I saw her sitting on the top step, cradling a head in her lap. She was punching holes in a woman's skull with a thin shard of ice protruding from her forceful palm.

"It is so cold," she said, "that the blood freezes before it can leave her head. Is that not fascinating."

"Chaelle, we're going."

"I could not find the little girl, my lord. I wanted to find her."

"Why?" I had to ask, and hoped this time it was sufficient.

"She gave me a dirty look with her face. I wanted to give her face a dirty look. Ha-ha."

There was so much more to it than that, now that I knew. To ask the Havenkeeper to change the name of his establishment, and to such a foreboding name – Vachaelle had planned this. All of this. How could she possibly have known?

"What was the name of this haven, Chaelle? Originally?"

"Something a little less happy, a little more wilted." She looked down at the head and asked of it, "Do you think he'll ever get it? No? Me either." Chaelle tossed the head over her shoulder. I heard it bounce and thump a few times. Then she rolled the dagger of ice down the stairs, which shattered once it hit the bottom. I knew exactly how it felt.

"One day you're going to give a straight answer," I muttered.

"Stupid *kind*," she replied, examining her nails. "What do you think *you* are?"

Again with the attempts at distracting me. Not going to work.

"The Haven's new name," I pressed. "It had to do with the girl, didn't it?"

My obstinacy paid off in the form of Chaelle digging her nails into her palms. Small victory but I enjoyed it for what it was.

"Such a pity I could not find her," she said.

"She ran off." I knew better than to say I'd seen her dead. Chaelle would check, and then she would know.

"Why did you not stop her?"

"She was too quick. Girl was hysterical." The lie began to form, and I loved it.

"So she ran outside?"

Would Chaelle give pursuit? Maybe. If she thought I cared. So:

"Yeah, the silly little thing ran right into the Night." I hated myself for sounding so casual, so believable. "I heard her scream. I imagine They tore her apart." Embracing the lie fully, I laughed and laughed.

"Hmph. That was her fate, either way. You should have been the one to do it, Charan. She had a soft spot for you."

And I for her, you loathsome whore.

"Didn't know me, did she? But you do. Only you can teach me." And I knew her well enough to know this is what she wanted to hear.

"A tiny bit of you awakens each passing second, and this playtime probably unlocked even more. But we need to take you further *and* farther, my lord." She stood, gave the woman's corpse a little kick and made her way past me and down the stairs. Little kicks, little flicks of her entangling blonde locks, little looks – she was all about the little things.

"Chaelle?"

"Hm?" She paused but didn't turn around.

"Don't forget the promise I made to you." *I'll kill you, Shai-Yeh, and you'll be so grateful.* "One day, I'll keep it. But until I am done with you. Until then," I stole a deep breath, and dove straight in, mimicking her unconsciously yet again. "Let us go."

I descended those steps for the third and final time.

I didn't look around as I headed for the exit. Not once.

On the way out, I saw the lantern on the floor. I reached down, took hold of the handle and lifted. It must have been a magical thing to remain intact despite the devastation. But at my touch it remained as dark as the slaughtered room around it.

One of *Them* had broken the magic as easily as it had the rules of the Haven. And it was *me*.

I hurled the defunct lantern at the floor, breaking just another thing.

Chaelle snickered. I stopped, seeing nothing but her insensitive mirth, wanting to let slip my smouldering rage, to send wave after incendiary wave into her smug face. To melt her too-knowing expression into a puddle.

Maybe she felt my ire? Because she said: "You have had a hard night, Char. A hard life. Relax. Let it go. Burn it all away."

She walked out just before I flung my hands like flexing claws, arms like glorious wings. The world burst into bright oblivion once more, and this time I was not afraid that it was my doing.

It was a big fire, but it takes a hell of a lot more than that to erase memories. Vachaelle clapped her hands at the inferno, giggling and jumping. I walked from the blaze, wreathed in flames that felt neither hot nor cold. They just were. Behind me, the beams and rafters succumbed to the rapacious tongues. Once I cleared the pillared exit and joined Shai-Yeh on the road, The House of Joyful Leave-Taking or Happy Departures or whatever the *Eph* it was called took its own leave of absence with one last flare of failing defiance.

Everything was grimly appropriate: my time in the House, the Haven, began with ignition, with the coming of light. It ended much the same way, give or take a hundred bodies, a few lessons delivered in both greetings and farewell. Zhang's profound death; Happy's choice to live and forget. Not much at all, really, not in the grand scheme of things. I'd come to learn about that as well, because my chosen teacher is truly a grand schemer.

"You know," she said as she strolled away, "there is a legend about a bird, my lord, that only attains its true form after it is burnt to death. The phoenix rises from the ashes."

"Some sort of metaphor, 'Priestess'? I don't care."

"Soon, you will understand that, as of tonight, you are a phoenix."

I turned to her as the Haven collapsed in the background. I tore my hood away and frowned at the girl-woman-witch-priestess (*goddess?*). She, of all the potent mysteries in my new world, actually fell back with a gasp, but then regained ground – stubborn planting of feet, fists upon petite hips.

What had she seen in me that forced her to withdraw? She, whom *I* undeniably detest?

"I don't care for your legend, Chaelle. It's shit. None of them," I waved in the Haven's direction, "will 'rise' from these ashes. They're dead, and that's that. I killed them." But I didn't. Yet I did. Permission was tantamount to action. "And I have to live with that, forever."

"Charan, my lord," Chaelle said around a smile, "I said that soon you will understand. Not right now. Tonight you died, and death is never easy. You are struggling with it, and that is fine. It proves me right."

"Right? Nothing about tonight has been right. Nothing about *you* is right."

"That's just your shame talking, my lord. You will not always feel this way."

"You think just because someone stops feeling guilty that they suddenly aren't?"

"No, but it will make next time easier. And there will be a next time, Charan. So you feel guilty? Good. Relish in it. Wallow. Writhe in angst. Indulge all those petty little twinges holding you back. And then *get over it.* Because compared to what lies ahead—"

Chaelle spun on her heel and faced the Haven behind. She snapped her fingers and it began to rain over us, over the razed Haven. There was no thunder, no lightning, not even any clouds. That feverish, unwelcome sweat sent no relief. We stood there, me tolerating the water, her guiding it onto the dying embers.

"—This is nothing."

"Chaelle?" I asked as the drumming rain tapered into an unfair drizzle.

"Hm?" Like a routine.

"When I asked what you wanted for helping me become who I will become, you didn't ask for my Fire." I wasn't afraid to offer that. I believed that she did not know about that other ability: the Window, the Door. Whatever it was. She exhaled with a thoughtful slowness, a sigh that was too long, too heavy.

"A question without asking? You *are* learning. Well, are you that eager to use it again, Char? That eager to become its pawn again?"

I did not bite this time: I was equally her pawn now as I'd ever been to the Fire. Submission *can* lead to empowerment.

"Who knows, Chaelle?" I shrugged, slipping away after replacing my cowl. "Maybe it will become *my* pawn." And I grinned, walking away from her, away from everything. I didn't know the way, yet she would follow, because we were pawns both, enthralled to and by each other.

"Where are you going?" she called, stamping her feet in the now damp dirt. The little-girl routine was back, but I knew it now. Just a routine. Still, good question.

Which way was I meant to be going?

What had Zhang said?

West. Seek the Swords.

Sword?

I made my left hand into a fist. It was ready. I would wait no longer.

Sword.

Then I *remembered*. For all her efforts, Vachaelle had failed to resurrect even a twitch of my true self, and a dying old man's final words unknowingly opened the one door she could never control. Now he was dead. I had killed him. Now he was my teacher. Now I knew I had had many teachers.

"You're going the wrong way!" she called out.

"I am if we want to go back to Kaifeng," I replied in yet another language, one that reminded me of picking purses, watching parades and stalking city streets at night. Of climbing and falling, of walls and love. Of flowers and knives. Apples and fire.

Dog-Ears almost choked on the word 'back.'

"But you don't, do you, Char Ah-Ran?" she replied in the same language. Not Charan. Char Ah-Ran. The name she was going to give in the Haven. The name I didn't want to hear. He's the one who knew this third language, who knew Kaifeng. He's the one who answered her.

"I fuckin' hate it when people call me that, Shai-Yeh. Wish I'd never told you my full name."

"Char, then? If you insist. So if you're not going home, where to?"

"Home, Fa Shai-Yeh? Home is where the sword is. Come."

I started to laugh. With each measured step, I remembered more and more, but I was withering inside, as Dog-Ears and almost everything about him curled up and died. I appreciated that it was he who'd gotten me this far, not Charan or Char, who for all their experience had not been worthy of what I truly desired. Only together, the three of us as one, would I reclaim her. Chaelle was half-right: the phoenix does rise from the ashes.

What she didn't know was that my fire hadn't even begun to burn.

Interlude

Kas'Daen-desne
Risingmoon
882 A.R.

The world inserts its darkness between possible sentences and the memories fall silent.

The Lady Dhiana reaches towards the prone figure upon the bed. Behind her, Arius Hawkstorm clicks his tongue. As though bitten, Dhiana withdraws her attempt at contact. She steps back from her subject, from 'Dog-Ears', almost placing a crooked knuckle in her mouth, but does not turn from him.

Arius, even now guarding the door, studies her as he has many times before. A single, high window allows moonlight to pierce the small room that might as well be called a cell. His Lady's choice of apparel is all-too-deliberate. She wears an effusive gown of reluctant opacity, an airy garment both gentle and imposing. The shadowy fabric contrasts her bone-pale skin, entreats luminary definition. Tall, thin and willowy: he muses at her apparent, and very misleading, frailty.

"So," The Lady opens, speaking in the same language as that which signalled Dog-Ears' surrender to Charan Jaydemyr. She glances down at her fingers.

"Yes," The Champion closes, understanding her. He takes a step forward, towards both Lady and the unconscious boy. Arius scratches his bristled cheek, rakes savage fingers through his pepper-spiked mane and scorns the air with those disapproving clicks. She finally looks away from the dreamer and at her Champion.

He remains armoured even in their concealed sanctuary. The burnished cuirass, greaves and pauldrons all bear devices appropriate to his calling: rending talons, proud beaks, unswerving avian eyes and that recurring arc and cross, the one neither of them understood until they heard it described so fully by the now-speechless voice.

"Shall we leave it there then?" The Lady tries again.

"I believe that is up to him." The Champion replies. *Why's she even asking?* He wonders. *This is her campaign.*

When she'd found him, perhaps five years ago, he'd been working – some menial task that seemed very important at the time. Cobbling, butchery. Maybe carpentry. A loner, Arius Hawkstorm chose to work at night because he suffered from insomnia, or so he thought. Evidence of a head wound explained the regular amnesia, or at least excused why he could remember his craft and name but not what he was doing a week ago. Then, as simple as a miracle, he'd heard a name in his head, and now he knows that name. After that, he'd slowly begun to remember who he really was, but dismissed much of it as fantasy and imagination. Four years later, she'd arrived, a hauteur maelstrom spun of quiet thunder and dim disclosure. Their first conversation had confirmed enough of those so-called fancies to guide The Champion back to the task at hand. Like a falcon perched upon a confident forearm, Arius rides Dhiana's motivation, smug and yet subordinate at the same time. When she announced the time to strike against this killer of their kin, this black-cloaked Scourge, Arius offered his services before any other, before even impetuous Ran'za, who was much-smitten with The Lady.

As are we all, Arius confesses to himself, now as then, when she'd made it clear his duty would be fulfilled only after The Scourge came 'home'. He'd fumed over the decision but acceded to her authority. He is but her Champion. She will make errors and he will stand by them, at least for as long as her arm can support the demanding claws of his loyalty.

"I want to leave him here. It would not be right to talk about him in his presence."

"He's asleep, My Lady. He can sleep through our conversation. I don't recommend leaving him alone. Not even here." This is, however, just his counsel and she is free to ignore it, to step past him and out of the room. Accordingly, he is free to follow, to choose her command.

It is a choice. Something inside of him recalls a betrayal, relishes in the chance of watching Dhivashes the Mindwarp suffer again. This twinge saves Arius *and* strengthens his capacity as a Champion. Without a latent disgust for the Lady's feigned weakness, the Champion falls into lust and an ancient triangle breaks itself. Thus Arius stays his hand, be it either in violence or virile longing. He loves her, hates her and, above both extremities, needs her.

He *needs* the boy, this self-styled 'Scourge', prodigy of the Nightsong's design. The boy remembers, and when he does, so too do they. It's beginning already; Arius wants more.

This is why he chooses to follow.

Dhiana prowls the length of a marble balcony, fingers glazing over the frosted railing. Beneath her, before her, the domain of her enemy, Kas'Daen-*desne*, stretches all around, as though she may be within God's palm, staring at Her infinite fingers.

"If God made all this," Dhiana says, placing her own palm aloft, "all this beauty, wonder and majesty, why did She leave it in such incompetent hands?"

"I don't believe in God," Arius replies. *Was that the wrong answer, or did she ask the wrong question?* "And Ephriem, The messiah? Flesh and blood, just like the rest of us, human or otherwise. He died, just like we all die – eventually. And he *stayed* dead." Arius has not come expecting a theological discourse – mention of death suits his purpose. What follows death if not rebirth? And that rebirth hinges upon change, upon development. *Maybe I am a phoenix too.*

"You do not bear God's mark, Arius. I know well your apathy towards Her, or at least Her existence. Ephriem's Flail doesn't suit your vestment." Dhiana bends her arms, leaning a little against the railing before pushing away from it. She resumes her pacing.

"The boy sees the Cross as well, Dhiana. He's seen it all his life, it seems." Arius is musing out loud now. To him, forks in the path are just tangents and any branches not selected remain secondary, whimsical. Hawkstorm gives little validity to the concept of profitable free will.

"Not his life." Dhiana is blunt in this denial, each of the few words acting as walls against the offensive idea. "That was not his life. Vachaelle told him so more than once, yet when I Delve, it is what he remembers so clearly. Even after he admitted none of it was real, he chooses the fantasy. Fantasy? Who would fantasise about being this Dog-Ears?"

"You buried the real memory, didn't you, Dhiana?" Arius attempts to encourage her, but if she's to continue, it will be by her own volition and in her own style. "And if you did such a thorough job, then it stands to reason that something else fills the void."

"I ask about his past, about where he feels it all started, and this is what I get. A mixture of fallacies and personalities. It'd be easy to shove him out of sequence, to simply skip to the point at which she began to tell him her version of the truth. But I have no idea if that would mean missing crucial aspects of these lives, and we need him whole. There was Dog-Ears, which I suspect I may have engineered, and then there was him, and finally a third, this Char Ah-Ran. Char. At least they speak different languages. Makes this a little easier."

"For all my years, I can't imagine living more than one life at once. One must dominate the other, mustn't it? Is he a village boy who dreamed of more, some petty street rat of a Mifūné city or the highly educated, painfully self-aware heir to a deposed, reviled Clan? It's not unlike the folktales, save that this *kien'dre*—"

"Do not say that word!" Dhiana gasps, a breathless wraith against his usage of the Noble Tongue. Then she composes herself, not realising that her need to compose herself just accentuates the slip. "We are at enough risk as it is. Besides, he is *not* a 'child', at least not hers. Whatever she might have intended."

"This is a good thing, Dhiana. That he so readily refutes Vachaelle's influence."

The Mindwarp, still inclined towards very human reaction, lets out a sharp laugh, a forced slap across the unadorned face of her Champion's simplicity.

"If he refutes hers, he can refute mine. Remember: my intentions are not so distant from Vachaelle's own."

" 'She's not my equal, Arius. She is not Jaydemyr,' " The Champion says, his mimicry of the Mindwarp's statement a week ago appropriately flawed.

"Exactly." Dhiana nullifies his sarcasm by agreeing. "So I must decide on where to Delve next. We don't yet know what happened between his meeting Vachaelle at seventeen and the murder of my Talons. We *do* know when they met. It's been nine years since. All that, yet to be revealed. And if the entirety of the Swimming Carp scenario was fabricated, just what was he doing *before* she met him at age seventeen in the Haven? This is why it is so important that we encourage recollection, not force it. If I simply said, 'tell me where you were at the age of twelve', I have a feeling we'd get at least three distinct answers, and each would be as real to him as the other."

"Why twelve?" Arius asks. "That year, that birthday, seemed so important to Dog-Ears, to Wong Shah-Long."

"Because that is when his visions and fantasies merged and he had his first true memory of us? Maybe. But something else. I think." Dhiana pauses. "Yes. We left the boy in Vachaelle's care when he was twelve. Or did she just take him? Of little consequence, if the result is the same: we trusted her, and she betrayed us."

In her frustration, Dhiana does not see the Champion's face twist in brief agony. For a moment, he remembers far more about Vachaelle the Nightsong than he is ready to accept, but like a sudden cramp, it passes, and is gone.

"She has planned," Dhiana continues, oblivious. "No, she has implemented her own means of using the boy, turning him into this lethal instrument, this Scourge who dispatched my personal war band effortlessly. A village boy, eradicating *us*. Just what was she trying to achieve?"

"Dare I hazard a guess and risk your wrath, *Mindwarp*?" Arius aims true with the barbed title; the Lady recoils – Dhiana Jaydemyr is no longer Dhivashes the Mindwarp, although the method of Delving hasn't changed. "It's clear Vachaelle can't destroy him. He found that out for himself and, I've no doubt, used the knowledge to great advantage. But she still found a way to wield him, even if he forced himself to believe it was the other way around.

"She has made of him a weapon. This can't be entirely a bad thing, Dhiana. I feel that some original purpose has been fulfilled. He realised his own Talent very early on, despite what others may have told him."

"And so he should have. *You* trained him for years," Dhiana says instantly. Then she smiles to herself. "I recognised the way he used his sword. When he killed Sa'hres'z, I knew him. But that was not your style. It was efficient to a point of sleekness, but also thoroughly ugly in its lack of concern. His father, Chara...Charas—" Dhiana actually stutters – The Lady whose command few dare question stumbles over a mere name. After a few moments of enfeeblement, she settles on a sterile pronoun. "His father was like that. Do you remember?"

"No. I trained The Scourge? I barely remember how to draw a sword. And you say *I* am responsible for that?"

"Perhaps Vachaelle augmented what you planted, but the basics, the foundation, are there. It would take far too many nights of Dreamsong for even Vachaelle to mould one such as The Scourge. Dreamsong only teaches the mind – the body must be developed over time."

Arius begins to ask, but Dhiana continues – or perhaps changes course. When she elaborates, she sounds as amazed as her Champion looks.

"Dreamsong. I mentioned it moments before we began, but now I know what it is. That is how she used to work, and it seems that much has not changed. How she ensnared you! I remember! She would sit by your bed as you slept. She was singing, no, praying, whispering, *poisoning*. And you would awaken feeling so worn out, so irritable! Think! The Scourge was near breaking point when he fell into my arms. How she must have denied him rest, abusing his prone stance by corrupting everything and anything he knew or learned while awake."

"If her Dreamsong is so potent," Arius says, not willing to accept the fact he himself learned years ago, "then how do we know *anything* he has said is real?"

"There are some things we knew before this. We know a Haven near Kaifeng was destroyed nine years ago – which means I must accept that everything he described about it, happened. For example, the Havenkeeper advised with his final breath that Charan seek 'The Swords'. The Havenkeeper knew my son, or at least knew of our Clan. Does this 'Swords' subject mean anything to you?"

"The Swords of Heaven," Arius replies, then shakes his head. "Don't know what it means. But if he headed west to find them, and we did find him west of Chūnko, here in Kas'Daen-*desne*, then maybe he was following the old man's counsel. Or the old man was primed to say it by Vachaelle."

"Entirely possible. And then this girl. This Happy Apple. Surely she would have been taken by the Peddlers if she were as curious and inquisitive as we have been led to believe. Vachaelle destroyed the Haven over his exposure to Happy Apple, but I am sure it was part of the plan. The girl managed to loosen Wong Shah-Long's tongue and mind, so when Vachaelle lured Dog-Ears into a game of questions and answers, he was ready. All a game designed to transform a lost, confused villager into a methodical killer. Dog-Ears into Charan Jaydemyr."

"Do you think it was at that moment?" Arius asks. "I detected hints well before that. Although I have no idea what 'before' means when someone remembers things out of sequence."

"No, you're right. He saw his name in that strange Plump Treat portion of the Dog-Ears scenario, saw her carve it into her arm. And I do not doubt that the so-called Maliscient woman was Vachaelle, just as Miss Master was. He couldn't read it, but he saw it. I buried the memories but memories have a way of digging themselves up."

"And that fantasy-dream he had. It seemed laced with imagery of true events, real things."

"His description of me in that 'warped' twelve-year-old true dream was too accurate," Dhiana admits, "and I must assume he saw what he thought was his father as well. The blonde woman was likely Vachaelle. Speaking of that event, he now actually has the sword he always dreamt about. The sword that meant so much. Even saying the word brought a smile to his lips. Do you recall anything about it?"

"Do you?" Arius counters, leaning against the door leading back into their secret abode.

"Yes…His father had it made, ordered it imbued by the most talented of Elementalists. The guard itself is the name Jaydemyr: moon and cross. But Charan trained with a wooden replica, because he was not ready for it, although it was all he ever really wanted. Why did his father have it made? This I cannot recall. There it is, though. Down there, with him. Why don't you go examine it?" Dhiana may be teasing.

"I won't touch the damned thing. It reeks of murder. Hot, foul murder."

"And what exactly do you think you are, Hawkstorm? You wear armour and a blade of your own: Talonslash. Your marks of office as the Captain-Guard of the Jaydemyrian Eagles." Dhiana pauses, lost in more impromptu, fleeting recollection.

"That was my duty. My burden. I do not stalk. I do not murder. I do not revel."

"He does feel that much, doesn't he?" Dhiana muses. "He is so mortal. By the Flail, he can even *cry*! But look at him. By any measure, Charan is at least related to us. His stature, thin and yet strong. His skin, like cold stone. Ears – well, that much is obvious. His eyes are most definitely not human. He seems to feel hungry but notice that he didn't worry about getting food in the Haven. In fact, during the fight with

Hua-Shi, Charan tasted his own blood and was, I believe, strengthened by it. That's unusual but not without precedent."

"On the other hand, Dhiana, he shows no real need for blood beyond that and, if we can trust these memories at all, he has no adverse reaction to daylight. You know as well as I what this means."

"No. Dear God, no."

"How can he possess *Feuermacht*, Dhiana?" Arius presses. "And you heard what he remembers Hua-Shi called him when they 'first' met. Hua-Shi, who also had pointed ears."

"Half," she says. "Hua-Shi called my son Half. I wanted to believe he was lying. He has to have been. But Charan is not full Noble. I don't understand it."

"Could you take a mortal's seed and then *not remember it?*"

"It seems I have erased my share of traumas even from myself."

Arius relents. "But we know that Halves are monsters, abominations. There's a reason the Peddlers hunt them down. Hua-Shi perfectly fits the description, and was exactly the sort of beast Vachaelle loves to use. And Charan is no beast."

"Or perhaps he is a beast of a different nature? It is time to return to him, to his memories. To unlock more of our own." Dhiana turns away from the world, gracing Arius with a view of her aquiline profile. She is at once haughty, defiant and sorrowful. "It is a shame we could not have just been a family, Arius. Even a clan of renegades deserves that, don't you think?"

But he is gone, back to the room, where her son awaits. For a week, the Dreamer has spoken of things she hopes he won't remember upon awakening – but she knows otherwise. Alone, she permits herself a sigh and one last heartful of this emotion – her private intoxication, her secret hope.

"You're home now, Charan, my son. We can fix things. Everything will be—" She stops, actually gnawing her lower lip as a mere human might, tasting the immediate blood. It does nothing for her. She completes the thought, and then sinks back into the comfortable if terrible role of irresistible inquisitor. "—Everything will be like it was before."

The Darkness returns and The Scourge dreams again.

"Have you remembered everything?" Her, in Ziegerian-Common.

"More," The Scourge Who Dreams answers.

"More than everything?"

"More *of* everything. All the time, more and more."

"What is your name?"

"Wong Shah-Long," whispers the Dreamer in crude, simple Chūnko-go. "Dog-Ears."

"Charan-Ra Jaydemyr," declares the Dreamer in Jaydemyrian. "Heir to the Blessed Clan."

"Char Ah-Ran," snarls the Dreamer in a harsh, thunderous Mifūn-go dialect. "Greatest Thief of Kaifeng. Char."

"There he is again." Him. "That third one."

"Charan-ra, have you ever been to Kaifeng?" Her.

"Only once, when I was seven. There are very good warriors in Kaifeng and specially trained Elementalists. The Ayakawa rule Kaifeng, which is the biggest city in the Mifūné Empire outside of the Three Isles."

"Not anymore." Him.

"You will tell us about Kaifeng, Char," She switches to that name and now uses a refined form of Char's chosen language.

"What's to tell? Kaifeng's a shithole but it's home."

"Dog-Ears?" She asks. "Have you ever been to Kaifeng?"

"I don't think so, but I might have forgotten. I'm sorry..."

"Char?" She uses the appropriate language once more.

"Yeah? What?"

"How old are you?"

The Dreamer starts to answer but his voice fails. His expression becomes savage in its confusion.

"Charan-ra?"

"Milady?"

"How old are you?"

"It does not matter."

"Dream now."

"Yes."

"Dog-Ears? Not much longer now, dearest. Tell me, how old are you?"

"I think I'm twenty...something? I can't...no, I'm sorry."

"Hush, sweetness. It's okay. You rest now."

The Dreamer dreams.

"Do you see, Arius? Because these personae do not occupy his entire life, at least not simultaneously, they don't know how old they are now."

"So which is the one that matters the most?"

"All. None. What matters now is that we make him remember everything, in any way that he can. The more he remembers, the more he tells us, the more we remember."

"And do you remember now why you captured him, Milady?"

"Some. We remnants of the Clan learned that a force moved against the Night, a force that destroyed Havens maintained by both the Tsukamoto and the Kas'Daen. There are other such vendettas of mortal insurrection, but this one was drawing far too much attention. It was too efficient — as though we were supposed to notice. Investigation revealed the name 'Jaydemyr', which I retained in jealous, frightened, lonely silence. I couldn't believe it at first — I knew I'd erased the name from existence, but there it was. Carved into the cadavers. Someone was signing their work and likely didn't even know it. I associated that name with my son, and that was when I remembered Vachaelle. I was struck with the notion of an unfulfilled purpose, that her usage of our name to defy the Night was, in some twisted way, the *right* thing to do. She always did have good intentions.

"That was also when I remembered you, Arius Hawkstorm. Not long after Blackcloak the Scourge moved against the Night's Own in earnest, which possibly began at the Haven, or during his duel with Hua-Shi, I reawakened the Eagles. In hindsight, we are very lucky I did not erase too much, was not so fully adept at my craft. We'd never have suspected that such had occurred beyond that awful sensation of wrongness, of not doing that which must be done. Charan, too, must do these things."

"Dhiana, I think we need to explore the relationship between the boy and Vachaelle."

She answers too sharply, "You still love her!"

And Hawkstorm bites back with equal surprise, "It is not as though I were permitted to love you! Charas'z-ra, that *rika fas'z!* He alone had that right, and he squandered it!"

The name and the insult — *'Dull tooth'* — trigger a sudden shift away from anger in Dhiana.

"Oh, Charas'z, my lord, my poor, deluded lord. You betrayed him, Arius! You and Vachaelle! You sided with the Three Beasts and that foul Hra'Xis of Sladaria!"

"Did I, Dhiana? Or did Charas'z and his fascination with forbidden history and useless questions call down God Herself to smite Jaydemyr? Look at me and tell me I would do such a thing without just cause!"

"So much for not believing in God, Arius! Listen to yourself – just another of Her tools!'

And they are almost completely human now, glaring at each other despite the breakthrough, fangs unsheathed from their fleshy home. Shiny-dark eyes gleam in the moonlight. Hatred populates the space between them with livid ease.

But the two share this one thought, beneath the fury and hurt: *perhaps it is best not to remember some things after all.*

"Stop fighting!" The Dreamer howls, interrupting them with his bitter, wounded Char attitude. "All you two ever do is fight! You wonder why I never came home that day? Damn you both. You are *not* my parents!"

Dhiana and Arius stare at him, at his shaking fists, held at his side in restrained ire.

"It may have been this aspect that slew so many of Kas'Daen's forces," Arius concedes with a very small smile.

"Don't underestimate your training, 'Mentor'," Dhiana snipes, also far too fascinated to maintain her resentment.

"What now, Dhiana? Continue with Dog-Ears, let this tortured 'Greatest Thief of Kaifeng' take over, or attempt bone before blood and ask Charan-ra Jaydemyr to speak?"

"Wrong way to look at it, Arius, my Champion. Watch."

The Lady steps back from the Dreamer and asks in Ziegerian-Common, the original language of the interrogation, "What do you remember now?"

"I remember the day I saw her," replies Char in Mifūn-go with the unmistakable ego of a brash young man tearing towards adulthood, "because it was my birthday, and I was turning twelve. I saw exactly what I wanted, and I went for *her*."

II. Char Ah-Ran

Kaifeng

868 - 873 A.R.

Chapter 10: *Attraction*
ONE, TWO, THREE

The last thing I thought about, sitting under a tree just outside the empty village that she said would be my home, was the first day I saw *her*, the reason for everything. Twelve years old, I was – not a day over. Five years ago. To see what happened, think that far back and look to the east, far in the distance. Over the forests, the roads, that Haven we passed on the way. Do you see? Kaifeng, the Imperial Capital. Now look past the multitudes milling around, living their lives until they run out. Closer. You can see the streets, the complicated guts of Kaifeng, intestines wrapped about the swollen Imperial womb. Now, further down. Sink into the slums. Smell the food that doesn't smell like food at all, rotting gently in the ragged stalls. Turn the corner. That alleyway, yes. Those kids pestering passers-by and loitering. Rats. And there's me, the tall one, next to the other two: a chubby boy and the scrawny girl by his side. I'm about to make a decision that's going to turn all three of our lives inside out.

This is the beginning of my great dream.

"Wake up!" Jaku snapped his fingers in front of my face a few times. "Char Ah-Ran? You in there?"

"You know better than to call me that. Do it again and I'll break your fingers one by one," I said, not opening my eyes. He didn't do it again.

"Char. You've been in a daze all morning. Are you okay?"

"Just thinking about this afternoon."

"The parade? It's going to be great! I've never seen a Gaikojin procession before. And on your birthday. You're lucky!"

"Yeah. Listen, how about you meet me at the south wall of the Palace afterwards?"

"You're not going to hang out with us during?"

"Nah, need to check a few things out. Got a job tonight. Big one."

Before he could say a thing, the other Rats, most of them younger than me, all of them shorter than either of us, reacted to the word 'job' like, hm, rats around garbage. The group tightened around me; the runts were all sudden experts on anything from espionage to appropriate fashion.

"If you're gonna break in, I'ma best lock-pickerer in the city!"

"I can climb a bare wall with my bare hands! Any wall!"

"Don't be a stupid, not even you can climb the palace walls!"

"Like, even treasure rooms. Easy. Aint no lock I can't—"

"Hey, Char, you gonna wear a hood like them ninja?"

"Ha, everyone knows a samurai could beat a ninja!"

"I can climb better than any stupid ninja!"

"Peddler, not ninja. Ninja don't exist," Jaku said, trying to intercede, not even managing to interrupt. The brats had no reason to listen to his voice of reason.

"I've heard that one Kasuden knight can beat ten samurai in a fight!"

The arguing became impossible to follow as they all raised their voices.

"Hey, shut up, the lot of you," I said, looking down the alleyway as if worried a Guard might be walking by. The lot of them shut up. "Enough talk about ninja and hoods and shit, okay? We ain't some buncha snotballs playing pretendies here." Well, I wasn't. "This is a real job. A real mission. You interested, Jaku?"

"You better not get im into more of your trouble," Wu Jen-Wah said, leaning around him to give me one of her stern looks. Futile, considering the way she talked. "I got plans for this one." And she nudged him in the arm with her staff. Lightly. He winced anyway.

"It's your call, Jaku," I shrugged. "I can do it alone, if you'd rather hang out with your girlfriend."

"She's not my fuckin girlfriend!" Jaku snapped, and the other Rats gasped at the harsh word. Despite this cheap bravado, Jaku didn't dare look at Jen. Gave him an excuse to look me in the eye. "Whatever it is, I'm in."

"I knew I could rely on you, man," I said to Jaku, who was going to turn thirteen in a few months. "Tonight, then. That's when we'll get *her.*"

Jaku might have been afraid to see Jen's reaction but I was glad to watch her bite her lip and tighten her grip on the staff. Then she said, "Well FINE but he's mine til then!" and dashed off, but not before grabbing Jaku and firing a hurt look my way. He, in turn, managed to miss this and let her drag him off.

"Jaku, I'll see you after!" With that, I let them both know that *I* made the call when we would see each other and when we would not.

The rest of the Rats started to press me for information about that strange exchange. I just threatened to hit the nearest one, waited for the circle to open, and stalked off.

To watch the parade and catch my first glimpses of *her*, I made my way close to the Palace and perched upon a nearby inn's slanted roof. The foreigners had started to enter the city a while ago, but what I wanted to see wouldn't come into view for a while yet, if the old man's tip was right. For now it was warriors and guards, interesting enough but nothing on what was to come.

I've never been any good at waiting. I started to fidget. I picked at the tiles with tender, cruel fingers thoughtfully, thoughtlessly. Never trust the quality of Chūnkojin construction: one of the tiles must have been loose, because it slid away from the others and down towards the street. I watched and half-hoped it wouldn't hit someone.

The offensive slab fell directly towards a Guard's head. Thankfully he had a helmet on, although I imagine the chaos caused by a wounded Guard during a parade welcoming tenuous allies from afar would have been pretty exciting.

Not that the chunk of tile even had a chance to bounce off the helmet.

The Guard barely seemed to move, and I didn't even see him draw his sword. It wasn't as if a mere chunk of clay would have done any harm. There was a clean flash of bright steel, a crack and then he was marching in perfect step once more, blade sheathed as though it had never been drawn. Behind him, my little accident rested, carved straight down the middle.

And that wasn't even what impressed me the most. That samurai's sword must have been somehow enhanced with *Huo-chi*. I had to concentrate, but I saw that the cut had melted the tile's edges. The road underfoot bubbled quietly, and then even that spectacle was lost to the spectacle of the procession.

Now the parade was interesting. I kept watching.

It was at least Eyesun when the women started to appear. Their otherworldly hair, tinged gold and silver, done up in curls or tied back with sensible thongs, glimmered in the afternoon sun. Their cheeks were not the ruddy, worn masks of weariness of a Kaifeng Rat. There was delicacy, frailty. They were like dolls, those ennobled young ladies.

And then, in an ornate palanquin, I saw *her*. Drapes of smooth, translucent brightness couldn't hide those perfect, shimmering curves.

I wanted to see her naked, more than anything else I'd ever wanted before.

But there was a boy sitting next to her inside the covered carriage. When he leaned forward to stare out the window, he blocked my view of her. Kid couldn't have been older than six or seven, but God, the way his nose seemed to point wherever he looked! His black hair, pulled into a braid, gleamed with immaculate grooming. A commoner's braid, for the love of Eph! There was Mifūnjin blood in him, in his cheeks and narrow eyes. He had probably only just learned how to wipe his own arse; what right had he to look at the world as though it were his to command? To wear such a fine gown? Arrogant little shit!

But these all meant nothing after he leaned even further out and I saw his ears. His pointy damned ears. He was Half too.

So hateful I stared, trying to see her, she who shared his seat, his world. What was she to him? He probably took her for granted. I can't imagine anyone that cold, that composed, loving anything. So, hateful, I stared. He passed, and once more she was all I saw. I forgot about the boy, because he was nothing. So, lovingly I stared.

Then she was gone. It was time to make my move. To complete my job.

"Your job involves breaking *into the Palace?* Are you absolutely sure about this?" Jaku asked, standing a few feet behind me.

I just kept staring up the wall of the Women's Quarters of the Five-Fold Imperial Palace.

"Of course I'm sure," I said. "Not like there's anything better to do, is it?"

"Not breaking into the Palace and not getting caught and not being executed sounds like a good plan, Char."

"Not getting caught and not getting executed *is* the plan."

He didn't answer.

Jaku was never really one of us, not with those clean clothes, his trimmed hair and smooth, vaguely scented cheeks. He was Terasawa: a refined Mifūné name with centuries of prestigious history. In the year Long-Time-Before-Now, the Mifūnjin had come from their homeland, *Mifūné*, 'The Three Boats', invading my native realm: Chūnko, the Middle Country. Lots of wars and betrayals and stuff later, the Mifūnjin, by the grace of their Emperor and God, took over. Most of their culture mixed with our primitive customs. Languages jumbled together, social structures and values tried to get along. We were all technically Mifūnjin under Clan Tsukamoto's reign, but some divisions remained.

If you were born into a *true* Mifūnjin family like Fujimoto or Ueda, or Terasawa, life was going to be good. And if you were a Chang or a Zhang or a Wong, you'd better get used to eating the crap the 'better' people threw away. That is the lot of the Chūnkojin, we true natives of the Middle Country.

I stepped forward and tapped the rock a few times.

"This seems easy enough," I mused. "Lotta handholds too. Almost like it was built to be climbed. We've done worse than this, Jaku."

But it was kinda high, and almost vertical further up.

"You're not stupid, Char. Everyone knows that," Jaku stressed. What the hell was he getting at? "But you're acting a little strange."

That did it. I turned around, reached over and grabbed a nice handful of his nice robe. A real Rat would have fought back. Not him, though — he just took it; let me pull him close, fist aimed right at his fat nose. He really was a well-fed little bastard.

Sometimes my temper just went off like that. Right there, right then, I could have killed Terasawa Jaku with a smile.

"Don't call me that. Okay?" I hissed. And if it's not okay, I thought, I'll be more than glad to show you just how not-okay I can make it.

"Yeah, okay. Sorry," he mumbled. "I guess I'm just a little worried about you."

Me, or you? I asked myself. And who was this 'me' for him, or anyone, to worry about?

"Worried?" I repeated, shoving him away. "Don't you mean *scared?*"

"No! I'm not scared!" Jaku's lips wobbled and his eyes trembled as I stared down at him. He was a bit shorter than me, but then again, most of the Rats were — that's one of the nicer things about being a Half.

"I am," I said. "Think of how boring things would be if you were never scared, Jaku. But I'm not scared enough to stop. Come on. We're going in."

I gave Jaku a grin, not really caring if he took it or not, and hoisted myself up to the first ledge of the wall. Walls exist to be climbed. Why else would they be so climbable? And when that fails, there's always rope and ladders. Doors are just the easy way of getting in – too many people think they're the only way.

"Jaku," I snarled over my shoulder, "get your fat butt up here or I'll tell Jen-Wah how much you like her." Not that I hadn't told her before, and then assured her I liked her even more.

"I don't like her!" he called in reply. "That much." His indignation was always a little too loud, always fell away a little too late.

"Fine," I answered. "I'll tell her how much you *don't* like her then. And keep your voice down. Have you forgotten about the not-getting-caught-and-executed bit?" That wouldn't really happen. Truthfully, the guards were far more occupied with the real criminals to care about us Rats and our antics. They knew we were harmless, and we knew that someday we'd prove them wrong. Deep down, though, every Rat wanted to join the Imperial Kaifeng Guard, to go from hunted to hunter, like a mouse being magically transformed into a cat. An Imperial Guard ate three meals a day, carried a sword, wore a uniform and got something like a real education. And all he had to do in return was hurt bad guys and help good guys. At the age of twelve, there's just nothing more a boy could want, or so I'd thought until this afternoon.

"And the guards," Jaku muttered, kicking the dirt. "They'd tell my parents, wouldn't they?"

Your blood is blue after all. I couldn't risk throwing this saying at him – not while I had him worried over what might happen if we got caught. If he didn't damn well *do what I told him to do.*

"Your parents?" I mocked. "God Herself is waiting to judge you, Jaku. Why the Eph are you so worried about your parents?"

Even though I 'knew' Jaku's parents, I still didn't like them, because they got to eat good food and threw most of it away. I think this was some sort of control issue, because when they found out he was giving his leftovers to us, they had Jaku thrashed.

What was the big deal with parents? I only vaguely remembered the two adults who taught me nothing other than how to run away, and they weren't my parents. I'm sure I had real parents at one point, but I didn't then and don't now and I don't plan on getting any either. Not if they are going to fight all the time like my pretend-parents, who'd decided to call me Char Ah-Ran, or be stuck-up and overprotective like Jaku's mamma and papa. Still, these may both be better than my *real* parents. God alone knows what name they gave me. I'm Half, remember? We don't have families, not from either side of the blood. It was easy to hate my real parents because they could have been anything, anything but there for me. So I made sure that *other* people were there for me, if I wanted them.

That's why I encouraged Jaku to share his food with us Rats. And when he stopped sharing, we still took what we wanted. His parents didn't get angry at him for being beat up and having his lunch stolen, and that confused me at first. They *did* start employing *gung-fu* teachers for their poor, defenceless boy, although this was apparently done without them asking him if he *wanted* to learn the art of fighting. Not that it helped. His tutors were relics, old like Grandfather Leung, although nowhere near as cunning as our caretaker. They didn't know how we street Rats fought, how form and kata, patterns and styles were pretty, sure: pretty useless against a good knee to the nuts. It only took three of those to teach Jaku how his otherwise awesome Four Cranes Playing With Themselves or whatever-the-hell-it-was technique had no use in the real world.

It was a good arrangement. We threatened to deck him if he didn't give his lunch, he got a chance to cross fists with the Rats, and always lost before anyone really got hurt.

But when you pushed him too far—

"Char, I can't do this. I'm going," he whined and then scampered. I'd get him for it later, but running away from me was better than risking the wrath of his parents. I didn't say a thing. He was gone. That and I'd been too quick with my words – what should have been fear of not following me became fear of getting caught.

Whatever. He'd have just gotten in the way.

So my little failure at coercion left me alone ten feet up a fifty foot wall. A gentle breeze stirred the darkening alleyway below. The streetlamps were not yet lit, but in the quick dusk, I expected that to change soon enough. This was my window of opportunity. By myself, I would take the chance and get the prize!

Behold Char, the bully who didn't get a family name because he didn't have a family. I call myself 'the bully' because that's just what I was, and I didn't care. You can't let people push you around, call you things like *'strange'*. If you do, they keep doing it, so you stop them before they even start. Controlling others is the only way to keep yourself safe.

But the only person to control on that abandoned wall was me, and I've never been very good at that. Ten feet wasn't that high up, but the other forty or so left to go seemed endless. Was this really worth it?

"Not like it was a dare," I muttered and began to scale down the wall. You can't run from a dare. Part of being the bully, the top dog. Show any weakness to the other Rats and they'll pounce like wolves. But I always rose to the challenge, as long as it wasn't too stupid. Then I'd just laugh and hit someone.

Nothing like a fight to distract eager, curious young minds.

"What exactly are you doing down there?" came a girl's voice from above.

I stopped, left leg halfway towards the ground. Don't move, just don't move. She can't see me, not with how this wall is built.

"If I call the guards," she continued, sounding more amused than anything, "they will come pull you down and chop you into little bits." It was a weird accent, a crisp way of using full words that was both condescending and, in its exotic nature, fascinating.

I looked up – taut, uncomfortable and in no position to change either. The girl was leaning on the railing of the first balcony above me, some twenty feet up. She looked about the same age as Jen-Wah's older sister, maybe sixteen or seventeen. Blonde hair and skin the colour of raw bean curd, of goat's milk: features of a Gaikojin – probably from the west, from another country, maybe even Kasuden. For a second I wondered if they even had a sun in Kasuden and if they did, this girl didn't get to see it very often. She wore a black and red silk getup that might have suited the local girls but just didn't accommodate her more developed, well, okay, let's not nibble fingers here: her boobs were big, way too big for the Kaifeng-style dress. What could foreigners like her wear and still be comfortable? Not all that much, I figured.

I was fairly comfortable with the thought of her not wearing all that much myself.

She rested her chin upon clasped fingers and smiled. I got the funny impression that she'd smiled at her dinner the same way.

"Up or down, then?" she asked. "I will give you one minute to either get up here or run away. After that minute, I *will* scream, and believe me, I am very good at screaming."

No doubt. One minute: plenty of time.

"How do you know I'm not an assassin?" I countered, trying to deepen my voice, which is *really* hard at the age of twelve.

"Well," she sighed, "assassins tend to be armed. They wear smooth, sexy black cloaks or maybe hoods that hide everything but their dark, intense eyes or a flashing, sharp grin. You, on the other hand, are wearing dirty, very *un*sexy rags and didn't even bother with the hood. Oh, and assassins usually do not care what their parents think. Fifty seconds, cutie."

I blushed. Maybe she saw this: she actually laughed. And blushing is one of those terrible things that just gets worse the more you try to stop it. Sweat began to line my forehead. For a calm spring evening, I was suddenly feeling the heat.

"So you were listening to that?" I should have thought of something smarter to say, because she frowned then. Her smile had been predatory, but her scowl indicated disappointment.

"How else would I have known what you had said? Forty-two, forty-one, forty…"

I hadn't moved. It was like a staring competition, the ones where you poke fun at each other, even fake a few punches but never touch, just to see who'll break.

And she wasn't the one with her arse sticking out, fingers slipping and legs aching.

"If you do not start climbing now, you will not have time. The ground is not far, though. Maybe you should just let it go. Maybe. Thirty seconds."

How could I let it go if I didn't even have it yet? I reacted in the only way I knew: tense muscles, assessment of height and then a second effort back onto the first ledge. Half-way towards her and no more stretched limbs or stiff joints.

"Keep going! I am not saying I will not call the guards once you are up here, but you have made the decision now. Can not turn back, can you?"

Oh, I could have. This outsider-girl didn't know my group, couldn't have told them the truth if I did turn tail. Although the guards wouldn't chop me into little bits as she threatened, they were tired of hauling me off to their guardhouse and putting up with 'that bothersome Char' for another night. I was probably on my last chance there – their offers to enlist me in the Tsukamoto Corps and send me to this Kasuden conflict or that border dispute with the Southern Dissidents were growing louder and more direct by the day.

"You seem to think a lot. For a kid, anyway."

When people called me 'kid', I hit them. They didn't call me 'kid' again.

I looked for the next hand-hold and took firm grip.

"Where was I? Fifteen? That shall do. Fourteen, thirteen, twelve…"

What the hell was I doing? Maybe imagining I was a samurai on a *shoji* screen, swarming these sorts of walls, banner bright and proud, armour polished and sword gleaming. I'll admit, I was working on the banner, armour and especially the sword, but I reckoned I had the climbing part down and mastered.

"Ooh, you are nimble too. When you get up here, you can tell me your name, and I shall tell you mine," she said, as though it were some gift from Hell Above. Ten feet above, anyway.

"Not counting anymore?"

"Oh, I am. I just do not wish to pressure you. You are coming up to the most difficult part."

"How do you know?" I didn't want to keep talking, needed to concentrate on the climbing, but that would have been too weak, too obvious.

"I have done it myself, both up and down. You saw me enter the city today but I have been here before. Oh dear, I think I have reached zero. Give me a reason not to scream, please."

She's been here before? How does she know I watched her this afternoon? I don't remember seeing her but then again I was looking at something else, and – a reason? Shit! Just say something!

"I'm almost there. I've almost made it." Not entirely true, that, but I *really* didn't want her to call the guards now. If I hadn't been so vulnerable and caught out, I'd have realised that was never her intention. Where would be the fun in that?

But I didn't know her then. Didn't really know me either.

"That shall suffice. Thirty second extension, and if you are not here by then—"

"You'll call the guards?"

"Nah," she replied. The flippant informality made her almost friendly. "If you are not up here within thirty seconds, I will pour boiling water on you." There was that smile again. I shivered even as I continued to sweat. What had I gotten myself into? "Or maybe just very, *very* cold water. Or rocks. Depends on how I feel. On how *you* make me feel."

That's another of her games. She likes to hurt people and make them think it's their fault. I understand now, because it was one of my games as well. It's just that I'd never played it from the other end of the stick before.

"You wouldn't do that!"

"Yes I would. I would not even get in trouble for it. Oh, look, there is an assassin on the wall!" She mock-wailed, delicate fingers against shocked cheeks. "Oh me, oh my, whatever should I do?" Then she winked and reclasped her hands, smug chin against comfortable knuckles.

"Yeah, okay, I get your point."

"I am glad you do! Oh, fifteen seconds. Why are you climbing this wall anyway?"

So she *was* curious. Even a bully like me knows when things are beginning to swing in his favour. Now was not the time for shyness. I responded even as I crept ever-so-closer to her parapet.

"I saw the most beautiful thing this afternoon," I gushed, probably because I was out of breath from the climbing. "And I wanted a closer look. I wanted to touch her and see how she felt in my hands." Now I was more than blushing – it felt as if my face might explode with blood and anxiety.

"Is that so." the young woman asked, but I didn't hear much of a question in her tone. "And what has that to do with the Women's Quarters? Or am I being a bit too obvious here?"

"Last I saw, she was brought into this building. Look, could you possibly give me a hand here? I'm just about there."

The girl lifted her chin and unfolded her hands again, this time waving as though greeting a stranger, or bidding a friend farewell. "This one? Or the other? Look, I shall be generous. You may have both." She twinkled her fingers in a too-cute gesture, giggling all the while.

"*Kono ama,*" I mumbled.

She frowned. Oops. Guess she knew Mifūn-go as well.

"Did you just call me a bitch? Oh, time is up!" And she disappeared. I heard her run across whatever room lay beyond the taunting balcony a mere two or three foot above me.

"I didn't mean it!" We bullies aren't very good at lying. Telling lies is for cowards and weaklings. They have to *talk* through things. I've never had much energy for that kind of crap. "Really! I'm sorry! It just slipped out!"

"As did this!" She snapped back, and then dumped what felt like an ocean of freezing water straight onto my head. I screamed and pressed myself against the wall. I heard nothing but the rushing deluge, saw nothing but the black insides of my eyelids, squinting and howling. After the water stopped, she called out,

"You never know when it might rain!"

That was when I began swearing in earnest. Didn't care that I was in full view, dripping wet and acting like a cry-baby.

"You!" I heard her gasp. "Why, how foul! Who taught you to say things like that? You should not – oh MY!" And that was about all she could get in between my cursing and shrieking. Had I been less focused on speaking my mind at the time (and what a dirty little mind it was), I'd have noticed that the girl wasn't all that disgusted by my torrid language. Just more fun and games.

Ten seconds later, her previous threat to call the guards no longer mattered. I'd gone and done exactly that. I fell silent with belated clarity. The blush, having deepened through rage and into despair, settled on a very embarrassed heat of self-consciousness. Not even her water could soothe me.

"Now we're in for it!" *We?* In her urgency, she wasn't quite so precise with her words, either. "Shhhh! Don't move."

"You there! What are you doing?" A man's voice intruded.

I almost answered, because I was extremely conscious of that sort of question. You just don't hesitate when Authority asks stuff like that.

"Sir, I was cleaning this area as ordered," the girl above explained, turning away from the balcony. I wouldn't have believed her so capable of humility, not from how she'd acted up to that point. "And then a drunken lout down in the street below began bellowing the most obscene things!"

"Let me see!"

"Sir, please, I have just finished polishing the floor! It took me all day. At least remove your boots before entering."

I didn't need this one given to me on a platter. Climbing down might have risked falling, but staying there guaranteed being caught. I sloshed over the stones, no doubt leaving a nice wet trail, like some sort of odd snail.

"But he is gone now, Sir. I scared him off with a bucket of water. See?"

And I could just imagine it: like a toddler showing off her first successful chamber pot.

"Well, you be sure to call us next time *anyone* makes a disturbance, girl. Her Ladyship dislikes being roused before nightfall. We don't need unwarranted attention."

"I shall certainly do just that, Sir. And you are right. I should have screamed and caused a scene like any other serving girl."

"Little smartass. You *are* just a serving girl. Don't mouth off at me! Hmph," the unseen Guard barked and then left the room, or so I guessed from the crash of a closing door.

"Well, that ruins that." The girl gripped the railing and leaned out. I call her a girl, but what I saw then wasn't the sort of thing 'girls' tend to display. I was torn between staring in unaffected admiration of her tits and—

Honestly, I wasn't all that torn.

"I told you to get out of here!" she hissed, unmindful that her body was telling me something altogether different. *My* body was just a little too young to answer in kind, even if my overactive mind could have taught it all sorts of things.

"You didn't!" But I was shimmying down anyway, because I didn't want another shower. She looked irate enough to give me one, too.

"Well, I sort of did. They're going to be watching me now, and they're going to be watching this street too!" By this point, any traces of the cultured, well-spoken young lady were long gone. "So – get lost!"

"But I didn't get what I came for!"

"Stubborn little brat, aren't you? And a Half, too, by the looks of your ears. Probably got no home, no one to care for you." Oh great. Now she was going to get all soppy on me. As if one of us dripping wasn't bad enough.

"Yeah, and I like it that way!"

I looked at the ground, judged the remaining distance and gave in to gravity. We all do, sooner or later – the trick is giving in on your own terms.

"Oh, be careful!"

As if she hadn't just done her best to make me fall.

"I'm fine. I'll be back tomorrow to get what I came for, Miss uh— what's your name?"

"In your language, I am Fa Shai-Yeh. Call me Shai-Yeh. I am no Miss. You heard the guard. Just a serving girl. And if you come back," she glared, but I could tell she was trying not to smile. "If you come back, say, tomorrow night at this time, or thereabouts, I will scream for certain! I will make you really regret it! Whoever 'she' is, she is not worth that!"

"Oh but she is, Fa Shai-Yeh. You wait and see. Char Ah-Ran, Greatest Thief of Kaifeng, will have her yet!" That was how the heroes of the stories would have said it. I was twelve years old – of course I wanted to be a hero too! And in my excitement, I didn't realise I'd used my full name.

With the introductions done, I felt it time to leave, and so I did. By then it was almost dark – wasn't hard to disappear, not in so poorly lit streets, and not when you know the city as well as I do.

I thought I heard *her* sigh as I dashed into the night.

"Morning, Char. Did you have a nice day yesterday?"

"Nothing worth celebrating."

"I'd disagree with that, but I'm a disagreeable old crank. Why don't you sit down?"

"Comfortable standing." Or leaning against the wall. I felt loutish, and decided to act it. Besides, his cramped desk in the back-room was strictly for business.

"What did you wish for?"

"You know damn well what I wished for."

"So did you get it?"

Had it been anyone but him asking, I'd have swung a punch.

"Didn't need to get *her*, Guan-Pi."

Only I was allowed to address the 'boss' in so familiar a tone. The other Rats called him 'Goong' – Grandfather, and sometimes, he even looked like one, with eyes that sparkled a glee all-too-often mistaken for good-will. Goong liked to stroke his long beard and say wise old things like "Ah, yes, it is that way." That was his act, but it was commonly known that 'Goong' was Leung Guan-Pi, one of Kaifeng's most notorious criminals and godfather of thieves. He was a true patriarch of a city's darkest angle: dozens of abandoned kids, orphans and cutpurses kept under the guise of an 'employment and care company': The Society for Disadvantaged Youth. Located in the grubby western suburb of Siu-Tsin, the Society was a legitimate refuge for us, the Rats, and that's why people in the know referred to the headquarters of The Society as 'The Nest'.

Rumours ran that Leung Guan-Pi was born into a Mifūnjin family, but no one could figure out his exact lineage. There are about forty established Mifūnjin clans in Kaifeng, although 'clan' simply means a family of any size with an established name. The Ayakawa, of course, is the largest, with members of smaller families vying to marry into the dominant family or prove through tracing bloodlines a substantial claim of kinship. Only real way to guarantee the favour of the Tsukamoto.

At some point in his younger, wilder days (so whispers the legend), Guan-Pi disgraced himself, and his esteemed Mifūnjin family erased his name from all records, forcing the nameless outcast to survive in Kaifeng's underworld as a Chūnkojin. As far as I was concerned, that was a step up. Something told me he despised it, though, because he paid for our education and always made sure we knew the morals of what we were doing even if we didn't quite agree. Leung Guan-Pi, I realise now, understood the juvenile criminal mind and tried to make sure it didn't develop into an adult one.

"Strange obsession you've gained, Char. What did you say it was again? Oh sorry, *she*."

"Guan-Pi, you're teasing me. Your little tip proved true."

"Of course it did. All my sources are good, although this one..." Sometimes, when we were alone, Guan-Pi forgot I was one of the Rats and let his mouth run. I was courteous enough not to wait at the finish line. Most of the time, his half-secrets just dashed around in a circle anyway. "Well, why didn't you need to get *her*, then?"

"I know where she is and I know how to reach her. In my own time."

"You're just the most arrogant little bastard, Char." But Guan-Pi chuckled, fingers toying with a single coin. Most of us could do the dancing-coin trick with our knuckles, but Guan-Pi had Talent to boost his efforts. He tossed the coin into the air, suspending it there, letting it spin, as though dangling from a piece of string tied around the rim. Then he winked and the coin flipped end over end, only to fall onto a thin tower of incense, the hollow square interior of the coin sliding down the shaft to meet with the other coins at the stick's base. I never got bored in Guan-Pi's musty little chamber at the back of his 'shop'. "What if someone else gets there first?"

"No one else saw her, Guan-Pi. They were too busy watching the parade of pompous Gaikojin."

"You really don't like rich people, do you, Char?"

That demanded a careful response. Guan-Pi was rich. Very rich, and because, not in some small part, of what we Rats could do. And he made sure we didn't go without. This made life comfortable, but money existed to be spent. I was usually broke only hours after being paid.

"I don't like rich people who flaunt it and don't do something good with their money, Guan-Pi. It can do so much more than just sit there."

"Careful, Char. You're starting to sound like a Revolutionary."

And that was my reward for being so honest! What an insult. No, worse than an insult: a threat. The Tsukamoto did not put up with any sort of counter-Tsukamoto thinking, and I say *thinking* because, like all the proper members of the Sladarian Overclan, the Tsukamoto employed Maliscients devoted to keeping their realm nice and clean of possible revolts. As large as the Tsukamoto Imperial Army was, the wars to the west and south kept most of the troops away from Kaifeng. An insurrection in their own realm would not be easily handled. Suspected Revolutionaries disappeared all the time.

"Going to turn me in, Goong-sinsan? And give up your best asset? Right." I liked to call him that as well: Mr. Grandfather.

"You think you're that good? Everyone heard about the 'assassin' who barely escaped the Women's Quarters last night, Mr. Greatest Thief Of Kaifeng. You may be quick with your fists, and you've even got some sort of vague, crude charisma about you, but I know for a fact you're next to useless at climbing. It's those long limbs of yours, you gangly Half."

I snarled; it wasn't *right* for others to point out my flaws. Not as if I can help being a bastard Half. Wasn't *my* fault, so no one should have tormented me about it. "Don't underestimate the worth of my reach, Goong-sinsan."

"You know I've no quarrel with what you are, Char. And as soon as you realise what that is, I'll let you go too."

"*You* know I'm going to take over your business, Guan-Pi." What better thing for a budding thief to become if not an established, *respectable* businessman? I'd seen Guan-Pi get dressed up and attend balls and functions well within bow-shot of Lord Ayakawa! But neither Guan-Pi nor myself were assassins — we liked stealing people's things more than people's lives. I guess you could say we liked stealing people's livelihoods instead.

Being paid to off someone sounded too much like real work.

"You could do better than that, boy. You're strong, quick, and far from stupid most of the time. You'd make a fine guard. Or even a soldier. Why not try it?"

The life expectancy of an enlisted soldier (be he an elite Elementalist or your average foot-soldier) is so low even a village idiot could remember it: six months of active duty. I'd be lucky to live to thirteen if I signed up now. And, well—

"Screw that." I pulled a sour expression. "Anyone can be a Guard, Guan-Pi. Fat louts, drunken no-hopers. It takes real skill to do what you do."

"I'm just not going to convince you otherwise, am I? Oh well. Report to Chu-Deng when you're ready. He's dying to hear about your escapades."

Ugh, speaking of drunken no-hopers.

"Yeah, I bet he is. Dying. Shame it's not true."

"He was a good man, Char, before the drink got to him."

"Before he got to the drink, don't you mean?" My *sort-of* parents had drunk. A lot.

"Smart as you are, you're still a kid, Char. You don't understand how hard life can get when it doesn't go your way." Guan-Pi tried to sound admonishing, but barely achieved melancholy. "If you *do* take my place, he'll serve you well. But you won't, you hear me? I'll make a respectable young man of you yet. *Anyone* can be a thief, Char." He was imitating me and doing it all too well. I growled a soft laugh. "Fat louts, drunken no-hopers. It takes *real* skill to be a civilised person in this world. You're wasting away here. If only you had my love of learning and if only I had your intelligence at your age, ah, I'm rambling. What I mean to say, Char, is you're a fighter but there are other ways to fight than with fists and foul language."

"Why 'fight' the world, Guan-Pi? If it takes malice and ruthlessness to survive, so be it."

"You really believe that, don't you? Well, fine. Do what you want. Get *her* as you will or will not. You know she isn't crucial to me. Oh, and have you been attending school lately?"

"In between scaling walls, taking things that don't belong to me, asserting my authority over the other Rats, contending with the Bloody Shadows and being a generally troublesome Half? Sure."

"I'd accuse you of lying if you weren't so well spoken." As if how a person speaks or what words he uses has to do with school, let alone whether or not they're lying. "So they're still giving you trouble, hm?"

He didn't need to say who. The Bloody Shadows were what happened when young street-wise kids could not benefit from old street-wisdom of a guardian like Leung Guan-Pi. More than thieves, they were brazen thugs, muggers and murderers. No one knew where they came from, or where they went — as soon as you shed light on a Shadow, it's gone. But in the dark, you could almost feel them moving, hear their violent thoughts. The other kids were just scared of them, as kids fear the unknown and make it more than it is. Having actually brawled with them once or twice, I feared that I *knew* them to be heartless, immoral scum.

"Those crud-eaters insult the Rats, Goong-sinsan. You wanna talk about *real* Revolutionaries? They're trying to rule streets that are free for all and I can't wait for the Guard to break every single one of them."

"What, and rob you of the chance?"

"Wouldn't know where to start. I'm just a thief, Guan-Pi." It was okay to let my defences down around Goong-sinsan, because there weren't any to start with. My first memory of him was a pair of hands upon my bony shoulders and a stern yet empathetic voice telling me what I was thinking. And getting it right, from the anger directed at my not-parents to the feeling of being not-understood. Leung Guan-Pi knew me without shadow. It's not hard to respect that.

"Just a thief for now. That will change, when you grow. You know what you really are. Don't forget it."

Was this one of those moments you never, ever forget? An exclamation mark upon the dull prose of one's life story?

"Yeah, I'll tell you what I really am. I really am tired of you people saying I'm just a kid!"

No, I had no idea where that came from — other than 'above'.

"I see."

He wasn't referring to that, but I was too young to recover from the indignant stumble. I was too much a kid.

"At least try to stay out of their way, alright? If a real war erupted between you Rats and the Bloody Shadows, my poor Nest would be— No, it does not bear thinking. Still, if. You would do the right thing, wouldn't you, Char?"

What a *strange* thing to ask of a thief.

"I hate them, Guan-Pi. IF there was war between us, you can bet I'd be the first to make those Shadows truly bloody."

He drew several breaths unburdened by words – yet each time he inhaled, I expected something. A confirmation. An agreement. A disagreement.

Leung Guan-Pi could not change the subject, so he let time and patience do it for him, saying at last:

"Remember: Wong Chu-Deng wants to hear about last night. Come back when and if you need work or money. Be good."

"Always, always." I flipped him a sort-of wave on the way out. Something had not just happened.

As I was about to slip out, Guan-Pi half-called:

"Char Ah-Ran? Happy birthday."

I stopped, fingers staying the sheet of deceptively poor cloth serving as a make-shift door.

"Yeah." And in that moment, I remembered the crazy girl on the balcony (Shai-Yeh, just a serving girl, right?), and Jaku's disloyalty, and that I had seen such an amazing thing during the procession, and I thought, *well, happy enough.*

Casting aside the curtain dividing this sanctum and the shop-front, I felt the sudden light drown me. Hesitation gave way to irritation at the apparently wasted meeting – like a deflated mood, the material fell back into place after my crossing.

"I thought I smelled something bad," the hunchbacked crook commented as I passed him on the way towards the bar. He was poring over the usual crap – accounts of some sort, filled to the scratchy edges with useless facts and figures.

"You should stop eating so much shit then, *Elder* Wong," I grunted in return, not bothering to stop. "Still, the way you kiss arse, I suppose it comes with the territory."

Jen-Wah, who was tending the bar, tittered. I heard Chu-Deng slam his fist and scrape his chair back. This would have terrified the other kids, since those poor brats were weened on tales of the legendary Elder Wong Chu-Deng. Everyone knew he could use a knife to take out a man's eye from two hundred feet with both of his own eyes closed, and everyone just *knew* Wong Chu-Deng had served years in the Kaifeng Lockup, which is where they send the *really* bad criminals – us Rats thought we were something tough if we scored a night in the local guardhouse. So Wong Chu-Deng was the sort of heavyweight most of us both feared and admired, into whom we didn't want to grow but whose skills were exactly the sort of things we all dreamed about. We also knew, with just one wrong step, that bitter lurch and mistrustful squint would be our destiny too.

"Guan-Pi won't be around forever, Ah-Ran." Same old threat. "And when I'm the man in charge—"

Blah blah blah.

I still didn't turn around. Jen-Wah appeared to be staring past my shoulder, but come on. How could she ignore me rolling my eyes, mocking lips mouthing Chu-Deng's every word? Of course, when she really wasn't looking at me, I was studying her unimpressive breasts. Maybe someday they'd be comparable to Shai-Yeh's curiously unforgettable assets, but probably not.

"Char, he's comin over," Jen-Wah whispered, fearful but excited. "Dun make him too angry. He'll take it out on the rest of us!"

Like I cared who he took it out on?

"Well, here we are," Chu-Deng said, clapping a harsh hand upon my shoulder. I winced but refused to respond as I wanted: with a fist. He *was* an Elder, after all. That, and when he stood up straight, Chu-Deng was one of the few people taller than me in the Society – at least for the time being. "The great Char Ah-Ran returns from his mighty adventure in the oh-so-dangerous Women's Quarters!"

Remember how I said I didn't really have the energy to lie much? This was offset by a very flexible concept of truth.

" 'We fear only that which we do not understand; we don't understand only that with which are unfamiliar.' Is that not so, good Elder?" I doubt anyone had ever used the teachings of a celibate *AkraVahm* monk in reference to women before, but I didn't see why it couldn't work.

Jen stared in absent comprehension. That's fine – I wasn't trying to impress her. Chu-Deng's hand slid away. *Good choice, Wart-face.*

"A Kashensan quote from a boy just now turned twelve? Words from a man who wasn't allowed to sleep with women used by a boy who probably never will. Now there's a joke. What would *you* know about them, you little turd?"

I couldn't win a pissing match with someone who drank so much. So much easier to just shut him up another way.

"I saw what Elder Guan-Pi has been talking about. It was in there, Chu-Deng." It took some effort to refer to *her* as an 'it', but I wasn't going to give the disfigured wretch another bone to gnaw.

He pulled a swift, surprised gust of air through swollen, fleshy lips. Poor Jen pretended to be busy with her cleaning. I noted her discomfort and laid it on hard and thick.

Not a lie, y'know. Just a story, of sorts.

"Yeah. Jaku chickened out before we even made it to the wall. Useless."

And, oh, did Jen's face just crumble? That's right, honey-cake: your rich wannabe-boyfriend is a pissant.

"Upper class, lower people," Chu-Deng commented, probably quoting someone else.

"So I did it alone. Scaled the whole wall, charmed my way past a dumb servant girl and snuck into the top chamber of the Women's Quarter."

"This girl," Chu-Deng oozed, and he did that too well, "was she one of those foreign pretties?"

"Yeah, but not my type."

"Attractive then, was she?" Jen-Wah asked, perhaps seeking a little vengeance for my curt dismissal of her beloved Jaku.

I kissed my middle finger at her: an insult we'd picked up from visiting Gaikojin – filthy barbarians, if anyone asked, but how we loved to imitate them!

"I was more interested in getting a look at her. She was heavily guarded, but I'll get her." My attempts to keep *her* unmentioned slipped in the spill of eagerness.

"The story I've heard doesn't quite run like that, little Thief," Chu-Deng taunted, hobbling back towards his table and his petty scribbling.

"The story you heard was spread by people who don't have the guts to do what I did, Chu-Deng. Not smart to let cowards be your source of information, is it?"

So much for not getting into a pissing match.

"Char," Jen almost whispered, shaking her head in what could have been disbelief. "You know the Elder'd tear you part. Besides, dun you member what happened last time you were caught fighting?"

See, that's another reason most of us wanted to join the Guards – they're the ones who were *allowed* to fight in Kaifeng. If violence did burst out in the streets or the alleys or wherever, as long as it was within city walls, the Guard were never far from hand to watch. They didn't always break up fights – sometimes it's good for people to take their anger out on each other.

And the last time I was *caught* fighting was about three weeks ago. I'd been staking a well-concealed cache owned by some equally cautious merchant. No doubt said merchant was crooked himself – it was illegal to trade with Gaiko-*jin*, and this merchant dealt in foreign weaponry: straight, two-edged swords, slings, chains. That kind of thing. The night came when I'd make my move into that merchant's vault, and I'd checked with all the right sources: no one else had designs on my mark. Always good to know, or at least believe, because it was an ambush, I tell you. A set-up; someone leaked my intelligence to the Bloody Shadows. I knew it was Chu-Deng, I just knew it – a shame he couldn't get any damn intelligence of his own! As usual, the Shadows hadn't taken a Rat seriously – I'd been hyped up and eager to make a killing and accidentally-sorta-on-purpose almost made five.

Another night of hard hospitality courtesy of the Kaifeng Guards; another bruised promise of retribution from the Shadows.

"They were knuckling in on my territory, Jen-chan." The Mifūn-go suffix added further endearment to the soft disagreement, but it also implied naiveté, childishness. Vulnerability. Three things I knew she loathed. "Just like Chu-Deng is now."

"If the boy wants a beating," Chu-Deng rumbled, "I'm there." And I looked at him then – his hands were encased in stone, hard and vicious.

"This int worth it, Char," Jen said.

"Our time will come, Chu-Deng. Try not to die of old age before then."

"Our time is already here, Half. By the time you see, it'll be too late."

He unclenched his fists, rock giving way to withered skin. It seemed a parting shot, and sure enough, he gathered close his precious ledger and limped away, deeper into the Nest.

"Mind pouring me a cup of wine?"

"Char," Jen said, gathering a handful of her long black hair just to toy with it, "you're a lil young for that."

"And you're a little young to be serving it, wench. Water then," I replied. The grin was too easy. "So where is Jaku?"

Jen knew better than to trust so casual a query. She put the cup on the counter, and I drained most of it immediately. The water was neither cold nor hot. It was nice.

"What happened last night?" she asked.

"I didn't get what I wanted."

"Lemme try that again," Jen said, wrapping her fist within a tumble of gleaming vanity. "What happened with Jaku-chan?"

"Chan, is it?"

Staring into the dregs, I didn't see her expression; didn't want to — knew exactly what it was.

"Char, there're lotta things I like about you."

But.

"But it's Jaku I love."

So what?

"You know, Jen — he's a coward. He'd never protect you."

"I'm a Rat," she retorted. "I can protect myself. But I dun wanna be a Rat forever. Fighting n stealing might suit you, Char, but I'm a girl."

"And?"

"And thas all." Jen released her hair but for a thin tress, which she twirled about an appropriately girlish finger. "Fine. This int how a girl should live. I can't go ten steps outside the Nest without my staff, without maybe someone like you to—"

"Protect you?"

"*Accompany* me. Kaifeng's so much more n this. I'm sure of it. Jaku, he might not be a tough boy, but he's gonna make a fine gentleman."

"Because he has money?"

"Because he int a savage! He dun just do things on impulse; he thinks twice."

"And that slows him down. In a fight, his *thinking* is dead weight. Isn't instinct better?"

She seemed to consider this — and I, in subtle hypocrisy, thought about it too.

"Why is it always bout fightin to you, Char?"

"You're the one who doesn't feel safe out there, Jen. You tell me."

We stopped talking then.

Dust accumulated on the rugged stone floor, a poor excuse for a spring breeze depositing dry flotsam upon tables and chairs of no great value.

"Let's go, Char." Jen eventually said. She discarded her apron, collected the staff that was never far from reach and stepped from behind the bar. "I wanna show you somethin."

She didn't offer me her arm and I didn't take it.

"And the bar?"

"Not my job," she said with a half-shrug, a few steps ahead of me. "Min-Wen was glad to take a few hours off, n she'll be back soon."

"Then?"

"Yes," she said, voice as steady as her gait – both assisted by the stern weapon's support. "I wanted to see you."

"And this 'showing' me?"

"Maybe I din plan that part. Come on – not much time left."

As we strolled out of Siu-tsin's bustle and into the tranquil streets further north, Jen twirled her weapon out of habit, not caring that if I strayed too close, she'd knock me out.

"I know where we are going," I attempted. I had to almost call it out. There was some distance between us.

"Shh. Listen." She stopped. "D'you hear that?"

Nothing out of the ordinary.

"It's getting late, Jen." *Late for what?*

"That's why we're here. Wait." And Jen just stood there, both hands about her staff, attention adhering to the grey brick almost-circle ahead of us.

I knew that there was a garden beyond that perfect arch, had played in it many times. We were in a part of town that did not require locked doors or gateways – the suburbs closest to the Five-Fold Palace enjoyed regular patrols by the Guard, prompt response times and, most importantly, housed the sorts of people who were clever enough to make their less-valuable valuables easy to steal. Robbing from these people was humiliating. It was a small step above begging.

Trying to take my share of these, but a few years before now, had been how I'd met Terasawa Jaku, whose parents owned the place. After threatening to beat me and discovering that wasn't happening without a very high chance of smashed teeth, Jaku had shown me where his family kept the 'to-be-stolen' goods. Shame kept me from obliging, but I did promise to drop by more often to keep the lonely kid company.

"I didn't even think to look here," I confessed, peering through the entrance. The afternoon was heavy with incomplete premonition; there wasn't a storm in the air, but it felt as though the cloud-smeared sky would welcome one.

"It's fine," Jen mumbled, distracted herself. "He's not home."

True to her words, the garden appeared abandoned.

"So why're—"

"You hear that?" she asked again, her expression wistful.

"Hear *what?*" I answered.

"Exactly. No one fightin here. No threats. Just birds n breeze. When I marry Jaku, this will be mine."

"Marry!" Shock amplified my voice, which in turn shocked me into cupped hands about insubordinate lips.

Jen laughed, but she didn't seem happy.

"You're so easy to like when you're not trying to be liked, Char."

Ouch. It hurt when she said it; it hurts when I remember it.

"I aint gonna marry someone I dun love," Jen continued, propping her staff against the wall of Terasawa's garden, "but I must marry someone who can help me n support me. Way I figure it, the chance of meeting someone I love who can do those is pretty low. On the other hand, I've already met someone with money who int so hard to love. Most times."

"I don't care for either money or love."

"You dun seem to care for much other than yourself, Char," Jen stated without malice.

"I care for you!"

"I think you care what I care, what I care bout you," she said, and it was, *I* think, a horribly sharp thing for someone who otherwise seemed so blunt to say.

"I don't care." Normally a good thing to say to get out of trouble, but in this case just made the hole deeper.

"I'm gonna meet Jaku now, Char. If you follow, I'll beat you senseless n you know I can. I want you to stay here n listen."

But I looked – at the garden, at where we'd played. Began to cross over, or under.

"I don't—"

"Yes you do," Jaku interrupted from behind, and I stopped a few feet into the playground of our resilient youth. "Heard you got into some hot water last night, Half."

Jen was right – she was, despite being a Rat, a girl. Soon, she'd be a woman and her influence, in presence alone, was already taking effect, judging by Jaku's haughty tone.

"Nothing I can't handle, Terasawa. Been looking for you." So why didn't I turn to face him?

"I'm standing right here, Half."

"Yeah, aren't you just so tough on your own turf? Won't be 'standing' right there when I'm done—"

"Both of you! Stop this. I dun even know what you're fighting over."

Oh yes she did. There was a smile in her false declaration. There was pleasure.

"This is hardly fighting, Jen-chan," Terasawa wheedled. He had more right than I to call her that, but it still chafed. "Why did you drag him along anyway?"

Jen was a distortion in the neglected corner of my vision as she retrieved her staff – then returned to Jaku's side, or so I presumed.

"He wanted to find you, n I've had enough, Jaku. Between him threatening you when you're not around n you crying about how unfair it is—"

She'd just insulted me – so why was I laughing?

There was a scraping noise behind me.

"—I think's bout time you grew up. Both of you."

I was too young and too selfish to realise that Jen was drawing a line in the sand, but when I turned around, this was made obvious.

"There." She stepped back, away from me, away from Jaku, and admired her creation.

"What? You think that's some sort of protection?" I asked, also considering what she'd done. It was about twenty feet across; Jaku stood in the middle.

"If anything," she replied, tapping the butt of her dirt-caked staff against the ground, "the opposite. Jaku, stay there. Char – step into the circle."

"With him?" I asked.

"With me?" Jaku's voice was only barely behind mine.

"Yes. Char, enter Jaku's circle n take him outta it. Jaku – stop him."

We both just looked at her, and she just smiled.

"The winner gets me."

That didn't matter. She'd already stated her real desires and I accepted that I probably wasn't part of her plan. *My* plan was to hurt Terasawa, punish him for leaving me to Fa Shai-Yeh's playful wrath. Whether he fell from the circle or not was beyond my concern. As with everything a bully does, the means was the end.

Did Jen cheer as I smashed my fist through Jaku's unsteady expression? No – was it expected? Underneath the veneer of brutal purpose, I *did* care, did seek approval as Terasawa's nose divulged runny red. Jen sniffled and cringed even as he did the same, as though I'd hit her as well. At once, I felt powerful and inferior – why was she not happy? This was what she'd asked of me!

"Bazdard!" And the Rat raging from within Jaku's pampered youth leapt at me.

"Stop," Jen-Wah said.

Again, I was doing what Jen wanted: my waiting elbow stopped Jaku. He went down, bloodied face first.

Someone was in my circle. Not that I planned to remove him, but that was beside the point. Or rather, within it.

I knelt beside him and started to bang his head into the ground.

"Char!" And she stepped towards the very division her 'desire' had created.

"What?!" I looked at her, and because my fingers held a tuft of Jaku's hair, so did he. "Don't start something you can't *God damned* handle, Jen!"

But her face was as dry as the ground her feet disturbed as she entered the circle and completed a triangle.

The three of us did not seem to fit within the loop.

"I love im." Jen knelt on the other side of the ruined fool.

His head thumped against the dirt, released from its numb hammering.

"Then you can take care of him."

"Thank you," she mumbled, leaning over her intended, "for giving me someone to care for. He's gonna need me."

"I didn't give you shit, Rat." She was not Wu Jen-Wah; she was not Jen-chan. As content as I'd been to pummel the one who left me to suffer Shai-Yeh, this girl's machination was clear even to me – and happiness always falters when it's forced. "If I see him again, I will kill him."

"What are you gonna do, Char?" My calling her 'Rat' provoked all the derision in Wu Jen-Wah. Beneath her ambivalent, flirtatious exterior, she had a terrifying reserve of insensitive scorn. "Run away? Leave The Nest?"

The incredulity of her voice clenched my fists for lack of sly throat between tight fingers, fingers already stained with Mifūnjin blood.

"Whatever I do is no longer your business. You know, as much as I hate Jaku right now, I pity him more – that someone like you loves him."

Three became two as I walked away, and one did not look back. The circle, broken by my uncaring stride, became a crescent.

Now I was free to do what I really wanted. *She* was waiting.

Chapter 11: *Obsession*
CLIMBING, FALLING, FLYING

The wall looked no more inviting than it had last night. It was darker this time as well – I saw my shadow trying not to look miniature against the uneven rock face and hoped it didn't see me wince.

"Well, I'm here now."

Guan-Pi's standard might have surpassed mine, but I was no slouch at climbing. I found myself reaching for known crevices and nooks as though seeking an old friend's assurance. They accepted my grip and kept me safe, providing the right position, the perfect extension. I passed Shai-Yeh's balcony within five minutes, and had my eyes set on the uppermost windows, behind which *she* waited.

At this rate, I'd be at the top in no time!

"Just how *stupid* are you?" she said from below. Like the wall, her voice was now recognisable, although I had not expected to hear it rising, hushed but edgy. Maybe even a little wondrous. "Seriously, Char Ah-Ran." She remembered my name? For some reason, this came as a surprise – then stayed as unwelcome displeasure. "I told you they would be watching, and they will not be just watching for long."

"I'll be in and out by then, won't I?" I didn't look down. This would have shifted too much of my careful balance. But I did stop. "And call me Char."

"But that is not the name you gave me."

"Yeah. Well. Char."

"…Alright then. Char, you are an idiot. Guard has been *tripled*, Char. Hearsay is 'a cunning thief' learned about some treasure we tried to sneak into the city. He was stopped, thanks to the efforts of a brave, humble serving girl," Shai-Yeh paused, as though waiting for me to laugh or grunt; I did neither. "But it looks like he did not learn his lesson."

"I don't care how well they guard *her*," I mocked, "I will have her."

"Damn you and your obsession, boy!" Shai-Yeh sounded so much older with the combination of cursing and the belittling usage of 'boy'. I hoped she wouldn't continue to call me that. Although I didn't like her, I held no real dislike for her either. She was like colourful scenery. There, but not really the point. "You are causing so much trouble, and for what?"

Trouble? What trouble? As brash as I might have acted, I didn't believe I had any real impact on the world around me. This attitude enabled all sorts of mischief.

And if I had no effect on the world at large, telling her 'what' surely wouldn't hurt anyone.

So I did.

She hesitated. I could understand laughter or anger, but not disappointment.

"*What?* You come to the Women's Quarters saying you're after 'her', and it's a mere—"

"*She* is no mere anything, Shai-Yeh. They wouldn't guard her so heavily if she were, *neh?*"

"You think your little toy is the only valuable thing in this place? You said yourself last night, in a fashion: they're more afraid of assassins here than thieves. Some pretty important people are visiting your city."

Like that boy?

"Either way," I said, "they, no, *you* are keeping her secure, but not secure enough."

"I serve them, Char, nothing more. Look, will you not just come down here? I can get you closer to 'her', but only if you play this my way. It is your decision, but I cannot pour water on you this time, not from down here."

And just how far beneath me was she? I risked a very brief peek, careful not to look down *too* quickly – wouldn't be good to get dizzy at that height, not with the only difference between Alive-me and Splattered-all-over-the-street-me being sweaty palms and uncaring lumps of rock. Ten, twenty feet? My newfound aptitude with this wall proved to be just another liability after all.

"Char, please? I would not have admitted this last night, but I need your help now. And *you need mine!*"

I stared at the sky above us both, as though fascinated with the same cloudy ceiling as I'd seen too many nights before. The answers didn't lie there, although many a lie might have answered me.

"Do I, Shai-Yeh? I don't think so. What's the worst that can happen? I fall, I die? But I won't fall, because I know what I'm doing."

"Your bravado is going to get us both killed, Char. Do you not understand yet? There are some here who believe you and I are working together! Why else would a low-born serving girl be even this high up in the Quarters? Come down and I will explain further."

"I don't give a crap about your problems, Shai-Yeh." And that decided that. I began to climb once more, pretending not to be bothered by her logic.

"My problems are your problems, you little scoundrel, now *get down here.*"

There were two balconies left, with the next being perhaps three feet up. I noticed that exactly two seconds before I heard heavy footsteps above me. Slow, steady footsteps. *Guard's* footsteps.

"Quickly, now!" Shai-Yeh hissed as I began to reverse my progress a little too recklessly. Overconfidence made sure I missed the next foothold; hastiness, prompted by the possibility of a Guard just above me, ensured I wouldn't find another.

"Ohhhhhh!" Not even the eloquent Shai-Yeh could get a single word out as I bumped and scraped down the wall. The world was a rush of pain and confusion. There was absolutely no clarity, no epiphany like people tend to think. My life didn't flash before my eyes, mainly because I wasn't dying. But I didn't know that.

The ground came much quicker than I'd expected. It was also quite a bit softer. I really should have let go earlier, if this gentle landing was waiting for me.

"Get up!" Shai-Yeh commanded. I didn't want to listen, but I heard, and so up I got.

Of course, I was on her balcony. There was really no way to fall down the wall without somehow colliding with the jutting landing, but that didn't explain why the abrupt conclusion had been so forgiving.

"Wow," I murmured, too dazed to say anything more important. "That was lucky."

"Luck was not an issue, Char, now please hurry! Follow me." She dashed into the room, the very same room she'd been cleaning last night.

I glanced behind me before obeying – and saw nothing but a bare slab of polished wood, a simple stone barrier.

"Char. Stop dallying and *come!*"

Right. No idea what we landed on, no idea why we didn't go *smoosh*. But what choice remained? I followed Shai-Yeh into the candlelit room.

After a few steps, I started to wince and hobble.

"What is your problem, kid?" She stopped and whirled around. I saw that she was wearing something a little less constricting tonight, a loose, pale orange dress and skirt thingy, and her golden hair was tied back in a practical braid. But for all the effort at seeming plain and unadorned, her tits were still obviously struggling to stay concealed.

"Nothing." I'd probably been less dreamy even in dreams.

"Then close your mouth and let us *go.*" Without even a bit of self-consciousness, Shai-Yeh turned on her heel with another peach flair and marched further into the room.

I just gazed at the balcony, at the strange lack of cushions or chairs or whatever the hell had caught me.

"Oh, why do you have to be so *fucking* difficult?"

I started. Did she actually say that?

"There." She sounded satisfied. "Now turn around and follow me. The Guards will be here at any moment."

"I didn't know people like you used words like that, Shai-Yeh." Char gone back lala-land. Yep.

"Only when things are really dire. Such as now. And you do not *know* people 'like me'. I am going, Char, and you can follow, or you can try your luck with the balcony, wall and twelve Guards at the bottom looking for your body."

Twelve? Why twelve? I looked away from the balcony, favouring the foul-mouthed girl with a distrustful glare.

"What about the Guards in here, Fa Shai-Yeh?"

"I will handle them. Oh dear, look at you!" She hurried towards me. I stepped back instinctively, as a wounded animal would. She couldn't switch moods this quickly and expect me to just crumble in acceptance.

"Don't. Just go. I'll be right behind you." I clutched at my grazed wrist and limped forward. I felt a million stings up and down my legs, but did not look down.

"This, all this. For a *sword?*" She shook her head and led me out of the small room.

And into a large corridor. Sliding doors interspersed the walls, failing to break the monotony of polished oak. Shai-Yeh led, but something else determined the course, perpetuated the progress of my otherwise timid feet.

"Where are all the women?"

"What?" She was annoyed, diverted, and not about to stop.

"Well, this is the Women's Quarters. Where are the women?"

"You surprise me, Half."

"Don't call me that."

"I saved your life back there, *kid.* I shall call you whatever I like. Are you ashamed of your heritage?"

More idiocy: I thumped the wall and then wondered why it made such a loud noise.

"Heritage? My mother was raped by some cruel Noble and you call it 'heritage'?" I nursed the offensive hand with contrasting defensiveness.

"How do you know she was raped?" Shai-Yeh asked. "Did you ask her? Did she tell you?"

No one had ever done this before. If anyone got close, I just shoved them back, hit them a few times to make sure they never tried again. But I knew better than to lash out at Shai-Yeh. Even then, it was clear she was in control, at least of that aspect.

"Don't change the subject!" Not easy to sound angry, righteous and resentful in a whisper. "Where are the women?"

"I guess we can resume that later." She just couldn't let it end without her final say. "They are downstairs, most of them, eating dinner and preparing for the night's entertainment. They will stay down there well past Highmoon. Our only worry is the Guards prowling these upper levels. You do not know much about this lifestyle, do you?'

"It sounds boring and stupid." She pricked my pride: there aren't many ways to get a boy to add chilli and ginger to his lies more effective than this.

"You *are* stupid and boring, kid, but you are also going to help me. Got it?" And Shai-Yeh fell silent, moving down the ridiculously long hallway with a tentative touch and frustrating caution.

"Yeah, I got it." And once I got *her,* I resolved, Fa Shai-Yeh would be the first to *know* it.

"In here."

After several passages (and no sign of these 'terrible' Guards, either), Shai-Yeh paused, glanced around then opened one of the many doors. The candlelight, granted by stands topped with thick, slow-burning tallow, revealed this door as no different to any of the others.

"But—"

"Shh. In, now."

I hesitated. I always do, even when I am being thoughtless and impulsive – that's just a hesitation towards thinking.

"But Shai-Yeh—"

"Shh! Listen!"

So I did, and I heard the rising sound of heavy footfalls down the hall, around the corner and hopefully quite far away.

"Right." And in I went.

I liked that room immediately – it was poorly lit, warm and quiet.

"Close the door behind you. Have you no manners?" Shai-Yeh's silhouette sank into the inviting darkness. I didn't think this at the time, but I should have: she navigated the room knowingly.

"But then it will be dark in here—"

"Oh yes. Are you afraid of being alone in the dark, Char? Or alone in the dark – with a girl?" Shai-Yeh purred. I never liked cats, because they'd yowl and hiss when I threw rocks at them, which I did, quite a bit, because I never liked cats.

"An ugly, fat girl with a bad mouth!" But I closed the door, and I was then in complete darkness, alone but for Fa Shai-Yeh.

"I am not fat. I will not bring light if you do not stop insulting me." Her tone didn't complement the words. *She was enjoying herself.* "Do I hear an apology?"

"For what?

"Slow learner, this one." She might have sighed, and she definitely clicked her fingers. A crowd of eyes glowing with mockery opened in the corner of my narrowed gaze. Shai-Yeh just smiled in that menacing way she never seemed to resist, no matter how nice she wanted to be.

"See?"

How could I not? I lowered my hand.

"Stop gaping! Have you never seen a bedroom before?"

Not *quite* like this one! Those glaring eyes were nothing more than now-steady candlelight. At first I'd felt their attention, but now I saw that they were locked upon the more curious sights in the 'bedroom'.

There was a huge bed scaffolded with sheets and drapes; lounges stuffed with cushions huddled against the walls. And it was all very, very pink.

"Guess your favourite colour is blue, then?"

"I never said this was *my* bedroom." Shai-Yeh slithered from one of those lounges, discordant in her orange dress. "I am not sure whose it is, actually, but it shall suffice."

"For?" My eyes took in whatever my hands thought they could; thief's instinct took over as I spotted all sorts of shiny little things.

"My purpose, but you need not know about that." And I didn't really care either. I was already moving, slipping around this dresser, that set of drawers. I guess my hands were busy, because when I stopped, they were heavy with newfound wealth.

"I hope you remember where that all belongs, Char." Was she behind me? Not in view, but that might have been because I was still studying the layout of a cluttered perfume and jewellery array. "I tell you there are Guards after you, that we are both in trouble, and you *steal* whatever is in sight?"

"Might as well," I shrugged, careful not to spill the precious necklaces, armlets and sparkling bracelets. "I'll be set for life with just a single handful of this!"

"But it is not yours, Char!"

"Is now." Loaded to comfort, I looked around for a window. Window meant 'out', even though climbing down a wall with a handful of jewels might not have been the smartest idea. One way to find out. "What are you going to do? Call for the Guards?"

Witty little brat that I was.

"Such petty needs, really. If you take off now, you shall never, *ever* get the chance to see 'her' again."

"Sure I will." I paced along the far wall, nudging aside curtains, only to reveal more wall. "Where's the damn window?"

"No, you will not, Char, because I can make certain you do not. Now stop being such a belligerent annoyance, put that stuff back and sit down! You impertinent bother!"

"Whatever! How in Hell Above is anyone supposed to escape this place if there are no stupid windows?" I might have listened if she hadn't acted like a snotty Schoolmaster. Fa Shai-Yeh used too many big words, which was, now I think about it, yet another thing we had in common.

"Are you really content with so simple a life, Char? Stealing, beating people up, getting into trouble?"

"Stop asking stupid questions!" She was making my head hurt. "Just shut up! I'm busy!"

"Fine."

I stared at the wall and muttered. What kind of wall doesn't have windows? A habit of 'deep' thinking: I began to rub my head in frustration, forgetting the precious collection. Jewels tinkled against the stone floor.

"Now look what you made me do! Why couldn't you have just left me alone, Fa Shai-Yeh?" It *was* her fault! All of it. "I had it all planned perfectly, and then you came along, and you ruined everything! I hate you!"

I threw the rest of my treasure down and rounded upon her, fists held at my side. I saw her leering at me through the faint blur of delinquent tears.

"Are you going to hit me, Char?" Still smiling, still acting so God-damned superior!

I snarled; oh, how I *wanted* to crack her dimpled cheeks, break them with blood and ruin. My feet, however, wouldn't respond. Looking down, I was sure I'd see chains or something holding my ankles in place, but there was nothing there.

"Here. I am right here, Great Thief of Kaifeng: ten little footsteps and you can do whatever you want to me." A quick but reluctant glance – she was sitting upon that disgusting, very-pink bed, legs crossed like one of those Noble handmaidens I'd seen on wall-scrolls and paintings and stuff.

"Let me go!"

"Let yourself go."

What in Eph did that mean?

"I am going to *wreck* you, do you hear me? Gonna rip you apart."

"A little louder, if you would? The Guards love hearing men say this sort of thing in the Women's Quarters."

Impotent, choked anger crippled even my enraged words. If only my feet were free, free to take me close enough. If only. I'd strangle her or hit her or just—

"Just kiss me?"

Ever seen a rampaging elephant tripped up by a single flower?

"—What?"

"Hm?" She picked at her nails. "I was musing that the other girls downstairs must miss me."

"That is not what you said!" *'O foolish, stubborn pride! O lamentable, immature pride!'* What a pity I didn't actually *learn* from all those obscure *AkraVahm* quotes I liked to throw around. "You said 'kiss me'!"

It didn't even occur to me that she had read my mind.

"I did not!"

"You did too! Stop *lying,* Shai-Yeh! Tell the truth!" I know, funny isn't it? A thief who finds the act of lying despicable. I was probably just jealous because everyone else seemed to be good at it.

"I am not lying. You are hearing things." She waved the notion away, as though she were an adult dealing with—"Just a brat! You are a child, Char, and the thought of you kissing me is totally *icky.* Besides, you are in love with a *sword,* of all things! I swear, by Ephriem and Shynsa and All the Holy Host, *Vahm en!*" Her piety aggravated me, right down to the gesture she made with a smooth, enchanting hand. I knew it, of course. Everyone did. We completed prayers with it, warded evil spirits with it. Probably the first and last thing we're taught in school:

Class, the Master will now teach you The Flail. She touches her right cheek with the tip of her left forefinger. She traces a path up, over her forehead and then down her nose, her lips, down the middle of her face with the edge of her forefinger. With her fingers straight, palm pointing right, she takes her hand towards her belly. Then she turns her palm upwards, cutting across her belly from right to left. Now do as she does, over and again. Remember Our Saviour, Ephriem, who suffered the Flail for our sins. May He protect us. Vahm en.

Shai-Yeh Curled the Flail at *me,* as though I were some wicked angel!

Maybe she'd cast some sort of magic over me? Was God Herself against me too?

"No! I am *not* in love with a sword!" Was it love? You tend to 'love' the stupidest things at the age of twelve, I guess, like a toy, or a dress, or a sword? Stuff we can't have but want more than anything in the world. "And that is what you said, I don't care what you say!"

"Yes, I did say you are in love with a sword! No arguments there!"

"Not that! You said, 'kiss me', For Eph's sake!"

"Shame on your blasphemous tongue, boy!"

"B-but you said the…that word before!"

"Commandment Three, Char! God Herself stated it thus!"

"The word you said is worse!" Wasn't it? Other kids said "Eph' and they didn't get in trouble, but the big ones, like *fuck* (I could think it, of course, but I'd never said it aloud!) would earn you a quick cuff from an Elder. She was confusing me even more and I hated her just as much.

"Not according to The Lord, Char. You are just changing the subject because you do not wish to admit that you find me attractive."

"You SAID 'kiss me!' and that is what I heard!"

"If that is what you want to believe—"

"It is, now shut up!" I raised my hands. They were still fists.

"You want to believe that I wanted you to kiss me?" She was so infuriatingly calm and amused, just like a damn grownup!

"Yes! I mean, that *is* what you said!" I think. Wasn't it? Maybe not?

"You are such a cutie." And she laughed. It sounded like glass breaking, or maybe a bird cackling.

I still couldn't move my feet. I needed to hit something. The wall was too far away. Had to *hit smash HURT something!*

"If I wanted to kiss a girl," I snarled, thinking myself oh-so-clever, "I could do *far* better than you! Now let me go!"

"I am not holding you, Char," she replied through a fierce grin. "Would you like me to pretend I am, and pretend to let you go?"

"Don't pretend, do it for real!" My legs twitched because I kept trying to lift those impossibly heavy feet.

"Ooooh kay then." Shai-Yeh lifted her hand once more, the same devout hand with which she'd Curled the Flail, and intoned, "Ooggeddy booggeddy blah blah bam—"

I was ready to charge straight at her, to pounce her and pummel her and make her say sorry for lying and for swearing and being such a confusing, terrible person! As soon as she let me go, I was going to *destroy* her!

"—I hereby release poor, little, baffled, angry, silly—"

"LEMME GO!"

"—innocent, childish—oh, *fuck* it." Shai-Yeh clicked her fingers.

And I was free!

Right as the lights went out.

"Oops."

All that pent-up energy propelled me through the thick, monotonous darkness and, at last check, I was aimed quite squarely at the vexing woman on the bed.

"Wrong hand, maybe? Well I shall have tooo—oooh!"

And even though the world was dark, I can imagine it was quite a sight.

The Great Thief was on top of Shai-Yeh, chest to chest, hands unclenched by surprise and pressed into the pink bed sheets. The smell of her perfume, some sickly-sweet strawberry mixture, made me want to gag. I listened to her breathing, I didn't say a thing, didn't dare move. It's ridiculous, but I was afraid of hurting her!

"Just as I said." Her breath stung my face with these words. "You cannot resist me. Here is your chance, mighty rogue."

I was going to tell her to get off me, but I couldn't manage even that illogical demand. I'd never felt so trapped in my life, so helpless.

"Well? This is not exactly comfortable, you know. Either kiss me or get off. Or both." There was more of that far-too-adult attitude for which I had no care, but she was *daring* me.

"I will. Don't push me, Shai-Yeh. You don't want to push me!"

"My breasts, at which you could not stop staring before, tell me I am not the one pushing, little boy."

"Stop *calling me that!*" And, for all my violent rebukes and denial, I was still frozen, pinned to her as though by some unrelenting weight upon my back.

"Then be a *man* for the first time in your miserable life, Char!"

Like she'd know? Like she knew anything?

Like she knew everything.

"Here! I am right here!" I felt her first caress the back of my head, then force it down with surprising strength. I resisted, because that's what I do.

"You want to play it that way, then? Fine! Get off me, you gutless worm!"

Not only did she lift her fingers from my head – Shai-Yeh used her other hand to shove me up and back. I flew through the darkness, wind hissing in my ears, soft and malevolent. Couldn't see a thing, of course, but somehow I knew I was in the air a little longer than a simple shove.

That I hit the wall opposite the bed might have had something to do with this woozy conclusion.

"Now, let's try that again," I heard her grumble and click her fingers a third and final time. I kept my eyes closed. Maybe if I didn't open them, this blackness, this forgiving blindness, would never leave.

No matter how hard I tried to clamp my lids, the lights were back on. Pale orange pupils were staring at me once more.

"Some guys just will not take 'no' for an answer!"

"Ow." I rubbed the back of my head, much as she had, and there was something warm and wet. Sticky. Another wild and stupid first-thought: *I don't normally sweat this much.*

"Ow? You try to molest me, and *you* say 'ow'? First you want to break in and steal some stupid sword, then you are stealing jewels and trying to escape, *then* you want to hit me, or kiss me, and when you get the chance to do either, you just lie there like a limp slug!"

"I think I'm dying," I croaked, still probing the soaked mop stuck to the back of my skull.

"You, you, you! What about me, Char? My delicate female sensibilities have been *assaulted* by a savage child of the streets and oh my God is that blood?!"

Oh. Blood. Right. That makes sense. Now I know why it hurts so much.

"Wow. Fragile little thing, you are!"

Her words were compassionate, but she just sat on the bed, expression that same rapt look, *almost* guilty, like she'd just heard a particularly naughty rumour.

"Hurts ooowww it really God-damn hurts!" A pity shock can't keep us numb forever. I wailed and ripped my hand away from my head, a head now clearly quite damaged.

Her voice finally gained a trace of concern, or maybe just fear.

"We need to get you help, real help. Oh Blessed Mother, what have I—"

Done for I'm done for and I didn't even get to hold her.

Then I felt nothing at all. For the single remaining second of consciousness, it was good.

Chapter 12: *Helpless*
FLOWERS IN HAND

That's when I woke up.

Upon awakening, there is always a voice, even if it's just the voice in your head. I used to wonder if that voice was what actually woke me up, maybe just before someone else's, or its silence. Eventually I figured out that it wasn't the voice waking me up – all it was trying to do was reason why I was awake, when I'd been asleep just before that.

Unfortunately, even that voice is a bit sluggish and useless upon first waking.

Up, get up, get out no, couldn't be bothered UP noooo you have to, find out what happened to—

"My head." Didn't want to open my eyes, still clung to the infinite sightless.

"Still there, I'm afraid," someone replied from only a few feet away. Snippy, effeminate, curt. An invitation to trust bewildered craziness: *I was out so long Shai-Yeh has grown up!* When she continued, however, I heard enough differences to think otherwise. Maybe I'd thought she'd been rude or scathing only because I'd just come around – her tone was suddenly far less sharp, despite her berating. "A little banged up, but you'll find it can do just about the same as it could before your accident. Although just how much, or how little, that was in the first place remains to be seen. What you did was very reckless. You're lucky to have survived the fall."

I didn't fall I was pushed thrown against the wall a really pink wall wasn't I I'm not sure—

"But I am sure you don't remember that…Char Ah-Ran." She hesitated, as though consulting some reminder of who I was. Enviable. And I was too…something to correct her. Or too nothing. "Short term memory loss isn't rare for that sort of wound. Do you feel any pain?"

I took time to think about this, although it was clear within seconds that:

"No, I don't feel a thing. But there's something pressed against the back of my head. Can I open my eyes?" So it wasn't really my decision to keep them closed after all.

"Not yet, and the 'something' is a dressing, my own work. Healing you will be a two step process, young man. The first is almost done: our help, a little bandaging, plenty of rest. The second bit is up to you, and I really don't want to see you here again. At least, not like this."

"Here?"

But I knew, could smell the flowers, the rich aroma of varnished wood – attempts to mask something more cloying, more *real*. Then I could *hear* the groans of pain around me. I'd been in a place like this before, but not like this. It made no sense, so I just let her give the only answer possible.

"You're in a Haven. You'll have to spend the night here as well, since it's too dark for you to go home."

"Don't got a home." Too dark? For me? Couldn't she see my pauper's rags, hear my street Rat's attitude?

"You've forgotten even that? How surprising. Well, give it time. Your sister will be back in the morning to take you home."

"I don't have a sis—"

Yes I do.

"Yes you do, now just relax. Healing takes it out of us all, and with as much as it took to keep you from slipping off to Heaven, you should still be asleep."

"Which Haven?"

"The Benevolent Hand. Not far from home, you see?"

No, not far. Just all the way across the city from my usual haunts, from Guan-Pi's urban fortress of curio shops and produce-hawkers. From The Nest, my own haven.

I was in another world now.

"I'm hungry."

"There's some food beside your bed but it's hot. You've just woken up; wait a bit."

"Ready now. Hungry."

"If you want to feel around for it and maybe spill it, okay. You can open your eyes now, but you're not going to see anything anyway."

So I did. And I didn't.

"Bandages, Char Ah-Ran. Don't panic. Would you like me to feed you?"

Full name again. Still didn't say anything. For some reason, I didn't mind the way she said it.

"No, thank you. What's your name?"

"Well, I like to be called Lily." Not really a name, not like mine. I heard her stand up, I think, and move away from whatever I was lying on. "I'll be in to check on you soon, Char Ah-Ran. Please don't disturb the others in here."

Others? Oh, Haven. Right. "I won't."

"Good boy." She might as well have patted me on the head and given me a treat. "If you need to sleep, don't fight it. See you soon."

I guess she'd figured out that fighting was what I did best, but against the after-effects of a life-saving Healing, not even Char Ah-Ran, Greatest Thief of Kaifeng, stood a chance.

Awake again, with an insistent throbbing behind my head or something. I moved to touch whatever was left of my skull. Had to raise my head away from the pillow, winced at the stiffness in my neck.

Just how long had I been there this time?

"I told you not to climb that wall, brother," Shai-Yeh's voice reproached, and naturally I couldn't see the pointing finger or hands on hips, tightened brow, lower lip pressed into upper: a most cross expression. "Mother is furious and Father, well, he has not said a word on the matter. I am sure he is going to—"

"Miss Fa," Lily, my newly-acquired guardian spirit against all things Shai-Yeh, interrupted with marked softness, "he is still weak. A little mercy, if you would?"

Yes, I was still weak, oh, can't even lift my head from the pillow, moan, groan.

"Well he has to come home *today*, Healer."

"Lily, Miss Fa."

"Whatever. Is he ready?"

When Shai-Yeh asked that, I know now all three of us heard a different question and settled on equally different answers.

"Provided he gets more rest. Say, a week or so."

"A *week?* What about school?"

Lily did not answer immediately.

"Sis," I croaked, and it felt as though I'd been calling her that all my life. "I'll catch up. Serves me right for being such a twit, doesn't it? Just gimme a second here. Can the bandage come off now, Miss Lily?"

I was a little more respectful when speaking to Lily. I knew this would irk Shai-Yeh.

"Yes. Are you able to sit up?"

"I'll try." And I did try, a little bit. For two, maybe even five seconds.

"You poor thing. Here." Her touch was gentle but not meek. For a second, I wished Shai-Yeh's lies were true, and that there might have been a mother waiting for me, someone who could hold me like that when I needed it.

Which was turning out to be more often than I'd thought.

"I could have done it by myself, Miss Lily," I protested with just enough insolence, just the right amount of bravery. All in a very feeble voice, of course. "Sis, you should take some lessons in being nice from Miss Lily here."

I wanted to see her teeth gnash, but again, imagination would have to 'suffice'.

"Feisty young man!" Lily said as she began unbinding the cloth from about my head. "But your sister did save your life."

Again? Shit.

But she also almost killed me. Again.

"That is right! I did!" Shai-Yeh jumped in. "*I* was the one who carried you here after you fell, Char!"

"Three nights ago, Char Ah-Ran, just before Highmoon," Lily supplied, still circling one hand around and around while the other cupped my chin. Her tone was too admiring for my likes. "A very brave thing to do, although under any other circumstances also very dangerous."

"God was watching over us, Lily. *Vahm en.*" Shai-Yeh was yet quick to invoke pious words. Probably Flailing herself again.

"*Vahm en?*" But Lily sounded sincere. "And she hasn't left your side other than to go home and sleep, Char Ah-Ran. You're lucky to have so loving a sister!"

"Hmph."

"Stubborn brat," Shai-Yeh said, not without some affection. Was she that good an actress?

"Okay. Close your eyes. I'm taking the bandages off now. This is going to feel a little weird."

"Will it hurt?" I asked – not a question I used very often, since the assumed answer was always 'yes, so deal with it'. I was learning how Lily worked, though, and what she expected of me.

"Not if you don't move. I need to cut some of them away, but it's only a little knife. Hold still."

For a moment I wondered why a healer would need to use a knife, because knives were weapons and belonged in the hands of Shadows and Rats, but I held my tongue. The sound of cloth being carefully nicked gave way to a strange sensation of suction as Lily pulled the last of the bandaging from my face – I envisioned blood, clots of flesh; that alone made me cry out. I suddenly didn't remember anything that had happened to me, how I even got to the Haven or why my head was covered in sticky fabric.

"Shhh, Char Ah-Ran. That was the last of it. Feel your face, if you want. It's all there, just as you remember it."

It was getting tough to trust Lily. My fear was rampant by then, skipping away from logic and reason with typical abandon. But without memory, what else *could* I trust? I lifted nervous fingers – mindful of how limp they were, yet how stiff – and brought them close to glutinous cheeks. Before touching the slick skin, which I expected to come away just as readily as the gauze had, I hesitated.

"I don't remember my face, Lily."

"Then you will not know even if something is wrong," Shai-Yeh muttered. "Hurry up."

So I sat there, fingers poised before my face, and opened my eyes. It was really like waking up. My eyelids seemed to be glued shut but soon peeled open. I saw another bed across from mine in the lantern-lit room; it was empty. Shai-Yeh was standing at the foot of the bed, arms folded. She had a red scarf tied around her head, was wearing something local and her skin seemed darker than I remembered.

She's hiding her blonde hair. Changed clothes. And make-up? Trying to look Mifūnjin to pass as my sister. Why such effort?

And there was someone not that much older than Shai-Yeh poised beside me. She was dressed in the unmistakeable red and white uniform of a Healer, and her expression was pure concern.

The slickness I'd felt was just sweat.

"Why are the other beds empty?" I asked.

"It's daytime, Char Ah-Ran," Lily explained. How odd, that her gentle, artless face so matched the soft voice. I'd seen angry women, cruel women, cunning women, even happy women, but never, ever had I seen a woman, or young lady, look so compassionate. Even her hair was unassuming: shoulder-length, tinted with the slightest hint of brown or red, or maybe that was just a trick of the light. "We won't have people here until tonight, and hopefully not even then. It's been pretty busy the past few nights. We're due for a lull." She looked about ready to stifle uncertain words with a knuckle; I saw her lift her hand reflexively, look at the small and slightly bloody instrument it held, then thought better of it.

"Time will not wait, little brother," Shai-Yeh took her cue – stole it with typical deftness. "And I am not carrying you this time!"

"I can walk." I swung my legs off the bed, ignored my tingling ankles and stood up.

"Careful." Lily looked like she wanted to steady me, but I wasn't going to play that game this time. Pride was at stake.

"I'm fine." And I was, for three steps.

"You think so, Char?"

It was Fa Shai-Yeh rather than Lily who asked this. Fa Shai-Yeh who caught me – my 'sister' was just too quick. She always is.

"Let go of me, Shai-Yeh."

"If I do, you will fall. Again."

Did I really want that? Bullies aren't supposed to fall over! The choice presented itself and I know now – once made, there was no looking back.

To quote once more the AkraVahm: The Fall followeth Pride.

Take away the pride, and no matter what remains, at least it won't fall.

Maybe because it already has.

"Fine. Thank you, Miss Lily. For saving me." I stressed that one, even though it was to Shai-Yeh that I clung.

"Go with God's grace, Char Ah-Ran. And don't climb any more walls." She didn't wink, didn't do anything but smile a bit. I smiled a bit back.

"Trust me, not in this lifetime."

As soon as we exited The Benevolent Hand, Shai-Yeh stopped. Since I was still leaning upon her, I did as well.

"Well?" she asked, avoiding eye contact as I stared at her in the flat afternoon light. The streets in that part of Kaifeng were clean and healthy, with people milling here and there, perusing stalls and chattering about the nice weather.

"Well what, Shai-Yeh?"

Then she did look at me, and I saw something I did not recognise right away: fear, fear tinged with a denial of hope, or maybe a fear *of* hope.

"Nothing. You know we are not going back to The Nest."

So she knows about that.

"Yeah, I know. You can tell me why as we go."

"All right. This way, then."

And she moved, slowly. As we walked, she would occasionally pause to let me rest before continuing.

"We're not going to some family, are we?" My head felt heavy – made it comfortable to let her guide me as I stared at the well-worn stones underfoot.

"No, Char. Not like that."

"What about my—" What exactly was Guan-Pi? Jen? Jaku? Chu-Deng? The entire Society? They were just: "—the people I know?"

"Will they look for you, Char? Will they miss you?"

I'd been known to disappear before – it was what I did. They always welcomed me back, but no one came after me, because they knew I didn't want that, or at least so I encouraged them to think. And after that seemingly fatal encounter with Jen and Jaku, I'd made it clear that I had better things to do than waste my time with their lot. So would they see me again?

"No."

"Good. Things have changed. The night you had your accident," she couldn't admit to what had really happened; was she feeling guilty? "your sword went missing."

Mine? How is it mine? She just means the sword I keep talking about? Yes, that would be it, because—

"It was probably too good for me anyway, Shai-Yeh."

"Well, someone thought it valuable. Despite the extra guards, that someone still managed to take it. Naturally they did not find you squished at the bottom of the wall, so one plus one equals two of us..."

"On the run," I finished with a bitter smile and plain chagrin. That explained her disguise.

"Sort of, yes. I have a plan, although you will not like it."

"Yeah? How bad can it be?"

"Look up."

Fearing dizziness, I did so very steadily – my legs, feet, cobblestones, edge of road a few feet in front of me, two doors. The wall.

The Sign.

"Are you shitting me?"

"I have a friend in there, Char. A few friends, from my previous visits to Kaifeng. They will keep you out of sight until things have blown over."

"Out of sight? This place! They take people out of sight and don't let them be seen again, Shai-Yeh!" People, like Jen's parents. Like most of the kids in the Society, she had more than enough reason to fear that which now leered down at me.

"That is their job, Char, but this is a personal favour I am calling in."

Best not to wonder about that – which is why I did.

"And you? Gonna just disappear as well?"

"No," she responded. "I have protection of my own. You will see me from time to time. We have work ahead of us, Char."

"You mean other than trying not to be arrested for the theft of an Imperial treasure?"

"Look!" She pulled me closer to the foreboding set of doors. I tried to ignore the ominous icon casting its shadow from above. "You were planning on stealing it anyway, were you not? Now it is gone. Did you honestly think people would not be after you?" She shook me. It hurt.

"I, uhm, you see—"

"Did you!?" She jarred me again, both hands upon my shoulders. Had it been her intention, she could have made a paper ornament out of me.

I folded anyway.

"—I never planned on stealing her OKAY?" I choked back a sob. Behold the mighty Char Ah-Ran, Greatest Thief of Kaifeng, terroriser of entire neighbourhoods, bawling his eyes out. "I just, I just wanted to look at her again, to imagine her in my hand. Then I'd tell everyone what I imagined, but I didn't really imagine it, did I? It felt so real."

Shai-Yeh grimaced but did not let me go.

"All this – and you did not even intend to take the sword?" Her tone held a solemnity I failed to recognise in my sobbing.

"No. I take stuff, sure, but taking something like her would be wrong, do you see, she is special, it's as you said, she is too good for a brat like me, she is a Goddess of Swords, a work of art, I'd just break her and then she'd be gone forever!"

"Amazing."

"What?" I asked through sleeve-drenched sniffling.

"Just amazing." She let go, stepped back. Smiled her awful smile but said nothing more.

"Go on, laugh. Tell everyone. Tell the world, for all I care." Anger always chased Shame around the room in which no children behave; Shame always ran into the wall. "You, Fa Shai-Yeh. Everything. Your fault! All your fault!"

I swung hard and wild, aching and sore but compelled nonetheless. I didn't even care who saw, not at this point.

She caught my fist, and squeezed as though it were nothing but a paper lantern.

I buckled, crumpling straight down, at her feet. The look in her eyes was complete savagery, complete glee.

But it only lasted two seconds. I was squinting in agony, yet even through those pain-thin eyes I saw her frown. Fa Shai-Yeh released me, but I did not fall – there was no further down from where I was.

"I am sorry. I have no idea why I did that." And I believed it. Her face shimmered but didn't reflect sorrow at all – as though she wanted to cry, but, for the life of her, couldn't. "Go inside and talk to the man at the desk. Do not say anything but the sentence, or they *will* make you disappear."

She began to walk away in a barren daze.

"What sentence, Shai-Yeh?"

The woman stopped, turned around. Her eyes were devoid of clarity. She didn't even look at me.

"The Life Sentence. Birth and death, just parentheses."

"—The hell?"

"Thought I told you." There was still no change in her tone. Were her voice a sea, a boat could have floated, frozen, upon Fa Shai-Yeh's few words.

"Told me what?"

"Tell them to listen to the Nightsong."

"Listen to the Night's song. Whatever that means."

"No. Nightsong. One word; a special word. See you later."

And she was gone with the most deadpan of farewells I had never imagined.

"I am so, so, *so* fucked," I muttered under my breath and looked up at the sign again. A solitary drop of painted blue blood fell from a cupped black palm, pointing downward. It looked as though the hand had let the blood slip, or was the hand itself bleeding? I had found the symbol fascinating until that point, even though it was a universal device of danger.

No choice now. Rising from the road, still hurting and ready to collapse, I nursed my throbbing hand and entered the House of Blood Peddlers.

I closed one of the two doors behind myself after entering, although all horrors howled in my head – *don't trap yourself in here!* The light encroaching from the street was sealed away, and I felt my salvation retreat with it. I expected darkness and saw precisely that: the shadows became swollen and threatening. There were, however, no true shadows, no defined silhouettes; it was a solid and consistent depth, made all the more deep because I couldn't see the bottom.

What to do? I was too scared to leave, too scared to stay. Out there, a world of trouble lurked in the form of everyone now after the stolen sword: The Kaifeng Guard, The Kasuden emissaries, Lord Ayakawa himself, and wasn't he in personal contact with the Nobles – with *God?* In here, that trouble was not so immediate. No – here was a different world in which 'trouble' defied conventional meaning. I wanted to be somewhere that was neither in here nor out there. I wanted to be nowhere.

But I'd made my choice. Shai-Yeh said what to do, I did it.

Why stop now?

"Anyone in here?" Of course there was, you idiot. The doors were unlocked. An unlocked door indicated either someone on the other side or nothing worth investigating. The latter was just not happening here – this was a House of *Blood Peddlers*!

Unsurprisingly, I forgot Shai-Yeh's instructions.

"I am. Come towards the sound of my voice. The way is clear." Where Shai-Yeh's voice was a discordant symphony of confident madness, and Lily's a damp cloth draped over a hot forehead, this woman used her reptilian tone as though she meant to dissect something with it, which of course she did. "No questions. Just come."

Disobeying that voice would have been worse than Talking Back To Authority, and we didn't do that either. Not if we liked our faces the way they were, you know, teeth still in one's mouth and all that. So I limped towards where I thought she'd be.

"Still on course? Don't answer. Just helping you." Disjointed sentences from her didn't even seem incomplete. "Hmm yes you are. Would you like to see something special?"

Louder. Closer. I stopped, but it was too late.

"Of course you would! Come here!" She cackled and grabbed my shirt, dragged me forward. Still couldn't see a thing – I wasn't sure whether I should be grateful or terrified for that.

I cried out but didn't have time to struggle. She must have had *very* long arms, because it felt like she pulled me clear across the room, even though I had no idea how large the room was.

"And the Lord said, 'Let There Be Light'," a new voice intoned. Deep, masculine, confident. I heard a laugh lurking beneath the contemptuous growl. "And there wasn't. Oh well."

I recognised the line, of course. It was from the first Volume of *Vahm*, except that it was wrong, it was supposed to be—

"Night!" I gasped, suspended in the air. "The Lord said, 'Let there be *Night*'!"

—song, you're supposed to say Nightsong to a man at the desk, what God-damn desk, shit, Shai-Yeh, I hate you – die – help –

"And there still is, and it is Good. Apparently." I saw a grin in the darkness, as certain as that gnarled hand holding me above the floor. "*Vahm en*. But sometimes, light is just as important."

He wasn't like Shai-Yeh – no snapping fingers, no showing off. It wasn't even instantaneous, but when the thin slat of white sharpness cut across the floor, I knew he'd opened a window. I saw that nothing was holding me up, exactly one second before that nothing dropped me.

I heard a hiss from in front of me: a painful, burning gasp.

"And sometimes," he continued from behind, "light is all that saves us. Thus, let there be more." He opened another window – two shafts of luminance, distinct in their crossing. Yet another shutter cast aside made it three strips, and a fourth provided so much light, the definition of the original intersection was lost. "And more, until—"

"Until the Light is just as blinding and confusing as the Darkness," a third voice, dry and desolate, concluded from my right. It was true – so much light, so quickly: I couldn't see any better than before.

"Can we find a balance then?" the smug instigator asked just before closing a few of the windows. My vision faced the challenge of the change, and I finally saw the interior of this infamous establishment. Furniture, like tables and chairs, even a lounge or two, cluttered around the edges of the room. It didn't look all that different to any other bar or tavern.

Near the far wall, ahead and to the right, was a desk, with someone in brown seated behind it, hooded head bent in scrutiny at whatever might be upon that ornate counter.

"Nightsong!" I squealed, crawling towards the desk before I could stand, and then hobbling once on my feet. "Listen to the Nightsong!"

The room went quiet. I didn't dare turn around, couldn't look away from the intent man at his desk. He didn't look back.

"Please, please. *Listen to the Nightsong!* Don't make me disappear, I don't want to die!"

But no matter how many times you admit that, no matter how much you believe it, it will still happen. All you can hope is that 'now' won't be 'when'.

"So she's sent us another one," he said, setting down his brush. The selective light revealed the hooded man as surprisingly young, calm and reserved. He kept his back hunched over the desk, as though concealing his height. He blew on his writing (if that's what it was) and then, perhaps displeased by what he saw, leant closer to the work. "Young, too. Ignore the others in here. They're just bored. Especially Chang there, with his little darkness and light riddling."

"Hssss. Little." Then 'Chang' eased past me. Tall, lithe, smooth. His hair tumbled past his shoulders like dark water rushing over a broad, snow-covered cliff. The coarse white attire was almost priestly in its simplicity; lack of armour must have permitted much movement. I saw no weapons, but this didn't mean he wasn't dangerous. If anything, he seemed all the more formidable for it. "Such matters as dark and light are never little. So says Chang Tong-Kut, The Knife! How ya goin', kid?"

He looked down at me without stopping on his way towards the desk. His features, while bearing something in common with Chūnkojin, were too angular, too pronounced, and his ears jutted out from the side of his head like handles. I coughed a small laugh – this was a Half who had it even worse than me. "Been better, thanks."

"Hs-s-s-s-s! He hides his fear with wit!" Chang turned a graceful pirouette on the spot then continued towards the desk. "Who's on the menu tonight, hm?"

Who? No! He said 'what', he said 'WHAT' didn't he? Don't ask, last time you heard wrong, Shai-Yeh made you suffer, just accept it and listen and don't cry, laugh, yes, LAUGH!

"I say we carve the boy up," said the woman who 'grabbed' me before – her voice was still incisive, still measured. She didn't *speak* words, this sinuous and as yet unseen serpent – she administered them. "His heart is still fresh and strong." I caught a trace of shadowed movement in my periphery – but couldn't hold onto it.

"She's joking," I stammered. "Isn't she, Chang-dailoh?" To someone who has little respect for authority and higher-ups, 'Big Brother' is about as reverent as it gets.

"No, Char Ah-Ran, she isn't." Chang didn't look up from whatever the man had been writing. Was my name written there? *Was I on the menu?* "Is this right? I thought we'd already taken care of it." He stabbed whatever was on the desk with a slender but forceful forefinger.

"So did I." The brown-hooded man looked up at him. "But there it is."

"Hsssssss!" But Chang smiled, first at the scribe, then at me. When he turned my way, the friendly grin turned feral. It was still better than what I imagined the woman to look like. "But you're right, Thorn. He is a young one. So, kid, which will it be?"

"Eh?" Okay, she wasn't kidding, but would Chang really let her eat my heart? I didn't want to believe it. He seemed nice enough, for a Blood Peddler. "Which what?"

"Great. He doesn't know. She's getting sloppy, sending us children like this!" Now Chang-dailoh didn't seem so friendly. "Do you know where you are?"

"A Blood Peddlers' House?" Get it wrong and he'll never see you as anything but a child, Char!

"Not 'A', kid. *The* Blood Peddlers' House, Malevolent Hand Chapterhouse, to be accurate. Do you know why we are called that?"

"No."

"He doesn't know," the woman shrieked from where I could not see. "Just a stupid little boy, no one will miss him!" She lifted me off the floor again, and this time, I knew it wasn't with her hand. I yelped in surprise as something sharp and cold pressed against my exposed throat.

"The last time you ate an initiate," Chang murmured, making no obvious move to save me, "you were Bound for a month. Do you remember how bad that was, Rose? I do, because I had to look after you, and it's not happening again. Put. Him. Down."

"Just a brat, just food, just like the rest of you." I'm not sure what I felt first: that tip penetrate the thin skin of my neck, the pain or the trickle of blood crawling towards my chest.

"Pathetic Rose. You're supposed to be better than this, than all of us." Chang did move then. At least, I assumed he moved, because when I blinked, he wasn't at the desk anymore.

Was that a creaking sound behind me? Like a shutter being opened, oh so slowly.

Then the room exploded into light. Everything was aflame, touched and consumed by cool, merciless fire. I saw only one thing in this glaring world, one taint, but I saw all of it. Rose: her pallid hand shrinking away, detached from the rest of her body even though she had two others, and her body, her twisting, awful body, clad in shreds of black rags, ribs poking from beneath taut flesh like fingers pressing against a funeral shroud; and her mouth – oh her wide mouth with its rows upon rows of glistening teeth!

"Ugly critter, ain't she?" Chang commented even as Rose scrambled against a wall, huddling and howling. "Behold, God's Chosen in all her glory. Bye-bye, Rose."

Something breezed past me and cut off Rose's rising wails with a very heavy thud.

"Show's over!" Right as I was able to see just what had happened to Rose, the dazzling radiance fled. Chang closed the windows again, but not all of them. Never all of them.

Rose was gone.

"See? Always nice to have a balance." He stalked by me once more.

Chang had called her 'God's chosen'. And that meant—

"Rose was a Night's Own, wasn't she? A Noble?" This didn't fit any of the stories. Everyone knew that the Nobles were, well, *noble*. Even Lord Ayakawa answered to them, they who commanded the Holy Night and conveyed God's will. They who travelled in great parades and flew upon majestic wings of righteous glory; They who accepted the truly faithful into their embrace once more, led us to Heaven!

All but one, the bastard who made me, who took my mother and brought from her demise whatever I am. I can imagine he was like Rose. Was he noble? Are all Night's Own noble? Am I?

"Noble?" Chang pulled his knife from the wall and looked over his shoulder at me. "That monster is noble as dirt. In fact, not even that. And not 'was'. She *is* Of The Night, whether she likes it or not. Would take a lot more than a knife in the chest to end her. And think, Char Ah-Ran: you and I, we're half that. Makes ya real thankful we at least have half a chance at decency, don't it?" Chang curled one corner of his lips upwards. I wasn't sure which half he meant.

"There are bad people," the cowled scribe, Thorn, noted with soft insistence, "and there are good people. So too are the Chosen of God. Just because God chose them doesn't mean they all choose God."

I didn't even have to duck for that to go over my head.

"So yeah, kid," Chang continued beyond the hushed cryptic comment from the clerk, "this is the Malevolent Hand. So called because the Haven not far from here—"

"The Benevolent Hand!" I interrupted, excited to know where he was going and that I could help. Then I realised how the names linked. "You mean Havens and the Peddlers. Oh. Wow."

It made sense. Havens, funded by the Empire, sheltered the good people, and the Blood Peddlers took evil people away, people like Revolutionaries and anyone who didn't believe in God and the Night and the Tsukamoto and all that other stuff I didn't learn at school. At least, that's how the stories went.

"Chang-dailoh, what do you do?"

"Me personally? Or the Peddlers? Both, I'm figuring you want to know. It's not like her to send so ignorant a kid, but you're here now. Not like we can let you leave, is it?"

"I wouldn't tell anyone!"

"You wouldn't have to. I'm sure you've heard of Maliscients. We have them too, of course. Anyway, you're stuck here, so you might as well learn what's going on."

"You have work to do, Knife," the official young man chided. Chang had dealt with a *Noble* and yet he took orders from a simpering clerk? I waited for my new hero to grab this Thorn person by the collar and hurl him across the room.

"Good point." Or not. The towering Chang stepped aside, gesturing that I should approach the desk. "Thorn will take care of you for now. I'll see you 'round, kid. Maybe you'll be lucky and get me for a mentor?"

"Doubt that," Thorn said. "She has plans for him."

She who? *Shai-Yeh?* A mere servant girl? She said these were her friends. Did that include *Rose?*

"We'll see. Is that Menu final?"

"Yes."

"Even the little girl?"

"Yes."

"All right."

Chang headed for the door, ruffling my hair as he passed. I smiled at him, at his funny ears. "We're brothers, Char Ah-Ran. You and me, same blood. Not like those snakes. We can choose when we bite, when we hiss. Hsssssss!"

I laughed and he laughed. If only it were true, and that we were brothers.

He left and I felt alone, even though I knew the room might have contained others like him, or like Rose.

The desk. Safety waited there, didn't it?

"What happens now, Thorn-sinsan?" 'Thorn' was clearly not his name, but it seemed right to be as polite as possible. Standing in front of the desk, I leaned over to peek at 'the Menu' and saw a gash of deep red before he covered the sheet of paper and sat up straight. Very up, very straight. Easily as tall as Chang.

"Thorn, Char Ah-Ran. That is my name as far as you are concerned. No 'mister', no 'sir'. Is that understood?"

Dailoh submitted to this one; I would do the same.

"Yes, I understand, Thorn. And you can call me Char." Well, not *total* submission.

"I can. I even may. Now pay attention. As Chang has already revealed in his uncouth way, this is a Blood Peddler House. You have seen our mark before, mainly because current law demands that we display it. Apparently this is so that people do not fear us *quite* so much.

"On the surface, we take the sick, the mentally incompetent and the dissident. We cleanse, as it were, the tainted. We *peddle* bad blood for good, even if 'good' and 'bad' are not always easy to tell apart. Having seen what you have now seen, I am sure you know that we go a bit deeper than that.

"Sometimes, a Night's Own loses the way, falls out of the Night's favour and goes rogue: becomes a Wild Rose. There are several illnesses that seem to afflict their kind, not the least of which we call 'doubt'. Such creatures are no longer fit to serve as God's spirits, and so they are also removed, plucked from the world like—"

"Like a thorn?" I asked, and then winced that I'd interrupted him.

"Yes." His slight smile eased my fear, a little. "So when Chang asked you, 'which will it be?' he meant, do you want to hunt people or rogue Night's Own and Halves? I present that question to you now. Think about it."

Of course, I didn't.

"This doesn't make sense! You say you got the power to fight *Nobles?* No way, no God-DAMN way at all!"

Thorn remained annoyingly tranquil. "I am sure she warned you about blasphemy. Look, Char Ah-Ran, you're Half. This means you have unnatural aptitude with a Talent, you're highly intelligent and probably pick up physical activities quicker than most. Good, you're not smiling. You know these are not compliments. All this means is that you're a threat. What starts as a feeling of superiority soon turns into detachment, and then it's only a matter of time before you think you're allowed to do whatever you want. If you don't accept our help now, we will be hunting you down. Next year, or the year after. Maybe in five years, Char Ah-Ran, if you're lucky. Why do you think Halves are so rare out there, in Kaifeng?"

"Because. Because being Half isn't normal, my mother had to die giving birth to me, and now I see the cause of her death every time I see my reflection." That's the way it is. That's why Halves are so rare, no matter what Thorn said. You know. *Everyone* knows, but I more than *know* it: I live it. A mortal womb is poor soil for a holy seed, but her body still can't help but give the twisted roots everything it can. And it's never enough. "You just don't understand, Thorn."

"Perhaps I don't." Thorn kept his eyes on me even as he pulled back the folds of his hood, exposed one ear. I nodded at what I saw; he replaced the fabric. Perhaps he did understand. "You will learn how it works. We will teach you the ways of the Night's Own, and you will understand our masters, our prey. Our parents, who have become lost."

"Are all Blood Peddlers Half?"

"Not even many. People don't work well with Halves and we don't work well with people. We generally don't even work well together either. You are a loner, I wager. But you cannot afford to be alone. That is why she brought you to us."

"You're talking about Fa Shai-Yeh."

"Yes, that is one of her names. But that is her story to tell. For now, you simply need to choose."

"Hunt people, or hunt Nobles and Halves."

"Yes." He clasped his hands and looked down at his desk. "We could give you a little time to consider."

"I want to talk to Chang-dailoh. Which is he?"

"He's both these days, but he started out as a Prick."

I laughed. To my surprise, Thorn chuckled as well.

"Do you see it yet, Char Ah-Ran? Thorn, Rose, Prick."

I stopped laughing.

"I don't think so, Thorn."

"Oh, that's right." He was disappointed – I could tell, because he made some effort not to sound it. "Our organisation is not limited to Chūnko. In fact, the first Peddlers were from the West, and in their language, 'Peddle' sounds just like 'Petal'. We tend God's Garden. There are chapterhouses all over Kaef're, coupled with Havens, like twins."

"Like a mother and father?" I asked, surprising myself.

"Yes, I suppose that is one way of viewing our duality. References to flowers, to plants, are our little code. Knowing this, you will never see things the same. It may save your life someday."

"So that creature. The Noble, her name wasn't Rose?"

"Of course not. Her name is impossible for normal people to pronounce. That was her label once she came here. Those we capture for return to the Court are Wild Roses, or just Roses. She was behaving well until you showed up, but you were not to know."

"And Pricks?"

"What happens when you touch a Thorn? But there's another meaning. When you are a Prick, that's exactly what you feel like, because your task is to take ordinary people from their ordinary lives and give them to the Night. Not all righteous jobs feel very righteous at the time."

Then, while the subject was on flowers, I thought of someone else but swallowed that question, because I didn't want to know the answer.

"But if Chang-dailoh has been both, he can tell me about both."

"He can, but he is just one man. You should seek other opinions. There is, you see, a third choice."

"There is?" I tried not to sound hopeful, but neither option so far seemed fitting for a Rat, even a 'gifted' one.

"Absolutely. You can die."

I laughed again. This time, Thorn did not.

"I expect you'll change your mind about that as time goes by. Welcome to your new world, Half. It all begins here."

Here. The room – empty but for him and me now. No sign of the Rose. Doors that lead to God-knew-where.

"Char Ah-Ran," Thorn said, regaining my attention. "Remember this: that third choice isn't going to be there forever, even if you are."

I nodded and returned to examining the Peddlers' main hall. I began to see, to imagine the room full of other Halves, hunters and shadows and rebels, all doing God's good work, trying to understand Her Greater Design and to pretend that individual people didn't exist, that the collective was all that mattered, that a child need not know that his now-absent father had thought the wrong thing, or that a man who had lost his wife because she was barren should seek more fertile soil for his seed. I tried to *feel* what it would be like to end one life just so that another could thrive and it was a proper, horrifying enlightenment. Such power, such terrible, luscious power.

And I realised that I was no longer thinking like a twelve year old, like a simple thug.

"She doesn't bring 'simple thugs' here, Char. Although you probably started out as one."

A Half Maliscient?

"Don't look so surprised. It is just what I am, but that is *my* story to tell, and you're not ready. What do you want, right now?"

And I thought about that too. Without a home, I didn't have *anywhere* to go, no one to run to, no one to hold me and reassure me. This is my world, then and now, and within it, I had to make a choice. But since I didn't have a clue what I could choose, I simply said the first thing that came to my mind.

"I want to rest."

"The door behind me leads to the dormitory. Most of us have homes of our own, but as you can appreciate, our work demands all hours. Take any available bed."

"Thank you, Thorn."

"You are welcome, Char. And please, stop thinking about windows. There are plenty, but none are for you."

I cracked a grin, but it was a rueful, nervous little arc.

"Not yet, they're not."

"Granted." He resumed his writing, a gentle but firm dismissal.

Just before I left, I had to ask:

"Thorn, if those who take people are called Pricks, what do you call the ones who hunt rogue Night's Own and Halves?"

"Anything they want to be called, Char. Chang the Knife, Orchid Witherheart, One-slash Butterfly. They all choose names like that. They *earn* such names."

"Okay, but what do *you* call them? What do you call Peddlers who hunt Those Who Hunt?"

Thorn didn't look up from his work.

"I call them insane."

Chapter 13: *Made For Each Other*

I expected a maze, but the Peddlers worked in straight lines.

The dormitory was comfortably boring. Beds lined the two side walls, uniform but not crammed. They were all clean and made. There was nothing else on the wooden floor. The walls were unadorned: people didn't need to post sticky reminders of "God's Glory!" here – there was a dedication beyond sycophancy and, although I didn't even know that word, its absence appealed to me.

My hand still hurt, my legs were bruised from being dropped by the Rose not once but twice and my head swelled with Thorn's words, or maybe Lily's healing. I flopped onto the nearest bed, face-first. The room's scent wasn't unlike the backroom of the Haven; when I closed my eyes, I could have sworn I heard Lily's gentle laugh. But she was not here. I smiled despite (or because of) my longing for her motherly ministration. Not here. Never here.

But I am here. Maybe I'll never see the world the same, as Thorn said, but does that mean the world itself has changed? Lily, and the Goddess of Swords, whose name I need to learn, whom I must rescue, for whom I am not strong enough. They haven't changed. I have changed. A bit, only a bit. Enough, though—

Enough.

I was just wondering how long it would take me to fall asleep when I fell asleep, obeying a lullaby too pure for any of my words.

My voice: "Not again. Let me sleep. I'm asleep, so let me sleep."

Not my voice: You're not real.

Are you?

I knew this voice even though I'd never heard it before. It was Lily with fangs, or Shai-Yeh in sweet adoration; all true things reversed and made true through a new logic, a fresh reasoning. In the lukewarm darkness, it all made sense.

She said: remember me; I need you, just as you need me.

"I remember you. I need you. You need me."

She said: I was made for you.

"Goddesses are not made, are they?"

She said: I am not a Goddess. There is only one God. She is love and hate, compassion and wrath. She is the Saviour and the Sword. I am just the Sword.

"And me? What am I?"

She said: The one for whom I was made. The Saviour? Perhaps.

"Not me. You belong in a hero's hand! That is why they brought you to Kaifeng, why they take you from city to city!"

She said: Yes.

"And, in other cities, they hold great fighting tournaments for you, and people bleed for the chance to touch you, hold you, own you, to use you. In Kaifeng, Lord Ayakawa wanted you for himself, and that's why he guarded you so heavily."

She said: Yes.

"But these people don't know that you use them, that the sword is made for a fist, that the fist is empty without you, and so no one wins, ever."

She said: Yes.

"Whoever gets you will lose. That is what it's really about, isn't it? People scramble to own you, but they don't realise to win is to lose. How do I know all this?"

She said: I taught you.

"Why? Am I special? Is that what this is? Just a fantasy! It's every boy's dream to be special, and I'm not—I'm just another boy."

She said: Yes. You are special.

"NO. When they write prophecies, they mean humble people, people who take the sword because there is no choice. I have caused pain and I enjoy causing pain. Give me the sword and I will cause more pain. I would cut the world in half, just so that it could understand how I feel."

She said: That is the fantasy.

"What? If not the little street-Rat-turned-hero, WHAT is the fantasy?!"

She said: That heroes do not enjoy their work. That when they draw their sword and plunge it into their enemy's heart, they do not feel ecstasy. I have been held by heroes in *my* dreams, and they all submit to the joy of ending another's life.

"That's not a hero. That's a murderer! And yet my heroes are murderers. Each kill Chang makes, each story he tells: I love it. I want to be him. I want to be a murderer?"

She said: Now you understand. You are special.

"Why? Everyone has these desires, deep down. Why not choose someone who will resist? Resistance is elastic – the more you pull away, the greater the force produced when you reach your limit, the more intense the attraction—How do I know that?"

She said: I taught you.

"When? When did you teach me, Goddess of Swords?"

She said: Now.

"Time doesn't work like that! 'Now' is a constant, and as soon as we acknowledge it, it is the past, so you cannot have taught me in the present, or in the future. So when did you teach me and how in Hell Above did I know that?"

She said: I taught you.

"Stop that! Your repetition is annoying enough to invoke the wrath of Xenides-Ra Kas'Daen himself Oh God WHO?"

She said: Your enemy. Tell me about him.

"Xenides-Ra Kas'Daen is the Clanlord of Kas'Daen. His age is not known but estimated at over two hundred years. Also known as The Fox, Xenides was one of the Three Beasts, great Clanlords who convened to plan the downfall of—" I stopped.

She said: Don't you know? Tell me.

"No. I know, I know, but I can't remember! Stop making me know things I can't handle this. Choose another. I beg you."

She said: You are tired.

"Of course I am! You've been doing this to me forever, and I sleep more than ever and I don't actually sleep, I learn things, things I never knew and forget anyway and I want to just go to—"

She said: Sleep.

There might have been dreams, but if so, I didn't remember anything about them.

I was exhausted, needed more sleep, but the more I slept, the more tired I was. Lying on my belly, I listened for a while, but not to any voice. There was noise, unobtrusive possible-speech, dampened by walls and distance. People in the entrance room; it was safe to open my eyes. Hadn't it been before?

It took a few attempts. Open, close. Open, close. Then, very carefully, like peeling an old poster from a wall, open once more. Blink, blink. Focus.

I stared at the bed next to me. It was unmade – as was the bed beyond it and all the others as well. That wasn't normal. Someone taught me how to make my bed. Blossom or Orchid. Or did Blossom teach me about laundry and Orchid about throwing weapons? No, Orchid had given me a wooden sword for practice, shaped specifically to my needs according to Thorn. Thorn taught me about the Roses, and, no, wait—

Did someone else teach me?

She taught me now.

The voices beyond the wall gained volume but not the clarity of words. Messy beds in here and raised voices in out there. Definitely not normal.

The usual reflex actions kicked in: get up, put on grey slippers and grey trainee robe, grab practice sword, take a few deep breaths and enter the world once more.

I yawned all the way.

Thorn was not behind his desk. A couple of the windows were open; it might have been mid-morning. There were quite a few people in the room, some of whom I recognised by name, most of whom were just other Peddlers I'd seen around.

They were busy discussing or arguing something, but that stopped when I closed the door a little too loudly. All stared at me as if I were a stranger, and that was fine, because I didn't think I knew them either. Not even the flushed young lady with the single blonde braid draped over her shoulder.

"Should I get dressed and then come back?" I asked with a grin.

No one smiled back. Someone had to give more, and it wouldn't be them.

"Is it my birthday already? I knew I was popular but this is too much! Throwing a surprise party for my birthday is just—"

"Not your birthday," Chang growled from near the entrance, his expression uncharacteristically stony. He didn't seem so tall anymore. "Your death-day, maybe, little brother of my blood. If this—" he paused, searching for an appropriate description for Fa Shai-Yeh, and settled on a very venomous: "—woman isn't full of crap."

Shai-Yeh rounded upon the Knife and glared up at him. I'd never seen her so livid.

"There are rules," Thorn rumbled, stepping from the crowd. "You both know this. A challenge has been issued by a rival faction and we must respond."

"Rival faction? The Shadows are not *our* rivals!" Chang said, and several of the others nodded and muttered assent. Orchid, standing to his left, pulled her lips back, revealing her pronounced canine teeth. She was the only female Half of Malevolent Hand, barely two years my senior.

"Since when do we answer to gangs?" she asked.

"You knew this was coming." Thorn remained typically calm. "It's why she brought the boy here."

"Brought me here?" A weak hand against rebellious mouth couldn't stifle the yawning. I came, when? Three weeks ago? A month? Two months? Six months? Quite a while, maybe, because I'd learned a lot during my stay in the chapterhouse. Fa Shai-Yeh had sent occasional word that she was still investigating the whereabouts of the sword, but I didn't care. It was just a sword. The Guards would find it sooner or later and punish whoever stole it and that was that. "Brought me here to hide me from the Guards, didn't you, Shai-Yeh?"

"Well, no. Actually, I did not, Char." Shai-Yeh's shoulders, tense from her possible conflict with Chang, fell with her sigh. She did not face me. "I brought you here to train you."

"I see." And I didn't. The game of actually becoming a Peddler wore off a week into my concealment, but they still treated me like one of them. Thorn's offer remained, and I continued to ask for more time. He gave it, and hadn't once mentioned the third option since that first day. "Then what's going on?"

"We found out who has the sword."

What sword?

"Great! Tell the Guards and fix things up. It doesn't have to do with me anymore. I'm going back to bed."

"The Guards already know who has it, Char," Shai-Yeh said as I turned to fumble with the door.

"And?"

"Look, Char," Chang said, "Hua-Shi is involved!"

Who? The name was familiar, but much in the same way as 'Ayakawa' was familiar. There was no connection between my life and that name, so I didn't recognise it in context.

"Chang. All of you, all of us: out." Thorn might have opened the main door, but he didn't leave any doors open with that statement.

"Char, sit down. Sit with me," Shai-Yeh said after I heard the entrance door close behind me. But I continued to fiddle with the handle, thinking not of swords, duels or guards but of sleep, sleep and sleep. When, after a little while, she added, "You cannot go back to that," I gave in, spine against unyielding wood.

"Don't really want to anyway," I admitted. "I wake up tired. Maybe I'm dreaming and don't remember. Doesn't matter. What's going on, Shai-Yeh?"

"Hua-Shi. Tell me about him."

Again? What? Not again! Not a hero, not a sword, just—

"Heard of him through rumours when I was in the Nest. He's the leader of the Bloody Shadows gang. Like me, he's a Half. Like me, he doesn't have a known family name. Hua-Shi is a prodigy, the master of his own fighting style and its signature attack, *Kuraiden-geki*, an airborne spinning kick which can break a man's neck. Wow, I didn't know I knew all this."

"You know more than you know. Besides, this is common knowledge."

She was lying, but how else could I know it?

"S'pose so. So he has the sword. The Guards going to get it back then?"

"Char, the Guards are not after the sword."

"Have they forgotten it?"

"How old are you, Char?"

"Twelve..?" Why did I ask that? Of course I was twelve! At least, I was twelve last I checked. When was that?

"You are almost seventeen."

"Don't be stupid. Seventeen is old! I'm the same size as before. I don't even have any pubes yet!"

"Halves do not get pubes, Char," Shai-Yeh replied with a small laugh. "And you are taller. You just have not noticed. Does your body really have to change for you to feel older, Char? It can be arranged, but you really do look like a seventeen year old. Well, almost seventeen. Sit with me."

"I don't want to be a child forever."

"What you want is not really important at this point. Unless you remember what you really want."

"The sword. Her. She speaks to me in my dreams."

I expected Shai-Yeh to mock me for the admission.

"You cannot forget her, Char. The Guards were not after the sword. They never were. They were not even guarding her. To anyone else, she resembles little more than a crass iron rod. Maybe that is what she really is."

"No! I saw her, and she was perfect, and there were Guards all around her, guarding her, and—" Remember, Char. Remember! "—And they hold big tournaments in other cities for her, because only a true hero should wield her, should wield the Goddess of Swords, and that hero loves to kill!"

Shai-Yeh said nothing in response. I nearly sobbed and didn't know why.

"I don't know what I'm saying." *But I believe it.* "I don't know how I know it." *But I do.* "And I wish I didn't."

"You see how important she has become to you, Char? The only thing you love and may ever love, and now she has a voice. She speaks to tell you a history, her story. Will you not share with me the tale of that sword?"

"You always have the answers, Shai-Yeh. Why don't *you* tell me about this 'crass iron' sword? Why don't you teach me?"

Now she hesitated, as though I'd somehow defied that which could not be defied, or should not be defied.

"That is what everyone sees," Shai-Yeh said after that unspoken stutter. "But everywhere I went with it, or it with me, I would notice certain people looking at it, like they were possessed or something. Of all the weapons in the parade, or in the armoury, they reacted to your 'Goddess of Swords' the most. None of them, however, actually went for her as you did. There has never been a tournament for 'her', nor have great heroes wielded that sword. The posting of the Guards during the entrance procession was to guard something else."

"Not true! What is worth more than her?"

"According to Lord Ayakawa and just about everyone else? Anything. But you were tenacious! I was cleaning, as you know, when I heard you and Jaku arguing. When I realised you were after that sword, and having noted how you used the fear of Guards against your friend, I decided to do the same. And the sword *was* stolen the very same night you came back to me. Five years ago, Char, you ran from an imaginary enemy after trying to steal something you never had any chance of touching."

"This is not true."

So why was I unable to maintain eye-contact with her?

"Sure it is. Think it through. It makes sense."

"I don't want to 'think it through'! It's nonsense. You're just saying this to—"

"Hm?"

"To toy with me. It's all you've ever done, right from the start!"

"Going to take another swing at me, Char?"

"No. But I still don't believe you. That sword is special. She is special."

I am special. She taught me.

"I never said otherwise. Now the sword is all the more special because someone is using it to lure you out."

"Hua-Shi?"

"Bah, he does not even know about you. He is just a thug. The one manipulating him arranged for the theft of the sword, the sword that has no value to anyone but you. Whoever had it stolen wanted to get to you."

"Wong Chu-Deng? Is he involved?"

"He is a major player, and Terasawa Jaku, and Wu Jen-Wah. They all joined the Bloody Shadows after Guan-Pi died."

That found bone before blood. "What? Dead?"

"I refuse to say any more until you sit with me, Char."

"Can't you just tell me what happened? I'm so tired of your games."

That wasn't the right thing to say.

"Better tired than dead. Better a game than nothing at all. I am sorry but this is the way it is, Char." Irony – the only time Shai-Yeh apologised was when she truly didn't mean it. "I realise it's all happening at once, but let me explain. At least look at me, if you will not sit with me."

"You look the same, Shai-Yeh, and I look the same. I arrived here about two, maybe three weeks ago. I've been planning on going to see Guan-Pi and the Rats but I've been busy. And I am happy here, because I don't have to be a bully to survive. I know I don't really belong here, and that's okay. I'm only twelve years old. I have the rest of my long life to find my place in the world."

There: all my honesty, laid out for her to accept.

Fa Shai-Yeh laughed.

"Char, I am going to prove something to you. You *have* been here for almost five years, training and developing yourself for the sole purpose of claiming that sword. I told you three years ago that the sword was worthless and you refused to believe me. You spoke of wild dreams, of how the sword talked to you. Your obsession grew dangerous. Only the craziest Peddlers still work with you, which is why Chang and Orchid are your only friends left. And now that we have found the object of your manic desire, the sword of your dreams, you do not remember. Typical."

"You're lying, Shai-Yeh. Guan-Pi isn't dead, and Wong Chu-Deng didn't join the Bloody Shadows. Jen-Wah's just a little girl and Jaku's a snot-faced brat from a rich family, do you hear me? I was never like them. I will do good things here, if not as a Peddler then in some other way. I will not be a hero. I will not take her, or any other sword. No matter how she tempts me."

"Very well. I can see this is going to take time – of which we have so little. One step at a time, then. Chang!" Shai-Yeh clicked her fingers and I shied away. What would happen this time?

The door opened. It was bright out there; I blinked a few times, but it couldn't stop the world from becoming nothing but illumination.

Then a familiar shadow blocked the light.

"You called, whore of God?"

"Oh but I do so love it when you are a gentleman, Chang. Close the door."

"This is all crap, right, Dailoh?" I asked, searching his frustrated, restrained composure. I knew, then, that something was up, because it wasn't like Chang to get so vexed.

"I haven't been listening, little brother. But if you're referring to Hua-Shi's challenge, then that ain't crap. Still, I wouldn't trust a single word she says." Chang impaled Shai-Yeh with his barbed glare.

"Ask him some questions, Char. Would you like me to leave?"

"No," I growled. "If you're here, you're not out there spreading more lies and causing trouble. You stay, and stay quiet."

She just smiled again, drew her knees towards her chest upon the bench and watched the two of us.

"Dailoh, how old am I?"

Don't lie, don't lie, tell the truth, I know the truth and she's lying, so just say my age and make me feel better, please, I am only a kid, only—

"Sixteen, but you like to say you're 'almost seventeen', y'know, and we—"

"No! I am twelve! I turned twelve a few weeks ago! On my birthday, the Kasuden envoys came to Kaifeng and I watched the march, the procession, and I saw a sword, and I tried to steal it."

"This is true," Chang agreed, now leaning on the front door. "But that was a long time ago."

"I'm twelve, just a kid, you're still taller than me and I haven't changed a bit!"

"Yeah, but we've talked about this lots of times, Char. We Halves grow at a different rate. Some of us grow normal-like, and some, like you, hardly seem to grow much at all. But you have changed, little bro. You have grown."

"How? I came here not long ago, fell asleep, and now I'm awake. I couldn't have slept for long. I'm still really tired."

"If I trained as hard as you, I'd be tired too. And there are those dreams you keep talking about. I think they've driven you mad, but with skill like yours, that hardly matters."

Was that awe in Chang's voice?

"None of that happened, because I can't remember it!"

"I can't remember lots of stuff, Char, and it still happened. Are you telling me you really don't remember a thing? What in Hell have you done to him, Priestess?"

Shai-Yeh just met his gaze, sullen and almost bored. Then she shrugged and returned her attention to the floor.

"Priestess?" I couldn't keep up. "Now what? She's just a serving girl in the palace!" But if she were a Priestess, then things would make sense.

"I don't know what games she might play, Char, but this is Fa Shai-Yeh of The Liquid Night."

She said: The Liquid Night. Tell me about them.

"The Sisters of the Liquid Night is a matriarchal, monastic society dedicated to enforcing God's Will and eradicating Her enemies. Through visions and prophecies, the Sisters supply the Blood Peddlers with the Menu. When the Blood Peddlers complete a Menu, a Sister conveys the Order to the appropriate Night's Own clan keeps. This occurs once a month, while the moon hides. There are several tiers within the Liquid Night. The highest tier is occupied by—"

She said: Enough.

"But I know so much more, let me tell you, I want to—"

She said: I know you know. I taught you now.

"Did I know that?" I asked.

"Yes, Char, you knew that. You told us, after you'd made your choice, that you and she met in the Palace, on your twelfth birthday. When you tried to seduce her, she subdued you and brought you to us. She saw the potential in you even then, and by Eph, was she ever right." There was that unwarranted admiration again.

"Choice? What choice?"

Die. I can always die.

I think.

"THE Choice, Char." Chang scratched his head, scowling at Shai-Yeh once more. "If this is your doing, your timing couldn't have been worse. He's supposed to duel Hua-Shi, and you've somehow taken his memories? I don't get you, Priestess, I really don't."

"What did I choose?" *Don't ignore me, don't discuss this among yourselves, I'm right here!*

"My God. You really don't remember," Chang said, looking at me and then her again. "He really doesn't remember!"

"Duh," she said in what sounded like Kasuden-go, or maybe was just a grunt.

"What did I choose?"

"The sword, Char, you chose the sword. Char Ah-Ran became Char, Blackcloak the Scourge."

Perhaps in my panic, I'd simply not noticed, but when he pointed at the wooden weapon thrust through my sash, I saw that I was no longer wearing the grey of a trainee. Black. All black. Long ago, Fa Shai-Yeh would have called my attire 'sexy'. I wasn't sure how it made me feel, but most definitely not that.

"The thought of taking ordinary people sickened you," Chang continued, "so you choose the sword against those who fall from God's grace. But you use that thing because you say you haven't got your real sword yet. You use a damned wooden stick against Roses."

"Very well, I might add," Shai-Yeh murmured.

Both Chang and I barked at her,

"Shut up!"

And she did, but even in silence her arrogance seemed to sing high praise unto itself.

"Still, she's right, little bro. You're a natural. That sword, your Fire. Eph's Bleedi—shit, sorry Priestess." All this, and he still deferred to her? "What I mean is, I ain't no poet so I can't say what it's like." He shook his head. "Any wonder Hua-Shi wants to face you. Your reputation's reached even his ears. Maybe that's not such a good thing, *neh*?"

I wrenched the sword free, closed my eyes and tried to imagine what it would feel like to be a master of it, as Chang seemed to think I was. The weight would have felt perfect, I would have been able to judge the distances and I'd have known how to—

Hold the sword. One inch between the hands, with the dominant hand half an inch from the guard and the levering hand near the base of the hilt. We call it the levering hand because it does all the work, with the dominant serving as a pivot. The grip itself should be loose to permit movement and prevent jarring should impact occur. This also minimises sweat due to friction. The practice sword weighs exactly one stone, which is approximately sixty five percent the weight of a true sword of the same dimensions constructed of the appropriate materials. This means that, given we strike with the top third of the blade and that the bottom third is slightly lighter to permit momentum, the exact movement to sever a head at three paces would best be commenced from a *Ryusui-Gedan* stance, sweeping the edge upwards and to the right, keeping one's body loose until the very second before impact, at which point you should become like steel, like stone. Don't cut the flesh, don't even expect it, aim beyond it, and with all your breath, expel your ki with a cry of

"—Eph's holy arse," I whispered.

Now it was my turn to be struck by awe.

I was away from the door. The wooden sword was frozen in an offensive, post-slicing attitude. I stared at the stick — something or someone was keeping it steady, just above eye-level, but it couldn't have been me. It felt like I was shaking all over, yet I held the weapon. My throat was sore. Was that an echo of exquisite force I heard? Shai-Yeh's face was pale; she looked away as soon as I caught her staring at me.

"A clean decapitation," Chang nodded. " *From nowhere, from nothing: expend all energy and waste none'*: your words, little brother. See? Only you know that, and only you can do it with a wooden sword."

There were nicks and dents up and down the slightly curved path of the blunt edge. "I cut heads off with this thing?"

"You betcha. Something to do with your *Huo-chi*, or so you say. Thorn says it's the most amazing thing he's ever seen, and you know how inscrutable he is."

"Bullshit. It's just a piece of wood, and I'm just a kid. If I want to hurt people, I use my fists. I'm a bully, yes, but I'm not a killer." I tried to drop the stick but my fingers failed to unfurl. They were beyond my command now.

"Sometimes things have to die, little brother." Chang shrugged.

"I don't want to be responsible for that. Sure, we all say 'I'm gonna kill you!', but we never really mean it!" And I knew, then, that I would never say it again without the full intention of the act. "I don't enjoy this. Do I?"

"Skill like that? Who wouldn't enjoy it?" Chang frowned then. "Maybe you're the one playing games, Char. You obviously haven't forgotten what you're doing with a sword."

"Okay." I took a deep breath and thought about putting the sword away. My arms, hands, feet, my everything went to work, spinning and adjusting, bodyweight shifting, tension draining from fingers to knees to feet and then gone altogether.

"You even flick the blood from the blade before sheathing," Chang said. "And there wasn't any blood, not this time. It's all second nature now. And you, you sly little bastard, won't even tell us who's been teaching you."

"She has," I replied. The wooden sword was, of course, once more tucked into my belt. "She taught me now."

"Same crazy answer as always." He sighed, refolding his arms. "Any more questions, Char?"

Too many, but this much I believed: I was a killer with a killer's ability. I was becoming what she wanted.

"If I am sixteen years old, and I have skill with a sword, and I have made my choice, and I tried to seduce Shai-Yeh, why do I remember something else entirely?"

"Got me there, little bro. Between her and you, I'd say. Who knows what mind games these Liquid Night witches play? That I don't envy of you, Char. But there isn't much I wouldn't go through to be as good as you."

His praise was exhausting. Yesterday (give or take five years?), Chang had been my hero, and now he expected me to believe this? Only last week, he'd taught me the basics of throwing weapons, or was that Orchid? I'd been useless, too, dropping the knife and often missing even the big, easy targets.

"Am I really that good, Chang?" I asked.

"Yes."

"I don't believe you."

"Mistress Shai-Yeh, Sister of the Liquid Night, I request permission to bear arms in your presence." Chang bowed towards the girl. I'd never seen Chang bow to anyone. Then again, what I remembered might not have been real anyway. He was a stranger to me too.

"A duel?" Shai-Yeh asked.

"Nothing so impressive. I promise your prodigy will not be harmed."

Prodigy?!

"Oh, I know that. I just do not want to explain to Thorn how you died. Well, it is your call. Permission granted, Chang."

"Char!" He called, eyes cold with the resolve of a determined foe. "I'm going to throw a knife at you."

"Uh—"

And he did.

Crack! Something tore my arms up and around. There was the taste of a sudden breeze upon my dry lips. I felt like a puppet.

Behind me, there was a thud that reminded me of almost-darkness and being choked.

"See?" Chang grinned, but I didn't see. The wooden sword was out again, and I was the one who'd freed it. This time, I held the edge before myself, arms almost straight. The 'blade' angled away from the floor, hilt at waist height, the tip seeming to pierce the enemy's throat.

"*Jodan no kamae,*" I whispered, and then wondered what it meant.

"Char," the dark blur across the room from me said. "Little brother. It was just a test."

One of their tricks, imitating people you know, care for. Only amateurs fell for it. I was no amateur. This Rose would regret underestimating me.

I shuffled a step forward, careful to maintain balance, keep the poise. Give the enemy no opening. Prepare a thousand assaults. Decide to win. To kill.

"If he cannot beat you," Fa Shai-Yeh might have said, "Char has no chance against Hua-Shi. You have my permission to kill the boy."

Was it Chang after all? Shai-Yeh wouldn't ally with those who have fallen from Night's Favour, would she? I concentrated and managed to lower the wooden sword, but couldn't drop it, not yet. It was like forcing a feather against the wind.

"Dailoh?"

"*Omeh no aite wa oré da! Ik'ze!*"

Roses didn't talk like that. *We* barely used Mifūn-go, but when we did, it always meant business. 'I'm your opponent! Here I come!'

I'd just manage to understand what he'd said when it happened.

Chang Tong-Kut, the Knife, became a typhoon. Shards of metal winked within the vortex, and then flew towards me.

The world spun and curled; the room itself seemed to quake. The ceiling caroused by; the floor rose and fell. The walls melted into each other. It was all clouded by a strange, thick brown mist. My arms began to hurt. Someone or something was squeezing them, releasing them, dragging them here, and here, there, here again. Everywhere, almost at once.

Crack! Crack! Crack! Crack! Crack!

I heard that weird rhythm. Like someone was trying to clap in time with the beat.

Then the storm stilled and there was silence. I wanted to be sick but managed no more than a dizzy yawn.

"*Mo ichido!*" he bellowed, and it did happen *one more time*. A final platinum sliver slid through the air. I saw it and understood my arms were too tired to make that crashing magic again. Instead, I caught it with my right hand, fingers closing around the hilt just as the point tried to dive into my heart. It was a beautiful thing, that dagger, but I knew a better shape for it. I held it in front of my eyes and forgot about the wooden sword in my left hand. Parts of the knife grew hot, buckled and then shrank. Other parts expanded, flattened and became concave. Others still bent slightly. It should have burnt my hand but did not.

I could doubt what happened with the knives – this last movement, however, was clearly me. It was so absurd. It was a joke.

"Do you have any idea," Chang sounded winded, and I wondered why. Throwing a few knives hadn't been much effort for him in the past. Then again: what past? "ANY idea," he paused, caught his breath and finished with great exasperation, "how much those cost to make?"

I smiled at the new shape of the dagger and licked it.

"See?" I said, displaying the new creation with justified pride. "Not a weapon at all. Not if you look at it the right way. Not if it isn't shaped like one."

"We're talking a lot of money here, little brother, just for one of them—"

"Char, look around you," Shai-Yeh said – a cat lounging upon her self-assured attitude.

There were little daggers embedded in the floor, in the door behind me, even a few in the ceiling. I knew how they'd gotten there.

"—And that's not including the cost of sharpening them, and the poison—"

"Chang-dailoh," I tried to interrupt him gently. He fell quiet but still fumed. "Don't you think this is more useful than a knife?"

"Maybe, but it WAS a knife, Char. My knife, you see? And you ruined it. I'd kill you if it weren't clear I can't." He wanted to be angry but was just amazed. Again. "Can I have my *spoon* back? Please?"

I grinned again and tossed it his way.

"So I did that knife-deflecting stuff. Whiz, bam, bang super sword skills and—right. Whatever." There had to be another explanation for Chang missing me with his knives.

I was forgetting again. Already.

"Yes, a fine display of swordsmanship," Shai-Yeh agreed with my sarcasm; I always hated her for that. "But you are still not ready to face Hua-Shi."

"Back to that then, are we? Okay. You've messed with my head, turned three weeks into five years for God-knows-what-reason, I'm a killer with a stick and I still want that damned sword that is apparently worthless yet is in my dreams, Guan-Pi is dead, Jaku and Jen-Wah and the rest of them now work for this monster Hua-Shi and Wong Chu-Deng is manipulating him? Have I missed anything?"

"That is just the start of it," Shai-Yeh sniffed, unfolding her legs with a feline stretch.

I started to laugh, knowing deep down I was tumbling into panic.

"Right, fine. Let me see – I'm a Half Night's Own, which makes me extremely strong—"

"Yep."

"And, hm. And my parents weren't normal either, in fact, one of them was a Lord of his own Clan, and my mother was a—oh, fuck it, she was a Maliscient wasn't she? Hahahaha!"

"Mock it all while you can, Char." Shai-Yeh studied her nails. Chang joined in my laughter.

"And it's my great destiny to take my father's place, but maybe HE is the bad guy? Yes, he rebelled against the other Clans and they removed him but secretly, secretly I was taken away and raised in obscurity so that one day I could take my revenge. Oh, my whole life is like a fable!"

"Char, Hero of the realm!" Chang cheered. "Saviour of the people and spoon-maker extraordinaire!"

"And in case I die, or cannot or will not fulfil my destiny as Big Hero Man, I have a sister, and she escaped too, but she's not like you, Fa Shai-Yeh, she's brave and honest and loving and this isn't funny anymore."

I gagged something between a cough, a laugh and a sob.

"Chang?"

"Mistress?"

"Thank you for your help."

"Yes, Mistress."

Chang left without another word. He wouldn't be waiting outside this time.

"Char, sit with me."

I dropped the wooden sword and stumbled towards her.

"Next to me. Here." She patted the empty space beside her, but that wasn't necessary: it was as far as I could go, falling onto the cushioned bench, into foetal frailty. I wanted to cry but couldn't. So that was how Shai-Yeh felt when she brought me here? When she crushed my hand and didn't even seem to realise it.

"You made a joke about who you are because that is all you can handle, but she has told you these things, has she not?"

"Yes." Then I remembered, and I'd believed her. Why would a Goddess lie?

"But you do not believe it now."

"Of course not." God, but my voice was small.

"Why not?"

"It's a fantasy, Shai-Yeh, and it's not even mine. Not long ago, I wanted nothing more than to be the strongest Rat, to lord over them and be Guan-Pi's protégé, and to beat the crap out of Wong Chu-Deng, but now that I've had time to think about—"

Five years of training, days of physical conditioning and nights spent in dreamy tutelage, and those rare times when they asked me to come along, when there was a particularly feral Rose, and I would think 'this killed my mother', and almost believe it. Revelry found in weakening the Rose's flesh with my fire, of driving a stick through its previously invulnerable neck – such a glorious clandestine murder, a defiance of all the laws, and I wanted to do this to everyone! Everyone, with me first and foremost. I believe that is my existence. I believe

"—it all, I believe I want more from life, from my life. But I don't want the sword."

"Oh, my poor Char. Why not?" She edged closer, and I just didn't have the energy to draw away.

"Because it would control me. She taught me that." Now. "I can't kill my mother again, Shai-Yeh, and I can't bring her back. For all I know, she might have been a bad person too. All I do know is that I love killing and I hate that love."

"You do not love *her*, then?" Shai-Yeh's voice matched my own in its tremulous weakness.

"Of course I do. She was made for me." I wanted to believe that, I really did.

"No."

Shai-Yeh reached over and touched my arm lightly. I was about to shrug her off when—

She said: You were made for me.

Chapter 14: *Girl Of His Dreams*

I blinked and then widened my eyes, looking at Shai-Yeh for what felt like the first time: her hair shifted from black to blonde to silver over and again, shimmering through a rainbow of glory; her face glowed with exuberance and her expression was unadulterated desire.

My voice: "I'm asleep again, aren't I?"

Not my voice: Yes.

"Are you the Goddess of Swords or are you Shai-Yeh, Mistress of the Liquid Night?"

She said: Yes.

"You are the same?"

She said: Yes, and no.

"No? You are confusing me, Goddess."

She said: It is simple. But it will be even simpler once you accept me.

"I can't, Goddess. I won't. I love you but I cannot do that."

She said: You hurt me.

"Can't you find someone else to do this? I don't even know what I'm supposed to do anyway! Yesterday, I was a street thug thinking thug things, and now—"

She said: Now you are worthy of me. You have been made so.

"By whom? Who would bother to control me?"

She said: Me.

"If you could shape me that easily, why not someone else?"

She said: I chose you. I revealed myself to you on your twelfth birthday. You saw me and then you came to me.

"But you weren't there! Shai-Yeh said – no, you said so!"

She said: I lied. I am a weapon, my beloved. I cause pain. Thus I can lie. Did it hurt when I told you I was not there, waiting for you at the top of the wall?

"YES. I felt betrayed, by Guan-Pi, by Shai-Yeh, by my own desire. I wanted to desire nothing!"

She said: But you still desired me. Your love for me endured even your counter-desire. I am pleased.

"If you loved me, you would let me go, because I do not want to want you. You're going to destroy me, enslave me."

She said: That is what love is, Charan. It is domination and submission, it is an infinite prison. Love always goes both ways. I understand love; it is a sword, like me. I am love, Charan. Love me as I love you.

"Char Ah-Ran? Why do you call me that? No one calls me that anymore. I have a name, and that's not it."

She said: Charan is your real name.

"No. I know my name. I've known it all my life. Everyone calls me Char. I call myself Char. You can't change my name!"

She said: That is not your real name.

"Who are you to tell me what my name is?"

She said: The one for whom you were made. You are Charan Jaydemyr, Heir to Clan Jaydemyr. I have told you this before but this time, you will remember. You will destroy Hua-Shi for the same reason as you will destroy everything else: simply because he is in your way. That is your fate.

"Clans? Heir? Fate? Who cares? The one who was made for me would love me enough to let me be whoever the hell I want to be and I don't want to be 'Charan'! I am CHAR, do you hear me? Char of Kaifeng, trained as a killer, but I will find another way. I will live a different life."

She said: Have you forgotten that you are Char Ah-Ran, the thief? The bully? That your answer to everything is a fist? What is a sword but a more effective fist? And effectiveness means you do not have to use me anywhere near as often as you did your fists.

"I was that, yes, but I've changed. You want me to change but don't realise I already have. You would request, demand one change but not permit another? You confuse me once more, my Goddess."

She said: Stop calling me that. A Goddess cannot be loved, only appeased, worshipped, idolised. When you hold me, it must be with a lover's intensity, familiarity and passion. I have a true name, but I cannot tell you that name unless you love me.

"What do I care for true names? A name is just a label. How we act, how we speak and think: these define us, not some stupid arrangement of slashes and dots!"

She said: You are wrong. Now that you know your true name, you will become it.

"I will fight it, Goddess. With every breath, with every resistance to kill. I will fight it."

She said: You will fight against me? No. You still love me.

"Yes, damn all sacred things, yes. But that love comes only when I accept that I must fight you, that through fighting you, I will be a better person."

She said: You have matured well, Charan. I will tell you my name. Your father gave it to me, because he understood what lies ahead of you.

"My father? How could he have known me if he never met me? He abandoned my mother as soon as he found out she was pregnant."

She said: I asked you once before. How do you know this? If she died giving birth to you, how do you know?

"Guan-Pi told me, because he knew the midwife, who was a friend of my mother!"

She said: Guan-Pi was a greater thief than you, Charan. And thieves lie. Great thieves tell great lies.

"Then I don't know the truth! Who cares? The past is done, gone. It does not affect the present."

She said: You have that the wrong way around. The present cannot affect the past. What has happened has happened. The echoes remain, whether you acknowledge them or not. The truth? I will tell you if you accept me.

"Your name, Goddess. My father gave you a name and it had to do with me?"

She said: Yes. My name is Oni-Goroshi.

" 'Demon Slayer'? Seriously? Sounds like a child's toy, or a really strong drink."

She said: Do not underestimate your father's complexity. He gave me a Mifūn-go name but spoke a different language. In his tongue, which is yours as well, a Demon can also be something troubling your conscience, a personal trial or moral battle. That doubt haunting the corner of your conviction like a mote of dust in a clear eye. My name is all too appropriate with that understanding.

"My native language is not Mifūn-go? Not Chūnko-go? What is it, then?"

She said: Jaydemyrian. Not unlike Kas'Daenne, since they were bordering realms.

"Kas'Daenne?"

She said: you knew it as Kasuden-go.

"Knew? Can you prove to me that this…Jaydemyrian is my native tongue?"

She said: We are speaking it now, and when you awaken, it will be our secret tongue. No one speaks Jaydemyrian anymore.

"Why not?"

She said: A great clan, Jaydemyr, defied the other clans many years ago. The other major clans formed an Overclan and eradicated Jaydemyr when you were eleven years old. And your joking about your heritage before was not funny – it took me a lot of work to get you out.

"You? Are you the Goddess of Swords, Oni-Goroshi or Fa Shai-Yeh?"

She said: Yes!

"I can't believe any of this. It doesn't make sense. I love you, oh but I do, and I want you, but I am not worthy of you if this is what worth means. No; if this madness is truth, if I grew up elsewhere and cannot remember, if I am not who I think I am, I don't want to be worthy."

She said: You are worthy, and the more you deny it, the more worthy you will be. Come. Find me. I will help you. Hua-Shi must die, and then we will move against the Tsukamoto. Against Kas'Daen. Against Zieger. Against Sladaria. Against all who brought your clan low.

"No. Vengeance is a heroic thought, and I am not a hero!"

She said: I will talk to you when you awaken, Charan.

"I'm not a hero, do you hear me? I will find another way to be me! Hell, I'll take up knitting, or sewing. I will find a proper use for the cut and thrust. My hands are not just weapons!"

She said: Such zeal! I will use it.

"I will not be used!"

She said: It is far too late for that. Remember.

"No. I'm happy. I deny the sword! Won't take it, take you—"

She said: As you so wish. Sleep.

I blinked and the world came into focus once more. Still on the lounge, Shai-Yeh leaning over me, cradling my head, fingers tracing gentle trails through my hair. She was no longer glowing, and her hair was a dull blonde again. I didn't draw away from her, not now that I had some idea of what was happening. No – my first impulse was to push myself closer to her, to snuggle against her warm breast, because she was a Goddess, or at least my Goddess. The only thing I should ever love, and even if I hated that, I had to accept it.

"Am I awake now?" I asked. And, of course, she hadn't lied: the language was not Chūnko-go. I was producing syllables which would sound like grunts or growls to a Mifūnjin ear.

"Inasmuch as you can be, Charan." She smiled, fingers pausing near my forehead.

"I remember you from my dreams, then."

"I have been in many of them." She reversed her hand's motion, combing back through my hair once more. It hurt. It felt good. It burned. I shivered.

"I don't sleep very much, do I?"

"No. When this is over, you can sleep as much as you want."

"I'm so tired. I'm afraid I'll fall." But I wouldn't, not as long as she held me.

"Not yet." She withdrew her hand. I trembled in sudden solitude. *"You know you cannot stop now."*

Was that a dare? A challenge?

"Watch me, Shai-Yeh." With the switch in attitude, my grasp of that strange new language became loose, weak. Unwilling, perhaps. I rose, disengaging myself from her arms, her bosom, and looked around. "I almost expected the knives to be gone. That much was not a dream, then. Hm."

"No matter what you do, Char," Shai-Yeh said, "you are not stopping. Time has passed, things have changed. You have changed, and not all the changes are to your liking. Some are not even known to you, as the knives prove. The evidence is right in front of your eyes. Is it that hard to accept?"

"It is. The dreams are real, and this is real. Does that make this a dream?"

"Simplistic but not unfair," Shai-Yeh conceded. "If this is a dream, and you are aware it is a dream, then why can you not control it?"

It was subtle, but that I understood her logic encouraged a strange belief – only in a dream could such nonsense make sense.

"Controlling myself when I am awake is difficult enough," I countered. "But dreams are not real. They're just fantasies. Craziness. We die in our dreams and then we're alive again and it makes sense. Doors open that were walls and it all comes together by falling apart."

"Now you are definitely dreaming," Shai-Yeh said.

"I'm not sure about that. You see, if I was dreaming, and I was conscious of it, I'd be able to wake up."

"Would you? Still dreaming, Char. You cage someone, you tell them they are caged, they understand it. Does that make the cage any easier to escape? You can study the details, the bars, the lock if there is one, but if someone else holds the key, ultimately, you will despair at your powerless situation."

"So I am caged." And I began to pace, ignoring the knives above, below and around me. "In other words, I have been put here, deliberately, by someone other than myself. There is no choice involved."

"Free will is God's greatest joke on the world, Char."

"So much for your piety and quoting of the *AkraVahm*, Shai-Yeh. You mock even God."

"Mock? No, sweet ward. I admire Her ingenuity. By giving us free will, She permitted us to produce our own motives, reasoning and justification. She let us dream, but there are some who understand that not even free will comes without a cost. This allows a manipulation of sorts."

"Are you a Maliscient then, Shai-Yeh?"

"No, this is not a Talent. Dreamsong is one of the Gifts from God. Faithful souls who submit to Her grand design are empowered, through great adulation and prayer, to influence certain others when they are at their weakest, their most susceptible. We are not unlike Her touch, quietly making sure things keep on schedule."

I wondered what other 'gifts' God might have given her and how she would use them, or was already doing so. She was just a girl, at least on the surface, and when I thought about what she'd done so far, the idea of Holy empowerment wasn't impossible to believe.

"You are a manipulator. Nothing more. You take away a man's greatest asset, his only true possession!"

"If God ordains it, who is a mere man to defy it? And God does ordain it, for Dreamsong is from Her!"

"Are you controlling this dream, Shai-Yeh? And all my others?"

"Yes. When you accept them and do what you must, I will let you dream in your own silly, insane way once more."

"You will, or God will?"

"In this instance, they are one and the same. Were She to deem otherwise, She would not empower me. It makes such simple sense."

"What if the power does not come from God?"

Shai-Yeh's voice changed then. It deepened, burdened with an archaic wisdom of equal sorrow and crazed rationalisation.

"Then God would stop it, Char. She would have stopped me long ago. I have asked Her, you see, to stop me, to end me. I do not enjoy doing Her work. My hands shake and shy away from the grisly task of re-arranging your life. Every time it seems that I can withdraw, She presents me with another angle to wear away. Your convoluted existence has long troubled me, Char. This is why I do not let you remember what I have done. It hurts me to do it, and it would hurt you to remember. Let me at least ease your pain that much."

"No. I ask for all your cruelty, Shai-Yeh." Because—

"Please. Do not ask this of me."

"—This is my simple sense, Shai-Yeh. When you are 'kind' to me, you rip me in half. You tie my memories in knots; you erase entire years from my life. So maybe if you are cruel to me, there is a chance you might just stumble onto a bit of *real* kindness."

"Char, you have the skill now, because I taught you. It is ready to be used. Why do you insist on remembering the lessons? Is it not enough that you have learned?"

"How can I have learned if I do not remember? That trick with the knives and the wooden sword? Well, it was a dream, wasn't it? We're still there, still in the room. I'm probably lying on my bed in the Chapterhouse. Probably twelve years old."

It was a gamble laid down by a sixteen-year-old mind taught so many such gambles. The thug Char of Guan-Pi's rearing wouldn't have been able to make an intuitive leap like this.

"Could a twelve-year-old act as you are acting now?" Shai-Yeh poked at the wager. Of course she knew what I was doing – she taught me now.

"In a dream? A normal dream, maybe not. But if you're controlling this one? Of course I can act any way you want. Assuming you are the master of this Dreamsong, and I think you are. By that reasoning, I have learned nothing at all, and when I wake up, I will be twelve years old and I will think, 'what a crazy dream!' and I'll forget the lot."

"You cannot forget! I will not permit it!"

"You can control dreams, Shai-Yeh, but I don't believe you can control memories. In this dream, you can convince me that I have forgotten, but, again, when I awaken, none of this will matter."

"Would you like me to wake you up and prove that it is not just a dream?"

"That made no sense, Shai-Yeh. You're losing your grip." It was time to reveal the extent of my original wager. "And if you are controlling this dream, then however I act, you are the one who wills it. I have no free will, remember? But understanding all this, I know I will be in control sooner or later, because I choose to believe you – therefore I can choose not to. And when that happens, I will be the master of my own dreams, and I will erase you from them. And it will be by your leave, your design! By encouraging me to question 'free will', you've authorised your own defeat."

"Try it." Shai-Yeh rasped in that other language. "Erase me and you will be stuck in here forever. I am your only way out."

Pride. It was all she had left, and I was going to use it. The fall would follow.

"I like it here. Your wild tales are just stories here. Then again, if they're real here, then in this dream I can play them out to my liking. That's your weakness, Fa Shai-Yeh. You toy with reality and dreams to convince me that your mastery of dreams is reflected in reality. Well, it isn't. And guess what?"

I sought one of Chang's little knives.

"This isn't real," I continued, twisting the knife in front of my eyes after turning around to face her. "Just a dream, and you're not the master of it."

"Going to kill yourself, Char? Do you think that will wake you up?"

"Only a stupid prisoner kills himself when the gaoler is within reach."

I considered throwing the dagger at her and then it was done.

She didn't bother dodging, didn't raise a hand in warding. There: a quivering hilt jutting out of Shai-Yeh's chest; here: my arm straight and fingers pointing right at her.

"You want my cruelty?" She fought against the blood rising in her throat. "Then have it! May all your dreams come true."

A quiet stasis followed, no longer than the dagger's fatal flight, and then her bodice erupted in a great gush of red brilliance.

I blinked, unable to endure the intensity, but finally opened my eyes to see.

"Nice throw!" Chang patted me on the shoulder and stalked past. Surging across the room in his white robes, he was so tall, so powerful. I definitely wanted to be like him when I grew up.

"You're improving, Charan," Orchid said from beside me, fingering a knife of her own. Of the girls I'd met since being inducted into the Chapterhouse, Orchid, with her short hair and unashamedly stocky build, remained my favourite fellow trainee. She didn't take crap from anyone, was as quick to react as I'd ever been and could really hold her own in a fight. In fact, she'd challenged me the very first day Chang introduced us. Arm wrestle? Full body wrestle? Not good enough for her. After school (the chapterhouse had its own full-time school) she'd grabbed me, called me a few names and then taken a swing.

After beating each other to a pulp, we became pretty good friends. Like me, her preferred weapon was the sword. Like me, she was a Half.

Like me?

"Maybe, Orchid," I replied, rubbing my head out of embarrassment. Chang knelt beside the spreading pool. "But I dunno."

"Charan, you're showing real potential. A clean puncture of the heart at forty paces. Wouldn't stop a Rose, but you'd have no trouble taking down a Weed." That was more slang. Weeds were people selected by the Night, placed on the Menu by Thorn and then pulled from society by the Pricks. Some, naturally, didn't want to be pulled.

"You know I want to be a Sword, Chang-dailoh." This was my way of dealing with praise. It wasn't a very good one.

"The skills you hone as a Prick will serve you very well against Roses, Charan," Chang said before frowning at the little scarlet lake. "I guess I expected you to miss again. Should have filled the target with something easier to clean than pig's blood."

Orchid released one of her almost-laughs as I struggled against uncomfortable pride.

"I should get used to the sight, Chang-dailoh," I admitted, now looking at the deflated satchel. It had been a dare. Knife-throwing in the Chapterhouse was usually forbidden. Thorn made it clear there were specific places for practicing our skills, and the dormitory wasn't one such place. Chang had hung the bloated sac at the end of the long hall and we'd all taken shots at it from the door. There were several little knives stuck in the ceiling and wall around the target — most of them mine.

Then, on a whim, I pretended that the bulbous bag had been Shai-Yeh.

Hadn't it been?

"It just doesn't feel the same," I added, as if I'd know, "throwing knives at wooden boards or dummies full of straw."

"Oh I agree, little brother of my blood, but did you really have to make such a mess?"

I laughed a little. I'd nailed a great shot and potentially picked a Weed but it was still just a game.

"He was getting away, Chang-dailoh. It was one of them whatchacallits."

"A fluke?" Orchid offered.

"Yeah, that. Wait, no. Oh I dunno." I grinned at her, unsure exactly how to feel. She reminded me of Shai-Yeh, whom I hadn't seen for months, but a Shai-Yeh without that horrible all-knowing attitude. I supposed if I could take Shai-Yeh and shape her to my liking, she would have been Orchid.

"Well, we'll need a new target now," Orchid sighed, sitting down on her bed. "And this time, I will be the one to make the kill. Wait and see."

"You're a bit older than Charan, Orchid," Chang said as he continued to scrutinise the blood. "And we haven't taken him out on a job yet."

"You could just get Butterfly to clean that up, you know," Orchid sniffed, supporting herself on the edge of the bed with slightly bent elbows. "She'd just love to show off her *Shui-chi*."

"Or Blossom could help you, Char," Chang added, winking at me over his shoulder.

"That slut," Orchid muttered. "Screw it. I'm outta here."

But she didn't move. In fact, they were both gazing at me with an unspoken query. I was being made to choose.

"No, Orchid. You stay. Butterfly and Blossom weren't responsible. We were." I was. "We'll clean it the hard way, right, Chang-dailoh?"

"Thorn teaches that sometimes, you should do things the long way around," Chang The Knife preached with mock piety, turning back to the spill. I began to smile when I saw, with insane clarity, a red horizon in my mind. It turned on its side, or did I lie down? Then it bent, like a bow, like an unfinished moon. That was the path I had to walk.

The need to speak struck me with the force of a granite epiphany.

"I have to take the long way around; I want to do so as quickly as possible."

Chang glanced up from his conscientious mopping again and gave me another of those 'you-are-acting-weird' looks. I'd long since learned to ignore it. Orchid fiddled with her throwing knife, poking it with a bored finger; little sparks jabbed at the blade. She was trying not to look at me.

What had I said?

I forced a cough, a failed laugh. I must have looked like a clown.

"I just don't get you sometimes, little bro," Chang conceded. "Get off your smart little ass and come give me a hand with this crap. And next time, close your eyes before throwing or something."

I did laugh outright then, honestly and happily, a third laugh to chase away the chills. What had me so solemn? I couldn't remember.

Although I was on my hands and knees, the menial task was fulfilling, as was the rest of my life as an initiate of the Malevolent Hand chapterhouse. There was always work to be done, lessons to be learned and, surprisingly, games to be played. Not all of the others liked me, but that was alright. I was different – Shai-Yeh said so the last time she visited. Thorn took me aside for special tuition, and Chang was my Dailoh, my personal mentor, my big brother. My friend. One day, I'd take the Sword and make my own way, but not for a long time. For now, I was twelve and every day was better than yesterday.

For an almost-thirteen year old, I had so much purpose, so much to look forward to. I glanced back at Orchid and caught her staring at me. A wink of my own made her roll her eyes but her lips twitched. Chang smirked to himself. I wasn't a thug anymore and, despite all my fears, not being a thug didn't mean I was nothing.

Are you happy with this?

What a strange question to ask myself!

Yes, of course you are.

But there was more. There would always be more.

My eyes grew dry and irritated from staring at the blood, the harmless pig's blood. I wiped them, gave Orchid another glance.

Her smile deepened as she slid off the edge of the bed. I blinked, and then it was just me and—

Orchid Witherheart sashayed across the alleyway towards me; for now, she was all that mattered. Moonlight elucidated the way her curvature augmented the loose-fitting jet robes, how each movement accentuated but a hint of what rippled beneath. Watching her was like witnessing the birth of an exotic realm of sensual shadow – gentle hills rose from the soft firmament, ebbed and became waves of irresistible magnetism.

"Here?" I asked and then wondered why.

"Here. Now." She was still smiling, but where once dwelt unaffected innocence now prowled a passionate immediacy. Orchid stopped a breath's distance from me, as she always did. For all her desire, she never hurried. In all things, Orchid displayed a patient diligence that teased even the most complacent of victims.

"Shouldn't we clean up first?"

"Why bother?" She murmured. "He'll be there after. Definitely not going anywhere."

This was true. Her circle of daggers around my sword pinned the Rose's torso to the wall across the street; its head sat in the middle of a steady, steamy pond of sluggish oil oozing over the well-worn stones.

Orchid stepped closer, taunting the possibility of contact. I lowered my gaze from the ruined Rose, drove it through a course that acknowledged the cobbles underfoot and then alighted upon the black hem of her robe.

"*Anata*," she whispered, and then repeated in a more common, less intimate language: "Darling."

She'd never called me that before, not even when we'd the spent the entire night exploring each other's warm, succulent treasures. Until this point, I'd understood that our relationship was one of improbable attraction. Killing aroused her, and her arousal sparked my own burning virility. We indulged in pet names and the hollow hyperbole of pillow talk, but crucial concepts such as faithfulness or love were unspoken wastelands. They lay beyond the golden borders, where consequences spiked the filthy trenches of absolute obligation and devotion. Promises like that were not for those who dealt with death.

I just breathed in, swallowing the word as though it might provide sustenance richer than any fleshly meal.

"Charan, look up. Look at me," Orchid insisted, reinforcing the command by first touching my chin and then tilting it up with the slightest of pressure. This treated me to a full tour of her physique. The pilgrimage almost took forever and yet it was the most direct route through a legion of gasping, entwined memories.

"Here I am. The one you chose. I am right here," she confided, and I started to draw away. Someone else had said that once, and I'd hated it. But there was no chance of escape, not once I found her face, her divine, alabaster visage. I opened my mouth and didn't know whether I'd kiss her, bite her or just breathe in again.

"Yes, now you see me." Orchid lowered her hand from my chin, marking a fine trail down my throat. There it lingered, as though her nails might penetrate the thin film of my neck and wrench forth a bleeding essence of gluttony. Then she leaned forward, bringing her lips so close to mine I tasted the sweet nectar of her hypnotic lust. "And I see you."

"What do you see?" I'd asked that before, but I liked to hear it. As much as I lived to hunt, to ravage, hearing her worship me was equally intoxicating. And she did then, describing my body in terms unfit for flawless statues, applying adulation to my muscles, the way they held her, the way I touched her. I demanded more, and she continued, even as she sank to her haunches and parted the folds of my black cloak. Orchid paused in the praise only to nibble my thighs, to creep upwards towards a stimulated pinnacle.

Then, as she placed her lips upon the firm bridge between us, I began to laugh.

What are you doing? This woman breathes you with every moment of her life! She defines herself by looking at you and thinking, 'For him I was made!'

My laughter was hard and caustic. Orchid's eyes, glazed with sweet hunger, flicked upwards from beneath full lashes. I eased her back – she did not resist. Her expression wanted to understand what I found so terribly hilarious. At the same time, I saw the birth of terror, and I knew what she feared.

She was not the one made for me. Of that I was certain.

She is anything you could ever want in a woman, Charan! You have known her for years, careening through the dance of courtship, and she is the one for you!

"Darling, what is it?" Oh, you poor creature. You could never understand why I'm almost hysterical.

What is wrong?!

"Darling, what's wrong?"

This wasn't real.

"Orchid, do you love me?" I asked after my mirth sank to a smirking undercurrent of amusement.

"With all my heart, being and soul," she replied.

See? What more could you possibly want?

"Have we ever had an argument?"

"Why would we, darling? You are perfect for me."

"You're not perfect for me." Because she was perfect.

I should have just picked up a hammer and shattered her. It would have done less damage.

Is there no boundary to your cruelty, Charan?

"No. No, don't say that—"

"Would you grow old with me, Orchid?"

"—What?"

"Would you give this murderous life up and live with me? Would you grow old with me as I worked as a tailor, or a baker or anything but this?"

"Yes." No. She wouldn't have, because without this, she wasn't special at all.

"Look at the corpse over there, Orchid. We did that. Look at it!" I couldn't.

So she did, and through her weeping, I saw a malicious glee. Orchid grinned at the butchered Night's Own across the street from us – to which we were both, in some grim, unspoken way, related.

"Yes, darling, we did that," she looked back at me, shivering with barely-contained rapture. "Now let me do you."

"Get away from me." I could have been anyone. She killed, she got horny, I was around. It was ridiculous.

I smiled despite her disintegration. She slid down my legs, unable to find a single handhold, and collapsed in a sobbing heap at my feet.

I wanted to laugh again, but I had to blink back a tear.

"Are you okay?" I asked, reaching down to help her up.

"I just had a bit of a fainting spell, Charan, that's all." Lily smiled in her quiet, brave way. That didn't stop me from helping her back to her feet. "They do happen at times like this."

"You shouldn't be doing housework, y'know, like you are," I stuttered, looking around our humble little cottage home. "The place is clean anyway. Why don't you just rest?"

"I can't stay off my feet, dear. I'd simply go insane," she confessed before giving me a quick hug and moving away.

"But—"

"If you really want to help, go check on the little one. She's been quiet for hours. And please do so carefully!"

"I'm always careful," I pouted and started to shuffle towards our bedroom. Well, it was ours, until what we did in there produced a miracle beyond the act itself.

"Hmm? Not always," she smiled and patted her precious stomach.

"Well, yes. Uh, I'll go check on the little one then, shall I?" I still blushed a lot. It was a habit developed back when I'd been an initiate in the Blood Peddlers, back when the Priestess had tried to ruin my life.

I paused by a small mirror on a cabinet in the living room. Who was the hazel-eyed man staring back at me? It had taken a lot of work to divest all semblances to Char of Kaifeng, the highly-trained killer of renegade Night's Own. A beard helped, but most of the change came in how I expressed myself. Before, my happiness was the grin of a feral beast, and when angry, actually, I did pretty much the same sort of thing. Now, nearing thirty years old, mature and content, I smiled with my lips pursed, and my anger was a quiet, subdued displeasure. Not that I had much to be angry about anymore.

Was this really me?

"Yes, dear, that's you," Lily teased, watching me study myself from across the room.

"Just making sure," I replied. "Wouldn't want anyone else to be in the mirror."

"Oh you!" Lily, too, was more settled these days. Of course we still talked about our amorous history, and it was always welcome nostalgia. We loved to regale ourselves with tales of how the professionally cold Half was tamed by a dove of kindness who had been serving the Night, waiting for something good to come of it.

"Why don't you come sit with me when you get back?" And that was all I needed to hear. Thirty was hardly over the hill! Between us, we shared a decent crop of grey hair, but Lily's stressful lifestyle in the Haven claimed responsibility for most of that. Besides, she looked wonderful with a few locks of silver.

I slipped into our bedroom thinking, this was worth all the effort.

What effort?

The 'little one' was asleep. In her mother's absence, she was sucking her thumb and curled up on her side on our bed. She must have been tired to not even bother crawling under the blanket.

I sat beside her, careful not to make her roll over, and reached out to brush a few strands of fine black hair from her face. She had her mother's hair, not to mention eyes, fingers and mouth. Her ears were almost round, too. A quarter was nowhere near as obvious as a Half. She would grow up to be a normal girl, then a normal woman, if such extraordinary beauty could be considered normal. No one would tease her about her ears or her tainted heritage.

"Perfect," I whispered, resisting an itch to take her in my arms. "Simply perfect."

But what if my blood was too strong? What if this little sprite, whose laughter sounded like chimes in the wind and whose smile outshone all the stars at night, contained the legacy of her grandmother's demise? Would she be a six-year-old terror like I'd been? Would she be drawn to what I had hidden in the closet, wrapped in a dirty cloth? I often thought about getting rid of it, but then someone else would have to bear it. I'd have to do something about it before she got too old, though. It'd only take one touch and she'd be seduced by Oni-Goroshi, by my Goddess. And then my little one would be— no. I wiped my eyes; the vision of such a cruel fate for my beloved child was enough to make me weep, just a bit.

I blinked as the tears fell like silent fireflies in a dead autumn dusk. What if she were the same way? What if those eyes would soon shine only in the light of violent conquest? What if she—

"—didn't go to school today?"

"Eh?"

"Daddy? Hellooo?" She waved a hand in front of my eyes from across the table. Lily laughed in the background, cleaning up after breakfast; we always ate as a family.

"Sorry, Pumpkin. I was. Sorry, what were you saying?"

"I was saying, Daddy, what if I didn't go to school today?"

"Well, if you didn't go to school today," I answered most solemnly, "you would get into the habit of not going to school. You wouldn't learn anything and then, in the end, you'd be dumb and silly like me. Now do you really want that, Pumpkin?"

She smiled, and that made every effort worthwhile. She knew I was joking – brat had her father's taste in dry wit.

"Daddy, I really don't want to go. The other kids pick on me, and I don't like it."

So this is how it begins. How old is she? Six? Yep, exactly as predicted. Nice work, Charan.

"They're just kids," Lily tried to help. "You should ignore them when they tease you. Be a good girl."

"Mother!" She never called me Father; Lily was never 'Mommy'. "This is really serious. They say I'm going to be a loser like Daddy, and my ears are ugly and strange, and I don't want to GO TODAY!"

"Honey." It was my turn to try, but having a bunch of absent six-year-olds call me a 'loser' wasn't improving my own attitude. "Your ears are fine. They're not strange at all. Or ugly! And the kids at school? They don't know any better. They're not like us. I mean, you."

"Charan!" Oops. Lily was rarely angry, but I was fairly certain I was in trouble now. My daughter gave me one of her Daddy-loves-me smiles. I grinned back.

"Sorry, dear, but it's true. No one is like our little one." *One.* Lily said nothing more for a long time.

"Daddy, if they call you bad things, can I call them bad things back?"

Shit. Are we hearing this right? A child is coming to a murderer, a liar and a thief for advice on how to treat others?

"Only sometimes?"

I didn't look at Lily – that was a lost cause.

"Like when, Daddy?"

"Well, when…no. Never, Pumpkin, okay? No matter what they say. You can't be like them. You have to be kind, no, twice as kind to make up for the kids who aren't kind."

That's the way. Be resolute! Stay strong no matter how weak they are – How weak you were, Half!

"Daddy, what if they hurt me?"

"Then I will hunt them down and rip them apart," I whispered to myself, and then raised my voice, repeating helplessly, "You have to be kind, Pumpkin…"

"That's enough," Lily almost yelled. "It's time for you to go. 'Daddy', would you mind walking her to school?"

"Well, I was planning on forming an army and attacking Kasuden before lunchtime, dear." A giggle from my Pumpkin. Worth every little lie! "But I guess so."

My daughter gathered her things, kissed her mother on the cheek and skipped out the front door. I followed – weary, drained but happy.

The sun was bright, too bright. I squinted, trying to make out my daughter's silhouette as she la-la-la'd down the street. I wouldn't blink, wouldn't lose sight of her – it was so bright, so strong and—

Then I heard her scream. The dimness returned.

I took off at a full bolt, but I wasn't a young man anymore. I was out of breath by the time I reached her.

She was on the ground, long onyx tresses hiding her face like a black veil. Her shoulders shook with restrained sniffling. There were patches of blood clotting her brand new white dress. I saw cuts and grazes up and down her bare arms.

"Pumpkin! Did you fall down?"

I squatted down in front of her, still wheezing, and tried to push aside the opaque wall between us. She swatted my hand away.

"No, Dad, they hit me again, okay? But you know what?" She threw her head back, causing the thick curtain to part, revealing the bruises and welts upon her face. She didn't have that ugly, arrogant smirk most young teenagers seemed to develop. But when I saw what 'they' had done to her, my poor old heart stepped outside its cage, laughed at me and exploded. I winced but refused to even touch my chest. "You know what, Dad? Next time, I am going to kill them. I am going to *fucking* kill them."

Here is where you're supposed to pat her on the head and say, 'that's my girl. That's my daughter!'

"No, Pumpkin, don't talk like that."

"Oh yes, Daddy. You see, Aunty Shai-Yeh has been teaching me a few things. And until now, they were just games. The others think they can pick on me because I'm strange, because I'm different. I'm gonna show them just how different I am." She sniffled again, but could not stop the thick blood seeping from her damaged nose. I reached out to catch it, but she gave me a look that exposed entire worlds of denial. "Don't. Just don't. You weren't here to stop them, and you wouldn't let me stop them. I trusted you; I was kind. But they never stopped. It's time someone stopped them.

"I can, Dad. I will."

If the Priestess has been training her in secret, Half, it's already too late.

"Did you tell the Master about this?" Now I was getting desperate. I'd never gone to the Master after fighting at school, not after I heard what happened to little boys who don't stick up for themselves. People had called me strange and I'd hit them. Now I wondered how this made their parents feel.

Such aptitude for impotent regret.

Is there any other type?

"Right, Dad. Not sure how school was when you were a kid," she said, bitter as only an intelligent twelve-year-old can be, "but it's a bit different now. You just don't understand."

I'm losing her. I'm losing the only good thing I've ever done in my miserable life.

Losing her? You lost her long ago, you fool.

"I did. No. I do, Pumpkin, I really do. You heard what I was like when I was your age."

"Yes, Daddy!" And, at great cost, she admired me once more. "Aunty Shai-Yeh tells me you were a fighter! She says that you were the best swordsman in the whole world, and that no one picked on you, not if they knew what was good for 'em!"

"And then I grew up and realised that every time I fought, I was not really in control at all. Fighting isn't the way, Pumpkin."

"Bullshit, Dad. If fighting isn't the way, what is? Getting beat up every day because my father is a Half and sews stupid clothes for a living? Having to take day after day of abuse because God hated your mother so much she was only allowed to have one—"

I shut her up with my hand two seconds before I thought about doing so.

So it wasn't enough that the other kids hit her? Now you're getting in on the act too. Great example you set, 'Daddy'!

"Not your mother, girl." Had I ever called my Pumpkin that? "You insult me all you want. But you do not disrespect your mother."

"Mother disrespects me by just letting you be such a God-damn weakling!" And with that, I knew I'd lost. I knew she'd lost. The world, so ignorant, uncaring, cruel, had won again.

You had your chance to change the world, Half. Do not cry about it now.

I looked down at the ground and wept anyway. I wept for us both – my daughter had not shed a single tear. I knew that when I raised my eyes, she'd be gone, but—

I looked up, feeling wetness on my cheeks.

"There's someone at the door, Charan." Lily hobbled away from the kitchen just enough to catch my attention. I must have been dozing. Dozing in my favourite chair. Could do that a lot these days. The business was going well and life was peaceful.

But at what great cost.

But at *what* great cost?

"Who could be it be at this hour?" I asked by habit alone, rubbing soft eyes. Seemed like I'd been crying in my sleep. Again.

"Charan, it's barely Risingmoon. You silly old man. Probably just the neighbours coming over for a chat. Go see."

So I eased myself out of the chair, grabbed my cane and ambled towards the door. The wooden stick felt good in my hands, supported my ailing weight well. Sometimes I'd sit in my chair with it across my lap, running my hands back and forth over the polished oak. I'd think about something hidden, but now it was something lost.

"Hello?" I asked without opening the door. "Who's out there?"

"It is me, Charan."

Not a neighbour, then.

"One moment."

I fumbled with the handle, ignoring Lily's pained wince floating in the corner of my oh-so-narrow and oh-so-blurry vision.

"My God!" I exclaimed upon throwing the door open. "You haven't changed a bit."

"Yes, well, I age in different ways. Hello, Lily."

"Mistress Shai-Yeh." And Lily bowed. With her arthritis, it must have been incredibly painful.

"I am not a mistress to you. Charan, I told you both that the first time we met. Have you not learned anything? Does she know nothing?"

"She knows how to make a pretty damn good stew." I smiled and stepped aside for my greatest enemy, my only companion from the very beginning.

"I have no doubt. You certainly liked it when you were in her care at the Hand."

Which hand?

"But we do not talk about that anymore, do we?" The 'young' Priestess contrived a shameful expression and crossed the threshold.

I moved to close the door behind her when she thrust out her hand against the wood. It was like trying to push a wall.

"Not yet, Charan."

No. No.

"Ask her in as well, Half." Shai-Yeh withdrew her palm, flexed the fingers and proceeded into the living room.

The night air mocked my bones, but I stepped out there anyway. So much darkness. Was it always this dark?

"Pumpkin?" Ridiculous of me to ask this of the empty street. It was a word I hadn't used for over twenty years. That was her word. When she left, it went with her.

"Hi, Dad." She was behind me. I jumped and stumbled forward. She laughed, and it was Fa Shai-Yeh's laugh.

"Well, uhm." And what exactly does one say to one's daughter after so long? "You're still beautiful."

"Am I, Father?"

It was almost true. She didn't look a day over sixteen, but that plated armour was deceptive with its moulded bodice. Her face was exactly as I'd imagined it to become, if one ignored the deep scars here and there, the very slight kink in her otherwise delicate nose. She had her black hair pulled back into a tight braid, and I didn't need to wonder who'd taught her that.

And she had my…a sword sheathed upon her back, the azure-wrapped hilt jutting from behind an unyielding left shoulder. I tightened my grip on the walking stick.

All of these, even the sword, were flawed but beautiful things. Her lips, wrought into a wry half-smile, almost tipped the scales the other way.

Lie. Just lie. You haven't seen her in years, you love her, don't hurt her. There's been enough pain.

"Why don't you come inside?" I shuffled past the young woman. "It's cold out here."

"Colder than you know." And she followed me in.

"Will you be here in the morning?" Lily asked my rotten Pumpkin after we'd all sat down. Not quite all: my daughter chose to stand, near the door. Her arms were folded; her eyes were illegible. She did not lean on the wall.

"Yes, Mother. I'm on leave for a few days. Mistress said it would be alright to come see you."

Since when do you need permission to see your own parents, Pumpkin?

"We shall not head out again until next week," Fa Shai-Yeh said. "But I will leave that up to Talon to explain."

"Talon?" Lily frowned in either confusion or disapproval.

"My name, Mother."

"We gave you a name. Wasn't it good enough?"

"Lily," Shai-Yeh stepped in, "it is not appropriate for people like Talon to use their real names. She detached herself from that weakness long ago."

"Mistress, requesting time alone with my parents." 'Talon' was not entirely heartless then; not even she could stomach Shai-Yeh's abrasive presence.

"As you wish. I will see you tomorrow." Shai-Yeh rose and bowed to Lily, a deep supplication. From a Priestess of Shai-Yeh's standing, it was an unparalleled honour. "The world owes you an infinite gratitude, Lily Jaydemyr. For giving us Talon. Thank you."

Lily neither met her gaze nor returned the gesture.

"Shai-Yeh," I tried to mediate, "we didn't give you our daughter. She went."

I expected Talon to comment, to say that we were talking as if she weren't there, but my one hasty, guilty glance revealed that she was still watching the door.

She'll never relax, Charan. Ever again. Never know a moment's peace, never just close her eyes and feel good about anything. This is the price she paid.

"Someone had to," Shai-Yeh sniped. "Thank God the Jaydemyr blood is stronger in her."

"I do believe my daughter requested time alone with us." I was just as acidic. "She'll be yours again soon enough, Shai-Yeh."

The Priestess shrugged. "She is mine forever, Charan. The world owes you too."

"Gratitude in the form of unending absence shall suffice. If I see you again, Fa Shai-Yeh, I swear, you will die."

She sighed.

"Goodbye, Half."

I relaxed in her absence, bravado falling from my shoulders like a borrowed cloak, and collapsed into my chair, latest knitting project within reach, a gentle fire lending the little room its welcome warmth.

"Mother, I want to apologise for saying that God hated you." Talon obviously had as much tact as her father. "God doesn't hate you, even though you only had one child. Apparently that's because I'm so special, but I never wanted to believe that. All who fight are special."

"What have you been up to, Talon?" I asked before Lily could start crying.

"Latest campaign was near Teristra, the capital of Teriss-Luniir," my daughter reported, just as if I'd demanded a complete assessment of the situation. "We've managed to push the Zieger forces back through Kas'Daen-*desne*. Our biggest fear is the Purashenan insurrection to the south. None of this breaches current intelligence restrictions. It is safe for you to know."

Look at that, Charan. She doesn't even speak the same language as you anymore.

"Yes, Talon, but what have you been up to?"

She was quiet for a while.

"Killing people, Father. Lots of people. I'm very good at it. Like you were." Were. "And I can't say I like it but it's what I was born to do. God saw that you were not the one and so She let Mother have me."

"Is that it then, Talon?" I fought against being angry and in that fight, let anger strengthen me. "You're some sort of chosen one? Is that the crap Shai-Yeh feeds you instead of breakfast or dinner?"

What next, Half? Going to ask if the Priestess has her house-trained as well? Idiot, idiot, idiot.

"Father, your hands are shaking. Relax, please." I insulted her and she placated me. Her tone was that of a Healer talking to a man dying on the field. Relax, it will all be over soon. "I am special, Father. This sword proves that. You should recognise it."

"I don't want to look at it, Talon."

"You don't want to look at me either, Father."

All this time, and she still knows the shortest route to my heart.

But I did look at my child. I saw her body mature and become that of a woman, that which Fa Shai-Yeh had denied. I imagined my child in a wedding dress, in a maternity gown, maybe just in a casual skirt as she watched her own children playing in the grass. Was there a man at her side? Yes, of course. A good man, someone who could carry on where I left off, a man—

Who loved her from the age six onwards?

"See? You are weak, Father, crying like that."

"Have you no respect?" Lily had been wringing her hands – but now they were fists, pressed into her thighs. Her eyes, buried within a nest of wrinkles, bore straight at this frozen maiden of war. My daughter.

"For him? Once, once I did, Mother. He was funny and strong and— God, I sound like a stupid little girl." She laughed that Shai-Yeh laugh; it made her a liar. "But not anymore. I'm not a little girl and he's nothing. Still," Talon looked back at me, and I'd never felt so worthless. "Mistress taught me about what you are, Father. Are. Not were. Physically, you're still stronger than just about anyone. Aren't you?"

"It doesn't mean anything," I mumbled.

"Not without the will to wield the sword, I know. I have that will, Father. That's why I took it. You, the one man who should have protected me, who *could* have protected me, did not. And look at the result. Look at it, Father, and love it."

She refers to herself as an object, an 'it', as a product, a result. A weapon. And you should love her, Half. You remember what it was like to love a weapon, don't you?

"I do. And I would give anything to protect you now. You deserve better, Pumpkin." And her eyes twitched. So – Shai-Yeh wasn't finished here. How strong my girl must have been to remain human after so long in Fa Shai-Yeh's twisted thrall.

"I think that all the time, Father. When I am standing in the mud, walking down the line of prisoners, dispatching them one at a time, or maybe spending a little longer with one or another, seeing how many times I can cut him before he breaks. When I stare at great maps where cities, thousands upon thousands of people, are just a simple word and I choose which word we erase next. When a friendship spanning a decade ends with a single arrow out of so many. During all these, Father, I say to myself: I should not be doing this. No one should. But then I think of the war, of the effort. Of our NAME, Father. Of my duty to the Clan. Of all that you should have done, but did not. And so I lift the sword once more, I choose another city to fall and I train another companion to die at my side, in my stead."

This is a hero, Charan. This is the result of all the good intentions you denied. Every moment of peace YOU enjoy, Half, costs your little girl another tear that cannot fall. Is it any wonder she is so cold?

"No. It doesn't have to be you. Someone would take your place if you left that world behind, my daughter."

"Aye, this is so," she replied, using a crude, foreign term. "Someone else's child. And for me to selfishly step back and let someone else endure this? Then I would be as bad as you."

"There has to be someone out there more qualified for this than you, Talon." How clinical of me. That wasn't what I wanted to say. But I didn't want to say anything. I wanted to let my heart go, laugh and cry, hold her and let her know that everything was—No. I forfeited my desires long ago.

"Not someone out there. Someone in here. You, Father. Only you. This sword was made for you." Talon lifted the baldric over her head, bringing the weapon before herself with more reverence and respect than she'd accorded Shai-Yeh, Lily or myself. "I love it, but it loves only you. Do you remember what it was like the first time you held it, Dad?"

Do you remember the first time I held your hand?

"No, Talon. I'm an old man and my memory's not what it was."

"You lie, Father. I suppose that is where I got it from." Talon continued to stare at the sword. The Goddess of Swords. My Oni-Goroshi. "You remember everything. Mistress taught me that. You remember everything and you are going to live for a long, long time. You are going to outlive Mother."

"No. I am old, and I will die at just the right time." How romantic. How utterly morbid. "Shai-Yeh never taught me how to control my ageing, not as she obviously taught you. How old are you now, Talon?"

That purchased a reaction. Her raven eyes glowered again – rage or fear, I could not tell.

"I do not care to remember. It does not matter. I see no reason in it."

"You're thirty-three years old, my Pumpkin."

There! Another sign of uncertainty, another sideways look.

She looks away, seeking answers. That is all she is doing, Half. She will not find them anywhere but here. Provide them. It is not too late.

"You kept count, Daddy?" my daughter asked, but then the killer she'd become stifled any further intimacy. "You wasted all this time remembering something useless like that, Father?"

"Nothing was in my mind more, Pumpkin. Thirty-three. But you look no older than sixteen. A teenager to the eye, an adult murderer to the heart."

"Such is my fate." She slipped even further away with that admission. "Would you like to hold the sword? It won't bite, I promise."

"Yes it will, Pumpkin."

"Why are you so bent on tormenting your father?!" Lily launched her last attack. "You know he hasn't the strength to lift something like that."

That's not important. What is, then? Whether or not I want to.

"Mother, you're just a normal person. You don't underst—"

I wasn't so old or decrepit after all, not if I could move from my chair, backhand the thoughtless girl so hard she fell to the floor, and then return to that chair before any of us had a chance to dwell on what my daughter had almost done.

"Do you remember what I said to you, girl?" I was trying very hard not to cry. Would she run again? "The last thing I said to you."

"I do, Father." She stood up – and she was smiling, a full grin: opalescence tainted with ruby fervour. Maybe she'd bitten her tongue. Maybe I'd torn her lips. "That was good. That was very good. How did it feel?"

"I just hit the most precious person in my life, 'Talon'. How the hell do you think it felt?"

"Not that precious, Father. You let other people hit me for years."

So it comes back to that. Twenty-one years and here we are again.

"Take the sword, Father. Hold it. Close your eyes. It's not your sword anymore, but you wielded it once and you loved it. Right now, I want you to show me that you truly have turned from it." She was still bleeding.

"Why are you doing this, Talon?" Lily shrieked. "I know I'm just a normal person, but I went through a hell of a lot for you. The least you can do is respect your parents. We devoted our lives to giving you yours!"

Talon turned to her mother and shredded her with an answer devoid of compunction.

"The Commandments don't apply to me, Mother. And the only thing you were ever devoted to were ridiculous ideals of peace and being 'kind'. This world has no room for that sort of infantile nonsense. I knew this when I was *six*. Here you are, so much older than me, and you still haven't learned that."

"Lily, Talon. Stop this. Please."

"You had your chance, Father. Take the sword, show me you can give it back!"

"Charan, darling. This isn't our daughter. I don't know who this is." Lily seemed to wither and shrink. The window which had shut out the world's sorrow was open at last, inviting a sigh, a soft demise of her frail, long-dying flame. "I'm so tired. It's time for me to go to sleep."

"Goodbye, Mother," Talon was suddenly respectful, but it was in the same chilly fashion that Shai-Yeh had channelled. "Rest well. You've earned it."

"Yes, yes I think I have. Farewell, Miss Talon. I'll see you soon, my Charan."

I moved to hold her, and didn't want to let go. I didn't want to let her fall. We were well past passion, but this tight embrace was beyond all the frantic kisses stolen under a Highmoon sky. This was the farewell for which any true couple could wish, the perfect goodbye which will, forever, be how one remembers one's perfect companion.

In the end, it was she who pulled away. I sagged back into my chair.

Lily's departure was the strangest smile I'd ever seen — it was what remained when all true joy had fled. An imprint of happiness. A smile like that did not belong in the present.

Then she was gone.

"What if I take the sword," I resumed, "and I like it? You know, don't you, Pumpkin, what Daddy was like."

"Absolutely." Talon was sucking at her split lip. "Shai-Yeh told me. Why you let the other kids hit me. I put on a front for Mother. She'd never let you go if she knew your plan."

Plan? Is that seductress STILL using me?!

"I have no plan other than living out my remaining years in peace, my daughter."

"Says the man who just landed one of the strongest, quickest and downright deadliest members of the Jaydemyrian Eagles on her backside. Drop the old man act, Dad. You let them hit me because you knew it would toughen me up, get me ready for the War."

Did I?

I stared at my hands. There was blood on my knuckles. That blood was hers; her blood was mine.

"Aunt Shai-Yeh revealed what you really did, and who she really is. She told me that before you left the Chapterhouse to be with Mother, you were the most feared Peddler in Kaifeng. Blackcloak the Scourge, they called you. You terrorised all who opposed God. You understood then that life was a war and the only way to survive was to win. The only way to lose was to do nothing. What happened, Father? What changed Char, Scourge of Kaifeng into whatever you are now?"

"I chose not to be Shai-Yeh's tool, my daughter. That is all."

"And put me in your stead?"

"You chose to go. You always had that choice."

"Daddy, I was twelve years old. I didn't know anything about the real world. You made sure of that. I was an ignorant little girl forced to find her own way, to open her own eyes, and you let me. You let me go."

"What was I supposed to do? Stop you? You'd have resented me even more."

Talon did not answer immediately. I saw her check the door with too-quick eyes, and that was when I knew what she was really doing.

Alright, Pumpkin. I'll do my best. I really will.

"Father, this is the last time you're going to see me."

"And I can't stop you this time either."

"That remains to be seen." Talon returned her attention to the sword. Now she held it at her side, as the Tsukamoto samurai used to do when I was a kid, before a genius, some unknown young leader of the 'Jaydemyrian Eagles', had disassembled the Tsukamoto from the inside out. I wondered if I were supposed to have done that. I wondered if I could have. "I can't allow any distractions now, Father. From this night onwards, I am betrothed entirely to the only thing I know how to love."

You killed her spirit when she was a child, Half. The least she can do is kill your flesh in thanks.

"And your mother?" I had to ask. Once again, the fates of my two most precious girls thrashed against one another.

"She's done her part, Father." The impossibly composed young woman nodded towards the bedroom, where once she had slept so peacefully. "She served her purpose and God will reward her soon enough."

And now, the same question we'd posed to Shai-Yeh the very night we tossed the sword away.

"What if you're wrong?"

"I'm not, Father. She will die, and soon."

"No. That I understand, my daughter. I've faced it time and again, and it just strengthens my love for her. If tomorrow is our last day together, I will adore her today. And if today is our last day, I adored her yesterday."

"How selfish. As if the world is just you and her. But you asked about my being wrong. What did you mean?"

"What if God isn't in this game after all?" I used that word on purpose. Children played games. My daughter played games, once. Games of winning and losing. I wanted her to think about what each meant. "What if the highest master you serve is the one funding your war, Talon? And even if God is the final word, She is still paying you. You're just a mercenary, no matter how you want to look at it. Your mother may be 'dead', but she never once lived her life through the will of another. I did, and you know what? That is death. God gave you nothing but free will, and you deny that of Her. You attach your act of killing to Her icon and that somehow lets you indulge without guilt. Take away that God, that divine right, and you're just murdering people."

"Yes, Father, you are right." Her answer came promptly. Shai-Yeh had used this stance on her before! And why? How? Because it had been my argument against the Priestess long ago. Fa Shai-Yeh had taken my shield and was now bludgeoning me with it. Through my daughter, no less. "We use God. No one likes to think about it, but how can God be good if this is what She wants us to be?" Talon raised the sheathed sword once more and shook it.

"Then give it up, my daughter, as I did. You say someone will take your place, and this is so, but that someone will give it up as well. As shall the next, and the next, until the sword lies in the dust, forgotten, until it's not even a sword anymore because no one will remember what a sword is. Do you understand?"

"Some won't give it up, Father, because like you, and like me, they love it. Unlike us, they are not afraid of that love. It empowers them. The sword will always be a sword as long as there is a fist to hold it. The world should not live under that fist."

"And that is why you want me to take the sword?"

"You couldn't do what you must without it, Father."

"I couldn't do it even with her, Talon."

"So, the blade is female. Mistress told me you'd always called it that, but I found it hard to believe. Just a weapon to me, Father. I can love it only that far. But to you, she lives, doesn't she? You love her because she loves you back."

"Long ago, my daughter. Then I found a greater love in your mother."

"Mother would not kill to save you, Father. All she can do is die."

I was out of my chair again, halfway towards her, one hand clutched at my side, Fire sparkling around the gnarled claw.

Do it!

"Do it, Father."

Talon closed her eyes and shifted her grip on the scabbard. Were Oni-Goroshi naked, she'd have been lancing towards my daughter's heart. Her sapphire hilt pointed at me, daring me to take hold, to take control.

"No. I will not be used, and neither will you." I clenched my flame-taunted fingers, crushing the fiery temptation with an audible crash. "It's all an illusion. When you wield her, you are not the one in control. She wields you. When you take Her, you—"

"Take my place, Father. You must. This is the plan," Talon whispered.

"Let go of the sword, Pumpkin."

"Daddy." Why wouldn't she open her eyes? Was I that much of a disappointment? "I can't. I can't let anyone else go through it. She was made for you. Anyone else who takes her will die and die horribly. Only my connection to you has kept me alive this long. I'm tired, Daddy. Tired of staring at the sword and wondering why it can solve all the world's problems but never mine. Why won't you let me sleep?"

Her voice faltered even though she maintained a statuesque stance.

"Your problem *is* the sword. Let her go."

"Father, draw this sword or I will."

That's when I realised.

I strode forward and tore *her* free; this was the only way my daughter *could* let go.

Talon's arms fell limp with the burden now gone. She opened her eyes and finally, after years of resolution, sank to her steel-clad knees and cried. Despite her will to fight me all the way, my daughter succumbed to the release and, for the first time in her life, won.

This is what she didn't let me see. That day, she had been the strong one. For me, for her mother, she endured years of abuse. Now that I had accepted what I should have taken in her stead, she could relax. She would be free.

For you, Pumpkin, and only for you.

I drew Oni-Goroshi close to my chest and all the memories of our time together came back into focus. I'd never forgotten, of course – in that, Talon and Shai-Yeh were correct. No, I'd managed to do more than forget: I had changed what I remembered. Just holding the sword sliced through any such self-imposed webbing. I recalled the thrill of skipping over the rooftops under a bone-pale moon, the joy of knowing that to kill was to be not killed, to prevent the death of more worthy people. I thought she would be clumsy in my hands after all this time, but there was a renascent understanding of balance, of equilibrium. She was weightless and ready.

Everything I'd ever loved was now with me.

I looked down at my broken progeny, saw through her and beheld her redemption beyond my thoughts, doubts and fears. She could have asked anyone to do this, could have done it herself. Not even Shai-Yeh had suspected it. And she'd chosen me as her guide. She knelt to me.

My child had come home to die.

"Daddy, don't let me go." Even with her eyes open, Talon looked relieved, almost relaxed. Just how heavy had the sword become to her? "Don't let her take me away from you again."

"Close your eyes, Pumpkin."

"No, Daddy. I want to look at the man who failed the world, failed me. I want to see the pain on your face as you prepare to kill again. Pain is the only emotion I recognise in the mirror. But I'm going to smile at your pain. I'm going to smile for the rest of my life."

I closed distance with my little girl, dragging my sword back over my right shoulder. But she wasn't really smiling; she wasn't looking at me. As she searched the sword, perhaps she saw something of whatever glory God had waiting for her.

"This won't hurt, my daughter. I promise you that." I could make it so easy. But could I live with myself if I killed my own daughter?

She said: *You have killed other daughters. Other sons. And that was by your hand alone, with me in your fist. Through your daughter, I have ended countless lives, murdered a multitude of families and destroyed entire bloodlines. Look at her, and see what happens when you deny me, Half.*

I wanted to say a thousand things, to tell her about the life she never led, about the grandchildren I'd envisioned and about how proud I was of her, every second of her defiant, tortured life, and how I'd take it all back, how I would have gone back to that moment when Shai-Yeh had told me who I was and what I had to do. I would not let go of the sword. I wouldn't let anyone else carry this burden again. I wanted to tell my daughter that I loved her so much that I would bear an eternity of suffering in her stead.

But she knew. It was inscribed upon her expression. Now she was looking at me, not the sword. At me.

And she smiled. There was no pain here.

"Thank you, Daddy."

I love you, my daughter. Smile forever.

Swallow. Close your eyes.

Pumpkin.

The ancestral blade fell.

Her edge clove straight down, through skull, face, neck and chest. Such was my skill: the sword continued to sink without slowing, knowing not the difference between air, flesh and doubt.

And I screamed. I wailed. Vision clenched against the sudden deluge of exploding gore. Oni-Goroshi was embedded in the ground, but I did not let her go.

A lonely crash of thunder shattered the thickened air. Was that my heart breaking?

"Charan, My Lord!" Shai-Yeh grabs my right arm, leaving the left free to wrench my sword out of the dirt. "We can't stop now. The battle has begun. Come on!"

"Don't just stand there, you twit!" Orchid Witherheart yells at me as she dashes past. "That was just the first! Be strong!"

You mean I have to kill my daughter again?

"Beloved, I will be watching," Lily whispers as she streams by. "I would die for you."

I open my eyes. There are droplets of blood upon my eyelids, my forehead, cheeks. A thousand flashes of light distract me, yet I can't focus on a single one. Bodies lay helter-skelter about the naked hills around me. The air is grey; there is no sun here, just a strange sort of luminescence pulsating from within the odious shroud overhead. Then a rip of white, surreal and brilliant, splits the chasm between a distant sky and an undefined horizon; another peal of thunder and another scream, but neither are my own.

I swallow again and looked down at what I have done. The thing at my feet has limbs almost as long as I am tall. Its flesh is even duller than the dreary clouds; black viscera sprawl over the carved ribcage and sundered abdomen. I've seen something like this before, somewhere, somewhen.

Rose. It's a Rose. And you're in the biggest garden in Kaef're.

"Kaef're. The garden is Kaef're," I whisper.

"Well observed." Shai-Yeh releases my arm. "And we must cull this garden!"

And off she goes to join the others.

I look around again and see my army. And I know all their names, as easily as a man knows every word in his head, but I notice only a certain few. Lily – running from one wounded warrior to the next, Healing where possible, praying where not. Past her, Orchid throws her tiny bolts of lightning; Chang, at her back, is once more a cyclone of knives. Shai-Yeh, even deeper into the steel-and-skin anarchy, sends bolts of ice through the aberrations, those made ugly through their denial of God's will.

Is there someone missing? No – everyone is accounted for, rightful warriors under my command. But who is that? There! – I see her: a younger woman, blonde hair bound in a severe pair of braids, body armoured in the traditional vestment of a Jaydemyrian Eagle. Her whirring flail seeks skulls as though driven towards nothing else. I don't know her name.

Now she is gone, absorbed into the melee.

I scream again, this time in complete exhilaration. I'm not sure why, but everything feels right at last. I am redeemed.

Tears of gratitude ease down howling cheeks and mix with mixed blood. Then, just before I charge into the mad fray, I cry my own jubilant elegy:

"For the one I love!"

I am a fury of perfect murder. One kill becomes ten becomes twenty and my laughter sings even as the enemies close in; it mocks their apparent victory. I have won. I have made the right choice.

For the one I love.

And she was Fa Shai-Yeh, whose fault it was, who showed me the way – whom I then forget.

And she was Orchid, who loved me for what I would never become – I forget her as well.

And she was Lily, who followed me and fought the only way she knew how, and would die for me – that was her purpose; after that, I forget her too.

And she was my daughter, who'd chosen the name Talon but would have been born Tzara-Min Jaydemyr, and never have touched a weapon in her blessed life. I don't have to forget her, because I didn't make that mistake, not this time.

But above them all, she is Oni-Goroshi, my true love, the only one at my side when I fall. Age will not weaken her and she will never betray me, not as long as I accept her. I will never forget her.

I close my eyes as the blows fall like iron rain. The agony is pure and real – the pain of life confirmed. My life. Exactly as it should be.

There is no more perfect dream.

"Good morning, Char Ah-Ran."

Shai-Yeh. Fa Shai-Yeh. I won't open my eyes. I refuse to see what she's done to me this time. I'll go back to sleep and wake up and blink and go back to sleep to wake up, over and again, until I die—

"Come on, sleepyhead. You have been out cold all night." No trace of smugness or concern. Just a stranger from a few days ago, with whom I'd now spent several turmoil-filled lifetimes. "Well, for a couple of nights – the Healers did say you would need rest, but now we need to get you in shape to help us get the sword back. Someone else stole it, remember? Are you even awake? Lily is coming by to check on you today. Again. Maybe she is fond of you. But you are only twelve years old. Oh, well. She *does* seem the big sister type."

Twelve years old. For how long?

"Char Ah-Ran, I know you have had it pretty hard recently, but things are just going to get worse."

If so, I wanted to face 'things' with unblocked vision. I opened my eyes and looked at her, she who didn't change once through all the dreams. People came and went, feelings settled and flew away, but Fa Shai-Yeh was, I knew then, the girl of my dreams. Kneeling at the side of my bed, she smiled the smile of one who had grieved prematurely. No, not a smile. A grimace. A thankful but still uncertain stretch of lips not daring to believe – upon being proven wrong, she still clung to that horror despite the reality. To her, I had died. Maybe she was right.

"There we are. How is your head?"

Fucked. Truly, completely fucked. Thanks for caring.

Maybe this wasn't a dream. She was never concerned about me like this before.

"It's okay. Shai-Yeh?"

"Hm?"

A promise made by a Rat meant nothing.

Even if it were just a dream, I was no longer a Rat.

"Die."

She was strong; she was quick. But now I was stronger; I was quicker. My nails carved bloody little moons into her neck; the flesh around each probing finger paled in ghastly contrast. A growl purred in my hate-stoked throat, where burned a fire no amount of swallowing could extinguish. Her jaw worked subtle motion, weak but reflexive, attempting to grasp snatches of air.

Still gripping her neck, I sat up, forcing the deviant woman-child back and down. Widened though her eyes were, something unexpected glistened in the amber specks. Had there been any other look, any other expression, there can be no doubt I'd have crushed her without a first or second thought.

But this – this succulent, indulgent scintillation! She was smirking with her eyes.

I shoved her away and up, but mostly away. And Fa Shai-Yeh, who had lied to me, given me everything I wanted then somehow taken it all away, chortled right up until she slammed into the wall. Hahahahaha. Ow. Then she limped towards a bed and collapsed onto it. I waited for her face to bleed.

All she did was open her mouth and start to sing.

Everything went blurry, so I blinked.

Shai-Yeh was silent, staring at me.

"How long have you been sitting over there, watching me?" I asked. Had she watched me sleep?

When had I fallen?

Had I dreamt? Something – but what? And why was my stomach twisting itself into nauseating knots just trying to remember?

"No more than a few minutes." She was smiling only with her teeth. The macabre mask made me recoil in all its cheerful deceit. "Well, maybe I checked on you a few times over the past few days."

That smile. Stuff of nightmares. Was I still—?

"I don't want to dream anymore, Shai-Yeh."

Her smile deepened as she slid off the edge of the bed; because I was twelve again, I had no idea how to take that self-pleasing grin. And that lack of coherence convinced me:

"I'm awake, aren't I, Shai-Yeh?"

"Yes, you are awake now. May I sit with you?'

Something about her asking for my permission made me bark a single laugh.

"Sure."

Fa Shai-Yeh hobbled to my bedside, collapsed just before she could sit next to me.

"Are you okay?" I asked, reaching down to help her up.

"Sprained my ankle and strained my back carrying you to the Haven."

But she'd been fine on the way here, to the Chapterhouse. When? Not long ago. Maybe something since then, before now. Something she didn't wish to share. Whatever.

"Oh," she said, "the reason I came in this time. One of the girls here heard you were the one after the sword, said you could have this."

Shai-Yeh reached under my bed and withdrew a wooden stick. The size, shape, even the type of wood was exactly as I'd known them to be.

"Would you like to hold the sword? It won't bite, I promise."

I did – so I did. It was cumbersome in my hands. I smiled to myself.

"Orchid Witherheart left this for me." Almost a guess. If it were true, then the fragment-visions were not entirely untrue. This meant, in turn, that Shai-Yeh might really have been a Priestess, and she might just have been able to manipulate my dreams.

But never my life – my choices shape that.

The remnant of a much older, wiser Char Ah-Ran (*Charan ?WHO?*) decided this, and the boy I was becoming once again found subconscious satisfaction.

"Ah, so you have met Orchid already. That is good. She's been assigned to help you fit in, if you want to stay here. You have that choice, Char. The guards are not looking for you anymore. They know someone else has the sword. You could go back to your old life. If it was much of a life at all."

Which one?

"No, Shai-Yeh. We have a sword to retrieve. She awaits. Can I go say goodbye to my friends in The Nest?" Before one of them dies and the others betray me wait,what?

"Nest? Oh, you mean those people. Yes, of course. Although I did not think a little thug like you would have friends."

"Friends and lovers, Shai-Yeh. More than I deserved." What the hell was I on about? "Anyway, did you say Lily's coming around to see me?"

"Yes, just to make sure your head *is* okay. With the way you are talking now, I have my doubts."

"So we're going to take the sword back from Hua-Shi of the Bloody Shadows, aren't we?" For all the horror of the multilayered dreaming, and as quickly as the details seeped away, certain peculiar facts remained clear.

"You were not asleep last night after all!" Shai-Yeh glowered. "We were discussing that in the other room. You must have listened at the door. Sly little thief."

No use in disagreeing with her; that much I remembered from the dreams as well.

"Thief for now. Someday, I may be something else." Killer, prodigy, lover, husband, father, failure, sacrifice. Saviour?

"I must have really rattled that brain of yours when I, you know, pushed you into the wall." She blushed. Ah, finally willing to admit it. A shame I was different, too different to notice. "You are acting strange, Char."

I hefted the stick again, but it was still unwelcome in my hands. Oddly, that felt good. It was time to get to know the sword, so that when I retrieved her, I would be worthy.

And that desire was all I could think about now.

"Hmm. From the looks of how you are handling that thing, you need to get better if you are to help me, Char. That Healer woman should be here. Don't be a baby around her. Tell her it doesn't hurt anymore. Tell her you are ready."

I *was* ready. Ready to search for *her.*

Chapter 15: *Comfort*
JUST GOING STEADY

Not even close to a day passed before she found me.

Shai-Yeh had left, and I had made no effort to keep her. I was just sitting on the edge of the bed, liking the way my fingers bumped over the nicks and dents of the sword. It didn't appear new but it was new to me.

I was still examining the wooden sword when someone burst into the dorm.

"Hey, are you Char Ah-Ran?"

I didn't look up at her voice.

"No."

"Excuse me? I was told there'd be a scrawny braggart who thinks he's some sort of hero in here, and you sure seem to fit that picture."

"My name is Char. Blackcloak. The Scourge."

I heard her snort. It might be possible to snort in a lady-like fashion, but whoever this was scorned the idea.

"And that proves that. Blackcloak? The Scourge? What a pile of dung. Even calling you Char Ah-Ran is too much effort. Char will do for now. Char, get dressed and come with me."

"Okay. In a bit."

"Now!" Then she seemed to notice what I couldn't stop noticing. "I'm really glad you like it, 'coz it was mine and you better not wreck it, because then I'll wreck you. Bah! We got stuff to do!" She stepped forward and I looked up.

Her black hair was short, the ends uneven, seemingly hacked with a careless knife. She stood with haughty forwardness, daring anyone to accuse her of lady-like qualities. I saw her thin ears, budding chest and stormy expression; Shai-Yeh's description of my would-be guide had been ruthless: "Orchid Witherheart: look for a girl with pointy ears trying to be a boy with boobs."

I smiled and raised the weapon, pointing it at her. "Mine now, Orchid."

I was just playing – she wasn't, and when her annoyed impatience gave way to a more hardened determination, I lowered 'my' sword, at least down to her navel.

That slip, that little waver, was enough for Orchid. Without a word she twisted forward, grazing her stomach past the wooden length. I tried to move it, though whether in her direction or away I wasn't sure. Orchid gave my indecision no second chance, knocking the weapon with what looked like a casual slap and felt like a full-bodied shove. The smooth hilt slid through my fingers despite any attempt at maintaining a grip – or maybe because of it.

The clatter, loud and mocking, was as condescending as a slammed door.

"Commandment Nine, Half-wit," she taunted.

I was too busy staring at the sword, too shocked at the shift in what was supposed to be a little harmless fun. A flirt, maybe. When she cuffed my right ear, I reacted with a reflex worthy of a veteran ruffian. As soon as I turned around to retaliate, it was obvious that turning around wasn't a good idea.

There was another blur of light and then a sharp, disorientating snap. I'd been hit enough times to know, just before I didn't know anything at all, that Orchid had just backhanded me. Bone shattered, skin ruptured and jaw wobbled. Not even Wong Chu-Deng hit that hard. I raised my hand to check the condition of my left cheek (or if I even still had a left cheek). Pain and embarrassment forced my eyes shut; I pretended to be someone else, anyone, just not some loser who let this bully of a girl hit him and then, maybe if only subconsciously, called for help.

Because that's when Lily rushed in.

"What was that noise? Miss Witherheart, what have you done?"

"He was being an obnoxious little shit." Orchid didn't sound repentant or even all that concerned.

"Oh, but you've hurt him! Now he won't be out of bed for days. Again!"

Days? Already? But Orchid was right – we did have stuff to do, though I wasn't sure what in my sundered state.

"A little more bed rest might do his attitude some good, Lily. Let me know when he wakes up. I'm supposed to be his 'friend' around here. That means I have to like him. I don't like this brat." Orchid slapped the back of my head again and walked out – or so it sounded. I couldn't see much.

"Looks like you've found another wall, Char Ah-Ran. It's time to grow up," Lily said, and I thought I understood her, but a lukewarm sensation engulfed me, and I went under.

"I'm over this, Lily. Can't I at least go watch?"

"Rest means rest, Char Ah-Ran. At least you're not stuck in bed, right?"

"Might as well be. And…did I ever tell you I don't really like people calling me by my full name?"

"No. I'm sorry. You should have said it sooner. May I ask why?"

I made a show of fussing over the book I was reading at Thorn's desk. Naturally he kept the more important documents – like the Menu – locked away. Not that I had any inclination to know anything about that. Or even reading in general. Especially not when I couldn't do anything else.

"It's the name my…parents called me. I don't think it's real. It sounds, I don't know. Mocking? Dismissive?"

"I think it sounds perfectly fine, but you're right, now that you mention it. So…Char then? That's what I've heard others call you."

"Sure. So you said I'm all better, right? Fit for duty and all that?"

I knew Lily'd give me that look. Even though she was probably almost twenty years old, and me, only twelve, I settled when she was around; to replace my habitual rebellion and aggression, I offered pouts and moping.

"See, now you're miffy." Lily sat back in the lounge near the wall, folding her hands. "And you know that bothers me. I believe you think you feel better but to be honest, Char, if you weren't Half, you might not have survived. First you try to climb that wall, then you get on that girl's bad side. It's almost as if you're intentionally doing this just to make my life difficult."

"Yeah, was just dying to see you," I mumbled. "Worth every bruise and cut, head wound and broken jaw."

I suspected Lily didn't really do sarcasm, but the stern rebuke in her tilted chin and lowered brow made clear knew it when she heard it.

"Nothing is worth those. My answer is still no. You can't 'go watch', but I can't really stop you. Did Shai-Yeh put you up to this?"

"Actually, I haven't seen her since I first came here." I looked around the main hall of the Malevolent Hand and thought how different it appeared to me now, even after only a few weeks. It was Eyesun; the windows were open and generous. I hadn't seen another Rose – in fact, I had hardly seen Thorn or Chang as well, either in this entrance room or any other part of the chapterhouse. Orchid alone came to visit me, saying it was her duty or something. She hadn't apologised for almost destroying my jaw, and I had the feeling she never would, either. "I guess Shai-Yeh is busy tracking—" Lily probably didn't know about the sword. "Tracking down bad people. Or something."

"Irresponsible of her, to leave you here just like that. I thought she'd take care of you, but—"

"Not her," I cut the Healer off, far sharper than I'd expected. Worried I might have been too harsh, I glanced her way. She wasn't looking at me, favouring her hands folded in her lap. "I mean, I'm bored, Lily! I want to stretch my legs."

"Then stand up," she muttered.

"You know what I mean! Everyone else is out there, training. I'm stuck at this desk reading crap about the importance of colours. What importance?"

"If you were more careful in your play, you wouldn't be 'stuck' inside, would you? You'll know better than to pick a fight with Orchid next time."

I pretended I didn't hear her and just went on studying the text spread open before me, but when Lily said that name it felt wrong; the two didn't belong in the same world.

"It's been quiet at the Haven for a while," she chattered. Although I hadn't been back to the Benevolent Hand, I had a feeling she didn't get the chance to talk much there. "Just the usual illnesses and accidents. I suppose that's a good thing – means the Peddlers are doing their job, but…" Then she did that thing where she found some reason to cheer up without looking too hard. "Hey, it gives me time to come and see you." I was wrong. Maybe she *did* do sarcasm.

"Come and annoy me, don't you mean?" I said. "You healed me, and that's good, but I'm healed now, right?"

"I'm annoying you? But don't you get lonely?"

"Wouldn't be so damn lonely if you'd let me go outside."

"It's okay. I know your story now, Char." Which one? Was there more than one? "Shai-Yeh told me she's not actually your sister, and that you didn't have a home, or a family. Just that Society for Delinquent Children or something. You're used to being alone, probably don't even know when you are lonely."

Oh, God, not her too.

"My story? If you mean that I'm a Rat from the Nest, that I'm a bully and a thief, then yeah, that's exactly it. Big fuckin' deal."

"Char!"

"Sorry. But that's the sort of things Rats say."

"You'd still be you if you didn't, you know. If you weren't."

"Hm. Very well, I will endeavour to refrain from further verbal violence, your Ladyship." Strange how easily grandiloquence came to me, not so strange how easily I disliked it. I'd behave, but only around her. That'd have to do.

"That should help you get along here better, anyway."

Did she know what 'here' really meant? Sometimes she was so naïve, but she worked at the Haven, and if anyone should know what the Peddlers do, what they really do, it was her.

"At least you're safe, Char. You're in good hands. Oh, I made a funny." And she smiled her small, almost shy smile. It suited her round face. I looked up from the words I'd barely been looking at to tilt my head, frown and then half-smile back.

"Yeah, you did. So you'll tell me when I can begin training, right?"

"Of course!" Lily wasn't adept at deception, but she could get huffy with the best of them. "I know how much it means to you, Char. It won't be long, I promise."

That sounded like a farewell; best to hide my eagerness.

"I guess I'll behave until then. Colours aren't that boring, anyway. Red and blue and whatnot." I sank back into the mock-study, trying to ignore the others outside in the back courtyard, with their laughter and shouting and occasional screams.

"You should know the basics of that already. Red is safety, blue is danger. That's kiddy-stuff, Char. What about green and yellow?"

Oh, great. I opened my big mouth to let her know I'm being a good boy and she took it for an invitation to quiz me.

"Green is the colour of my puke after I'm done being sick of all this reading. Or was that yellow?" I chose to fail her quiz so grandly that it couldn't be anything but a deliberate show of intellect. My time with Guan-Pi and lording over the Rats had taught me this well.

"How vulgar!"

"How true."

"I'll be back tomorrow," she sniffed with what could have been disdain and then stood, smoothing her skirt self-consciously.

"You better be. Come and tell me it's okay for me to play already!"

"That's all you care about, isn't it? Oh, how I miss being so young and carefree."

Was she really going to leave with that insult? I tried to retort, but by the time I could muster something worth saying, she was gone.

Alone now in the entrance hall, alone as everyone enjoyed the pre-dinner hours outside, I cursed my head, Shai-Yeh and the stupid, annoying lesson about colours ten times over, then went back to reading even though it made my head hurt because Shai-Yeh had scrambled my brains. Was it going to be like this forever?

"Always such a baby, Char. I didn't hit you that hard," she said, resting her practice staff upon a bare, sweat-laced shoulder, even as my own shoulder throbbed and ached. "What in Eph were you doing, closing your eyes like that?"

"I don't know. Thought it might help me focus."

Orchid rolled *her* eyes. "On what? The insides of your eyelids? Don't be stupid, Char. All it'll do is stop you from seeing your enemy. You're distracted today. What's up with you?"

"I was just thinking," I replied, staring at the sullen parade of clouds above the courtyard's walls.

"About?" Orchid wasn't really curious; annoyed, yes, and probably impatient.

"That's the thing. I don't know." Was that a rabbit floating by? Someone's face?

"Look, you're not supposed to know this," she confided after glancing around the abandoned enclosure, "but Thorn's going to offer you a place on a Weed-Pulling trip in a few weeks."

And there I was, thinking about rabbits in the sky! Invited into the field, and barely after my fourteenth birthday!

"What?" As if I hadn't heard her.

With a rising growl, Orchid twirled the stick around her head, crying out as she drove it down towards me. I thought I should have used my sword to block her attack, or maybe—

"That's a bit better," she grunted after I'd somehow extricated myself. Evasion had once been a conscious effort: rolling, bending, tucking, twisting. All those little mechanics practiced over and again until they were one action, and then not even that. Bruises, both from mistakes in technique and the rigours of repetition, were tattoos of unnoticed achievement. I was a little tougher now, though, after the hours, days, and then months of physical conditioning, of meshing painfully slow theory with awfully fast sparring. I'd wanted to leap right into things, of course. Thorn himself said I was unusually apt, and I'd been better than the other Rats at just about everything. As with everything else before Shai-Yeh and my fall, that had been nothing but the basics.

"How would you know?" I bit back, knowing she'd used my anxiety of becoming a real Blood Peddler to rip me out of the daydream. Several feet from Orchid now, I fell into a loose defensive stance. I should have been out of breath, but we Halves have an uncanny aptitude for defying what 'should' be. "Why would Thorn tell you?"

"That," she barked, leaping towards me with a fresh series of swings, hacks and thrusts, "is my business!"

"Tell me!" I demanded as Orchid overextended herself, maybe seeing a chance to shatter my ribs. Curling into a crouch and feeling the wind of her strike pass overhead, I lashed out with a backhanded swipe straight for the back of her knees. The slash struck home: she would have lost her legs from the thighs down if the sword had been real. I contented myself with knocking her off-balance, but did not pause to enjoy the success: it was no success until she, my enemy, was out of action.

Orchid staggered forward onto all fours; now her cry was one of surprise and dismay. Momentum carried me through a natural circle, gathered my sword into a second arc – this one designed to crush her right collar bone.

Prone but defiant, Orchid raised her right hand, the left still supporting her weight. Wooden edge and naked palm drew together. I envisioned her knuckles and fingers crumpling in the weapon's path and tried to pull the blow. A shoulder wound could be treated easily enough, but a broken hand would take longer to heal, and that might have affected whether or not I'd be welcome to join a Weeding.

Her eyes condemned mine, flooding with tell-tale darkness as she exerted her Talent. Orchid's brows clenched and my attack stopped. There was something between her hand and my sword, something unseen but impenetrable – a forceful, denying something. I knew what it was.

"That trick again?" I asked under my breath. There was no use in fighting her Aerian defence: that was precisely what she wanted. Instead, her attempt to block my assault would become a deflection, in good time. My pushing against the thickened air coerced her into applying more repulsion. Grinning at her teeth-gnashing effort, I pressed even harder. All she had to do was withdraw her denial, flow with the attack and counter – that was the gamble. But she wouldn't. By then, I was intimate with Orchid's stubborn expression, her obstinate reactivity.

"*Saseruka!*" she cried.

She 'wouldn't let me'?

"You have no choice!"

Her response was to bend her elbow a bit, just so she could straighten it with renewed vigour.

That was my sign. Her push became unknowing propulsion: I wrenched in the other direction suddenly, as fire is known to do when the wind changes. The wooden sword sailed through a new crescent. I released my right hand from the hilt, adding flexibility to the weapon's very brief journey. With my now free hand, I decided, mid-spin, to punish Orchid's inability to adopt a new strategy. Amidst the accumulation of this latest strike, I tapped my own Talent, collecting a sheath of Fire around my fingers.

Orchid, for all her uncreative reactions, had used the few seconds to resume her feet and set safe distance between us. The oak weapon carved naught but air. I'd expected that. This was about momentum again, about turning an attack into nothing other than a feint – or a planned counterbalance. If one is quick enough to learn and adapt, there are no failed attacks.

"No choice at all!" I laughed as my fist, incandescent and triumphant, hammered against her staff. What could she do now? There wasn't time for either Aerian measures or even a more mundane alternative. She would have been better served, again, by not trying to meet my power with her own: by holding the stick firm, Orchid made it all the easier for me to snap it.

"Now tell me," I breathed, looking up at her through the flutter of embers. "Or do I have to break you too?"

"You—you wrecked it." Her fingers tapped the tip of her now-halved weapon.

"It's just a stick, Orchid." She wasn't easy to defeat but it was over. At least until she got her hands on a new staff. You never knew when Orchid's idea of 'done' might become a decision to get back to the singular task of beating the crap out of whoever she decided needed it. "Were you serious?"

"I'm always serious, Char. My God, it's hot." But she didn't let it go.

Feathers of flame faded from the air around me; it was safe to approach her. Or so I thought.

"Let me see." After placing my own redundant stick on the ground, I padded towards her.

"Here, touch this," she instructed, tapping the singed, splintered end. I moved to do so, but instead of wood, found myself feeling skin. I looked away from her hand, towards her face – a blush? The brutal Orchid Witherheart, blushing? And biting her lip? Perhaps this was my reward for besting her at last.

"Not that, Half-wit," she whispered, pulling her hand back so that it rested at the base of the broken staff. I resisted the temptation to chase her retreating touch. Orchid nodded at the tip of the weapon. "This."

She was right: it was hot, but cooling swiftly enough. Annoying. I tried to finish the job, channelling a stronger flow of Fire.

"Not that," Orchid repeated, dropping her end of the staff; it fell limp in my own hands then clattered to the courtyard floor. She breached the distance between us, taking my yet-warm hand in her own and placing it against her chest. "This."

"That was quite the show."

"Eh?"

"You and Orchid," Blossom said, mincing down the steps into the courtyard. "How long have you two been like that?"

"Like what?" How much had she seen before Orchid slipped away? "I'd kinda like it if you didn't tell anyone."

Like asking a dog not to bark.

"You think they don't know?" The supple girl was somehow sensual despite the standard drab robes of a trainee, an absence of makeup and thick, untended hair – at most times, so carefully combed and pinned:

she would tie it up so that men could enjoy letting it down. Rumours were that she was already working in a reputable house of pleasure, but since she was the biggest gossip in the Hand, there was no telling either way. "You're both Halves. No offence, Char, but no one else could or would even want to fill her role."

"Yeah, we're abnormal like that," I said, taking offence and rubbing it into the dirt.

"Well, maybe Chang could," she mused, sitting on the bottom-most step.

"What?"

"Don't look at me like that, Char. I'm just saying that maybe Chang might be able to keep up with you as well."

"You mean. Oh. Oh!" Good thing my feet were scuffing the ground, because I'd almost rammed them into my mouth. "Yeah, I'd like to see how that turns out."

"Mmm. Or you could watch Orchid and Chang going at it, just so you can see what it looks like. You probably have no idea, huh? Being in the middle of the act and all."

Now I had to look. Blossom, however, was just sighing at the courtyard.

"I don't get you, Blossom. 'Looks like'?"

"Pffft. You're Half. Unnatural? Sure, but not in a bad way. It's hard to watch you two move that quickly. I can't even tell you apart. It's all screaming and smacking and—" she sighed. "God, but I wish I could get some action like that."

Oh, come on! Now she had to be teasing me.

"Maybe you and One-Slash Butterfly could?" Go on, Blossom. Bite that one. If I see even a twitch of lips, you're so dead.

"Oh, we used to," she said. "We were like this, y'know?" Blossom clasped her hands together, almost smiled and then, fingers limp in her lap once more, sighed again. "Now she's busy with Chang, since they both share the same interest in knives. I'm just whatever I am."

Was it worth pursuing?

What a shame I didn't ask myself that at the time.

"I bet whatever you are knows all sorts of moves you could teach me," I teased, beckoning her with a few waves of Orchid's old sword.

"Oho, I hardly think myself worthy, My Lord!" Blossom bowed her head, then raised her eyes with a playful grin, which froze almost immediately. She didn't need to lift her finger, because those eyes were now looking not at me but past my shoulder.

Don't turn around, don't think about it, don't—

"Don't stop on my account," Orchid said in a pleasant, light voice. "Char, Thorn wants to see you about what we discussed before, when you broke my sword, or was it the other way around?" Fitting words for a swift departure.

"Oh my. She's claiming you already," Blossom giggled. "Do you know what happened to her last boyfriend?"

"I'm not her fuckin' boyfriend."

"Fine, fine. I can see I've done enough damage here." She was such a sharp girl sometimes. "Best not to keep Thorn waiting."

"Remember what I asked!" I called, but she'd already left.

Right after that, Thorn announced that Chang The Knife would be in charge of the Weeding and that I was to be part of it. Our paths hadn't crossed much in the past two years, so the chance of seeing him, perhaps showing him how much I'd learned, made me even happier than just being included in the Peddlers' true business despite my age. My role was to be a guide: the Weeds in question were a childless couple who lived in Siu-Tsin – suburb of the Rats' Nest, of my grotty upbringing.

When I read the address, I knew why Thorn had chosen me.

'Don't forget to cover your face," he said before I left, knowing I wouldn't.

As we made our way through the streets of my unruly childhood, my bullying of Jaku and none-too-graceful courtship of Wu Jen-Wah, my wasted adolescence, I felt very little nostalgia and no regret in leaving it all behind.

When we arrived just before Highmoon, I moved to open the door.

"Char," Chang hissed, pushing in front of me, "you've done your bit. Go home."

"I am home," I said, moving past him and into the house. Of course, I could navigate it better than any of them, although Chang and the other two Pricks had no doubt studied the layout to a point of flawless, silent infiltration. I stalked through the living room, the ill-kept kitchen, up those crude stairs upon which I had sat and listened to their arguments and down a hallway that had never seemed so short.

I stared down at my sleeping 'parents' – could smell the alcohol on the man's breath, saw the moonlight stab the woman through a gap in shutters of disrepair. A silvery shaft cut a fine slash across her cheek, revealing a large bruise. I never pitied her: she was stupid enough to stay with him even after I'd run away. I raised my wooden sword and waited. Someone, or something, had to intervene, or I would revisit years of abuse upon these two who had evaded righteous retribution – and that, only because I had hardly thought of them otherwise.

"Why?" Chang limited himself to a single, soft word – probably worried about waking the pair up. I'd heard that conscious Weeds could be reluctant to accept God's will.

"Need them alive, right?" I did not share his apprehension, wanted them awake so that I could see the fear in their eyes, fear I'd shown them for far too long.

"Yes."

"Good. Block the exit, please. Now." The final word was both a reiteration and an announcement.

The first attack broke my adopted father's leg. I felt it give under the thin blanket. Pain woke him up; he howled from what I figured was a mix of pain, confusion and disbelief. The woman I once called 'mother' screeched herself awake, fell from the bed and backed into a corner.

The man's almost-words of protest fell under a fresh tumble of screams and gibbering as I swung at his chest. Ribs caved.

"Isn't that enough?"

No, Chang-dailoh, it wasn't. The arms went next. Then a single sound blow to the face demolished his nose and mouth both.

"If you kill him, we're screwed," Chang noted. There was no tone of warning – maybe he understood what I was doing. He, too, was a Half – and he, too, had no idea who his real parents were. Few Halves did; we were a product of shame and abnormality. Chang, Orchid and I had all sworn in our hearts if not to each other to someday find our more Noble sires, hunt them down. But then what? Kill them? Perhaps that's all the training was for.

Until then, this would have to do.

"Done with him," I said, advancing on the woman as Chang motioned for the two other Pricks to 'help' the man out of the room. Amazingly, he struggled. Chang responded by giving him a smart, efficient knock on the head with the blunt of his knife.

"Why?" the woman managed, raising her hands in futile defence.

"You are a Weed. Worse than that, you are a BAD mother!" I drew my sword back to teach her what this meant when she asked,

"Who are you?!"

I wanted to uncover my face so that she could see her 'son', who had come back to show her what a fine young man I'd turned out to be. But that was against the rules, even though wouldn't matter what she knew or thought come the morning. Both would be gone by then. And I'd broken enough rules tonight.

"Char, we have to go."

"There. Now you know who I am," I spat upon her and turned my back to leave.

"Who?"

I refused to give her the answer she wanted and left my 'home' for the last time.

"Your parents?" Chang asked after both of them had been hauled off to the chapterhouse.

"Yeah, I think. But why. Why didn't?" I stopped, determined to collect a whole sentence from the mess of my feelings. "She didn't recognise me, Chang-dailoh." I shook my head and melted into tears. "Why didn't she recognise me? They treated me like shit, and then forgot me."

Chang held me for a long time as I blubbered, but when he thrust me back, his words were stern and final:

"This didn't happen. You went home after you guided us there and the Weeds tried to resist. You understand me, little brother? Dry your eyes and waste no more pain or thought on them. Go home. This time, do as I say."

And that was my first experience with Weed-Pulling. It would remain my most traumatic experience for several years, if not necessarily the rest of my life.

"Life? What does that mean to you, hm?" The old man asked around a mouthful of apple.

He was being typically curious; people loved to talk, and they loved to be given permission to talk – about themselves, all too often. I felt something not unlike love for him, but wariness responded to his effusive interest. More than once, he'd been both the teacher and the lesson.

"Duty. Work. Learning. I'm a Guard now, did I tell you?" The usual cover story. Not exactly a lie.

"Only three times so far. But seriously, what happened the last time I saw you? When you were going after her, was it?"

Was he faking this vagueness?

"Just a sword. Not a 'her'. I was a stupid kid. After the Kasuden envoys left, the Guards released me. What threat would I be to their precious weapon if it isn't here, right?"

I reached over, plucking a persimmon from the array of morsels between us. He did not stop me, although it was rude to do before he suggested it. Nor did he offer me anything to drink – Leung Guan-Pi was never known to drink anything but tea, and that was his alone to enjoy. "Then I was asked to join them, join the Guard. Asked, with notable incentive."

The Godfather of the Rats leaned forward, out of the shadows slightly, just enough to leave the half-eaten apple on the table. He looked older, inestimably older: stretched skin, slow movement, belaboured breathing. I saw the way he scratched his knobbly knees beneath the unassuming robe, the attention he allocated to rubbing his heavy shoulders. His sporadic, almost self-reassuring caresses of a wispy, altogether useless beard.

But it was still an act: the affectations of age hung over his bones just a little too effectively. That sly gleam lingered in his half-shaded eyes.

"A Guard who hides his face under a hood. But I know you, Half. That voice, those fingers."

"You were right, that time, Goong-sinsan. Not everyone can be a Guard."

"Is that so." Was he proud or despondent? "But your story doesn't end there. It starts, I think. Why are you here?" Guan-Pi leaned back and even that sharp sparkle of intellect in his eyes lost itself to the darkness. This was starting to feel like an interrogation.

"I missed you." I think I meant it. "I missed this room. Our talks. What I was to you."

"Me? Not me, Half. You miss being better than everyone else." Guan-Pi did not hesitate; with his acute response, battle was inevitable. "You miss the way Wong Chu-Deng tried to hide his fear of you by always pushing you around. You miss lording over the Rats, and you miss me giving you special treatment. But that is all in the past. Why are you here *now*?"

I absorbed this with conditioned aloofness. Why? A whim? I could have said that and probably even sold him on the idea. Nostalgia was no flimsy tether about Guan-Pi's conscience.

I decided to tell the truth.

"You know what I am, Guan-Pi." I reached for another piece of fruit from his delicate assortment; let him understand I was welcome here and knew it. This time, I retrieved an apple of my own and tore a healthy portion of its flesh. The juice was cold upon my chin. "You said it yourself: I'd make a good Guard. Maybe I'm here to arrest you? Ha! You almost laughed. You know better. I'm here for one of the kids, actually."

"Is that Menu final?"

"Yes."

"Even the little girl?"

"Yes."

It was the truth – and it wasn't.

"My kids get arrested all the time, Half, and I take care of that too. You should remember how many times I bailed you out." With this, Guan-Pi made a feeble fist and pounded his thigh lightly. What did that mean? What was he trying not to tell me with so obtuse a gesture? "I don't even really know what sort of Guard you are – still in training, though. They wouldn't send a trainee into the Nest."

"They would if he said he had inside information. But you're right. I'm just a student. I pulled a few strings to get here before anyone officially." There – my gift to you, old man: I'm not the dark storm come. Just the first breeze, or maybe that stillness of air before the catastrophe. "One of your kids has been conspiring with Revolutionaries."

"I see. Revolutionaries. Hm. I won't ask how you know, because I know." Guan-Pi sent his sunken eyes roving the dark corners of the inner sanctum. I wanted to follow suit, but could not look away from him, not for a second. What if he did something I could not read? What if I were not looking when he revealed his true intent? "Do you know a Guard came for you once?"

I remained silent, palms dry against my own tense thighs. A different Char would have wiggled in discomfort by now, adjusting his feet to alleviate the weight upon bones not designed to support an entire body. He would have been glancing around as well, but, as I said, that's what a different Char would do.

"It was just before your twelfth birthday."

So was everything else! I wanted to yell; the wave of serene momentum almost broke. But that's what I thought, and it was only thought. And when your boss can read minds, you learn very quickly how to layer your thoughts, how to make some 'louder' than others.

"That's a long time ago now," I said, but I knew he wouldn't respond to that. A pity: I would've liked to know just how long.

"Same accusation, too. I tried to tell you, do you remember?"

"Yes." And I'd been a child; I'd missed his real intention.

"You were so bent on getting that sword."

He laughed. I didn't.

"In fact," he continued, "the same person who provided me with information on the weapon tried to take you away. She strode through my Nest as though she knew precisely where to go, what to do. As though she'd been here before."

Were I anything but a Peddler, a devotee to the grander fate dictated by God, I'd have reeled at the sudden understanding. And all I could feel, despite everything she'd done, was bitter admiration. I knew, then, that I would accept whatever she wished to teach me. She could make me a Prick, could give me what I needed to overcome even that, to become a Sword. The Scourge.

"But you didn't know her name, did you?"

"She knew mine. And she knew yours. I'd always known you were special, of course."

That wasn't praise – it was a lament. He went on:

"She wore no uniform, carried no sword. Do you understand? She was a Priestess, Half, a Kasuden dignitary with all the authority of a thousand Guards. Even though she was young, she threw the name of God around like *it* was a sword. Said that you would abandon me after your twelfth birthday. She advised that I kill you to avoid this.

"I tried to dismiss her, Half. You can't understand how I tried. It's not easy to deny the words of a Priestess. She had no obvious reason to want you dead, and believe me, I kept a firm list of those that did – and do, but that's neither here, there nor anywhere. Her knowledge of you was frightening, because it far eclipsed my own. She named your parents and she cited precisely what I'd done upon finding you at my door. I can't make it any clearer, Half: she knew you with the intimacy of a dedicated, obsessed enemy. I couldn't curse her and I couldn't agree with her.

"Still, I did agree, didn't I? In my silence, I agreed with her every word."

"You had no choice, Guan-Pi." No choice and no chance.

"There's more, Half. She said that she herself would put you on the path that'd lead you to destroy me. Two days after learning that, I told you about the sword. I told you because she said I would. For every moment until then, I swore that I wouldn't tell you, that your twelfth birthday should come and go in quiet ignorance. Then you were here, bright as ever, sharp as always, and I felt I couldn't hide from you even that which you didn't know you sought."

"This isn't about me, Guan-Pi," I said. "I'm here for one of the kids."

He said nothing more for some time. I could see some strain of forbidden knowledge dragging his conscience through a thick, heavy web of angst. Here was a man who, if not for age and influence, would have been Weeded long ago. This sort of double-standard failed to bother me – God had a plan for him. It wasn't a pious thought, any more than conceding that maybe I was an integral part of that plan.

"There's more, Half," he repeated, saying something completely new. "I've named Wong Chu-Deng my successor."

What? Did he expect me to quake and thunder? To cry denial and challenge?

I listened.

"He'll move against you." Now he was more than resigned to his impending demise – he was trying to arrange the method and the time. "The Society's vision will falter." And he squinted, blinking furiously. "With me, it dies. Just another gang, just another brick in the demented wall of Kaifeng's seclusion. I had such visions, Half."

And now he'd start about how close he'd come to success, about how his end was nigh, if only, if only, if only.

"But she made it clear to me."

Or not. Shai-Yeh was still in control even though I had not seen her since joining the Malevolent Hand chapterhouse.

"And we agreed – you were not my proper heir. Too good for this world of deception and dubious dealings. Not pure, no, but talented. Capable beyond your means, and so I tried to provide you with other means. She knew that too. 'Stop trying to make him what you couldn't be', she said. And I, proud and foolish, asked in turn, 'What's so wrong with trying to show him how to be better?' Her answer, her last words to me, was a fitting elegy for my illusions."

Silent once more, Guan-Pi neither fidgeted nor glanced around. His former nervousness had succumbed to a small death. I almost mentioned my reason for being there again when he breathed in, hovered on a state of fullness, and then exhaled.

"So you went. And you are a Guard, or so you say. Where is your uniform, I wonder?"

And he did wonder, because he was staring at me, me in my too-plain grey robe. I was no real Peddler yet, but that transition was assured. I wore their particular vestment already, under insignificant cloth and skin.

"I didn't have to wear it today. Might have scared the Rats."

"Where is your badge? Where are your lapel-pins? What rank are you?"

Had he done this before, assisted by implements of cutting, digging and breaking? Not difficult to believe. I chose to meet his rote queries with standard disappointment.

"Left it at the station. Don't need to wear them when I'm off-duty. Trainee Third Class, Heavenly Kaifeng Enforcement. And to save you asking, Guan-Pi, I won't tell you the location of our secret base, no matter how much you torture me."

I laughed. He didn't.

"Where is your sword, Half?"

I was too ready to play now. The question didn't sting as it might have half an hour previous.

"Trainees only get wooden swords, and I didn't feel like bringing it on what is technically a social call. I just want to talk to the kid in question, Goong-sinsan."

"You do not get to call me that in the same breath with which you lie to me, Half," he snapped, once more the confident, potent Godfather of Kaifeng's little moral abortions. "Haven't I already shown you that you do not have to lie to me?"

I didn't think he had, didn't believe he could. I would not concede that he wanted something as simple as the truth.

"I'm here to talk to one of the kids about the dangers of associating with Revolutionaries, Guan-Pi." After taking one last bite of the crisp apple, I deposited the core upon the low wooden table and looked an old man in the eyes. "And just as you had no choice the last time, you have none now. Let me go to him."

"You're just like her now, aren't you?" The befuddled nature of his flustered babble might not have been altogether forced. "No uniform, no weapon. But a warrior nonetheless, waging your war against a young man's hope, against his chances of a good life."

"I'm not like her, Guan-Pi. She—" This would not be easy. "She is close to God. She knows her purpose and commits herself to it wholeheartedly. I'm just doing my job, knowing neither why nor what. But I am doing something, Guan-Pi. I have made something of myself. I thought—" Not easy at all. "I thought you'd be proud of me."

"I believe you will end me, Half. I believe that Chu-Deng is the last hope for my Society, and that he must forge it against those whom you now serve. I believe that God has chosen different sides of the field for you and me, Half, and that She means this to be our last meeting. And for all this, I am proud of you, boy. You used to talk with your fists; now you've learned the value of a conversation. You move like a man who knows his worth, and yet you are only eighteen. Nineteen?"

"Seventeen in two weeks."

"Sixteen, then. So young and yet so purposeful. You've come here to take away a kid who is really not so much different to what you were."

"What, he's a Half too?" I snorted, deliberately sweeping a long fringe back, knocking aside for a significant moment the folds of my dark cowl. "Nothing like me, Guan-Pi. Do you know which one it is?"

"I'd guess it's your old friend Jaku."

"That is correct." In my memory, the flabby little bastard had become nothing but a reminder of what a hopeless waste I used to be. When I'd seen his name on the Menu, I begged Thorn to let me handle it. "He's been consorting with—"

"I know!" Guan-Pi almost wailed. He should have been stronger near the end. "With Revolutionaries! You said it already! I know it!"

He should not have been so fragile as to make his own traps. I didn't even need to use bait. I felt sick at how gladly my former mentor leapt into the pit.

"Members of the Bloody Shadows, actually, Guan-Pi. They happen to be Revolutionaries, of course, but now you see the dangers in keeping Terasawa around."

And it should not have been so nauseatingly easy to break this pillar.

Then Leung Guan-Pi cast off his garb of elderly frailty one last time.

"Half," he declared, "the Bloody Shadows are mine. Their Revolutionary ways – my idea, my teaching. I hate this city just as I hate every single Mifūnjin. I would remove the Tsukamoto from power and then from life, one by one. Do you think the Society alone could achieve this?" He smiled, and there was the predator once again, diving fang-first into its final hunt, its last great strutting domination of the urban wild. "You were to be my heir, you and any I could turn against the ruling classes, they who turned me out. Rejected me because I saw straight through them.

"And I was not so much older than you are now when they came for me, as she came for you and you come for Jaku. They sought the rebellious Tsukamoto Genma, they whose thoughts are always on the thoughts of others. I knew that my blood would save me, just as I knew that same blood had betrayed me. They came for the firstborn of Tsukamoto Tatsunojo but could not find Leung Guan-Pi, who slipped their chains and defied their bonds. I ran and ran, deeper and darker, never once losing my ideas, my faith. But in the end I betrayed all values and morals, all save one, and to that I say farewell at last."

Perhaps I should have been taking notes.

"An army, do you see? I have an army now, recruited from the very streets of the city I hate, and I will topple the pyramid, Half!" His beady gaze narrowed into shrewd sharpness. Lips gave way to a ginger sneer. "With the might of the Bloody Shadows and those I have trained – you were not the only one in whom I saw potential – I will teach Kaifeng the greater way. The way of the people, unified against an elitist, outnumbered aristocracy."

For which I cared not even a bit. This, however, was Guan-Pi's finale. It deserved neither protest nor interruption.

"You'd have made a good leader, Half. Chu-Deng, a proper advisor for the darker aspects of government. And all the Rats, they'd swarm the abused courts and ornate seats of office, stripping the Palace room by room of all opulence, dispersing among the many the wealth of the few and I, I'd die to see that."

He sagged, as if mention of why he would die reminded him that he *would* die.

"But now everything's changed. She's taken you from me; Chu-Deng dismisses my grander ideas and seeks to merge the Society with the Shadows into a private war clan to rule the underworld. And with him, go all my Rats. Your Jaku and Jen. Changed. All changed. "

"Of course." I said, tired of his tirade. "Doesn't change why I am here." Or did it? Would my unspoken battle, my vendetta, against the Bloody Shadows now become an official campaign? It was not unheard-of for Peddlers to work with the Guard, with any who accept God and

The Night, accept the Night's Own hierarchy – even if the greatest of Peddlers actively fought the Night's Own.

"Maybe not, Half, and maybe so. Who am I to say? Just a rebel who entered the system to change it, to destroy it, and then found himself using it, abusing it. Dependent upon it."

"Is he here, Guan-Pi? Is Jaku here?" I felt it more than actually seeing or hearing the symptoms: the old man was about to fade.

"Of course not. You know where he is. The Den. The Ways of Life." Codenames for where the Bloody Shadows lurked. Their lair, for they were beasts. Not even the Peddlers knew the exact location. Shit. "They all are. Didn't you notice how quiet the Nest is now?"

And I hadn't! Were my memories of a frenetic, crowded Nest stronger than the abandoned reality?

Shit and shit again!

"Enjoying the fruit?"

Wha?

Then he coughed blood, a great glob of black mirth. I moved – and I moved quickly now, around the table, across that which divided us. I cradled him; it took no invitation for him to rest his spindly body against my chest.

"What have you done, you old fool?" I wanted to shake him so hard, to make him talk – but he was shaken enough. "I didn't do this! Do you hear me? This isn't my business anymore!"

"Oh no, Half. You did this. You and that witch of God. Curse Her! Her and all Her hosts! To hell with Afraen and Adael, with Shynsa and the lot of them."

He cackled, producing another drooling mass of forced disease.

"And you, and you too, Half. You whom she came to take." Guan-Pi clawed at my shirt, shuddering but determined to stare up at me. His eyes alone were alive, unyielding. "Tsukamoto Genma curses you most of all. Take you to Hell Above with me."

The fruit. Was that not a strange burning I felt in my chest? The onset of the toxins lacing each and every sliver of sweet goodness on the table clutched me, or was that just the power of belief that I had been poisoned?

"Good, eh? Good stuff." He burped, of all things, and there was something solid in the belch. A limp slice of dislodged tissue clung to his lower lip like a bloody worm squeezing from of an infested orifice. "I know my stuff. Invited Jaku but he didn't come. You gotta find him for yourself. Him, Wong Chu-Deng, their new master. You know him? Another like you."

"He is like me. A Half?"

"More than just that."

"You mean he was a Rat, don't you?"

"Thinks he was." The failing old man retched and hacked, but it was mostly dry. "She has him thinking he was. Now he rules my army, my Shadows. Now he's breaking my Rats."

I fought, desperate to know before the poison could carve its fetid trench through my resolve. "What is his name? This pretend-Rat. Fa Shai-Yeh's messed with him too, and you helped her! Damn you, old man, damn you for this!"

Then, no longer able to contain myself, I turned away, still with him wrenching at my clothes, and spat what should have been a flood of blood and saliva. Instead, a simple gobbet of dark green fluid splattered against the floor. It was too thick to spread, too heavy to fade.

"Knew it," Guan-Pi said, "I knew it. You're too strong for even my poisons. So you're not coming to Hell with me quite yet. When you arrive, I'll be waiting, Hua-Shi. I'll gladly attend your throne."

So he knew the other Half. The Pretend-Rat. Leader of my hated Bloody Shadows. And – he mistook me for that monster?

"What did you call me?"

"Trained you good, we did. She said you'd be different, but who are you? Hiding under that hood."

Why wasn't he dead? For how long had he been dying? I almost broke his neck – that was how much pity I now felt for the fallen Godfather of Kaifeng.

"Not enough time. Diary. You can figure out where it is; you're a smart kid, Hua-Shi."

"Stop calling me that."

"You used to say the same when I'd call you 'Half'. Do you know, Half, do you know what she told me last?"

I shook my head, though not as an answer to his question. It was all I could do to not laugh in acidic disbelief. To end like this: no fitting fate for a man I once admired. It should have been me to do it.

"I said to the Priestess: 'What is so wrong with trying to show him how to be better?' It was always about you. Both of you. All about you."

But this isn't, I thought. This is your story's end, Guan-Pi, Tsukamoto Genma. Anticlimactic, banal and insignificant. For your ideals, you denied glory and real power, and now you're about to die in the arms of the one person who understands that choice.

Words I'd never said stirred: I will find another way to be me!

Then something I should have never said made itself known.

"It's about me, to everyone but me."

Guan-Pi trembled in my arms. Horror of all horrors, he smiled through the accumulation of fluids and flesh around and coming from within his mouth.

"This is what she said, Half. 'Your way only teaches him to disrespect his teachers. Mine will show him how to kill them.' She was right. So right."

"And that's all she said?"

"My diary, Half. Everything you need is in there. You'll stop him, won't you? Hua-Shi. Let me." With a strength sustained by determination alone, Guan-Pi lifted a thin, wasted hand. "See."

What would it hurt to grant a dying man's wish? But I suspected something, just as I had not that night, years ago, when dealing with my 'parents'.

What his weak hand could not do, mine completed, easing back the cowl.

"You look. One of them now. Nothing like you should be. Like him."

"Who? Who do I look like, Guan-Pi?"

"That pretend-Rat. Bastard. Half. Char."

"No! I am a real Rat! Tell the truth, old man!"

If everyone tells the same lie, is it still a lie?

"If I'd known. You. Would've used stronger poison, hehehe—" laughter dissolved into bloody coughing.

"But it is me. I am me! Not Hua-Shi, just me. Char. Greatest Thief of Kaifeng, do you remember?!"

"Hua-Shi, Greatest Thief. Kaifeng. Not you. You're changed. God, your eyes!"

"What about them?"

And I shook him, because I wanted an answer. Didn't want him dying yet.

But he did. Not the most poignant of deaths, but surprisingly restrained for an old fart who thought, to the last breath, he'd lost all control.

Now that he was dead, I had no need to hold on any longer.

Shortly after tapping memories that mightn't have been my own to find even more, I walked out the front door and turned around, regarding the Nest in all its complex balconies, windows and walkways.

I saw a lot of wood.

"Did you hear about the fire in Siu-Tsin?"

"What?" I glanced at Butterfly across the dining hall table. She, with her plain ponytail and inclination towards shapeless, baggy clothing, was all that Blossom could not be. Quiet, passive…forgettable. Not hard to believe those two were best friends – one sword is often shorter than the other.

No one else paid either of us any attention. They just kept on eating – meals in the Malevolent Hand were hearty and appreciated. I'd already wolfed down my bowl of succulent rabbit, was picking at the vegetables with no real intention of eating them.

"Fire, Char. Big one. Say, isn't Siu-Tsin the suburb you're from? That Rat's Nest place. Oh, all those children. You must have known some of them."

"Hmmm." I pushed a mushy mass of green around the bowl, watching it form mounds of mulch.

"Don't you care, Char?"

"I have other things to care about now. Other people," I replied, not looking up at her. *Other people. People who matter. To me. The real me.* "That was a different life."

"That's cold," she said. "Maybe they got out in time."

"Or before that," I muttered.

"What?"

I shrugged and waited for her to change the subject.

The topic of the old man's diary was two Halves, separated by a few years. One, a foundling left on Guan-Pi's doorstep; the other, a free-spirited bully eschewing the Society. Perhaps worried (or certain) that someone would find and read the journal, he never once referred to either boy by name. One description was Hua-Shi, and the other seemed to be me. One Half took over the Bloody Shadows, the other was trained to be a Blood Peddler; both were at her instigation. Both Halves matched how Guan-Pi had treated me, either from before I was twelve or that last meeting. My name was Char Ah-Ran, but I could not tell which of these two the old man thought me to be. At times confused, at times quite funny, the journal gave me everything I needed and even more that I didn't. It was a manual of my creation, a schedule for my destruction. Conversations I remembered having with Guan-Pi were in there, word for word, but again, I had no idea who Guan-Pi thought he was talking to, all that time. It would all be madness were Fa Shai-Yeh not present throughout the account. No rules, no logic, no common sense applied with her in play. You just took things as they were, even if they probably weren't.

While deciphering the diary, I stepped up my solitary espionage upon the Bloody Shadows. Within the words were enough hints and clues to make it almost easy. I watched, learned and planned.

Guan-Pi's memoirs would have been evidence, but against whom? Fa Shai-Yeh? I wanted nothing to do with her, and yet she alone could help me. Other than that, the little collection of secrets was dangerous. I had what I needed. I knew when I'd move, with and against whom.

So I burned Leung Guan-Pi's diary, sending it to the hereafter right along with the Nest in which it had waited for me.

"You seem a little troubled. Was it too difficult an assignment?" He caught me on the way out early that morning. By Lazysun, his desk would have been unattended – like most of us, Thorn obviously had duties beyond that of mere clerk. Who could say what a Maliscient would get up to? "I send you there to scout, and somehow, the place is burnt to the ground. And you still have not located the Weed."

"I will add to the quota this month, Thorn."

"Char, why did you choose a childhood friend from the Menu? Why is Terasawa Jaku your first Weed?"

Why was he on the Menu in the first place? Not worth asking, but worth thinking about.

"You know that's not your business, Char."

Oh. Of course. Maybe not worth thinking about after all.

"No one else knows where he is, Thorn. It's that simple."

"You're hiding something."

"You tell me."

The moment he went silent, I forced my mind do the same. It was far from appropriate to use a skill designated for handling potential interrogation situations by hostile Maliscients against one's superior, but I needed to have secrets. I wasn't sure if what I was hiding was all that important. It was enough that I knew I knew things that no one else did. Not even Thorn. Especially not.

After a while, Thorn blinked.

"I don't approve of this misuse of the defences we've given you."

"A gift to another, Thorn, is yours only until you give it. That is to say, it never is. I'll tell you this much: I want Chang, Orchid, Butterfly and Blossom when I head out tonight."

"That many, for one Weed? This is not protocol. Are we looking at a Garden here?" He seemed almost put-out by being reduced to actually asking for that which he could normally just take.

"This is my test, Thorn. I ask that you trust me. I promise I won't forget a thing you've taught me. I will earn my title tonight. I'd do anything for that…but this is not worth committing the entire Chapterhouse."

"You've proven that she was right yet again, Char, and that my impressions of you were not astray. But—"

"This is not like you, Thorn. Either yes or no – but if you say 'no', I go alone into what might become a Garden."

"For you to request so much help? Yes. I will have them assemble in an hour at a Haven of your choosing. You have the day to prepare them. Just bring them all back in relatively working shape, alright?"

"Separately, they've Pulled hundreds of Weeds, Thorn. They're my heroes, do you understand? This isn't just a test to see if I'm good enough to be a Prick. I am. This is something else. If we come back, I assure you, we'll be in no other shape. One last thing."

"You're full of demands today, Char. What is it?"

"Have you heard from her?"

"It's been years, Char, and still you ask. Perhaps you should pray for her return; I hear you have been lax in your Temple visits. But your obsession with her is unwarranted. Are your dalliances with Orchid not enough?"

Pray for her return? Thorn wasn't one to suggest so overt a reliance on faith. I never thought to ask him for elaboration: Shai-Yeh had taught me nothing if not the value of figuring things out for myself.

"Not enough time to explain. Next time you see me, I'm going to be different, Thorn. One way or another, everything changes tonight."

Chapter 16: *Reinforcement*
WHAT LOVE IS

This wasn't the most precious thing I learned from Guan-Pi's diary.

The Ways of Life, where the Bloody Shadows rested between their nefarious dealings, was actually an abandoned village several miles west of Kaifeng.

"You're kidding." Chang pored over the map, rotating one of his darts between hypnotic fingers. "Swimming Carp. Never even heard of it."

"Yeah. Apparently they've recently set up there," I said, sitting opposite him.

"Makes sense, when you think about it," One-Slash Butterfly said from across the room. She was straddled over a bench, sharpening the sword that was her namesake. "No one's kept count of how many Shadows there have been since the Society and other gangs all joined Hua-Shi's cause. That many people couldn't stay hidden in Kaifeng. The Nest was bad enough, and now we have to deal with a whole village of them. A shame the old man died. He was a crooked bastard, but things worked with him around."

I glanced at her after tracing a path through the parched streets with a blunt finger. She tried to look away, but in the small room, one of many private chambers within the Benevolent Hand, there wasn't much else to look at but the irate Half piercing his stare through her. "Well, you know what I mean."

She returned her attention to the map.

Orchid, dressed in her customary and very practical Peddler wrappings, passed her throwing weapons to Chang for examination – she hadn't taken up the sword again, not since that time in the courtyard. I did not bother to watch. After relinquishing her arms, Witherheart rose and came around the table, kneading my shoulders with the very same hands that had, and would yet, become fists against my will and wish. I tried to shake her off, finding the gesture inappropriate in front of the others, but she made it clear with an almost affectionate slap about my head that I was, as usual, overreacting.

Last to arrive was Blossom, breathless and breathy.

"Whew! Busy day!" She cast back her bright green hood and revealed her sweating, listless brow – and contrastingly satiated smile.

"I don't know how you do it." Butterfly shook her head, bringing one of her legs over the bench to make room for the exhausted girl. "Sex before an assignment? And knowing you, more than once."

"Five times!" Blossom said with a languorous stretch. "Figured we'd be too busy tonight."

Orchid, against a nature I knew to be unrestrained in its carnality, sniped, "Better not be tired tonight, Blossom dear. This is Char's initiation and if you fuck it up, I'm going to personally bring your escapades to an end. Physically, emotionally. Totally."

Great. Not only was she calling the shots with how affectionate she was in public, now Orchid was my God-damned babysitter?

"Orchid, leave her be." *And me, while you're at it.* "It's going to be very different this time. I've accompanied you all on your Weed pulling, even helped Pick a few Roses. Despite this, tonight is mine. I say what is okay and what isn't, and if Blossom wishes to arrive late, let her."

Butterfly laughed, glad that someone else was receiving my scorn. The girl in question poked her tongue out at Orchid, who was standing behind me. I could only imagine my occasional plaything's scowl. *I cannot afford to play favourites now. Not now, if ever.*

"I wish I'd gone out and done the same then," Orchid sniffed and sauntered towards the wall. Chang guffawed, acting even now the elder brother to my bumbling errors. I ignored each of them and yet regarded the whole. My team. My warriors. My chess pieces. Something about this felt right even though they were all older than me, and I was the only one in the room wearing trainee grey…for the last time.

I tugged unruly hair back from my face, securing it in a short pony tail. Let them see my ears for once.

"This is what is going on," I began, rising to pace the room. I would command them – this meant I had to be among them but never, ever one of them. "I was once a member of the Society for Disadvantaged Youth under the tutelage and care of Leung Guan-Pi, recently deceased. And you all know what happened to the Society immediately after that.

"Before he returned to God's dark heart, Guan-Pi revealed to me that there is an army in development, an insurrection against not only Lord Ayakawa, whom we serve indirectly, but against the Tsukamoto, The Night and God Herself." I was, of course, telling them a lie with a series of carefully selected truths. "The Bloody Shadows, the Society: their number is now several hundred strong."

There were perhaps fifty members of the Malevolent Hand and, at best guess, five or so Peddler Chapterhouses in all of Kaifeng. Ours was the only one with Halves. The Peddlers were specialists, not expendable soldiers. They did not hold with rank and pomp. This was not a war any of them were prepared to fight – and they made this clear with a mix of grumbling and downcast, crestfallen expressions.

"Don't worry. We're not going to try and take them all out. This is a Weeding, not an all-out battle. I won't drag you through your various skills – you know them well enough. Mine, however, remain unknown. I've studied the maps, I know my quarry. But if you do not get me in there, I cannot do this."

I then elaborated a little on Hua-Shi, disclosing that he, too, was once a Rat and Guan-Pi's former protégé – another mix of truth and not-quite-truth; since I myself didn't know the truth in the instance, figured it best to just use what I needed. I brought the *Dao-sha*, Elder Wong Chu-Deng, into play, and then, having softened them with these little blows, claimed quite clearly, "Tonight I will defeat Hua-Shi, leader of the Bloody Shadows."

Did I mean to say that? *This isn't right. Why am I so eager to destroy him? This isn't part of any plan, not even my own!*

"Char," Chang interrupted my thoughts and a long, solemn silence. "I don't mean to spoil your great idea, but he'd massacre you. And that's assuming we even find him. No one even knows what he looks like. All we know is that he is Half – he could be you, Char; he could be me."

The others seemed relieved that The Knife had revealed their collective sentiment.

"Do not forget that his teacher was also mine, Chang. And that I have had better teachers since. Hua-Shi is a primal, undisciplined Half who refuses to accept that at least part of him is Holy."

"Like I said, it's not a bad thing, Char." He let the 'but' speak for itself.

"The main goal is to weed Terasawa Jaku. Given. Yet Hua-Shi will be there and he will oppose us. I know a way to get close to them both without contending with the majority of the Bloody Shadows. I am confident we can get that far without trouble. Thugs do not stay home at night. They like to go out and play."

I smiled then, reminding them without a word that if anyone would know what a thug might do, it would be me.

"Truth is, they're expecting me."

"Just how long have you been planning this behind our backs, Char?" Orchid narrowed her already thin eyes at me.

"It wasn't 'behind your back', Orchid. I just don't want anything to go wrong, and I have to admit I haven't been entirely confident in my planning. Not confident enough to share it, anyway. We're taking a huge risk tonight. I have very specific tasks for each of you, so listen up."

So they did. Although I had no idea if any of this would be put into play, it sufficed that I told each of them that their roles would suit their abilities. By the end of the briefing, their despair and anxiety had given way to eagerness, excitement. Not for the first time, I marvelled at how easily people consume possibilities as certainties provided it gave them pleasure to do so.

"This is going to be fun," Blossom gushed. "Good work always is."

One-Slash Butterfly was studying the map, tapping various locations with the tip of her slender blade. "Why did you make such a big deal of it, Char?"

"All I gotta do is knock a few sentries out?" Chang sneered. "They stand there, begging to be put down!"

"And me," Orchid sniffed, "stuck by your side. They all get to do real work — and you want me to pose as your girlfriend?"

Ouch. I saw Chang's smile die, felt Butterfly's sudden distance and paid no heed to Blossom's knowing grin.

"Will it be that unpleasant, Witherheart?" I asked with deliberate neutrality.

"Stop acting like you care, Char. I'm a better lover than girlfriend and you know it. All that mushy shit. Do I have to hold your hand?"

"I've saved your orders for last, Witherheart. The others don't need to hear the details. If there are no questions, we're done. We meet at Westgate, Risingmoon," I announced to the group. Each of them departed, both knowing their work and understanding that a certain pair of Halves needed a whole moment alone.

"Yes, you have to hold my—"

Orchid crushed her lips against mine. It was a passionate bonding of frenzied, almost desperate theft. I responded with burning abandon, reflecting the Fire I bore even in what was nothing more than heated lust.

"I'm really proud of you, darling," she whispered after pulling back and then leaning in, licking my ear. "You're going to be great. Ha, remember how we met? You said your name was Blackcloak. The Scourge. I didn't believe you – who would? – but now, now I believe in you."

Typical vacuous praise. Each time, I believed *her* a little less.

"There's something very important you need to do tonight, Orchid." Now was not the time for endearment. I was cold in tone if not the way my eyes lingered upon her shoulder, her neck. She continued to tease my ear with her tongue.

"Mmmm?"

"I need you to kiss me in front of Terasawa, really kiss me. As though you love me. Can you do that?"

It was a sobering request and even Orchid paused. My ear felt wet. She didn't need to lick it anymore.

"But what if I do?" she asked, releasing me to turn her back in uncharacteristic meekness.

"You don't, so don't."

"I could," she stressed, sounding small and almost hopeful. I realised, were it her true self, I could fall in love with that.

"Why would you offer what I cannot give back?" I wished it hurt me to say this, but all I felt was relief: dead, dense relief.

"Why can't you?" her voice was still soft, still demure. Still clinging to the act. "Am I that unlovely?"

You can't compete with a Goddess, I almost replied and then forgot.

"You know better than that." It was true; her tomboyishness had flourished into physical self-confidence, and it's almost impossible to question a nature that never seems to question itself. "Besides, this isn't about you."

It's about me. Everyone knows that but me.

"Oh, now there's a line!" She laughed, finally reaching for that caustic composure that had seen her through time and again, perhaps not realising I'd seen through it before. "Then what am I? A toy? Is that what I have become after all?"

"Orchid, we shouldn't feel anything. You face Roses and I will soon follow that path too. Anything other than resolve and dedication to the task clouds the mind and weakens the fist." I meant to say it in a way that sounded less clinical, less detached. Less forced, but that's all this was: clinical, detached, forced. I was sure of it.

"What in Eph…are you quoting Thorn at me?" She snorted.

"Kashensan."

"Whatever. Afraid to use your own words? Maybe you do feel something more, but choose not to."

"Don't hope for that either. I'd have asked one of the other girls if I thought they could do it half as well as you."

The intimacy between us had not dulled Orchid's speed, either of temper or fist. She spun around, open hand whistling towards me. She was a Half – her acceleration defied natural limits and made her movement a blur.

But I, too, was a Half, and my training more intensive than hers. I had a choice then.

It had been a terrible thing to say – one aimed at her heart with unerring brutality. And I'd meant it, which is why I would not reward her reaction.

"If you loved me," I said, gripping her wrist with firm but not digging fingers, "you would not try to hit me."

"Let me go!" Her cheeks were dry and yet flushed. Her eyes shimmered but did not spill.

"Let yourself go." Where did I get that from? Why did I feel so guilty for saying it? I released her and once again she turned away. I expected a second attempt. Anytime now.

"You cunning bastard." That sounded more like my Orchid. There were no tears in her voice, but she kept her back to me. "You use everyone. You don't tell us your plans, your schemes. All you do is manipulate."

Why in Eph's bloody name was everyone comparing me to Shai-Yeh these days?

"I have a job to do, Orchid, and so do you. When we're not doing that job, we are free to do whatever we want. Look at Blossom – does anyone make a fuss about her other activities?"

Bringing up another girl was probably a mistake. Orchid began to laugh. It was not a happy laugh.

"I bet you do look at Blossom. She's a whore, Char, and though I love her like a sister, that is all she is. Why would you choose her over me? I'm all yours. You suffer no rivals and neither, I thought, would I."

"I didn't choose her over you!"

Because I had no choice. Neither did you, Orchid.

"I'm starting to think you never choose at all," she pressed, returning her eyes to mine. The amount of sincerity I found in her expression was both a surprise and a threat. "Someone else always chooses for you, and you just make the best of that. I see you for what you are now. There's nothing real about you, Char. Not your actions, not your desires. You're a fake, and I can't fake it, Char. I never have. So find another bitch to play your games with you tonight."

Fuck!

"Not a game, Orchid." I was out of moves, so I stopped playing. "Which is why I felt it had to be you. Also, whatever your desires or choices, you're still assigned to this mission tonight, and I'm still in charge."

"And I'll do what I'm told," she replied through her teeth. "So are you seriously commanding me to kiss you? Has it come to that?"

"No. I didn't command. I asked. You've said no, and I'll respect that. But you will be by my side. There's a girl from the Nest, and if I'm right, she's going to perceive you as the greatest threat. She's going to try to come between you and I. That's where I need her. So that's where I need you."

"As you command."

"Has it come to that, Orchid?"

"Has *what?*"

Good question. I just sighed, walked over to the door and opened it for her.

Dismissed, my lovely flower.

And she left, giving me a wide berth where once she might have brushed by.

It wasn't until she was gone that I started to think about her.

"What are you thinking about?"

I opened my eyes and looked up. I'd figured the Haven's main room would be deserted that afternoon. There wasn't to be a Hunt for some nights yet.

"Just going over things in my head," I replied. Another truth – I'd been rereading Guan-Pi's notes.

Memorising the lot had proven impossible, but I had burnt the relevant material into my mind with a clarity I couldn't begin to understand.

"You've grown into such a serious young man," Lily said. Unlike my rejection of Orchid's exaggeration, I accepted Lily's words as what she believed, and so it was easy for me to believe it too. There was nothing duplicitous about Lily. She was incapable of being anything but herself. "Mind if I sit with you?"

I could have said yes, and she would have not sat. That, too, was part of my growing power: awareness of influence over the innocent as surely as the guilty.

"Of course not." She chose the opposite end of the couch, leaving plenty of space between us.

"Good. The bedrooms are done for now. I can rest a bit. So what does the great Char think about?"

"Everything and nothing," I answered, smiling. If she wanted to make me 'great', I could quite easily fit that position with cryptic answers in abundance.

"Psh. One thing at a time."

"Fine. I was wondering if you would care to assist me tonight."

No, I wasn't.

Involving Lily in my malicious scheme had felt, until then, *wrong*. What could a Healer do for me, when I needed warriors and killers? Still, she would die for me. So there it was – the last game-piece was on the table, and I knew I'd need an entire set against Hua-Shi and the Bloody Shadows.

"Judging by what you wear, Char, I suspect you have some dark work ahead," she said, her gaze seeming to tiptoe over the simple, sinister outfit that I would make my namesake. "I would be lying if I said I did not want to help, but is this really something I should be getting into?"

No, it wasn't.

"You'll be no more involved than you are each night you Heal those who are caught in the Hunt, those whom The Night does not take."

"Then I will be at your disposal, my Lord!" It was playful, as was her tone and deep lowering of onyx-framed face.

I chuckled, but only briefly.

"Some of my people may be wounded tonight. I'm trying to make sure there is as little violence as possible – despite their wishes for a little melee. This is all or nothing, Lily. If there is an outbreak of combat, it won't be a small foray. By that point, we will be running for our lives. Running here."

According to the map, there was another Haven closer to Swimming Carp, but it might not grant sanctuary to an entire band of Peddlers without questions, questions we simply couldn't answer.

"Alright, Char. I will be ready."

"Even if that doesn't happen, I'm planning on having someone brought here. He's going to be distraught, maybe even traumatised. He must not die, Lily."

"What's his name, Char?"

"Terasawa Jaku, Lily. Why do you ask?"

"The best way to calm an upset person, even with Healing, is to use their name, Char." As if I should have known that. "Can you tell me what sort of wounds he will have?"

"Ever seen a man thrashed by a wooden sword, Lily?"

I couldn't have said it more plainly.

"I will be ready," she repeated, conviction penetrating her sudden hand-wringing. "Char, I want to tell you something."

"Yes?"

She kept her face down, but I saw her through the veil of her hair. There was a rare conflict in her normally clear, guileless eyes. "I've grown very fond of you."

I waited, more full of unspoken anticipation than I'd have considered proper.

"That's all."

No, it wasn't.

"Why didn't you say this before?" I asked, and it was a stupid thing to say.

"Oh, Char," she said, laughing and sighing as only she could. There was melancholy without melodrama, self-consciousness without self-loathing. "Your eyes find Miss Witherheart, and I've seen how Blossom's find you. And I know you still think about Miss Fa, that you two have a connection of some sort. What about that girl from the old days you talk about, Jen was it? I am nothing like them."

No, she wasn't. She was better and I'd never know. For whatever reason, Lily was not part of this pathetic harem into which I'd been thrust and out of which I was quickly tearing myself.

Still, I said something, because at some point I had made another choice, back when I hadn't realised how much it mattered. The only time I *can* choose.

"I imagine we'd be *that* couple, Lily. Holding hands, flowers and candlelight, simple meals and evenings curling up in front of the fire, doing nothing more than enjoying each other's company. Sounds about right." It was tempting, God how it was. And yet I was young, hot-blooded and impetuous; why would that sort of boring stuff lure me?

But it must have, if only because I could imagine it in such detail.

"Maybe you do know how it would be. But that's not for you. It's not for us."

Was there even an 'us'? I extended my right hand towards her. There was no way I could touch her, not with that distance. It was as much an invitation as it was an effort to cross the chasm. If only she'd look away from *her* hands; if only she'd stop wringing them as she tried to put words to thoughts. We were both reaching.

"Still, it'd be nice, wouldn't it? Imagine if we could—" Then she did look at me, perhaps ready to embrace the fantasy. "Oh! Is there something wrong with your hand?"

I started to pull it back when she moved closer to me and started to examine it.

"Looks okay to me. Does it hurt?"

Too much. Too close. I wanted to make a fist, but then I was gripping her fingers, not so tight that I'd break anything, but tight enough to break the confusion.

"Oh." And then she did something I'd never expect: Lily took the initiative and forced my fingers apart, so that hers could slide between them. In almost the same movement, she shuffled away from me a bit, so that we were just sitting next to each other, rather than anything more complicated and tense.

"I will always accept whatever you are, Char," she whispered after a very long, very pleasant serenity – shared warmth devoid of hot, stifled longing. "Always accept whatever you're willing to be. Whatever you must be."

"But I want you to remember me like this." I, too, was whispering. Something in my throat denied anything louder. "Not who I may become, but who I am." Who I was. Maybe I wasn't him anymore already. "Please?"

"Alright, Char Ah-Ran." Never a flicker of doubt, not even a single question of what I meant. She could have held my hand forever, but she couldn't have. "I cannot be with you tonight," she repeated, disengaging her fingers from mine, and of course I didn't resist. "And you might be changed by whatever happens. If I am to remember you as you are now, I want the same."

What did she mean by that? I imagine my expression saved asking that, because she just stood up and walked towards one of the many sets of drawers lining the walls. When there was a Hunt, it would be prudent to have all necessary supplies within reach. After a brief rummage, she slid the drawer closed and returned. Lily stood before me, brought one hand from behind her back, held it between us, palm up.

"This is how *you* will remember *me*," she said. "Do you remember?"

My first time seeing her. Before the unveiling, the necessary cutting.

It was only a little knife.

"You said it wouldn't hurt," I replied, staring down at the instrument. It was no scalpel, no real blade at all. She'd used it to cut thin fabric, but I doubted it'd be able to do much damage beyond that. For some reason, that seemed right. "And it didn't."

"Only because you trusted me and held still." She waited until I took the knife before sitting down next to me again, but this time there'd be no hand-holding. "I didn't use it again after that time. We've enough knives and blades for the usual purposes." Even now, she would not divulge any such details, the grisly reality of being a Healer whose Talent only went so far. "I thought that someday I could give it to you, maybe as a parting gift, something important and significant and special. I'd say something clever and that's how you'd remember me, as the person who saved your life *and* could be witty about it. But I dreaded that thought. The only reason I didn't throw the knife away was if we *had* to say goodbye, I could at least leave you with a memento, something more than words."

She had no idea, then or ever, how little love I had for words. Words were Shai-Yeh's knife, and I would never so happily hold that vicious weapon as Lily's impotent little shiv. Still, I knew by then that however reluctantly I was using Shai-Yeh's method, I was using Shai-Yeh's method. When I spoke, it was to control, coerce, convince. The only person it never worked on, of course, was me.

And the only person I felt no need for it to work on, of course, was her. I tucked the knife away and looked at Lily of the Benevolent Hand. She looked back. Silently, we did our best to find things to remember, pleasantly unaware that what the present wants and what the future recalls rarely agree. Still, we did our best.

So passed my final afternoon in Kaifeng. She accepted me without reservation, with a love that defied lust: a woman I would never kiss, never know beyond a held hand and a sensation of unrestrained concern. Lily – who will, forever, dwell in that sanctified land beyond the bleak scape of my mind, a golden fire in the corner of my eye, promising that tomorrow, maybe, I will be a good enough person to enter there too.

"You are not allowed in."

"I have neglected to attend Prayers."

"Everyone is welcome here, seiyansi, but you may not enter the sanctum."

"May I at least use the Common Altar? I have need of it."

"Everyone is welcome here, seiyansi."

The gaunt attendant stepped aside and I stole into the Respite's entryway, grateful to be out of Eyesun's glaring wrath. Clad in shade once more, I Flailed myself with a cautious bow before the First Arch. Murmurs were a process of rote passage – I could not recall the words under any other circumstance.

I shivered upon crossing the First Arch. Always did, and that was unpleasant enough to encourage the absence Thorn had noted this morning. It was not the quaver of devotion; my faith lay in the practical aspects of God's will, relied upon the legitimacy of all my otherwise underhanded tactics. I was not like these priests in their flaxen robes and their chanting, but the First Arch must have somehow humbled them too, if for very different reasons.

Of the three Arches, it was perhaps the most important, representing God's invitation into Her house of worship, the Respite. Passing under the First Arch reminded us we were all inherent sinners and that only Her benediction could alleviate the heavy suffering. I'd thought it all quite certainly a great deal of crap before my steady absorption into the

Chapterhouse, my initiation into a world beneath the veneer. But when they'd forced me to attend Prayers, a month or so after I saw Shai-Yeh last, after first meeting Orchid, I fell to my knees as soon as I saw the First Arch; I had to crawl under it even though it was easily twice my height, and no one said a thing. No one laughed and no one cried. Afterwards, I learned how common a reaction that was, and I didn't feel so bad about it.

Each time after that, I was a little less eager to remain on my feet in God's gaze – thus She had no need to make me kneel.

Holy script adorned the marble stonework of the First Arch, running from the base of the left edge all the way to the base of the right. If you stopped to look, you could see the symbols clearly, but no one could read them anyway, not even the priests. Considering how the First Arch unnerved me, I wanted neither to understand the intricate writing nor linger within the threshold long enough to even try.

But that was just the initial trial and though it was disturbing, it was necessary to enter the Common Altar hall. I felt lighter for it. People with an easier belief than mine often referred to emerging from the First Arch as Darkbirth, considering the world outside to be a womb of limited spiritual value. Perhaps we Peddlers, and the Night's Own who Hunted each month, who did not become Roses, were less 'in' that womb than an actual part of it. Fa Shai-Yeh said I was special; what better way of confirming this than considering myself above the rules by being one who enforces them?

Even as I lowered myself before the Common Altar, I realised I was thinking about the Priestess. Knowledge of her true calling came in dream alone, dreams that continued to snake around the knotted branch of my 'awakened' life, coiling like undulating scales, chromatic under a too-real sun. Like hair, surreal and enticing, memories of what-was-not choked me with a promise of something greater than air to breathe, some sweet mist I first had to die to taste, to swallow. The sight of a musty stone floor the colour of a crumbling yesterday failed to placate rampaging senses – the scent of succulent deceit, the sound of a knowing laugh. Presence of overwhelming cunning sprinkled with the tangy sugar of easy success.

No more thoughts of Fa Shai-Yeh. Must not. Not here. Focus on the pain. Knees grinding into the floor. Suffer before the one who suffered before.

The supplication before the Common Altar was an act of willing abasement. The Altar, stark with the image of myriad messiahs, each a stylised Afraen Who Was Ephriem, armoured in plate, in faith, and in bloodied robes, demanded of those kneeling a tiny agony with its every scene. Under the jutting slab, Afraen before the Shining Legion claimed Him – a warlord of glory and conquest, figure of awe and majesty; a blink away but still on the surface facing the room, First Warlord Afraen Pleads to God for the power to quell the hordes of He Who Shines – His face a design of piety and yet longing, desire. And then, nearer the corner, one sees the threat of Tangariel, the seraphic poseur, archangel of treachery with his seven wings – three per shoulder and the last straight down his wretched spine – pointing at Afraen, condemning Him for the Plea soon granted. A shuffle of aching shins and a glance closer to the base of the Altar reveals the grim Battle of Ocharaya: masses of angels and Nobles struggling against each other, with the now-augmented Afraen soaring even higher than the great hosts, and Tangariel, Bitterspite of Shamain, smashing his fiery sword against Afraen's own heroic blade.

The Common Altar only stretched as far as the Battle of Ocharaya. Common – so called because, as the attendant said, all are welcome to use it. All seiyansi – a meaningless word that some said was as close to the Noble Tongue as a Chūnkojin could ever manage; it meant 'people', and only the mysterious attendants used it. The Respites of God and those who kept them were as enigmatic and intriguing to the Peddlers and Havenkeepers as we were to the common folk. But the true extent of that curiosity only began with the fantastic (and yet very real) episodes carved into the Common Altar. Further into the Respite, two more Altars sat silent, one singing in stone the creation of Ephriem, who was Afraen – the corrupted Holy One; the other lamented His anguish both as Ephriem and as Afraen, the first at the hands of His former faithful and the final torture enacted by Tangariel, by knife and hook, by fire and Flail. These deeper vessels were used only during official prayers, of which there were many per week. They were simply not accessible when a person wished to offer private or solitary thanks to God and Her Own.

Which is what I was trying to do, truly trying, but words of prayer wouldn't come. Had to settle for mumbled half-praise, for the occasional clap and pressing of forehead against a floor frozen in disbelief at my failure. I wanted to say something else, to apologise for my lack of zeal.

To be honest with God in Her own house. To be humble, with eyes closed and voice subdued.

"I'm sorry," I began, and thought: crap, why bother saying that? She will know you're lying. But saying it was a start. So I continued, still not opening my eyes for fear of distraction. "Sorry that I don't talk to You very often. I just wonder. Are You listening? Are You there? Where are You?"

She said: "Here. I am right here."

Chapter 17: *Proposal*
ON ONE KNEE

She made me an offer that I could refuse – not that this did any good.

"Do not bother getting up," 'God' said from above me. "I appreciate seeing men in this way: on their knees. And you are a man now, are you not? On your knees, no doubt full of questions."

I opened my eyes and smiled at the floor, deciding to remain there, though for an entirely different reason than her overbearing presence.

"That all depends on what defines a man, Shai-Yeh."

"In this case, as in all cases of worth? Not what, but who, Half. And who am I?"

"I have been asking myself that for almost five years. Are you here to answer it at last?" I didn't like how small my voice sounded in the cavernous interior of the Respite.

"Any answer I give would be right only until I give it. No, that is not why I am here. Glad you picked up Thorn's clue, Char. I am impressed."

She sounded anything but. I looked up and was utterly unsurprised to see that she hadn't changed. Not in five years. Not one bit.

"Still indulging in distractions, Shai-Yeh?"

But I was not distracted, pointedly watching the young woman slide from the altar. Strange. Although her departure from the sacred slab should have ended the sacrilege, even the way Shai-Yeh tapped her nails upon the chipped stone seemed a casual mockery.

"There are no distractions, Half, just subtle changes in topic."

"Then let's change the topic away from this airy bullshit," I replied, straightening my elbows and following her vague pacing with dry, stubborn eyes. "What's going to happen tonight?"

Her only reaction was a laugh that lacerated the air — I'd almost forgotten how harsh the sound had to be. Before I could adjust to it, however, her words, edged and honed, sliced even that outburst.

"You have been planning this little excursion for months, Char, perhaps even years. I, on the other hand, have been busy handling the fires in your wake.

"Or were you really so single-minded as to think Siu-Tsin put itself out?"

She wasn't referring to the blaze, either. Or perhaps she was. It was always an error to take Shai-Yeh literally, yet to do otherwise was equally dangerous. Hell, taking her at all was a risk I made only with the confident resignation that I had no choice.

"You lit that pyre, Fa Shai-Yeh. Guan-Pi!" Just saying the old man's name carried the bulk of my impending anger. "He didn't recognise me, but he knew my name. Thought I was Hua-Shi until he saw my face. And our roles, Hua-Shi and I, were reversed in his eyes. You know all this, don't you?"

"Of course, Char," Fa Shai-Yeh sighed. "Hua-Shi was the Half protégé of Leung Guan-Pi. I needed his position for you before you arrived, and so I gave him a gang of his own. With a few delicate conditions, of course. And the old man thought — well, he thought a lot of things. But surely you realise you were never his student."

The eagerness to demand that she give a straight answer, just this once, collided with the almost scheduled understanding that maybe she was doing just that. Her capacity for rhetoric defied my ability to discern — I was lucky if only that I knew this and kept my mouth shut.

And when I did speak, it was not what I expected.

"Yet I killed Leung Guan-Pi. Tsukamoto Genma."

"Not everyone you end will have been your teacher in name, Char. But you learn. You know what he knew, and could not have known it until he was removed. Did not reading his journal feel a little like picking his brain apart? It validates the death. Besides, the stupid old goat killed himself. It is not pertinent."

"You're right. He doesn't have what I want. So I ask again, with this 'want' in mind: what's going to happen tonight?"

"What is going to happen tonight, Char? You are going to meet Hua-Shi and he is going to blame you, rightfully, for the murder of Leung Guan-Pi and the destruction of the Nest. Then you will do battle, and if you win, you will own that which you have owned only in your dreams."

"The sword."

"It need not be said."

Then I remembered: the sword was her. Made for me. Or I for her.

"What of Chang, Butterfly, Blossom? Orchid?" The pause was unintentional but pronounced.

"Now who is indulging in distractions, Char? What of them?" Shai-Yeh's muted footfalls surrendered as she stared at me. The intensity of that look would have arrested the most capricious of children, and I was certainly not that; at least, not anymore.

"Don't they matter?" Didn't I know? I lowered my eyes again, letting them sink beneath the shameful weight.

I almost missed the abject shift in Shai-Yeh's behaviour – but for a moment, she appeared actually exasperated. I liked her, when she was confused or uncertain.

I didn't like her much.

"They matter in the same way as the hammer matters to the hot, malleable metal that will become a sword. In fact, that is precisely what you should think about, Char, because you will be *my* sword. From the forge of youth, I have been shaping you, disciplining the reckless, crude ore that you were into what you are now. Fuming, hissing, steaming. And when you burn brightest, I will plunge you into the still, freezing water of the Night, and you will soak in Its depravity, drench yourself until you, too, are cold and hard. Once you are submerged in that black pool, Half, you will purify both it and yourself."

Her final words were as a fist. My timid glance of attention became a prolonged gaze – not only were Shai-Yeh's hands clasped into potent little rocks, trembling, righteous; her teeth bore down upon an out-thrust jaw, as though grinding any opposition into a mouthful of dust.

She believed every word, and because her conviction was so complete, I began to accept them too. If not about becoming a sword myself, then at least seeing the sense in how the hardships of being young and the trials of growing up can shape, mould and ultimately strengthen a would-be adult. Too young I understood the necessity of discipline and punishment, could justify why people hurt each other, or—

"Or something like that," she interjected, but I wanted to think there was no way she could have known that her flippant words and shiny grin would interrupt my tumult of developing despair. Maybe it was not yet time for righteous fallacy, for portentous solemnity.

Shai-Yeh resumed her pacing.

"And how do you know any of this?"

"Ask something else, Half."

"Why?" I asked that far too quickly.

"Ah, now that is a proper question." The Priestess was appeased: she clicked her fingers, punctuating a profound statement, but the light did not change. "And the answer is: because."

Now my teeth took their turn to gnash.

"Because why?"

"You invite the circular trap, Char. There is your answer. Ask something else."

"No! Tell me why!"

And by now, I'd forgotten why I'd asked 'why'.

"Why? Because! Why is that because? Because that is why! Because? Why."

The offensive laugh broke the cycle, made my entire angry complex into naught but a soapy bubble.

Pop.

"So this will all happen, because?"

"Exactly."

"Because I want it to be this way?"

"Irrelevant, Half. Coincidence."

"Because you want it this way?"

"Sadly, that is also irrelevant. This we share, Char, as possibly significant players: our desires do not really have much impact. That is the cost of being someone."

"I thought being someone would mean we have the power to get what we want."

"Maybe it means having the power to give others what they want. They can not all be somebody. Lucky them."

"Everyone is someone, Shai-Yeh."

"Do not take refuge in generalisation, boy. You are special, like it or not. You are some one."

"Some people are no one? Then who are they?"

"I would not know." Yet another laugh.

"And here I thought you knew everything."

"Sarcasm or stupidity? Either way, you are wrong. If these people are no one, it is only in the eyes of those who are not."

"So a person is worth nothing if those around him fail to see that worth?"

"If those around him includes God, absolutely. But She is infallible. To Her, are not all special? But some can be as nothing, as I said. A good thing She cares where we do not."

"God doesn't care," I muttered.

"She *does* care, and no one is nothing in Her eyes," the woman affirmed, her nascent piety lending the words a sharpness unrivalled even by her acute laugh. "But if She does not, as you say, then who is caring? To whom can you turn for an explanation of what I know, what I have said?"

There was no immediate response, not in God's Respite, anyway. I nibbled incomplete defences as Shai-Yeh whisper-toed back to the altar and hoisted herself onto the consecrated stone. Despite my consuming frustration, I noted a curious inanity: she was bare-foot.

"He Who Shines? The Morning Light?" she asked, voice tempting blasphemy. The walls didn't shake; the high, raftered ceiling of the Respite didn't peel back to admit God's thunderous rage. Shai-Yeh glanced around with remorseless guilt anyway. "Oops. Probably should not have said that. But maybe God does not care after all. Or maybe She knows how unlikely it is that anyone would turn to that damned usurper for answers."

"That leaves other people."

"Oh, and they care, Char? About themselves, perhaps."

"Orchid?" Why did I bring her up? Ah. Witherheart's caring actually meant something to me. Of course, when evidence had arisen that she might, I instinctively rejected it. So why would Shai-Yeh's words change anything?

"Ooh, selfish to the core, that one. Using you for sex – a pity you cannot blush, Half, or have you failed to notice that? Too busy checking for pubes?"

"Orchid," I repeated.

"Orchid Witherheart, your Half lover, gets jealous if anyone else shows you the least bit of attention and yet she is incapable of caring for you as anything but a pet, no matter what idiocies she might have told you in moments of reckless passion."

"Lily, then?"

"A more subtle case. The woman can Heal, and does so selflessly, but her heart understands the selfish reason – it gives her purpose. Without the influx of wounded people each Hunt, Lily would have no idea what to do with herself. She needs people to suffer, so that she can make things all better."

I had to deny this. I couldn't.

"And you, my dear Half, are the worst of all. Who do you care about, when we strip away the mantle of superiority and solitude you have assumed? Yourself? Even that I doubt, sometimes."

"But it can't be that no one cares at all!" I protested. No, I whined, and Shai-Yeh's scathing down-the-nose condescension was well-earned.

"Perhaps it would be best if people cared less and did more."

But she didn't believe that – the words came with too much sincerity. I waited, and the silence demanded that she continue.

"It has to be God, Char. Even were it not, you would not know. If a neighbour shows no interest in something you have done or said that concerns them, it would not be hard to notice. Say you are passing the time with Orchid—"

Why couldn't she just let that be? My nails impressed holy firmament as I struggled not to think about Witherheart.

"—and she is just not paying attention, you would at least hope to notice. But if God does not care – what indications are there for you to see? What would be out of the ordinary? If She does not care now, She never did, for She exists in all times, at all places. And if She never did: again, would you know any different? She may as well not care at all, but compared to the belief that She does, the reality is almost just a shadow."

I was lost then. God cared, but maybe She didn't, and if She did, I'd never know, and if She didn't—

"If She doesn't care, it makes no difference, because your belief that She does—" I half-whispered, refusing to be awed by the magnitude of what Shai-Yeh had led me to realise. If God did not exist, and people still believed She did—

"It means She does!" Shai-Yeh declared, opening her small arms like outspread wings, preparing to receive the embrace from the very God I had begun to doubt – be it a blessing touch or a punishing crush. "That is what you cannot forget."

"But I have a different God."

The timeless girl's hands sought solace in her lap, shoulders receding in quiet sorrow.

"Yes. Yes, you do. A Goddess. So you remember."

"Some. Enough to justify my hatred of you, Shai-Yeh. I couldn't fathom it until now. Why would I hate the woman who introduced me to the Peddlers? To Orchid?" And here it was only proper that the tone change: a decrescendo guided by uncertainty: "To Lily?"

"It hurts me personally that you hate me," Shai-Yeh admitted, and because there was so little emotion in her voice, such a lack of energy and conviction, I knew she was telling the truth.

"Wish I didn't, Shai-Yeh, my false Goddess, my true mentor. Everything I am, I owe to you, and we've already covered how selfish, faithless and callous I've become. It was not so bad when I thought I was a Rat, because I was also young and ignorant, but now I have seen – felt – the texture of loss and sacrifice, caused death and loved it, and now I still choose to be what you have made me. Ha, that made no sense. But I am an educated killer, a well-taught destroyer, the greatest of abominations: the knowing bringer of pain. I'd rather hate myself, you know, instead of you. Maybe I do, but apparently I am the only one who cares for me. So I love myself, then? And you made me, made the thing I love. How can I not love you for that, my Goddess of Swords?"

She did not giggle, squeal or mock, as the girl upon the balcony that dreadful, wonderful night had done. Perhaps Fa Shai-Yeh was not so completely immune to time's vicissitudes after all.

"But what a fucked up kind of love!" When her illegible silence breached tolerance, those sick words I spat out, a proxy for apology I breathed in, self-chiding coarseness I coughed up and any chances of escaping her I put down.

"Yeah," she agreed, sinking into a single word where her grandiose, formal speeches usually complicated everything.

Just that one time, an elongated lecture contradicting me would have been nice.

But Fa Shai-Yeh was not nice.

"It is your love for the sword that counts now. Whether you choose her to be me, or me to be her – or Orchid, or Lily. I really do not care, Char. Without the sword made for you, for which you were made, you will die, and die soon."

But Hua-Shi has the sword. My sword. How can I get it (retrieve her?) and prevent my own death if he will kill me for trying to do just that?

Fa Shai-Yeh wouldn't answer that – too simple, too useful – so I did not ask. No, she would answer it because it was a useful question, and in her eyes that deserved a useless answer. Best to let her tell me in her own time, in her own way. Shai-Yeh had invoked the possibility of my death, but she had made me, had made something for and of me: she wouldn't risk my failure by omitting some 'minor detail' I didn't know to ask about. I knew she was watching, waiting for me to take the skewered morsel. Just another God-damned test.

"How can I love something I have never known, Shai-Yeh?" I asked instead. Her relief was blatant: this was the sort of vague query within which she revelled, giddy and yet completely controlled. And yet Shai-Yeh's disappointment in my failing to fail was almost as obvious.

"Ask a priest how he can love God. Seriously, Char. What is this 'knowing' that you find so important? You can grow up with someone, spend years with them, and then, at some crucial moment, discover something about that person which totally proves you knew nothing all along. Or so you feel at the time."

She stopped, but I waited. This was more squirming rawness, and she must have thought me someone other than the would-be Scourge to even consider tasting it.

"You want an example? Remember that fat kid, Terasawa Jaku?"

The one I'm supposed to extract from The Ways of Life tonight, somehow infiltrating the very core of criminal concentration in Kaifeng and then deliver to the Benevolent Hand? Whom I've never met and yet whose blood has made my hands wet and my smile deep? Hell no, don't remember him at all but—

"How do you know him, Shai-Yeh?"

A sharp intake of annoyance squeezed through her teeth.

"You had to make a mistake sooner or later, I suppose. I know what the old bastard told you before you killed him. Well, you assisted in his demise. I said that it was not pertinent, but I am a bit pissed off about that whole situation, Char. The outcast Tsukamoto was of use yet – rearing Hua-Shi was not the extent of his utility. Terasawa Jaku knows this too – he is the only true Mifūnjin to ever be welcome in the Society. Hua-Shi 'recruited' him, although you remember otherwise. Terasawa Jaku wants the Bloody Shadows, of course. And he is very close to getting them."

There was a lot to consider, to rearrange, cross-reference. I had to think very quickly then – Shai-Yeh had almost imperceptibly intensified the situation.

So I thought.

"That shut you up, eh? Now you are thinking. Good boy. You take your time."

But that was all the time I needed. People tend to forget that just because they don't think while they rant and gloat, others are taking full advantage of every precious second.

"I did not plan tonight."

"That is true."

"My original question wasn't stupid at all. You know what's going to happen when Hua-Shi and I meet."

"Yes. Everything is pre-destined, by my hand."

"This is familiar."

I felt sick.

"Then change it."

"Terasawa Jaku. He has taken Jen for a lover."

No guesswork there; Guan-Pi's diary revealed to me just how lurid the dirty Godfather could be.

"So?"

"She is in love with Hua-Shi." As she was with me. As she never was.

"A common little love triangle, Char? Pfft. Do better."

Think. Think some more!

Hua-Shi took the sword meant for me. Guan-Pi, or whatever his true name is, raised him. I remember this although it wasn't me. We are Halves. Orchid is a Half. Three Halves? What? No. There's Chang as well. Shai-Yeh mentions Terasawa Jaku, I bring Jen into the picture. What a messy picture. And she planned it all, but why, can't figure that out, does it matter? Yes, and no, and yes again and—

"Thinking doing you any good, Char?"

"No. It doesn't make sense at all."

What could I do? Ask her what it all meant? Even in dream, she had not clarified that.

I was still falling.

Would she catch me?

"Of course," she said, "you could just do whatever I tell you to do."

"Or the exact opposite."

"You think I have not planned for that as well, Half?"

Shit.

"That about sums it up, yes." Maybe I mumbled the foul word to which she responded – and maybe not. "There is one thing I do not know, Char: what you will do when you take the sword, when you are made whole. And because I cannot see it, I know it is going to be something spectacular. But until that moment, I can tell you whatever I want, influence you or irritate you, love you or hate you. Equally, you cannot change what I will do – or did you think I would not be there to watch you destroy Hua-Shi, the Half-man who dared to fuck with me?"

"Terasawa Jaku," I said, ignoring the abundance of bait for now. Time to do a little fishing of my own. "He was a childhood rival of Hua-Shi's? Something like that. More like an underling. Now he's a Weed. That's your doing."

"So?"

"The people I thought were my parents. In Siu-Tsin. They also became Weeds. You did that too."

"Are you forgetting Whom I represent, Char? Putting all these acts onto my shoulder is hardly fair."

"Since when have you been one to deny the greatness of your machinations, Priestess?"

"My glory is Hers, Char. If I feel any exultation, it is through Her permission." Now Shai-Yeh was unperturbed, fortified – prepared. My fish turned out to be a shark, and I'd treated the fishing pole like a sword. It's all I knew.

"But She gave you free will too, Shai-Yeh. I remember – you said: if God did not want me to do this, She would stop me. Didn't you say that?"

"You remember something word-for-word, Half – clearly you believe it was said."

Sharks aren't always destructive; they've been known to play, should a cruel whim take them.

"But if it is free will, God would not stop you. If She did, it wouldn't be free."

"My, my. The boy is thinking again."

"You won't stop me."

"Of course not. All I can do is watch and hope you do the right thing."

"Which is?"

"Oh well – the thinking could not last," Shai-Yeh sighed at the beam-crossed ceiling.

"Jaku, my not-parents. You removed them for a purpose."

"Do you not notice their absence more than their presence?"

"Clearing the way for something else?"

"It is all I ever seem to do," Fa Shai-Yeh agreed with a nod emphasising the 'ever'. "As soon as the hole is filled, something better has come along."

"Won't it always be that way, Shai-Yeh? Eventually, you have to settle," said the young man eager to rock the Bloody Shadows and their Ways of Life. Fa Shai-Yeh's sceptical look wasted no time in proving that she caught the hypocrisy too.

"Death awaits those who settle. Those who 'make do'. That is not my way and we both know it is not yours either."

"Knowing what my way is 'not' doesn't clarify what it should be, Fa Shai-Yeh."

"One less option can only clarify, Half. But you are arguing simply for the argument itself. Proof is there: you are not one to rest. Your history is one of agitation and disturbance."

"That which is done to me still doesn't constitute my 'way', Fa Shai-Yeh. I have been agitated and disturbed in the same way a bored child will agitate and disturb the water of a puddle."

"And there you were espousing free will, Char. I do not mind if you take sides, even if that side is your own. But would you kindly stick to one stance? You are not adept enough to hold more than one."

"Yet?"

"Your eyes are not ready to see more than one thing at once," Fa Shai-Yeh replied, and I wondered what my eyes had to do with it. "Why is it so important that you understand my way? Your 'not-parents' and Jaku are just a few of the people I must sweep aside. For you."

"You say you do it for me, but you're just using me as an excuse to do whatever you want, Fa Shai-Yeh."

"Well, if you happen to be a particularly poor Clan Lord, you could always take that attitude and apply for position of God," she said and then laughed her breaking-glass blasphemy laugh.

"Clan Lord? What the—oh, Eph In Hell." I remembered then because she said it. Some memories are like that, and sometimes, I wish people would keep their God-damned mouths shut.

People like me.

Fa Shai-Yeh was now in front of me, above me, slapping down the top of my head. Hard. Like punishing a dog and not much caring if she caused serious damage.

"That was for God, and for Ephriem. Stop wincing – you got off lightly. I have killed men for less."

"Ow! So it's okay for you to make jokes about God but I'm not allowed to say—"

The Priestess drew her hand back to hit me again, her expression a too-accurate picture of wrath. "Grr! That is what really gets to me with you, Char," she said without stomping her feet even once; she relaxed her hand but I didn't relax at all. "You can not tell when something is truly serious. It is no joke that you are the heir to Jaydemyr and it is no joke that very soon, you and I will not be the only ones to know it."

But what did I care for this? Tonight was about a sword and truth.

"Does this have anything to do with Hua-Shi?" I asked, now that she had turned her back and couldn't be so swift in meting backhanded justice.

"Of course!" Up went her hands: not quite a shrug, not quite a huff. "Maybe I have pushed you too hard, too fast. You are not thinking again. When you have her, certain things are going to happen, things that you do not and cannot know about."

"So why tell me?"

"Love?" She looked at me, one eyebrow teased with the upswung word, the grotesque question-answer. "No. Maybe not. Then because I do not want you unprepared. This is assuming that Hua-Shi does not kick your head clean off. It is possible. After all, killing you is all he really wants."

"Me?" Idiot. Of course – she'd have told him exactly what I'd done. The me-that-I-wasn't had been a foundling Half, taken in by a compassionate if practical mentor, and then at age twelve I'd done something very stupid involving a wall after watching a parade, then I'd— no. None of that. Because Guan-Pi had never met me. Which meant that: "I do not remember anything of my life before waking up in the Benevolent Hand."

"That is a lie," Fa Shai-Yeh said. "You remember. You are just not sure if that was your life or not."

"I can only go on the evidence," I reasoned. "Any memories I have of Guan-Pi, Terasawa Jaku or Jen-Wah, of being in the Nest at all, do not mesh with how the old man treated me last time. But we spoke a while and I did not seem to make any mistakes. So while the memories are false in that they are not mine, they are real in that they are someone else's. Hua-Shi is the natural culprit. But why?"

"Well thought. I will reward that. Because when I brought you to this city for the second time, it was to hide you. And where better to hide someone than in someone else? Hua-Shi was not happy with the Nest and he is Half. Those two conditions are why I singled him out for this. It was he who climbed the Palace wall on his twelfth birthday, he who tried to steal your sword." She hesitated, and then added: "When you were only seven years old, visiting this city for the first time, along with our-then Kas'Daen allies."

She knew exactly what that would do to me. I remembered how I'd felt about that little bastard during the parade. I'd hated myself even as a stranger; I tried to steal the sword from myself. Yet I refused to ask what she knew I wanted to ask. She wouldn't answer that. The age difference between Hua-Shi and me was hint enough.

So I asked a lot of everything else.

"How did I get hurt, then? Why was I unconscious? How did I come to be in the Benevolent Hand?" Not that she couldn't lie. The game was now figuring out which lie was the most difficult to disprove.

"Someone tried to cut your head off."

So much for calm logic.

"It would be foolish of me to ask how any of this is possible, wouldn't it?"

"Very, but I do understand. You need to know the 'how' before you can properly find out the 'why'."

"Not always."

"In this case, as in all cases of worth?" And she smirked. "Best to know neither and just do what you must. That is how you felt before today, is it not? Sneaking out of the city, night after night, not caring for the reason, if at all any existed. And you using people – just using them! That is the way of a Clan Lord, like it or not."

"I do not wish to be that," I said then and didn't recognise my own voice. So who really said it? "I absolutely refuse!"

"Then your daughter will take your place, in exactly forty years, and you will kill her for it."

Pumpkin.

"Well, look at that," Fa Shai-Yeh said. "Mr. Righteous is trying to cry."

Wasn't I? There were sobs, shoulder-quaking wracks of remorse for something I remembered so clearly not-doing, but my face was dry.

"No pubes, no sweat, no blushing and no tears," she said. "This is what you are and have become. More than human, less than anything else. You are the Half, Char. One foot on each side of the chasm, and the gap will only widen. You are the necessary bridge between, and people are going to walk all over you. All the while, as you struggle to maintain your footing, whatever is lurking in the divide is staring up at your crotch and thinking about dinner."

Yet again, her seemingly irrelevant rant gave me time to think.

"Of course Halves can cry," I said. "I remember that much. After I joined the Peddlers. There were times." So why not now?

"And that just makes you all the more special," she replied. "Why can you not accept that you are just unique and move on from there? If I told you that everything you remember from since you met Lily in the Haven was real, and that Thorn did tell you that Halves who are not properly handled go a little crazy, become a little homicidal, would you believe me?"

"Really, Fa Shai-Yeh. Have I done anything but believe you?"

There I was, and there she was. Both facts hinged on the hypothetical nature of this question. She knew better than to answer it directly, because everything she said answered it.

"Most Halves do lose their sanity by your age if they are not reined in. And I handed Hua-Shi a small army of less-than-stable followers. He is nothing like you, and yet he is what you would have been. May yet be. Will you even recognise your demented reflection upon seeing him?"

"Yes," I said and believed it.

"And Terasawa Jaku. You have never seen him, but you think you know what he looks like?"

"I see no reason for my borrowed memories to be altered like that."

"Does not mean there is not one," she countered.

"A fair point. Got a meeting with him either way. I'm sure he's dying to look his old teacher's murderer in the eye."

"Well, you did beat him to the punch there. Look, Char." So I did, and she was looking back. Her face was unusually puzzled. "You know what you are going to do tonight. Whether it happens or not does not even matter right now. So why did you summon me like this? Not that I mind – I feel quite at home in here." Here she looked around, appraising God's house as though it were her own.

"I needed a few answers."

"Did you get them?"

"More."

"More?" She was not interested; her gaze wavered like the candlelight around us.

"More, and less. Different. I will have to change a few things, but overall, I'm confident in my plans."

"Infiltrate the Ways of Life, have your expendable little Peddlers take out the sentries and clear the way, meet with Terasawa, maybe beat the shit out of him with that silly wooden sword of yours, draw Hua-Shi's attention and try to do the same to him? Oh yes, Char. Great plan. Let me show it to you from the other side."

I was resolute, no matter how she simplified and mocked the idea. Let her show me, then.

"Kaifeng is a tainted city in which Lord Ayakawa and his clan, Tsukamoto, are using God's name to maintain their ill-gotten power and wealth. You know this because you have grown up among the poor, and you have seen how many they are. As your teacher said, it is a pyramid inverted and must fall. But you can not do it legally – the Guards are as bent as anyone else. When the wind of corruption blows that hard, few people have much choice. But not you, Hua-Shi. No – you remain on your feet. You gather close those who agree and you begin to play the system against itself. The law does not apply to you because the law is wrong. God Herself has told you this through a Priestess, who delivered into your hands a weapon so coveted by the enemy. You are powerful because you are right. Your time is now.

"But you must beat away the wolves who would steal your treasure. In the case of Terasawa Jaku, it is best to keep him on your side, because he is too closely tied to the Tsukamoto. Wong Chu-Deng? He is a ravenous boar you must not let out of your sight. Your real fear, then, is a threat you cannot see, cannot predict. And he is out there. The Night has trained him and he somehow believes that what is yours by right is his. But you have work to do – a city to cleanse. You leave him alone, partly because you can deal with him later and partly because he just does not matter. But then he started to be a problem, harassing your soldiers and attacking your past. When he murdered your old teacher and burnt your childhood home to the ground, you decided that a confrontation was no longer avoidable. It seems this nemesis agrees, because now he has negotiated a meeting with your lieutenant and rival, Terasawa Jaku, right in the heart of your home.

"He is clearly insane, remembering things that did not happen and worse, acting upon them. You do not think you are a cruel or bad person – just efficient and necessary. Killing this poor boy is not really on your agenda but if he tries to take what's yours, you will not hesitate. It is yours, because God told you so. And if She is not right, who is?"

And, before I could digest any of it, I accused: "You told him all these things!"

"Of course. Pillow-talk is sometimes a bit loose like that."

Blood pooled around my knuckles; pain streaked up my right arm. There was an echo of some impact.

"Careful there, Half. You are going to need both of those soon enough."

"You have been *sleeping* with my enemy. While I've been waiting."

"For me?"

"Yes."

"You were waiting for something else, Char, not me. I offered myself to you first, in so may ways, and you rejected me every time. He did not, and so it is he who gets me. For now. Not that this has not caused its share of problems. The triangle has become a very unstable square. But that is alright – you are going to break it tonight. My beloved, you are so much more worthy. I would not be much of a weapon if I did not enjoy a fight, and Hua-Shi provides none."

"So that is where you have been all this time." I did not remove my fist from the floor, blood thick like glue.

"Oh, hardly. Hua-Shi is just a distraction. No – mostly I have been dealing with those who were trying to cut your head off. Once you 'became' Hua-Shi, as it were, they had a far harder time tracking you. They were not following 'your' tracks so much as following your thoughts. The thoughts of a fledgling lord, and the trail stopped dead here, in Kaifeng. But you could not remain anyone but yourself, obviously. Now they are close, and you will need your sword."

I offered myself to you first and you rejected me. I wanted to feel dejected but thought only about control. Until now, the sword had no say in who it killed, or why. You raised it, you brought it down. It did its job. But maybe it had objections, and simply lacked the means to disagree. Or worse – maybe we lack the means to hear its cry. And maybe we just wouldn't care. A sword is not for caring; it is not an emotional thing.

"And will you have me killed when I, like Hua-Shi, am no longer useful to you, Fa Shai-Yeh?"

"No, darling Half," she answered, kneeling in front of me to examine the damage I'd done to my hand. "I will have you killed when you are most useful to me."

She didn't move to touch the little wounds. Saved me snarling and waving her away. Saved me from fighting the pleasure at her concern.

"How about a little help then, hm?" I asked, wanting it to be a joke. The girl-priest shook her head, slow and sad. I tried to rise, but only made it to one foot when she placed her hands upon my cheeks. She held my stare, although not even she could stop time long enough to make it anything more than a moment. But in that moment, this is what she said:

"Tonight you will be alone, Char, because that is how it has always been. You will have neither friends nor allies, not once they know what you are. Poison, my beloved. Your very essence is lethal, especially to those foolish enough to love you, or those sorry enough to know your love. But this is what you chose – I want you to remember that, when everything feels empty and hopeless. Remember that, and follow the choice."

Was she going to kiss me? Strangle me? Just how long could it last?

I could not last, and closed my eyes.

"Butterfly, Blossom, Orchid, Jen, Chang," she whispered.

I meant to blink, to contemplate the significance of this sequence, but I couldn't raise my eyelids in time.

A hesitant touch roused my shoulder, and an equally hesitant voice stirred the air.

"Seiyansi?"

Was she that afraid to let me see her walk away?

"What is it?"

"Evening service is about to begin. We respectfully ask that you conclude your prayers and withdraw."

I had been there that long. This explained the pain I felt upon standing, the stiffness in my legs and the crack of my joints.

"Thank you, attendant. Enjoy the offering."

"In Her Name, we thank you, seiyansi." He moved around to where Fa Shai-Yeh had been standing, had been sitting, between me and the Altar.

"Yeah, and what a name it is," I muttered, stepping back to give the attendant room to scrutinise the quickly-drying specks of my blood. Normally one would make an offering into an appropriate chalice, but blood is blood. Down he went, eager tongue scraping over the dark-flecked stone I'd punched instead of Shai-Yeh's face.

I looked towards the door, beyond the First Arch. He was right – it was getting dark. Sure, Shai-Yeh couldn't stop time, but that didn't mean she didn't have a certain way of screwing with my perception of it. A few would-be worshippers dotted the pews, and I had no idea when they'd arrived. A woman here, a man there. None together, but together in the Respite. I looked at each, and they looked back. If they were unnerved at the strange discourse just now ended, there was no sign of it in their flat expressions.

Behind me now, I could hear the attendant shamble my way. Time to leave.

"Seiyansi?" he asked as we passed under the First Arch.

"What?" I had business, and he wasn't it.

"Most people pray in silence."

Well, wasn't this rich? An attendant pretending to be subtle. Their lot was no more a role of delicacy than anyone else who served the Night.

"I wasn't praying, attendant."

"Then to whom were you talking?"

"Who the fuck do you think, priest?" I rounded on him just as we reached the exit. This was where we parted ways, whether he liked it or not. "I was talking to God. You got your offering, and I doubt you taste the blood of a Half very often. So stop with the questions, priest."

Of course he flushed. I'd just insulted him on his own ground. But would a mere Respite-servant really face down a Half?

"Mmm," he said, licking his lips. Strangely unsettling. "Be with God, seiyansi."

He made a half-hearted Flail as I left, pausing on the threshold. Maybe he was waiting for me to bleed some more. After I crossed from the endless shade of the Respite into Kaifeng's warm twilight, I made it exactly three steps before the attendant gasped, coughed a few times and then fell over.

"Not before you, it seems," I mumbled. That'd be the last offering he'd enjoy. Should I have been surprised? "My very essence is lethal." Trust Fa Shai-Yeh to deliver a virile truth in hushed hyperbole. Had to laugh, even as I walked away, and walked towards whatever insanity waited for me in the west.

No longer sovereign of the sky, the sun had begun to take refuge under the horizon, but the moon overhead was not yet full. How many of those fledgling stars would bear witness tonight? How many would die before it ended?

Chapter 18: *Rejection*
THE BREAK UP

"Five."

"That's right. Like a hand, eh?" I half-joked. The Gate guard's tired expression didn't change. "Imperial business outside the city. Village called Swimming Carp."

"Never heard of it. But that's your job, not mine." He raised his lantern towards the manned ramparts above us and the large wooden gate groaned open. "Five heading out at Risingmoon. Don't see many leaving on any night, let alone five."

"Wanna make it six?" Blossom taunted, reaching out to caress the wall as she passed through the gate. I stood aside, waiting for each to go before me. "You can, hm, clean up after us."

"Not as if you'd share," Butterfly said, treading on Blossom's shadow.

The guard just studied the thin alleyways around him.

"I thought you'd outgrown a taste for my leftovers, sister," Blossom shot back, giggling.

Butterfly made reference to Blossom's easily-parted legs and gave her a hard shove from behind. Unseen trinkets of pretty death rattled under the pastel skirt of a girl not easily rattled.

"Both of you, cut it out," Orchid admonished, entering the brief passage with a determined pace that suggested neither of them be there when she arrived. There was something familiar about what she'd chosen to wear: a low-cut robe the colour of the sky on a Hunting night. I suspected she was trying to tell me something with her change from the usual curve-concealing apparel. Whatever it was, I wasn't listening.

Chang, of course, just laughed and gestured with an inviting sweep. Refusing to acknowledge the necessary antics of those soon to bleed, I inclined my head, pulled the black cowl over my face and assumed my place in the single file. Dailoh came last, had my back, like a pallid guardian spirit.

"Lock the gates behind us," he said.

"That's my job," replied the gruff sentry. "God help us if you don't know yours."

"God help you if you ever do," Chang said, just as the gate into Kaifeng began to close in our wake.

It was a nice night for a walk. The moon was a sickle carving the thin gauze of pale cloud. Nice night for work.

"I wish we'd brought horses," Butterfly said maybe a mile out of town. Not that we weren't fit, weren't predators in our prime. There was an issue of speed, but I'd already told her. Maybe our resident pessimist needed a reminder.

"Only reason we'd need horses," I said, voice filling the abandoned road with careless abandon, "is if we get lost and run out of food. There's no rush. You're not even going as far as the village anyway, remember?"

"Who knows if any of us will make it that far?"

"Oh, come on, Butterfly." Just as I wasn't prepared to entertain Orchid's volatile moods, there was no need to let One-Slash ponder the worst-case. "Who in Hell Above could give us much trouble? We're out of the city, where even now most of the Bloody Shadows are having a grand old time misbehaving. This will be a simple matter."

"If they know we're coming," Orchid said, choosing Butterfly's side in a rare show of sisterly loyalty, "then what's to stop the whole lot of them lying in wait?"

Both Butterfly and Blossom began to notice the trees on either side of the road then – or so I figured, by their sudden skittishness. *Good work, Orchid. Because nervous warriors are exactly what we need right now, y'know?*

"If a callous, power-mad Half can rise to lead them," Chang suggested, and then it was clearly a little skirmish between the sexes, "then they can't be that strong, can they? We'd probably rip through the Shadows like a knife through mist."

And there was mist, gathering between the greenery. I wouldn't join the others, wouldn't look at it, wouldn't read into the unknown around us.

"You were all so confident before, when I'd told you the plan," I goaded, taking the lead simply because none of them were moving. "They know I don't have an army of my own. And this is about personal vengeance. Don't forget what I am to them now, at least as of the departure of Leung Guan-Pi."

"Isn't that all the more reason to want to take you out, Char?" Blossom asked. I glanced her way – she was staying close to Butterfly, and I realised then that I had no idea what sort of relationship those two had. If Butterfly were bothered by the sudden proximity, she didn't bother to say so. Then again, her eyes were still creeping about the thick woods enveloping the solitary road.

"Hey, if anyone wants to go home, there's the door," I said, pointing back the way we came. Back at the gate locked behind us. "Somewhere thataway. I didn't think any of you would come if you didn't trust me. Told you they're expecting me. Hell, they're expecting you lot too. When you read a note that says 'come alone', the first thing you do is wonder how many friends you can fit in your shadow. Well, you're not hiding and neither am I. As if I'd be dense enough to 'come alone'. I want to take them out; they want to take us out. I much prefer things out in the open like this."

"I just figured we'd be, y'know, a little quieter and stealthy-like," Butterfly continued, hand twitching towards the pommel of her sword. "In, get it done, out. Like we always do."

"There's something to be said for taking your time with in-and-out type business," Blossom quipped, ducking away from Butterfly's swat in the same breath. As usual, the girl had done me a favour with her harmless antagonism – my warriors began to laugh. Even Orchid.

I almost joined in when my ears told me that another course of action was appropriate.

"Hsss. Horse approaching. Hide, now."

Could they hear it? Chang and Orchid had already sought cover like rats avoiding torchlight. The two girls looked at each other, still giggling, then at me. I made a hasty shooing motion and they, too, removed themselves from sight.

I stood in the middle of the road, legs slightly apart, and looked down. No chasm. Not yet, anyway.

I knew it wouldn't be Hua-Shi – no Half needs to ride a horse, not over so short a distance. Besides, it wasn't allowed to be Hua-Shi.

The sound of rolling hoof-beats preceded the appearance of a cowled rider, who in turn reined the nickering beast's gait to a mere trot. He didn't appear armed. I still didn't move.

"You're shorter than I remember," the rider said, and I recognised his voice in the same way one can recognise a relative one has never met before. "Did you come alone?"

"Of course not. What do you think I am, crazy? Get down off that horse and let's shake hands at last."

Of course, he didn't. His control over the horse kept the circle it stamped around me tight and steady. When it wove behind me, I didn't turn around.

"You *are* crazy. Doesn't matter how many you brought. These woods are ours, much as the city will soon be ours."

"You can have 'em. The old man wanted you to take over. Why do you think he tried to put me down?"

No snappy comeback; no smart reply. The young man had come to learn.

"You found his diary, didn't you?"

"He all but gave it to me. All but gave himself, too."

"See? He *did* favour you," the lean horseman admitted, yanking the reins. The horse stopped that very moment.

"Not me, Terasawa Jaku. Look at me – my face. It's nothing like the person you grew up with."

And I removed my hood. Knowing the gesture, four Peddlers appeared from their nearby concealment. I didn't need to look to know that knives divided Chang's fingers, that Butterfly was brandishing her sword in typical backhanded fashion. She was supposed to use two, but never had. One was enough. Blossom would be at her side, a slender length of chain drooping between her casual hands. And Orchid was at *my* side, exactly as requested. Her left hand slid into my right, cold where once it had merely been cool.

"That's the thing, Half," Jaku mused, not bothering to flinch. Yet again, my expectations had failed to keep up. "No one can remember what your face looks like. You could be anyone, at least anyone who is also Half. But I know your name. I know your expression. It knows mine."

His boots were no less heavy upon the dirt than the now-silent hooves before them. I stood there, palms open at my side. The wooden sword in my belt was just wood, just as a threat is only breath. Confident and easy, he strode towards me. I saw then, under the loose cowl, his smile. I recognised that too, from the garden of a youth we'd never shared.

It wasn't the sort of smile you give a stranger.

"Hmm. Only four?" Terasawa sniffed and cast back his own hood. Lithe silhouettes began to slide from branches, from behind thicker shadows. No need to count – there was more than four.

The hardship of never being the favourite student, of rebelling against his pampered upbringing and, finally, of losing what little prestige he had in the Society had done Terasawa a lot of good – there was no trace of the fat my memories so despised. That too-smart hairstyle was gone; Jaku had recently shaved his head. Only his nose, which apparently never fully healed, denied his aspirations towards handsomeness. He wasn't the gentleman Jen had felt he would become, this harsh, prematurely cruel taskmaster. But she chose him, and had stuck with him – because there she was now, beside him.

Just as the rigours of being a Rat in Kaifeng had hardened Jaku, whatever Wu Jen-Wah had been through seemed to have weathered away any capacity for kindness. They called me crazy, but her eyes, not quite able to narrow in thought, made me feel horribly sane. She, slightly shorter than Jaku now and dressed in ragged Rat-fashion despite the sure wealth of the Bloody Shadows, stood beside him, right hand gripping a plain wooden staff, the other seeking his hand thoughtlessly. They looked like a couple.

"Well, we always knew this wasn't going to be pretty," I said. It didn't manage to break the silence. "Wu Jen-Wah, Terasawa Jaku. Pleased to meet you at last."

The other Peddlers just breathed; this was my night. They knew the Shadows around them were no real threat – a real threat would have done something by now.

"So she wasn't lying," Terasawa replied. As always, I didn't have to ask who. "You really don't remember us, do you?"

"Probly for the best," Jen said to the ground, long hair blanketing her vapid stare. "What with ow things ended n all."

It's never really about what you do or don't remember – I know this, because she taught me. What matters is whether or not what you remember actually happened. You always remember something, and if you don't, the first thing you do is start believing otherwise.

"Nothing ended because nothing began. But it's about to. I promised that I'd bring you the man you seek tonight. The one who killed your master, Leung Guan-Pi. The one who burned down the Nest. The Half agent working for the Tsukamoto, for the Guards."

And everyone knew it wasn't me.

"That's only half the deal," Terasawa said. "The diary. Where is it?"

"I burned it."

Jen started forward, her staff describing arcs of incomplete purpose, and Orchid mirrored her move to engage, but Terasawa restrained the feral Jen with a simple, "Not yet.

"That is so like you. To keep things to yourself." There was that smile again. "I hated you for it, but you're the one the old man always trusted. I believe you when you say he tried to kill you, because she told us that you'd come back and kill us all. I figured you'd bring more than four friends, though."

"Four's enough. You're as good as dead, Jaku. But you don't have to die here. At least, not at our hands."

"That is true, Half. Have you told your 'friends' there who you really are?"

"No need. They've made up their own minds." And that's another thing she taught me. Taught me now. "Either way, you've got one thing right. I am Half. I'm not the untrained thug you faced in your garden, so long ago."

Jen's face resisted nostalgia with an omnipotent dam of denial. No, not even denial — there was nothing so forced, so conscious. She just wanted to start swinging her staff. Maybe that's why I recalled such affection for her: Orchid was much the same way. Orchid, at my side: I could smell her eagerness, gathering about the lurid curves of her muscles like steam from seething coal — a perfume that had long informed my instincts when another, richer scent was about to nourish the needs of our shared ancestry.

"Where's Wong Chu-Deng?" I asked next, giving vent to the theory of violence by sliding my wooden sword from its latent position, left hand about the 'blade'. I held it more like a walking stick than a weapon, harmless tip pressing into the coarse debris of passage underfoot.

"Who cares? He's a nobody," Jaku replied. Rather than leaping into my suggestion of conflict, he turned away, towards his horse. Jen began to tap the ground with the butt of her staff. The vague Shadows in my periphery defined themselves with deceptive distance, this blade glinting luminescent, that ripple of dark cloth obscuring a body of tight intent.

"Change of plans," I said to my Peddlers. "I don't think we need so many witnesses."

"And me?" asked Orchid, still doing nothing more than taking orders. Fine.

"Join them. I can handle these two."

"Fine."

Orchid got her wish. She wouldn't have to kiss me after all. As though she loved me.

Freed from her frigid anchor, I walked away from my friends. Towards Wu Jen-Wah, but never close enough to invite a single swing of her inert stick.

"I see that choosing Jaku over me didn't work out so well for you," I said to her, to her dishevelled clothing, and to the fact that she was here at all, and not living in luxury as she'd assumed would happen when she chose Terasawa. "Or was it that hard to stop being a Rat?"

"No Rat now," she retorted. I thought I heard the first clash of metal behind me. Very far behind me. "After you left, Elder Leung dint seem to care much bout the Rats no more. Wasn't a hard choice, yknow. Become a Shadow or oppose what had to happen. Theys always givin you trouble, Hua-Shi, but you looked for it too. Lookin for it still."

Far too late to tell her that wasn't my name.

"You drove me away," I accused, conveniently forgetting that it never actually happened. "You made *me* choose, and so I did. What – did you expect me to disagree when you said that Terasawa was the one for you? I had other things on my mind. Better things to do."

"Like getting mixed up with the Guard? The Peddlers?" she spat. "With that Ephin blonde bitch?"

"It's not as if you hate *all* Peddlers," Jaku said to her over his shoulder. It was both an admonishment and a placation.

She actually blushed. No idea what was transpiring here, so I turned my attention to what was transpiring there. Around us. Away from us.

No distant chorus of screams. If the underlings, the nameless Shadows, were trying to take me out, then the Peddlers were doing a fine job of keeping the attempts to just that.

"I'm over im," Wu Jen-Wah said without looking at her Jaku-chan. I thought she meant me; I was wrong. "But Hua-Shi *did* go to er. Said he was lookin for er, member? And we never saw im again. Then she comes long, poisonin our master with er talk bout God and destiny n all that crap. Bout the sword you went n stole, Jaku."

On cue, Terasawa returned from whatever he was doing by the horse. He was holding something. Something wrapped in a dirty white sheet. Long. Thin.

It couldn't be *this* easy, could it?

"Yeah," he muttered, and I knew from his expression that he'd lied to her. However he'd come by the sword, it wasn't anything so bold as theft. "It was the one thing you wanted, Half – Wong Chu-Deng confirmed it. And you took from me the one thing I wanted." Whatever that was. Guan-Pi's approval? Jen's secret love? Didn't matter. Was the Weed holding *my* sword? If it was my weapon, my Goddess, shouldn't I have somehow known? Felt it? "I went back to that wall, a week after you disappeared. Can you believe it? I actually looked for you. I called your name. Do you know what happened?"

Of course I knew. Of course I thought I did.

"She was waiting, Half." As always. As ever. "This Kasuden Priestess who seemed to be everywhere, to know everything. I'd seen her prowling about the Nest, and I'm sure if you think about it you'll remember as well. But this night, she said she had a gift. For me? Not necessarily, but for now. Take this for now. That's what she said and this is what she gave me. Then she told what you were going to do, and I laughed. Bitch was crazy, everyone knew that. But it all happened. All but one thing, the last thing. I'm meant to give this back to you, here and now. And then you're going to kill everyone with it. Really. She said that. And I knew if I'd done anything but come tonight, that'd be me believing her and trying to stop it from happening. But I don't. I want you to take this damn thing, Hua-Shi. Show me there's enough of you left in there to hold a weapon without using it."

"So it *is* my sword?" I pressed, unimpressed with his little speech.

"It's your sword if you can take it," Terasawa said, stepping back. With each shuffle, he removed a little more of the fabric concealing the weapon. "It's your sword if you can keep it."

Whether or not it was a bluff, whether or not it was real, no longer mattered. Wu Jen-Wah swept her staff around. I hopped back, saving myself a shattered knee, but that wasn't her intention. The ground between us gritted its teeth as she dragged the end of her stick through the dirt. She was drawing the line.

"You member what has to be done, Hua-Shi," she said after completing the ritual. "Cept this time, you don't gotta fight for the circle. You gotta fight your way into it."

And this time it wouldn't be a fat little Mifūnjin snotface, either. Jen had drawn one circle in the road; now, her staff cut thousands of others through the howling air.

The stage had been set, but not for me. Fa Shai-Yeh had underestimated my ability to define myself beyond her machination, and I finally had the chance to prove it.

"I'm not Hua-Shi," I said and tried to turn my back on both Jen and Terasawa Jaku. "And that's not my sword, because I won't take it from you."

I will find another way.

But.

She said: Here, Charan. I am right here.

The wooden sword clattered to the ground as I stepped forward, prepared to break the circle once again, to complete the triangle.

"Where the hell did everyone go?" In front of me, where Jen and Jaku had been: empty road. Around me: empty forest. I couldn't even smell a suggestion of sweat, of blood.

I heard the lilt of a voice – not words so much as a distorted hum; no more a melody than the sun is a fire. My eyelids fluttered; the road and the forest and the night broke away from continuity, like I was watching the world through a snapping curtain.

The voice rose. I fell.

Her song grew louder. My eyes tried to shy away.

I did not blink.

I did not open my eyes.

"On your knees again, hm?"

Her.

"Seems to happen when I'm around you, Goddess," I said.

"What a strange thing to call a girl you hardly remember."

But I did remember her. So many dreams, so many moments. An infinitude of now.

"You can change your voice all you want; wear whatever masks you choose, Goddess. I know you."

"No, Half, I don't think you do."

She laughed and it wasn't her laugh. No sensation of someone planting pins in my ears.

I opened my eyes and saw that whoever was standing over me didn't have much of a face at all. There were features but they didn't seem to fit together. Like a blind man's collage. And if she was nobody, then there was only one nobody she could be.

Butterfly. One-Slash.

"You taught me, didn't you, Butterfly? You taught me now."

"Didn't teach you a thing. You were always too busy with Orchid to notice me."

Her face wanted me to define it, but every blush of cheek, every slant of jaw and every tilt of eyes belonged to someone else. No matter how disparate the combination, she never became someone – just a disconnected combination of other people.

I knew who I was looking at – I just didn't know who was looking back. The fog around us, grey with a recollection of nocturnal foliage, eased my watering eyes.

"Yeah, you look away, Half. Look away in shame," her voice said, and it was hers. It was a start and probably an end.

"Shame?" I started to see something in the nothing. "Why exactly should I be ashamed for how *I* spend my time and with whom?"

"Because we're more alike than you think, Half, or want to think."

She sounded like someone else now. Of *that* I was ashamed.

"Let's see. You're not Half, you're not male, you've no idea how I think most of the time and you're dead." What? "Yeah, Butterfly. We might as well be twins."

"Is that the only way you can deal with anything you might share with others, Char? Sure, we're not *that* alike, but there's something. Something special."

There were a million things I could have asked. There was only one question.

"And what is that?"

Still couldn't look at her. As long as I kept her in the margin of my sight, there was an excuse for her obscured profile.

"We're both morons," she said, her tone glazed with self-deprecation. "I let go of someone I never meant to want, and you want someone you were never meant to let go."

"So that makes us like everyone else. I wouldn't say that's sharing something special."

"Look around you, Half."

What? Darkness. Forest. Night.

Or.

"What is this?"

There was no need to ask, not to know. But she wanted to tell me. To show me what linked us.

In front of me was a window. Through the window I could see a floor and on the floor were two people. They were whispering, naked under lazy folds of fabric. Clothes or sheets. Their positions alternated between various arrangements of pleasure: sometimes cuddling, sometimes fucking, sometimes just talking. No matter which position, their faces. Their faces I could see. Where Butterfly's face refused definition, now there was an exaggeration of two – his pointed ears, her sunlit braid; his coarse growl, her delicate insistence.

"What is this?" I repeated, now whispering.

"Moron," said Butterfly's voice. Was she still here? If I looked away from the couple, would they disappear? "You don't have to worry. They won't see or hear you. Do you know why?"

"Because I'm not really here," I answered. "This isn't my memory."

"Ha. You think it's mine?" Butterfly's voice started to dwindle. "You don't even remember me, Half. Couldn't place my face and you dare assume this is *my* memory? Let's say it's your imagination dealing with what you think you know. And you know now, this is how it works. Shape one person's dreams, and you can shape anything, even the truth." She'd never talked like this. Not in all our conversations. All…three of them? "It's time for you to know that truth, because for you and you alone it will remain true. All the others now know only one thing: you don't belong, never did. Their world has been forced around you, but now it's all about to snap back into its proper shape. But not for you. For you, there is only one dream after another. Not even knowing that will stop your madness…"

Her voice was almost gone now. Bye-bye Butterfly. Whoever you were. "You know the others too well. Guess you're using me to tell yourself what you've always known. Without so much as asking. *Saa, hajimahteh imas'*."

How odd, that she would say 'it's beginning' as a farewell.

Someone was about to talk, and I was about to listen.

"It should be safe for you to go out soon," said Fa Shai-Yeh.

"Not yet though." said Hua-Shi.

Don't tell me you're done already – that's how the sentence was supposed to end. And then I would see.

And I saw.

"He's watching us," she said through her smile. "And soon he will come in here and kill you."

"But not before feeling such shock at who we are," Hua-Shi added, lips slithering in delight. "Besides, he won't kill me. Just give me a bit of a fiery tickle."

They laughed together.

"Now, show him," Fa Shai-Yeh insisted, but it was she who dragged the material back, exposing her feet, legs, thighs—

Blade. His hand around the hilt. Her edge, grinning.

She is the sword. The sword is the Goddess.

For all my effort to tear the window apart, to crawl through that hole and claim what was mine, the world turned away, down. I sank to someone else's haunches and hated myself for it. How dare this body I occupied disobey my desire?

And whoever I was took in the surroundings, a village or something. Swimming Carp. I was in Swimming Carp, and not for the first time. Behind me was my house. My home. My sword. I have never had a home, but homes have had me. Like memories. Like dreams. Like borrowing a past; like stealing a future.

I stared. Knew what would happen if I faltered, but my sword was right behind me. Hua-Shi – right there. Both at once, just like Fa Shai-Yeh had said. That was her will, so why would she? Would she betray me, work against me, just to help me?

Yes, I thought. That is precisely what she did.

I stared, but not forever.

"No," I heard myself say after I blinked.

One-Slash Butterfly looked up at me. I knew it was her, because she wasn't any of the others. She was lying on the ground, and I was kneeling beside her, my shins saturated in spreading blood. It is never easy to be with a stranger as they die, but it's even harder when you realise they're not the stranger at all. You are.

"If, if I'd known," she said through scarlet spasms, "that you'd do this, I would've stayed home tonight."

Do what? Why wasn't I at least holding her?

Because my hands were busy holding a sword.

"Butterfly?" I said, turning her name into a question. But what would I ask? Why? – no, never anything that coherent. Not at first. "What?" was the only word I could manage. It was obvious – I killed her. Now I had my sword and I'd killed her. She was dead and my free hand was shaking her.

"Don't know why you're bothering," Blossom said behind me.

So, at least I hadn't killed her as well. Yet.

Sounded like she was humming, some naïve tune I almost knew.

"Get away from me, Blossom," I said through a warning of clenched teeth. "I don't know what I've done, or what I might do."

"Testy this morning, aren't we? And you're not the one who had to stay up all night pretending to *enjoy* sex with the human version of a long-legged dog. Dog-Ears. Mmmm."

Morning?

I rounded on her, armed fist raised in warding, but when I looked at it, of course my fingers were empty.

Blossom, on her knees, was not smiling at me, but she was smiling.

"I see that the sleeper has not yet awakened," she said, the words coming from lips that barely moved. That was Blossom's way. "I could hear them from all the way down the hall. Lucky man, that Char. Poor taste, but fortunate."

"He's allowed to have whomever he wants," I found myself grumbling as Butterfly, behind me, shuffled in her sleep and murmured the names of nameless pleasure. "The Priestess says his time is soon."

"I can't believe that she has so much say in the matter," Blossom replied, transfixed smile losing meaning around the resentment. "Doesn't the old man have any backbone left?"

"He's been acting strange too," I said. Other than a satiated Butterfly wrapped in silky bliss, an amused Blossom, and myself, the little room was empty and serene.

And full of memories.

"What were you doing in here anyway, Hua-Shi? I *know* it wasn't you with her last night, because, well, not even you're that stupid. She's one of his."

"I wish you wouldn't call me that here, Blossom," I said. It was a better answer than the truth. I didn't know what I was doing in Butterfly's bedroom that morning. Had I been watching her? Envying her? Envying *him* again? Ah, that little brat. The Priestess told me I had to play my role. Both of them. One known, one not. One always close to him, the other always out of reach. With the way she tortured him, what was there to envy? This, all this. Just temptation. Teasing. Tests. It wasn't worth questioning. A good way to get her attention, that. Questions as statements: Oh, so you want to sacrifice the Rats, the Peddlers and the Shadows to shape your saviour. You say this sword is going to change the world, but only if the right person wields it. And that that person doesn't even exist yet, but will. Are you mad. No, please, stop. Stop.

Statements only: you're right, Fa Shai-Yeh. I'm sorry. Of course I'll do it. No, really, it's nothing.It's…fine.

"Fine," Blossom said. "I guess we all need our little masks. He'll know who you really are soon enough. Come on – let her sleep a little more. I can keep you occupied."

The hands of a whore reached for me.

"Hssss." Where was it? Had I left it behind again? I began to move around on my knees – that was when I heard the comforting rattle of a scabbard.

"You're doing it again," Blossom pouted, lowering her fingers. "*What* are you looking for?"

No need to tell her. It was with me. Funny how I didn't notice it, slung over my shoulder, until I panicked, feeling like someone had stolen my arms and not told me.

"I'll pass on that offer, Blossom. Time to see the old man again. Maybe I can change his mind. Maybe it's not too late." I could understand Guan-Pi getting caught up in Fa Shai-Yeh's clever web, but it was just not like Chu-Deng. I'd expected him to ally with me, but now he was about to hand power to the one person who never deserved any of it. Who didn't even *need* it.

"I wouldn't know," Blossom shrugged, leaning back until she was squatting on the balls of her feet. The girl could make eating gruel look sensual. "Not one of you 'Rats', am I? Or Shadows, whatever it is you call yourselves. That's your business. Mine, well, I can pretend your rejection of me is just because you're busy. Or distracted."

Blossom didn't have low self-esteem – she just liked the idea of it now and then.

"Speaking of, where's Orchid?" I asked.

"You know full well where she is and with whom. He might sleep with Butterfly now and then but it is Orchid he's chosen. Then there's that docile cow from the Haven."

"And Jen," I sighed, cutting the *chan* off with a hiss. "The Priestess has certainly given him enough fruit to pick. Well, if she's not full of shit, it'll all be over soon. He'll have to *really* choose then."

"I have no idea what you're on about," Blossom shrugged. "You're all mad. Things are fine the way they are. Change is only needed by people like that Priestess, people who always have to meddle and twist things around."

I agreed with her instantly in my heart, but the muscles around me stiffened in defiance.

"No, Blossom. Change is coming and everyone needs it. Kaifeng is ripe for revolution. Leung Guan-Pi had the way of it there. Wong Chu-Deng knows it too. And the boy is the key. Him and his ridiculous quest for some sword."

There was a sword with me, but it wasn't the one. I knew where that was.

"Like I care," she mumbled. "Screw it. I'm outta here."

To leave me alone with Butterfly, dead to the world.

"Wait, Blossom," I said. Wasn't like me, but then again, I wasn't sure which me I was supposed to be like.

There is only one me. Me.

"Huh? What is it, Char?" half her face asked over a lithesome shoulder, deciding for me.

"Do you remember, in the courtyard, that day—"

"When Orchid broke your sword."

"No, I broke hers."

"Yeah?" Blossom winked, or maybe it was just her profile blinking. "Guess you're not her 'fuckin' boyfriend' either?"

"Not anymore." Never again. "Do you remember any of those moves you didn't get to teach me?"

I heard something delicate jingle under Blossom's robe.

"Follow me then, Half."

I saw nothing but her as I gave steady but impatient chase – Blossom was an intimate ideal. A flutter of subtle flower encouraged me out of the room, down the hall, onto the walkway that ran all four sides of the courtyard. After wading down the steps, Blossom stopped a few feet into the square enclosure, into Fallingsun quiet.

"What is it?" I said, aware only vaguely that the few trees in the training ground were further apart than usual; no matter how wide the gaps, Blossom and I were on the inside, together.

"Shh. Do you hear that?"

She wasn't supposed to say that but what if she had? If she did, then next there'd be three of us and a circle and blood—

"She's out there. Just behind you. If you turn around," – Blossom still didn't – "there she is. But here I am. Choose."

As if there was ever any choice. No, there was, but each one I made, *she* changed. Might as well enjoy whatever was in front of me. In front, behind, around: all the same thing in the end. Not my thing.

I completed my descent and drew the sword.

My sword. Oni-Goroshi. The Slayer of Demons.

Wet with blood. Drunk on it. Soaked and slippery.

No, just some trick. No sword can be drawn that way.

Blink, blink. See? Clean. Shiny. New.

"Is it safe to spar with real weapons, Blossom? I mean, I wouldn't want to hurt you." Depending on what sort of moves she wanted to teach me, of course.

"Would you like to see something special?" Blossom asked in a voice that didn't belong to any girl, Half or whore or *anything*. Words doled out like venom, honed with a confidence of simply *knowing*. And I knew exactly what to say, even as I readied the sword and leapt towards her.

"Of course I would!"

The Rose emerged from what was Blossom, and what was Blossom? A tattered explosion of silk and scented hair; a beautiful cocoon for this dread symbiosis of claws, teeth and madness. Shreds of the Peddler's robe clung to her corrugated ribs, pasted by an aftertaste of perfume and sweat. Any further detail coagulated into a shriek of grey lightning.

But she wasn't as quick as last time. It wasn't dark and I wasn't the same boy. As then, the Rose lashed out with an arm that wasn't hers, and I didn't have time to wonder where it came from. Behind every thrust is a fist: something less inclined to keep its grip when you do your best to slice it off. And then a sword is just a piece of metal on the ground. I landed from the opening jump and lunged left, towards the Rose, swept the sword's edge around, up, left hand, backhand. Had her outstretched arm been a real sword, my retaliation would have severed her wrist instantly.

Instead of cleaving flesh, Oni-Goroshi met with metal; pliant links yielded to her push. I heard the unnaturally long appendage whip around behind me as I all but barged into the Rose's wasted body. Metal? Clinking? I thought: *chain,* and then it was too late to deal with it. I kept going: leaned forward even more, followed through with the swing until my sword was angled away from the ground. The weighted end of the chain grazed under my left arm, and then it was above it, under it again. The Rose stepped back, giving the links room to swing, to bind, to strangle. The whirring grew quicker and then ended with a snap as its leaden weight smashed into my elbow. I howled but could still feel my fingers around Oni-Goroshi's hilt.

"Char," The Rose said, mimicking not only Blossom's weapon but voice as well. "Calm down."

Yeah, right. There she was, one hand keeping the chain taut, the other poised with a dagger just in case I decided to give in and rush at her without control of my sword, and she said 'calm down'. What — so that she could end it nice and quickly? This won't hurt a bit, I promise.

Oh, it was going to hurt alright. I bent my knees and started to lean back, forcing her to pull just that much harder. There wasn't much time – if Blossom concealed a Rose, anyone else could do the same. As she stepped back to maintain control, I turned the hilt, which no amount of chain could prevent, until the handle rested on my palm and the blade faced forward. She noticed, of course, and heaved a Blossom sigh – *men! Why are they so useless?*

Now I followed her backtracking, and the links slackened just enough. I did the one thing neither of us expected.

I let go of the sword.

Perfect weighting pulled her point down; links of grating metal pinched and burned my skin. The Rose with Blossom's everything came at me, knife seeking whichever part of the soft 'stupid little boy' it could. But, quick as it was, the fallen Noble could not keep up. Oni-Goroshi's hilt was almost vertical; the glimmering fang wanted to bite the ground. My left hand, wrist and arm were all but torn. Again, I gave in and threw myself in that direction, grabbing the hilt with my other hand. Mindful of the Rose/Blossom's approach, I could now grip *her* with both hands once more. The chain no longer mattered – it was loose, as I too had to be, knees unlocked, all fingers calm around the rich blue hilt, the blade's edge at thigh's height, almost horizontal.

Ryusui-Gedan no kamae. The perfect stance for sweeping the edge upwards and to the right. *Keep your body loose until the very second before impact. Become like steel, like stone.*

I didn't cut the flesh, didn't even expect it. I aimed beyond it.

A clean decapitation. Expended all energy. Wasted none.

And just behind the sword's arc:

Blossom's head, forced away by a bloom of gory petals shooting from her neck. The torso teetered, legs failed without the expected command to remain upright. I had to lean over the corpse to disentangle myself from Blossom's snare.

"No." Not Blossom. The Rose. Fa Shai-Yeh's illusion was still going – could hear its warped rhythm around me, far away but not far away enough. No matter her effort, I would not believe any of it, even though the body was no longer a gangly doll of pasty skin, emaciated limbs. Somewhere under the sundered remains was Blossom. "NO."

The deceitful thing twitched, and I aimed Oni-Goroshi's tip to pierce its heart, to needle between a ridge of ribs. She plunged into the valley of its breasts instead, sucked into the sternum as though she belonged there.

Somewhere, the song hit a giddy little trill, less a voice than a flute, and I knew everything was laughing at me.

Couldn't wrench her free – she wasn't done with her bath of bones and blood – so I just stood there, watching her. Waiting for the next set of instructions.

But.

"Jaku-chan," Jen's voice said, closer than possible, closer than if she were leaning right over me, whispering in my ear. So this is what had to happen next. As ever, I didn't want to be away from *her*, object of all desires, but now I knew that the next now wouldn't happen otherwise. So of course everything was different when I—

Looked up, saw a small set of drawers against a wall, with a mirror on top of it. I trod over the soft, thin matting of the bedroom to stand in front of the polished surface, gripped my left arm but the pain was gone, must have just been nerves. Now the mirror didn't see anything beyond me, me with my short, neat hair, which is how I'd always worn it, was how my parents said I should wear it. My face, which I didn't mind, was pretty handsome, except for the nose, couldn't help touching it, running my finger down, until it hit the bump, the bend, the mark of that day, that bastard, that—

"*Bastard*," I swore, as I often did when looking in a mirror these days. She, behind me now, just tittered, put her hands around my waist and squeezed with hands that were better off wrapped around a stick, had a fine grip, but no real grasp of the situation, why Fa Shai-Yeh hated her so much, I almost understood sometimes, but.

Tonight, then, there'd be reunion, reckoning, resolution, to this issue and all issues, because the sword said there would be, and she knew, and shared it, shared it with me, told me I would wield her, forever, that I was Kaifeng's destined ruler, and my time, near, so near.

"If it bothers you so much, Jaku, I dunno why you spen all that time n front of the mirror. Not as if you're gonna forget what you look like, is it?"

Six years together and she still talked like a fucking peasant.

"Just reminding myself."

Except for the nose, all except for that, I was decent enough, normal ears, normal eyes, but I guess that just wasn't enough for Jen, although she always said I was the one, I'd take care of her, do better by her than those thugs, and that's all Hua-Shi was, whatever they said about him, now or then, whether they were talking about the little shit who thought he could impress Jen by beating me up, lucky hit or two and suddenly he thinks he's better than us, or whoever he was now and then, some lackey of the Guards, some fetchboy for the Peddlers, oh yes I knew about that, she told me, told me what I know she told me I know what she—

"Why int the city nough, Jaku-chan?" her face asked mine in reflection; her eyes couldn't pretend anything else, couldn't understand something worse, even though it was her pity for me back then, now it was reversed, backwards, nostalgia alone made sense, I felt like she was holding onto the waist of a man I didn't become, well no guesses needed there, but at least. At least.

"We've been over this."

Offer a man the world but not the one thing he really wants, that's what She did, knowing exactly what a man wants, it's such a power, like I thought of it this way, She can define a hole by building a world around it, and of course all you really saw was that hole, and everything else existed just for that, it's enough, Kaifeng she said, beautiful paradox, hole that is a hole, around a hole, yeah, whatever, the question was when do I get to deal with Hua-Shi, what I want, all I want in the world.

"No, you tol me but I dun get it." That's when she pulled her fingers from me and stepped back, made sense, I got it. "You got me, n you're gonna get all of Kaifeng. Why aint that nough? Smore n we ever dreamt of back then. Member?"

So that's why she did it, so she could touch my back, trace some memory up and down, up and down, and maybe I was supposed to stiffen or smile or turn around but no, she didn't get it, couldn't feel the thrill of tension I didn't let her feel. That was Jen — touched, touching; unfelt, unfeeling. I should've known this that day, but there was a circle and pride, and things needed to be handled, taken care of, yeah, me.

"I remember. What time is it?"

"Gettin on twards Fallinsun."

"You know what to do, then."

Jen could know but not understand, just like she could do and not know what she's doing, it's a talent, not thinking, not asking, wish I'd somehow been allowed that, but never, not as firstborn of the family not as onlyborn, not as Terasawa, when that meant almost nothing it was almost enough.

"We're goin to die tnight," she said. I should, I guess, have taken her seriously, but if I had I wouldn't have this chance to realise that I should have, so who cares and what does it matter? Let her rant. "We're goin to die all coz you couldn be happy with what you got. Tempted to tell evryone to jus forget it, jus have a normal night n the town. Let's do that, Jaku-chan. You n me, us alone, goin to meet Hua-Shi. It'll be the good ole days. I'll draw a circle n you two can fight over it." Giggle, giggle.

Appealing to a memory for a memory, the girl was insane, yet she was with me, and I with her, so maybe it made sense in the end and came again, a circle and how she loved those, gold and sand and skipping, hearts and hands, held one, held the other, squeezed not knowing which was which.

"As long as Hua-Shi lives, there are no normal nights. There are no old times."

"Like you can kill im," Jen said.

I didn't hit her because she wasn't thinking, I hit her because she was. Her tongue tried to reach the future of a scar, not yet, only a taste, a trickle. Smiled, she smiled, not like this hadn't happened before, it's wrong to hit girls but she was a Rat and a Shadow and if I went too far she'd know what to do, sometimes I wished she would, but she didn't ever and I thought, no I knew that if she had, just once, then I'd have won. My knuckles and her cheek, her lips, had a pact and she never once fulfilled it.

That day after Hua-Shi left the circle, and I bled, she knelt over me and wiped the blood with her fingers, smearing some on her own face. She smiled.

"Can't even kill me," Jen goaded, stepping back and swirling the red into a curl in the corner of her cut lips. "I'll do what you wan, Jaku-chan, coz you're the one I chose."

Like that 'Ephin' blonde bitch'. Like a sword. Not like she had much choice, Chang rejected her and who can blame him, when you run with the Blood Peddlers you don't settle for leftovers, but I guess I was first and she was doing that settling even if she was never settled, could tell this even by the way she walked out, touching things as she went. Jen disturbed things to keep herself company.

But she was really alone and so was I now with most of the Shadows heading off for another night of Kaifeng carousing. I realised I wasn't thinking right hadn't not since that night I'd left him there, hanging from a wall. I wanted to remember that time as real, before Fa Shai-Yeh and the Peddlers, before the fight. Before Grandfather just gave up and gave everything to the cripple, the usurper, Wong Chu-Deng. Before she left me with this thing.

This thing wrapped in dirty cloth and lies lies on the floor. Couldn't ever draw it, but now and then I tried again, and the first sparkle of silver was enough. Too heavy. Had to drop it, and it landed silently. Didn't break, didn't even rattle. Hidden blade, hidden burden, fully sheathed, it allowed me to lift it once more, all I had to do, all I could do, all I did.

Look after this, she had said.

Can I use it?

You can try. You will fail. There will be a night, years from now, when someone else comes to take her from you. And you will want to give her. You will be desperate to be rid of her.

Her? It's just a sword. Is this ugly thing what Hua-Shi tried to steal?

She's not supposed to be beautiful to you. That's why she has chosen you to be the one to wait for the one who was chosen.

Whom has she chosen? Hua-Shi? Is he the one? Light enough to carry, until you try to, well, only a Half could wield this.

You'll find out on that night. She will make all things happen.

That night was this night.

Why not me? I didn't want to give her away. Not now. Not after years of listening to her, hiding her, of wondering why I needed to hide her, and maybe I didn't. Hua-Shi was getting stronger, now a Guard and a Peddler. Now planning to take the Shadows. I'd need a weapon against him this night tonight. No amount of Shadows would stop a determined Half, and she said that four of them were coming tonight. *Chang? Why do I care? I don't!*

I need a weapon. Why not this one?

I tried to draw her again, but I couldn't free even an inch of her. Her, when did I start calling her. I called her, then, now, and she asked my name.

"Char," I answered, meaning to lie but failing, and for that she answered at last.

Now I have drawn her, draw her close, she is ready and it's not her and I it's us, we, together and alone tonight the way it's meant to be, and the way out is in sight, just out that door and—

Orchid's knife, crackling with lightning, whizzed towards me. The sword flicked upwards and I heard something like a spoon hitting a floor. Another came, and another.

I'm your opponent. Here I come.

Armed with the now-compliant sword (she, mine, *now*), retaliation wouldn't be hard, just duck and lash out, just like a game we called practice, just so I could move onto him, for whom *she* waited but got tired of waiting, and—

"*Hua-Shi!*" Is that who I was?

This is what was:

Orchid, fallen to the ground.

Jen, yelling a name, appearing from nowhere, now there, between us.

Her staff where Orchid's skull used to be, covered in what used to be in Orchid's skull.

My sword halfway through Jen's side, stopped only by a sudden spine.

Her, Oni-Goroshi my sword that used to be, covered in what used to be in Jen's stomach.

Jen, bleeding a name, stumbling somewhere, sword and air between us.

Orchid, fallen to the ground.

I began to approach her, trying to concentrate on the crumpled fabric, the unmoving girl's breasts, anything but the mess around her neck, but that was like staring at a page and not seeing the words, only a straight ripple of nonsense, all lines you can't help but read between. Chest, shoulders, throat—

No. She had nothing like a head left. No face. No lips. No need to look.

Just another crushed Rose.

I stepped over it and after the staggering girl taking my sword away.

"I would have kissed you. As though. I love you."

This came to both my ears, the last remnants of Orchid spiralling around me and then drifting away. I wished I could choke back tears or say something heartfelt, but I'd already said goodbye to that Orchid with an absent kiss.

Dismissed, my lovely flower.

"*Jen-chan!*" Two someones cried out, and neither was me.

Hard not to feel some gratitude at this distraction, even if what the simultaneous cry announced was nothing to be thankful for: Chang Tong-Kut and Terasawa Jaku, emerging from the nether of dull combat, struggling to maintain their melee even as they headed towards Jen, whose dwindling back seemed so much smaller than the blade stuck in it.

Wu Jen-Wah, Rat and Shadow, girl and woman, tool and temptress, toppled forward. Chang sent Jaku sprawling with a boot to the chest like an afterthought. Then he was simply at Jen's side and she did not fall.

It was then that I knew that Hua-Shi had been with me the whole time. And I had called him brother.

The vicious Half, enigma even to me now, and Jen, object of an affection I'd never owned, fell into an awkward embrace. If he tried to remove my sword, the girl would be done for. But wasn't she anyway?

I trudged towards them, feet lifting only when they hit something heavy and uncompliant. Someone's arm, someone's leg, someone. Jaku hadn't brought too many Shadows but enough to turn the road into a shallow massacre. Didn't want to look at them but I knew – they'd *all* died to the same weapon. And when I did drop my head to examine this body or that, I recalled, no, relived a moment of death that wasn't allowed to be mine. That's what it means to be a killer, voluntary or otherwise: you become the most significant thing in any number of lives until someone does the same to you. That last slash, that breath-stealing hack. There is nothing after you, and yet always something *after* you –

death itself. Like the sword stuck in Jen's flank: you wield her, she wields you. Even when you leave her quivering in a future corpse – all you can do is negotiate the puzzled expression of a dying daze to get her back.

Someone's arm, someone's leg, some—Jaku.

I kept walking and then turned around, looking down.

"Get up," someone said with my mouth. "You are not dead yet."

Unlike his Shadows, those hapless twigs floating on the dark, wet gravel, Terasawa Jaku moved of his own volition, whimper-scampering away from me, battered eyes casting about for something to take, to use, to keep. He probably knew some of the bodies around him.

"Stop that. Jen is dying. Go to her."

Because I couldn't. Didn't have the right. Even if I didn't remember what I'd done, I had done it. Some part of me chose to end her. End everyone. Just peering at Jaku recalled the decision to accept. And once I did, nothing – not Butterfly's sword, not Blossom's snare, not Jen's staff, not Orchid's knives, not Jaku's fall – offered resistance, denial. Worse still: when somebody raises their defences, I know now that it is my instinct, my way, to justify it by becoming the offence.

He didn't speak, but not for lack of trying. Maybe one of Hua-Shi's kicks dislocated his jaw.

I knew what he meant to say, though. Jaku might as well have deposited his every word straight into my head. His eyes accused my tongue responded our hands mirrored as fists.

Why.

"Because!"

Did you do it.

"If not me, who?"

Because you care.

"This is caring?!"

Whatever she tells you to do.

"You had her, why didn't you damn well do this?"

You did it.

"Jen's dying, Jaku. I'm unarmed. Couldn't stop you even if I wanted to."

Without regret.

This deserved no answer. What could this person, who didn't know me precisely as I didn't know him, say about my regrets? Then again, with that pulpy mess for a mouth, what could he say at all?

"Not dying anymore, little brother," said someone behind me, the only someone who *could* be behind me. "And you're about to follow her."

And what could *I* say that would mean anything to this last instrument of vengeance? The sword spoke louder than even the meaningless scream. Didn't need to do anything but wait for her visceral sweep, just as I had seen (just as I had *done*) with Jen. Halfway between a drawn breath there'd be a single sharp smile biting into my side, evicting organs from their soft, complacent home.

Jaku's face rearranged itself around the truth before I had time to finish that rising breath. The moment Hua-Shi gagged into a frustrated grunt, I felt all the air destined to swell his triumph gather in my chest, my chest that remained indecently intact. Too full of borrowed hope and wonder, I looked down, away from Jaku's shivering eyes and towards what made Jaku's eyes shiver.

My gaze reflected in glistening steel: two shiny, apathetic black holes, caught within a sliver of emasculated rage. Only a few inches of mere air challenged the sword, but it made no progress. I blinked and the slash of face looking back at me assumed familiar elements: two worried, pathetic brown eyes.

"Are you satisfied now?" she asked from somewhere I could not look. When there is a sword struggling to embed itself in your guts, there aren't many places you can look. You *can* follow the arc, turn around just enough, check the fists to make sure it is not really *her* fault. Note the tense arms, the taut shoulders, all robed in white peeking through posies of dark red. And behind it all was Hua-Shi, who was Chang to me, and would be forever. My Dailoh, my brother.

He would not look at me, his eyes narrowing as though that alone might reduce the gap between stomach and stubborn sword.

"Why?" he asked, and I knew it was not my place to answer. Somehow I was once more just a witness in my own skin.

"Because he taught you nothing," she replied, and it was from behind Chang. "Would you like to see how things might be if the roles were reversed?"

It was enough for her to ask. I saw and I knew. I saw his expression and it knew too. Still he tried to drive the unwilling weapon into me. That was not the merger she had in mind, however.

"One wears black, the other white, and each bears a surplus of red," a third voice said, and I should have expected it. Reason and wisdom held

Thorn's observation steady, even though he was now pacing around us, himself clad in the same unassuming brown habit as ever. I didn't have to look at him directly to understand his attitude – now I wasn't a witness; my other and I were both exhibits, specimens, subjects. "Yes, I am satisfied, Your Holiness. Displeased at what it cost to prove it, but knowing always comes at such a high price. Chang Tong-Kut, this is not your task. Give me the sword."

"He'll kill us both if you do," I said to Chang as softly as I dared. "And then he'll tear Kaifeng apart. He wants revolution but she'll give him chaos. Give the sword to *me*, brother. It's mine. *She was made for me!*"

"Either way," Fa Shai-Yeh added, because she had to, "choose this world's salvation, Knife."

Chang Tong-Kut, whose relationship with our aloof leader remained a mystery to me, caught my eye and then, just then, all our differences ceased to matter. Whatever madness we were in, we were in it together. His wink said 'little brother'; it was the last thing Chang-dailoh never said to me. As the wind is known to do, he changed direction, launching himself at Thorn. The whipping of his white robe was a shroud of preemptive mourning. Our cowled teacher just stood there, and although I remembered thinking of him as little more than a clerk, he was Half.

Everything said about Halves – the accelerated learning, the aptitude, the physical superiority – revealed itself not through Chang's violent shift but in Thorn's reaction. He wasn't just standing there when the sword came to divorce upper from lower. There was no denying Chang's ability, but he was a clumsy savage with a club to Thorn's graceful descent – who didn't so much duck the horizontal swipe as let his knees bend and his spine turn. Since I was focusing on him, my own faculties tuned themselves to his pace. I even saw him glance up, watch the lethal edge skim overhead, just before he rose at precisely the same speed and, once more, just stood there.

Chang Tong-Kut, the Knife. He was no Sword.

I stole a look back at Jaku – and saw Fa Shai-Yeh tending to him. It took me a moment to realise it was her: the woman was dressed in such a strange array of colours and tones as to resemble an exotic bird with pretences of outshining a rainbow. She was normally so concerned with fitting in, so why this abrupt choice of eye-wateringly bright apparel? Her presence alone was unexpected, but this was something else. Then again: why shouldn't she be there? If anyone belonged in this distorted scene, it was her. And I trusted her, implicitly against all explicit denial. So whoever I was, had been, would be, I turned my back on the girl of my dreams and watched the fate of my sword.

Again and again: Chang spun, slashed, hacked, struggled. Each time: Thorn was a thought ahead, true to his Maliscient capacity. Although I'd been able to veil some intent from Thorn's prying, Chang had given himself to recklessness; no doubt the master of the Malevolent Hand was following the Knife's lead before he even made it. It was a spectacle, reminding me of how, as a kid, I would try to cut a wind-loft leaf with a stick. I'd twirl and swipe and make myself sick with futile fury. The leaf always fell to the ground after me, in its own good time.

Before long, the white-robed assailant was tired, heaving his breath not amid attacks but between them. Brown-cloaked Thorn slowed down too, as condescending now as he'd ever been during the increasingly rare lectures in the Hand, as if his body was just an extension of his attitude – or façade. What wasn't 'normal' was this playfulness, this teasing. Then again, no one really knew Thorn personally. Maybe this was years of repression manifesting in a first and possibly last clash with the Hand's most prolific Peddler. That was it – I was watching the decision between who was the master and who was the student the only way it can be decided. Thorn was not a very good teacher.

Seconds after the mockery began, Thorn chose his moment. The next wild blow saw him step back, fold his hands like a Respite Attendant and wait. Chang tried to lower the sword but its growing weight beat him to it. Knowing that I had to watch this, I shuffled around so that I could see more than Chang's back, but of course did so without approaching. No one likes intrusions from the audience.

"Is that it?" Thorn asked. "That sword's not very good with you."

A terribly Shai-Yeh way to put it.

"Your death will change that," Chang replied, and started to raise the blade.

"Don't, Tong-Kut. She'll never accept you. You've played your role. Leave him to me." Him. Me. "You knew all this when we took him in. Tonight didn't have to happen, but remember the alternative. What she said."

"*Kono ama!*" Chang's hatred of 'the bitch' lifted the sword to waist-height.

"You'd have more luck trying to kill me." Thorn answered a question I couldn't hear but it made sense, much more sense than Chang's exclamation. "I've lost almost all of my finest warriors tonight, Tong-Kut. Please don't."

"I don't want to see her future," Chang said. Then he began to smile.

And then laugh.

And then roar.

He lunged.

Thorn's whole body seemed to sigh, to sag. The heavy steel bar, once liquid, once a dazzling wheel of carnage, prodded his mid-section. No longer trying to prevent the inevitable, the Maliscient Half moved out of harmony with the sluggish push. Before the sword's tip could even pierce the thread of his cloak, Thorn leapt, straight up and around. Chang finally released the sword and stepped back. He knew what was coming, because he didn't try to run. Now it was his turn to just stand there, even as Thorn's leg sprang from the dizzying vortex and drove a slippered foot towards Chang's head.

"*Kuraidengeki!*"

The first and last time I ever heard Thorn use the language of our ancient masters.

Most kicks make a thud. Some crack or crunch.

I heard a snap.

Thorn landed, limber and ready – perhaps he wasn't sure his enemy was dead. Chang remained upright, so maybe he wasn't. But the way his cheek was resting against his shoulder wasn't something someone who was alive should do. Thorn lashed out with another kick, this time driving his heel against Chang's chest.

I heard another snap. And then a splat. I saw Thorn's foot buried in the corpse, up to his ankle. It looked ridiculous, like he was practicing his kicks against a dummy made of wet clay. Maybe I laughed, but if so I had no reason for it.

Thorn's lips twitched in irritation, but a few shakes dislodged what remained of Chang Tong-Kut. My Dailoh, who wasn't Hua-Shi after all. Finally I understood Guan-Pi's diary and could name both Halves, and of course neither had been me. Hua-Shi, who had left the old man's care to join the Peddlers *and* took over the Bloody Shadows, and Chang Tong-Kut, a Half Peddler recruited from the streets who was simply convenient for Fa Shai-Yeh to add to the confusion. Not hard for her to encourage some flirting between Chang and Jen-Wah, who no doubt saw some of Hua-Shi in the tall, powerful Half Peddler. Just another game within the game.

And once again, we were playing Fa Shai-Yeh's favourite game: three had been reduced to two, two who would now circle each other to be the one.

With the hem of his cloak saturated and both feet squelched with gore, the true leader of the Bloody Shadows retrieved the sword. As he turned it here and there, moonlight slicing along the untainted bend, one thing was clear: he did not find it heavy. She had accepted him.

One thing led to another: I was without her.

"Excellent," said Hua-Shi, who may yet be a Thorn to me again. "Maybe the future will be different after all."

From what? – I almost asked, but there was no time. He was a Maliscient, but moreover, he was a Maliscient flying towards me, following the sword as though it were dragging him into fatal proximity. Equally there was no time for me to raise the usual defences against against Hua-Shi's prying – any move I made he'd be already there.

So I made no move at all. As before, when I'd been attuned to Thorn's velocity, I was operating at a pace that permitted an almost unpleasant level of reflection. An older, stronger Half had decided my life was in his way. All his Peddlers were dead; all his Shadows were dead. All because of me. But everything was a message – neatly arranged in a convenient sequence of anarchy. A message, and a lesson. Of course Fa Shai-Yeh was singing again, and maybe she'd never stopped. And that was the so-called 'flash before your eyes' in the moment of mortality I was long overdue. If Fa Shai-Yeh stopped singing, I'd cease to exist. So if her Nightsong's next verse was about how Char was felled by his own blade, so be it. Maybe someone else, much later, will hear snatches of the rhythm and rewrite the lyrics so the bad guy in black wins only to be forever tormented by his demons. But here, now, a mass-murderer was about to be spared a long life of regret, fear and solitude.

Don't forgive me, Hua-Shi, because only I can do that. And you know I never will. Let me live and I'll come for you, you'll come for me. So kill me, my Other, and take my place. I'm ready.

No, there had been time to raise the usual defences, so I decided to raise an unusual offence instead.

Hua-Shi blazed past me but his attack never landed. I knew better than to relent, to give in to some sort of triumphant attitude. Even as I followed him, even as he had to stumble in order to stop, I believed that if he killed me, he'd be the one forced to dance to her woeful melody.

Was that what changed his mind? Close, all too close: that's where I stood, easily within range should the Maliscient change his mind *again*.

"No," he said, but not to me. Not even at me. *About* me? "But it was a good idea. You are right. I am Hua-Shi, protégé of Leung Guan-Pi: the old man you killed."

He pushed the sword into the ground, releasing the hilt after letting her sink a third through the dirt. And then Hua-Shi faced me. I noticed the spatters like wet flames creeping up the bottom of his robe, but even darker than this reminder were his eyes. I'd seen eyes like that before, in dreams and in steel, owned by the Night.

"Why did everyone attack me?" And yes, when I asked this, I had a fair notion what the answer would be. Hua-Shi tapped the very top of the sword's handle with one finger, and then folded his hands behind his back. Pacing away from me, he resumed his lecture.

"They were defending themselves. I didn't tell them what was going to happen tonight. We all hoped for the best, whatever she said."

He kept his voice at its usual subdued level; I kept up with him just to hear it. This, of course, brought me directly to the weapon.

"What did she say?" There were fangs between the layers of blue spiralling up and down the handle, diamonds whose bite punish the greedy thief, the impulsive would-be hero. Would be not me.

"I said: Yes."

Hua-Shi stopped, knelt. I pulled my hand away from almost-touching her hilt, imitating Thorn's habit of clasping his fingers. Maybe it would lend me some of his serenity.

"Yes?" I asked.

"Yes. They asked, I answered. But they already knew." She entered the corner of my eye then, and I did not trust her there. So I looked, and once more noticed…all that colour, all those layers. "Are you ready to take what is yours?" Fa Shai-Yeh held the sheath out, her smile revealing neither teeth nor temptation. "Do you think you can put her in her place?"

So that's what it was really about. Not just taking the sword – I'd done that, and then I'd done this. The challenge was controlling her. And was this why I couldn't get her back until now? Until everyone was together, and I had to learn the cost of not 'putting her in her place'. Could I?

"What if *I* said yes?"

Half her smile lifted, transformed pressed lips into a dare. "You are not afforded the luxury of words-as-deeds. Do it, then it is done."

The cadavers around us – they were what had been done. And if it wasn't the sword, it was me. And even if it hadn't been me, if I'd somehow blacked out while someone else went berserk, one fact remained: when I 'came to', I was trying to cut down an Orchid but severed a Weed instead. Most importantly, I believed I had done it, and since no one else stepped up to accept the responsibility, what else could have happened?

"I almost preferred it when he wasn't thinking at all," Hua-Shi said. He walked past me, a body slung over his left shoulder, and lifted the sword from where he'd left it. "So it didn't work, Priestess. This isn't him."

"Apparently she was right the whole time," Fa Shai-Yeh said. She turned the scabbard so that Hua-Shi could, with no apparent effort, slide the sword home. He put her in her place, accepted the loaded sheath and then began to walk away.

With my sword. Of course I had to follow, but Fa Shai-Yeh's sneer gave pause to belated pursuit. She knew that I'd had my chance to take it (again). What right had I to cry denial now?

"You will never be ready for it, Char Ah-Ran," Fa Shai-Yeh said. "My plan was not enough. Still, you may yet make a difference."

"Where is he going? Not back to Kaifeng."

"Swimming Carp. You will face him there."

Somehow I already knew that. Instead of pursuing the course, I asked the one thing she'd taught me to ask.

"Am I awake yet?"

"From whose dream?" She canted her head. "You have to sleep before you can wake. You have to dream before you can know."

"What *really* happened, Fa Shai-Yeh?"

"What you believe, happened."

"So the Peddlers, my friends, turned against me, transformed into Roses, murdered not only the Shadows but also tried to kill me, and then each other, and I was me, and another, and another— no! That can't have been it." I stopped shaking my head but continued to study the ground. "No."

"Fond of that word, are you not? So negative. I say yes, you say no. Somewhere in between is the truth. The truth that once you touched the sword, you went insane with fury. The truth of you being Char, Hua-Shi,

Chang and Terasawa Jaku, all at once. The truth of you being not even one of them. Which would you like? If this is a dream, any of those can be the truth."

"There is only one truth, Fa Shai-Yeh, and that is what has happened."

"There is only one truth, Charan, and that is what will happen."

That name. Not quite mine. Only in dreams, and even there I wasn't sure if it was the truth. Had it been this Charan who allowed the sword its indiscriminate feast?

"My name is Char, and I didn't kill anyone."

"That is not what Terasawa Jaku is going to say when the healers of the Haven ask him. You have made this all about you, when in actuality you are only who did it. What was done: so many lives gone, and you did not even know many of their names. When you end one life, you affect dozens more. How does that make you feel?"

"I wish it hadn't happened."

"There! See, was that so hard? Listen," she said, closer now, arms outstretched. "Listen and I will tell you the secret. Come to me."

There she is, Charan. Right there.

"But it did happen! Look! Look at what I did!"

Closer still. Touching. Enfolding, somehow smothering me despite her slight stature.

And me, collapsing.

"The secret," she whispered, "is just a matter of letting go. Do you really wish it had not happened, Charan? That this truth is not truth at all?"

"If I am Charan, then yes," I answered, waiting for her to stroke my hair.

"Hmmm. Then I will fix everything. You have but to ask."

When someone says that, in all sanity you should worry what they're *not* telling you, what might be written on the back of the contract. Why the name must be signed in blood. Why the wording is so precise.

But if it's reached that point, sanity is not something you worry about.

It went something like this (I only remember it now):

"Fa Shai-Yeh, Goddess of Swords, please, I don't want to be Charan, or Char Ah-Ran. I don't want to be the one who did any of this. Will you give me another chance? Let me make the right choices next time. I don't want to have killed my friends. Can't you give me a better dream?"

"If I change one thing, I change everything. You will be someone else. Someone I tried to prevent you from becoming. From going through. But I see now. Char was not enough. You must suffer so much more before she will accept you. Last chance, Charan. If you are going to change your mind, do so now."

"What can be worse than this? I killed everyone. What can I do? I'll do anything."

"Shh. If you will not change your mind, then I will change it for you."

She began to hum. There was no resisting it now.

This was the beginning of the better dream, the truth I chose.

I saw a road. It ran in two directions: backwards and forwards. I wanted to walk forwards.

She sang: When you are ready, you will come back here. He will wait.

I saw a tree. It grew in two directions: up and down. I had to sit under it.

She sang: You will look down, and then you will look up.

I sit under the tree and look down at the village. I remember Dog-Ears *will hate it* and Father *will hate you* Plump Treat and Elder Leung *alive and not-alive* Marriage *moon* and separation *cross.*

She sang: That is why you are here.

I reach for something small, something I always carry *hold still* and must remember *it won't hurt trust me.*

She sang: That is not why you are here.

I put the knife away. I stand up and I go down. I saw the village. It was alive and not-alive. I must have been there.

She sang: It is called Swimming Carp, and you will hate it.

I saw a house. It was my home and prison. I grew up there.

She sang: They will call you Dog-Ears, and they will hate you.

I see a village Swimming Carp *I see a road* Come back here *I see a tree* Look down look up.

I make more memories, emptying the village and filling the night with pain *Hua-Shi* and fire *Me.* Now I am walking on the forward road going backwards. I know where I am returning to and who I wasn't, and who I am, because I know who I will be

Because

I am.

III. Charan Jaydemyr

Kaifeng

856 A.R -

"Where are you going?" Shai-Yeh called again, but I didn't stop laughing. A memory of the Haven's blaze lingered in the air, smoky and thick, despite the momentary rain she had called down. "Come back here!"

But I already had. I did exactly what you wanted, Vachaelle. Look, listen.

"*He has my sword,*" I said back, using that language Shah-Long never learned. Char of Kaifeng had known it without knowing it – and Charan Jaydemyr was nothing without it. "*And he's coming.*"

Because now I'm awake, he won't have a choice.

"*Him and so many others,*" Chaelle replied, making haste to catch up to me. Truthfully, I wasn't going anywhere specific at all. He'd been in the Haven, watching. Waiting. And Terasawa, his pet, the two of them, telling the story of the Rose named Charan Jaydemyr. No, Chaelle, you didn't have to tell me any of this. I just knew it. Better than that, I knew it didn't really matter either.

"Guess I should hurry up and get my sword back then, hm?" I continued to use that language, but no longer with any stress or poignancy. It's just how I talked now. "Alright, Chaelle. Where is he?"

"You had better hope he is the closest. Any of the others and it will be over before it begins."

She was right. The moon was no longer just the crescent of cracked eggshell I remembered from a week ago, and the destruction of the Haven would have alerted the local predators, *them* as poor Happy put it. I could only hope she was more adept at negotiating these dark woods than that useless idiot yet cringing somewhere between the events of Kaifeng and Swimming Carp. Dog-Ears – was that what we Halves were called in the real world? Barely Noble, but that's precisely what a Half is. Barely *anything*. But barely is still more than nothing.

"The sword is useless to him while I live. But you did a fine show of it in the village," I said, sending a grin her way. Dog-Ears had feared Hua-Shi; Char hated him. But Charan? I knew Hua-Shi, leader of the Bloody Shadows, was nothing but a failed prototype, whether he was Thorn or Chang. It was all so petty now. "But you should have known how he'd react to it."

"He? Oh. Charan?"

"Mm?"

"Here he is."

He? Oh. I stopped and, as I had done so many times before, turned around. There stood Hua-Shi, next to Chaelle, looking much as before in his customary brown robes. The Healers in the House must have been good at their job. I imagined Havens outside the relative safety of the city would have sported hardier stuff. Still, there was a gauntness to the man I'd known as Thorn, a hollow vacancy that seemed like the afterimage of determination — not at all helped by his lack of hair. Guess Healers can't help with that: splotches like liver spots pocked his raw scalp. Scars. Maybe he had learned.

Then I knew something else. That brute from the Haven who threatened Happy Apple. Wu Ming, they'd called him. 'Nameless'. I glanced at his wrist and wished I'd broken it when I had the chance.

"*Dohsh'ta no, shisho?*" I asked, switching to Mifūn-go for his benefit. If being insulted like that is a benefit at all. Asking him 'what's up, Master?' in such a sarcastic tone was all about letting him know. "Back to finish me off?"

But he, too, had changed — or was this our first meeting? Didn't matter. The other Half glanced at the priestess, who, true to form, just shrugged and folded her arms. Hard to believe they'd been rutting in Swimming Carp only a week ago, but who can say who he thought he was then?

"That's twice *you've* tried to finish *me* off now, little Fire-slinger, but if you're the one meant to wield this," he said, drawing my sword and holding her just as he had last time — ready to run it through my guts, "then yes. If not, I believe I know that dance too."

You're in here, but you know there's more than one voice to listen to. And guess what, Hua-Shi? They rarely agree. So which voice are you going to trust?

"My own." With that, Hua-Shi — former leader of the Bloody Shadows, original prodigy of Leung Guan-Pi, Greatest Thief of Kaifeng, rival to Wong Chu-Deng, stealer of swords and later teacher to fellow Half Chang Tong-Kut — cast away the sheath and sprang at me.

I had no idea what I was going to do next.

It was a bit like all those dream-battles in Kaifeng, the training with Orchid, and a bit like the beatings I'd never received in Swimming Carp. Wherever Hua-Shi sent the sword, I wasn't there, but now and then Dog-Ears let the edge nick my skin and gave the other Half hope. If he overextended himself, exposed his ribcage or an armpit, I drove my fiery reproach deep into the flaw, scolding him with a little more bite than he'd ever dared. Before long, he was repeating movements; Hua-Shi was no swordsman. I left scorch-marks up and down his torso, his sides — and speckles of my blood on the sword. He leapt, I ducked. He flurried,

I dodged. He missed, I slapped the blunt side of the weapon away effortlessly. Some newer and yet older part of me was taking care of the fight, that part I call Charan Jaydemyr, who is a weapon of impulse tempered with experience, a weapon with no mind to read. This left Char free to fantasise what sort of state Hua-Shi was going to be in when this was done, and Dog-Ears rode the ebb of terror, convinced that each time Hua-Shi attacked would be our last. Neither Char's arrogance nor Dog-Ears' pessimism could have been doing the Maliscient any favours. He wavered between overconfidence and doubt. *You might as well get out, Hua-Shi, because what you see in here will only confuse you. God knows it's confusing us.*

"You little prick," he panted and lowered the blade, as distant a creature from the calm, composed Thorn as I was from tortured, timid Dog-Ears. Yes, she had made us anew, broken us, reshaped us, but I was something else too. "Why are you so smug? You're a murderer, a traitor, a hypocrite. Even if that is what she wants you to be, it doesn't change the fact that you are. That you are still guilty, and should pay."

True. But I had better things to do than quibble with a glorified thug. Oh, that stung him. He winced and looked at her again.

"Yes, Hua-Shi, that is what he needs to be. And you are going to help add to his tally of sin." Chaelle had killed a man with a look, and then so many others with the mere flick of her frosty fingernails. Why should Hua-Shi be any different? "You were never fit to lead the Shadows anyway. Leave Terasawa to that task. Your reward for service to the Night comes now. Look." She nodded at me.

Damn – and I'd almost caught him by surprise. What did his blackened eyes see when they returned to that 'little prick'? Wings of flame in the wake of my raised arms – *you are a phoenix, Charan* – and bolts of sizzling light crackling between my fingers. *Remember this, Hua-Shi? Last time had been reflex and I still humiliated you with it. Look what I can do now.*

This aptitude came from no Kaifeng teacher, no clumsy fooling around in the dream-fields of Swimming Carp. Earlier, and later, lessons stalking between one self and the next, through a Window and behind the Door. Chaelle stepped back, her face warped by the ambient heat. But Hua-Shi, ah, so proud. Char remembered, then, more of what she'd tried to erase but had only buried. Restless nights of early apprenticeship in the Malevolent Hand, me wandering the halls. And him, Thorn, in the courtyard, doing what no one expected: training. I thought: this must be why Chang-dailoh is afraid of him, because his body was a machine of grace and ferocity, fending off countless enemies of silence and shadows. And later, in a street between Siu-Tsin and the Five-Fold Palace, Thorn was duelling with a Rose, and that time I'd been less worried about being caught, but never got the chance to tell anyone what I'd seen because I hadn't seen anything. So many songs, so many blanks. Only a few came back, but there'd be more. If I survived this, and I would, because now I'd seen what Thorn, Hua-Shi, could do. And what he could not do.

He could not back down. Steeling himself, he lowered his head, bent his knees and erupted into a charge. Char scowled and made ready for the onslaught. Dog-Ears was already trying to imagine life with a broken neck. Charan waited.

Never let it be said Chaelle has no sense of humour. I heard her click her fingers, and I knew that this trick had never been used on me. Hua-Shi was too committed to his attack to react, but he was affected by her power nonetheless. Between one loping footfall and the next, Hua-Shi began to shimmer, the air around him forming shards of moonlit ice. Char cursed the Ephin whore for making things difficult, Dog-Ears amended his vision to include frostbite and shattered bones. Charan? Charan laughed briefly.

All three of us stole a peek at the priestess, and sure enough, she was twinkling her fingers in a now-familiar gesture.

"*Kono ama,*" Char muttered and brought my arms together, forearms crossing in front of my chest. Inside its heart, fire is warm but not intolerable – it is the tongue and claws that do the damage. I couldn't see much of Hua-Shi through the orange-yellow mist, but then he began to give off a furnace of steam. And he did not slow. Charan dragged my right foot back, extended my left hand. Waited. Breathed. Thought for a moment about eggs.

Now Hua-Shi was drenched in scalding fog, screaming and bearing down and screaming. Dog-Ears, whimpering in pity, withdrew the Fire. It was too late – the enraged Half's flesh bubbled like a broom's bristles. Charan giggled; Char pulled Dog-Ears to the back of my mind to beat the shit out of him.

I thought about eggs again. I hate eggs.

Hua-Shi gave me back my sword in the only way he knew how. A backhand slash, a downward chop, a straight thrust – who knows, who cares? Probably all and more. Once you avoid the dangerous bits of a sword (roughly half of any given weapon is dangerous – the rest is up to the wielder), it's all just a matter of taking control. No doubt in a great deal of pain from the burns, Hua-Shi was slow, almost inanimate. Without his Maliscience to tell him what to do, he really was a pretty average fighter.

"Shut up!" he roared and swung yet again. Dodge. Yawn.

I suppose it was the mental version of trying to attack three different people at once. Dog-Ears had managed to fend off Char, who was in turn trying to call forth the Fire again and fry Hua-Shi to a twisted lump of black lumpiness. So while those two were grappling, Charan made my move: the sword whistled through air unfortunately devoid of me. I reached out and let my left hand follow it. A blade's width might not seem much from front-on but there was more than enough to grab onto from behind the blunt spine. Four fingers and a thumb formed a neat vise, but Hua-Shi was still a strong opponent. Before he could get over his shock, I shoved the sword down and stepped in, right foot coming from behind to carry all the weight of a straight right fist. Char ignited my knuckles; Dog-Ears pulled the blow so that all it did was send Hua-Shi sprawling rather than penetrate skin, bones and heart, or so Charan supposed.

Somehow none of us kept hold of the weapon, our mutual object of affection, of obsession.

We...I bent and finally, after decades of her absence (Dog-ears says five years, Char grudgingly agrees and the dreams of both say many more on top of that; Charan doesn't care because that's the past), I took up my ancestral sword once again. She was weightless, perfect; I lifted her with my left hand and stared down the hilt towards the blade, but the crossguard, the *tsuba*, was in the way. Between my fist and the beautiful tooth stood a charred moon and a burnished golden cross, and no matter which way I tilted the sword, the crescent never became a straight line and the cross never stopped shining. Visions and dreams. A scar. A name. I remembered now – with this, I could kill even my father. If I had to.

For Dog-Ears it was fear; for Char, excitement. For Charan, it was completion. Whatever the reason, I was weeping.

Charan knew what to do. I held the sword in front of me, left hand keeping it level with the ground, right hand travelling the length, palm not quite touching the smooth steel. I was drawing the real sword from within the physical illusion: a weapon of air-searing flame. What I expected to happen, did: the metal glowed, caught alight and simmered with a fine haze. Satisfied with this reality, I withdrew the Fire and Oni-Goroshi was cool and passive once more.

"Now, Charan!" Chaelle had unfolded her arms and was pointing at the fallen Hua-Shi. "Now!"

Dog-Ears clamped his teeth around Char's arm, who was more than happy to step forward and wreck Hua-Shi's plans for tomorrow on a permanent basis.

"Why?" I asked. "What did this nobody ever do to me?"

"What? Nevermind what he did to you. What did you do to *him*? You beat his parents over half to death, killed his adoptive grandfather, not to mention his former lover and several of his top students and, because that was not enough, burned him so severely no amount of Healing can remove the scars. Char, this is your *enemy*. End it."

"My name is Charan, Chaelle. Call me that or 'My Lord' – whatever suits you. And this is not my enemy. He's not even my teacher."

Taking both Dog-Ears and Char by surprise, I turned my back on whoever I'd been fighting and headed down the road, looking up and down. Moon and ground. Between, a horizon. My destination.

"What about the sheath?" she asked, and it made sense. I had to put her in her place. I sighed and, determined to make this the last time, spun about.

What we saw was not Chaelle.

Dog-Ears cringed; Char widened his eyes; Charan dealt with it.

Maybe Hua-Shi was trying to catch me off-guard, and since I was walking away, he'd chosen a good time to do it. Unfortunately, the difference between ambushing someone from behind and leaping at them once they've turned is all the difference that matters. I didn't really think about it. The sword was at my side, cold in my left hand. He was airborne; and then the sword was at my other side, seething in my other hand. I was bent over slightly and Hua-Shi was gone. No, not gone. There was half of him, waist and legs and a tangle of intestines toppled to the right. I didn't really want to look, but sure enough, the rest of him must have sailed right over me, because there was his torso, arms and head making a mess of the road behind me.

Chaelle crept towards the lower half of him, her face contorted with horror. Then she looked at me.

"What?" I asked, examining the sword's edge for any specks of black residue.

"Who *are* you?"

As if she didn't know?

"Charan, heir to Jaydemyr." There were other answers but they wouldn't have been as true. Satisfied that Oni-Goroshi's heat had rejected Hua-Shi's leftovers, I held my right hand out to Chaelle.

"Are you okay? Not going to be sick or anything?" She looked a little green herself. Weird, considering what she'd done in and to the Haven.

"I am who I am because of you, and now you expect me to go back to that?" I was still waiting, arm outstretched. "Sheath."

"Well, no, but I had no idea that you would be like this. What is the—oh. Here."

"Thank you," I said, sheathing the sword and slinging it over my left shoulder. *This* was the weight my shoulder remembered. Any wonder wearing a travel bag that way felt so familiar: thumb under strap. Turn. Stare at Chaelle. Chaelle, staring past me. "What is it?"

"Behind you."

I could feel them. *Them.* Drawn by the scent of Hua-Shi's murder, and already called by the moon. I looked up at it. Round. Pale. Ready to hatch.

"Fuck I hate eggs. Did I ever tell you that?"

"What? Look, they are getting closer. I suggest we make ourselves scarce and let them have their dinner."

"Eh? But I am the Blackcloak, Scourge of Kaifeng, Fa Shai-Yeh," I said in Mifūn-go. "I used to rip Roses to bits with a wooden sword. Imagine what I can do with my real one."

"That was just a *dream*, Char!"

"I told you. My name is Charan," I said in Jaydemyrian and shuffled around. How many of them out there? Not many. Five, maybe. Less than I'd faced in the last dream, the Garden that is Kaef're. Five: like a hand, and I would break this one too. No, not a hand: a claw, Talons rushing towards what they thought was their prey. Dog-Ears fainted and even Char of Kaifeng was devoid of his usual braggadocio. Which left me. Charan. With my sword. My Goddess. Oni-Goroshi. I was complete. There was no greater dream than this.

I had to blink back more tears of relief.

"Charan, you *have to wake up!*" the air says, and I feel my body grow heavy; at the same time, something is shaking me. I know it isn't her, not this time, but I have to say it anyway.

"Quit it, Chaelle. No more games. Leave me alone!"

So she did, so she had. So I did what had to be done. I know They will be closing on the drop of blood by now. It is the answer to the question their own blood forgot to stop asking.

My very essence is lethal.

The full moon fails to hinder Their greedy pursuit. Not even the guidance of the night's sun could rein in the madness of the Night's Own. One little sniff of Half and they lose it.

But as I move, low and quick, I see: a solitary Rose, separated from its gaggle by some measure of hesitation.

I do not hesitate. Don't even need the sword now; no, she had said: *do not do this.*

Don't even need her now.

Leap. Grip. Snap. Leap away.

Run.

"This has already happened," says the wind as I race through it, but now it isn't her voice. I didn't listen to the air and I wouldn't listen to the night. Whatever way she chose, it is not my way. Still, the voice repeats: "It has all already happened, so wake up! They're coming!"

Up ahead, three more, soon to be no more.

Pause. Those filthy aberrations. All I can do is stare. Poor cat. I like cats more than eggs.

No. I do more than stare.

In my head, I find room to arrange a transaction and wait for the response.

Three Roses are the price, plucked and shredded, scattered red and forgettable. Their bits and the cat's pieces tell me that the deal has been struck.

I know another is coming for me. I am patient. Try to find in the puddle of lumpy paste the cat's silent purr.

"Yes, yes I came for you and now you are with me! Open your eyes and see."

I'm not being shaken anymore. Forced to face this other her. I almost ask her the same thing we almost ask of the Roses, so many there have been. I almost ask for their names. But: you are not my mother. Even if you look like her. Even if you sound like her.

She said: *Yes.*

"No I didn't! I named you."

Yes. I have names. Char Ah-Ran. Rat. Shah-Long. Dog-Ears. Half. Charan. So?

"So you are the Scourge. That is what I called you. That is what you call yourself."

She never called me that. Not then. A new trick. There is no use in picking up the sword. That'd be like trying to write with a piece of paper. What if it is not her? Yes, I ask myself that. A closer look, for the revulsion that was compulsion. In denial, the ground closes between us.

"No! Turn around—"

Too late I obey; too early I move. No severed Half this time – just a premature query and another Rose, diving into the idiocy of my thoughtless-stupid-Dog-Ears question.

He stops. Something has stopped him. And then I stop his everything.

So why do I imagine him landing on top of me? Why am I now on my back?

Why are my eyes *still* closed?

Which me is taking over now? Which part of my self is going to let this Rose just slice us like a kitten in its sleep?

Dog-Ears? No. Something is making me afraid. All of me.

I want to stand, but all I can do is tremble. Can't even move my arms. My sword. My sword. My sordid hands are empty. Am I having some sort of fit?

Just as the Rose lands on me with all its ungainly weight, something slaps me across the face but it isn't the Rose, because a slap from it would have knocked my head clean off, so what—

"OPEN YOUR EYES!"

Ah, so it's just another dream after all. Well played, Chaelle. Fine. I will open my eyes and you'll be finishing your song, I'll be in bed in the Malevolent Hand, twelve years old, I will wake up and I will say—

W. James Chan

Epilogue

Kas'Daen-desne
Highmoon
882 A.R.

"What the fuck?" The Dreamer isn't dreaming anymore, but he's still talking like it.

"There is no time to explain," Dhiana says in Ziegerian-Common, leaning over the young man. "You are awake now. Charan Jaydemyr, I am Dhiana Jaydemyr. Your mother. I promise that I will take care of Char and Dog-Ears, but it is Charan we need now. Do you understand? It is time to be you."

The black-cloaked young man blinks his black-filled eyes a few times and then sits up. Still blinking, he pulls the cowl over his complicated expression and says the one thing Dhiana wants to hear.

"In that case, I will need my sword."

Arius Hawkstorm first heard reports of the approaching enemy not long after the Dreamer used his own real name again. Each time he says it, as Dhiana had stated, both Champion and Lady remember more, not just about the boy but, more importantly, about themselves. About that night. By the time Charan Jaydemyr is awake in the basement of their tower, the former Captain-Guard of the Eagles is staring at the dark, twisted forest not far from the tower's base. The dream-tale was still deep in a teenager's view of Kaifeng when Arius had been forced out of the intimate interrogation and into the gloom of Awakenmoon. He is no longer uncomfortable in the armour, and his gnarled fingers are at home around the pommel of a sword. At his side stand the remnants of the Talons, but he knows that other allies of Jaydemyr are coming, now that the bar jamming their cognisance has started to slide.

They won't be here in time.

The first Kas'Daen warrior emerges from the night, but the gangly Noble hesitates. He was not expecting to find others of his kind ready to oppose him. Arius knows now: since the eradication of Jaydemyr and formation of the Overclan Sladaria fourteen years ago, there has been very little fighting between the Night's Own. This is why the Scourge's appearance has caused so much trouble. And whatever his Lady locked away by burying Charan Jaydemyr under at least two layers of personality, it is obviously coming forth in more than just the Jaydemyrian allies. Tonight is the beginning, and this is just an advance force. Little more than a scouting party. More than enough to take a serious bite out of the Jaydemyrian forces, Arius reflects, sour for good reason: there can be no more than five Talons and twenty Eagles left.

But when the boy awakens, that won't matter.

"Nehraz," The Champion says in Ziegerian, avoiding the inflections unique to the Noble Speech, and oddly enough it feels natural. "Head downstairs and see what's going on."

"As you command, sir." Arius is now used to being called that as well. He doesn't so much as nod before the Talon slips back indoors.

Even now, Arius is more comfortable using a mortal mode of communication. It was what he'd used before the Overclan's rise, when Jaydemyr negotiated some sort of 'peace' with the *nse'ante*. No – that word bothers him. They are human. Yes. Not 'vermin', and that is precisely what the word meant before necessary association softened it and the translation became 'people'. The Noble Speech is entirely too honest in its lack of ambiguity for Arius. Although he is a straightforward creature, the Hawkstorm understands the need for linguistic secrecy.

"Sir, an archer has been spotted."

"Mm." The old Captain-Guard groans to his feet and glances up at the tower's only rampart, little more than a balcony, where he and the Lady had debated her son's fate. He shakes his head and gives an order – this time in the Noble Speech to ensure there are no misunderstandings. As yet, there are no 'people' in their ranks.

Satisfied that his own marksmen are readying their unerring bolts in case that archer decides to loose an uninvited gift, Arius settles himself upon the stairs leading up to the weary tower's entrance and waits, hoping. Hoping and, yes, praying to God Herself that the dreams taught the boy what they all need.

Dhiana, ancient mistress of not one clan but two, a Maliscient so powerful she is called Mindwarp, is afraid.

As vivid as the retelling had been, either the trials of Dog-Ears or the tutelage of Char, no amount of words from her son's tortuous tale have prepared her for what she now sees. Upon his capture, he had been sapped, undermined by the driving demands of Vachaelle's agenda. Certainly, he had made short work of her Talons, but that was the Scourge's last moment. She keeps her distance as this creature, who is at once the Scourge, Dog-Ears, and Charan and yet something else, retrieves his sword and just stands there, staring at her. Through her.

"I regret hitting you," she says, irked at the banality of the first conversation with her son in sixteen years.

"We've been through worse," he replies. "Although that was a first."

"How so?"

"In all our dreams, we've never been hit by our mother." He pauses, and then his voice is different: "I don't...mind. I probably deserved it." Dog-Ears. It has to be. Dhiana sighs and switches to the Noble Speech.

"Charan. I'm sorry." Now she's just stretching it out, selfishly trying to keep him down here as long as possible. Dhiana, a full-blooded Noble, tears herself in half: she needs to forbid her only son from entering the deadly fray; for the sake of the family, she must command him to be the Scourge once more. "I'm sorry but now you have work to do. After that, we can talk. I will tell you everything. No more dreams, no more nightmares. I will give you every choice." She will be everything to him that Vachaelle wasn't.

"Yes. That shall suffice," The Half says, showing her with his choice of words that Vachaelle's influence will not slip away that easily.

Then comes a knock on the door. Dhiana knows what that rap signifies and turns her back, ostensibly fidgeting with something on the desk behind her. She waits until the message has been passed, until she is alone, before she tries to cry.

Five minutes later, as Charan is meeting his mentor for the first time again, there is another knock on the door.

"Who is it?" Dhiana asks, feeling terribly mundane. Who would be down here at this time? They should all be upstairs, preparing for the first of so many attacks. She herself is clad in the same armour as she'd worn that night, what she thinks of as the first night. Soon she will join them in battle, wielding neither sword nor shield. She needs nothing more than a will to change reality and the fingers to shape it.

"It is me, my Lady."

A female voice, speaking *Jaydemyrian*. Dhiana is certain she is the only woman on Kaef're to know that language.

Or she was.

"Enter then."

No matter how many times she remembers seeing the other woman, the fact that the traitress never ages always gives Dhiana a rare chill. It is accepted if not expected that the Night's Own learn how to slow and eventually stop the decay of flesh reserved for mortals alone. But for this girl-witch to forever appear barely twenty years old and always in that same dirty white dress is entirely *unnatural*, if a monstrosity such as Dhiana is permitted to even think the word of others.

"Vachaelle Nightsong reporting, my Lady."

And it is just the same as it was before: complete submission, a bow that falls into a kneel, a kneel into almost a prostration. Dhiana cannot see the troublesome girl's smile, but it's there. It's always there.

"Say what you have to say, *nse'ante*, and then slink back to the Kas'Daen."

"My Lady, in all the years you have known me, have I ever betrayed you?" The Nightsong remains close to the ground, looking up only to make her voice clear.

"More times than I can remember," Dhiana lies. "But you have brought him back to me. Did you have to do it in this way?"

"No, not really, but I saw no use in delivering a half-finished product. Now you know what he can do. Even to his closest allies. It will take a firm hand to keep him in check."

"And you are that hand, Vachaelle? You've done nothing but torture my boy."

"Had we gone through with your plan alone, My Lady, he would not be Half the weapon he is now. But I will concede – my own design was not enough either. So there you have it. He is at once Shah-Long – your Dog-Ears, and Char Ah-Ran – my Scourge. And now he is Charan, Blackcloak. One plus one equals three. Or one."

"You and your word-games. So you are posing as a Priestess of the Liquid Night again?"

"It is a fitting role. Better than most of my others. Permission to sit, my Lady?"

Dhiana knows it's all routine, all ritual. Vachaelle, in league with Arius Hawkstorm and the Three Beasts, gained enough power to all but erase Jaydemyr from Kaef're. But it is an important ritual, and so the Lady Jaydemyr gestures negligently and the Nightsong makes her way to the pallet upon which the Dreamer dreamed his lives.

"You have more to say, Nightsong. As I said before: spit it out and leave."

How crude she becomes when dealing with her old nemesis.

"Did he tell you what happened after he got his sword back?"

"There was no time. I presume to ask him about this after your Kas'Daen have been turned back. After he has used that sword to kill them all."

"I recommend you do not ask him, my Lady. I was forced to be even more heavy-handed with the Song after that. There was so much he did not want to remember, and some things he should not have to."

"Who are you to decide what my son remembers and does not remember? You are not my equal, girl."

Both of them bristle at the sudden return to this time or that, the verge of an all-out argument that inevitably ends with Dhiana dismissing the human girl and the human girl going behind Dhiana's back anyway.

"As you wish, my Lady. Ask him. No matter what, it will be a jumble of all his voices, because he was rarely one of the three for very long. Charan Jaydemyr killed, Char enjoyed it, Dog-Ears kept your son from turning into a mindless murderer. Besides, all we did was wander. Now and then he would throw a tantrum and try to give up the sword, but it never lasted. Oh, and I taught him how to knit."

"Dog-Ears must have enjoyed that. He is the strongest of them, I think. He even influenced Char's dreams." Dhiana smiles, but it is not for Vachaelle's presence. "He made that violent bully become a tailor. A husband. A father. A good man."

"I was there. I did all that. Maybe you are forgetting this."

Dhiana's smile dies.

"And yes, he did enjoy it, my Lady. Took refuge in a small town for over a year, doing nothing but dressmaking and fixing patches in people's pants." Vachaelle half-shrugs. "Then they found us and everyone died." Matter-of-fact. People die. People who don't die, watch. Until they die.

"Nightsong, your old allies are out there, no doubt remembering all about the Revolution and that not every single Jaydemyr died that night. Shouldn't you be off so that I can join *my* allies against them, and against you?"

"Dhiana. He encountered *her* last year."

As fulfilled as her memory may have become, Dhiana has to concentrate to decipher Vachaelle's emphasis.

"In what capacity?"

"She was in the hunting party sent out by the Tantamonian monks to investigate 'The Scourge'. The collective pagan temples are very interested in the possibility of a Half slaying his supposed superiors – full-blooded Nobles. There have always been Peddlers but we both know they do not really have anyone at the Scourge's level."

"A good touch," Dhiana concedes, and the Nightsong dips her head in acknowledgment. "Although making him think he could do it with a piece of wood was a bit extravagant."

Vachaelle grins, absolutely proud of herself.

"He believed, and so he became. But to conclude my report, my Lady: he is starting to figure out who she is after just that one time, but I have managed to distract him thus far. I would not be surprised if he mentioned her in the Delving." Dhiana does not respond to Vachaelle's own delving. "I leave it up to your wisdom to decide how to deal with this."

"In other words, you're dumping it in my lap and running again?"

"Perhaps, my Lady," Vachaelle replies, no longer penitent. If anything, she is now quite impish.

"When was the last time I tried to kill you, Vachaelle?"

"Two nights before the clan's fall, my Lady, you attempted to strangle me."

"Hmm. And why did I stop again?"

"As I recall it, my Lady, your husband and Clanlord personally intervened."

"Oh, Charas'z."

"Indeed. I suppose had he known what we were planning, he would have let you end me after all."

"No, no he wouldn't have. But he might have been less eager to name Arius as his blood-brother at the ceremony. What dreadful timing.

But perfect. I'll grant you that. So why now? Why bring him back, if you were so determined to bring Jaydemyr low?"

Now that Dhiana is asking questions, the true division of power between them is revealed. Vachaelle giggles and the Lady Jaydemyr recoils.

"Surely he told you about the phoenix. Goes for clans, too. That and Charas'z— well, he was not the ideal Lord of Jaydemyr."

"The clan was doing just fine before you sold it out to the Sladarian."

"Were that the case, I would not have been able to sell it out to the Sladarian, as you put it. Besides, I did not mean the Jaydemyr that was. I refer to the Jaydemyr that will be. Your son, Dhiana, is going to rule the world."

"Another of your Liquid Night visions, Vachaelle? Not a single one of them has come true yet."

"And *yet* you yourself are worried what will happen when he and she get together."

"That is just common sense. He is dangerous enough alone. I will believe you Sisters when your so-called prophecies are fulfilled."

"That is the part you never understood, Dhiana. We do not wait for the predictions to come true. Much easier just to make them come true."

"And if a clan happens to be in the way, you conspire to destroy it."

"If I had not believed it would eventually lead to the true rise of Jaydemyr, My Lady, I would not have so much as said 'hello' to Lord Xenides-Ra."

Again Dhiana seems to wilt – that name. And her old name: The Mindwarp, *Dhivashes-ra Kas'Daen*.

"That doesn't matter anymore," she asserts. "I can't kill you and you'll do whatever you want anyway." Can't she? Surely a single word in the Noble Speech would deal irreparable damage to the woman's mind; a whole sentence would destroy it utterly. But somehow, Dhiana knows that won't work either, if only because such an obvious idea must have been tested before. "You have my leave to go. If I wish my son to see you again, or if my son wishes it, then you will."

Although it is her intent to exit by the same door and to do so very soon, Dhiana returns her attention to the small desk opposite the bed and waits, yet again, to be alone.

"I am not leaving, my Lady."

"I said you may *go*, human."

"I may but I will not. Charan needs me."

Vachaelle watches her Lady's shoulders quake and smiles.

"I thank you for completing your mission, Lady Vachaelle, but it is done. It is his mother he needs now."

"Ah, but I *am* his mother, Dhiana."

And so distraught is the former Mindwarp, so displaced, she wonders: *is that why is he called The Half?*

"What did you say?"

"I am the mother of who he is. You entrusted him to me fourteen years ago. With a mix of your plan and my talents, I have spent over fifty years with him since. Me, Dhiana. Not you. You are an ideal to him, and I do not think even you can live up to it. Stay out of his life and he will become a Clanlord, and so much more."

The laugh from Dhiana Jaydemyr is one only of bitterness and suppressed fury.

"Even now you want to Corrupt him with your Song. It is enough that you manipulated one generation of Jaydemyr, Vachaelle. You may stay with us, if the ranks of Kas'Daen do not want you, but I will *not* be an 'ideal' to my son."

"That is entirely up to him, but as you command. I will see you upstairs."

And then a tiny pitter-patter of bare feet, a creak and a gentle click.

Dhiana still cannot cry but, as she rubs her eyes, blood from her nail-bitten palms streaks her cheeks nonetheless.

By the time the Lady Jaydemyr arrives at the entrance to the old tower, Arius and Charan have already met the foes in combat. Vachaelle is seated near the base of the granite steps, elbows on her knees, chin in her hands. Ignoring her, Dhiana assesses the situation. Naturally most of the Eagles are dead – they have not had the benefit of Arius' tutelage, let alone everything else her son has experienced. But not far from each broken Jaydemyrian warrior lie the limbs and remains of a Kas'Daen intruder. At first it looks like the fight is already over, but then she sees Arius, who until but a night ago claimed not to know one end of a sword from the other. He is doing Jaydemyr proud, even though his regal style is far less vicious or cunning than the feral hit-and-run tactics characteristic of the Kas'Daen. Her own Talons, now all but slain, had been trained not by Arius but by Xenides-ra Kas'Daen before she left him. But past Arius, who meets every sneaky slash with a forthright opposition of straight steel, she recognises Neh'raz, the youngest Talon, too young to be pitted against the Scourge before, dueling with a former comrade. She smiles, seeing that he is not hesitating, not letting anything but his loyalty to her and to Jaydemyr dictate his severity.

"Where is Charan?" she asks of herself, treading down the steps and preparing to protect him, if need be. Dark though the night is, she will know his black cloak immediately.

"There," Vachaelle says from under her, pointing into the clearing around the tower. An obvious answer, and yet Dhiana has no choice but to trust the conniving sorceress. She follows the direction of the finger and sees nothing more than one of the Kas'Daen by himself. But what is he doing? She focuses and then it is apparent. He is blocking, dodging, attacking, fending. Struggling.

"You see?" Vachaelle asks, and Dhiana refuses to say either way. Remembering how much she had to concentrate when the Scourge mutilated Sa'Hres'z, Dhiana bends her will upon the space around the beleaguered Noble.

"I see," she says when it is finally not a lie. He'd been quick and efficient with Sa'Hres'z, but this is the Scourge, after a good rest, not riding on night after night of Vachaelle's relentless fervour. It is more than just the Scourge, however: Dhiana knows that Dog-Ears is holding him back, Char is encouraging him. And Charan is mocking the Kas'Daen like a hornet stinging a bee, over and over.

"Beautiful, is he not?" Vachaelle comments, and again Dhiana holds her tongue. If this is a straight line, then her son has learned how to stretch it and make it a spiral. This, she realises, is 'the long way around, as quickly as possible'. After the Noble falls to his knees, Charan stops his apparent circling and becomes quite visible in his steady approach. Dhiana cannot hear but the way he pauses in front of the downed enemy, she suspects he might be asking for surrender. Dog-Ears, surely. The terms are not met and the sword, briefly lucent in the moonlight, divides head from neck.

Then her son and his sword disappear again, having spotted another Kas'daen foe.

"They are here for him, but they had no idea what they were after," Vachaelle gloats. Dhiana, still of half a mind to provide her son with her protection, realises that *she* had no idea either. To lend him her aid, she would have to have some clue what he plans, how he works. Right now, she knows she'd just be in the way.

The Lady sits a few steps up from the Nightsong.

"You are taking him to Xenides, aren't you, Vachaelle?"

"No. I am staying here."

"Here? But you said he needs you."

"He does, but I am already with him. Each night, he will hear me, in his head, just as he hears everyone else he has met. I will miss singing him to sleep, but this is something he has to do alone. Somewhat alone."

"So why stay here?"

"You know why. You know who."

"Do you actually love him, Vachaelle? *Can* you love?"

"Arius? What do you care? Do *you* actually love him, Dhiana?"

"I need him."

"Well, so do I. Let us leave it at that, eh?"

One of them grins and the other grimaces, and neither knows which.

The battle is done, but it is only the first.

"You are too playful," Arius scolds as he staggers towards the tower. "Dog-Ears alone would have been more efficient. You take risks. I am ashamed to have taught you, boy."

Charan, anything but exhausted, surveys the clearing. Only dignified scorch marks scar the grass. Fallen enemy and ally both, reduced to ash. Arius cannot tell if the boy's practice of cremation is one of habit or respect.

"You taught the son of Charas'z-ra Jaydemyr from age five until twelve," Blackcloak replies. "I have had other teachers for many more years. Sometimes I will be as your student, Mentor Arius, and sometimes I will be the progeny of very different schools. And sometimes," here Arius glances at the Half and sees his dour lips curl into sardonic amusement, "sometimes I will be your teacher."

"Impudent!"

"I have my moments," The Half says, and walks up the steps, into the tower. Then he pauses, and says over his shoulder before disappearing inside: "Thank you for the lesson, Mentor Arius. I hope there are many more yet to come."

"Count on it, boy. The night I no longer have anything to teach you will be—"

"A very sad night for us both," Charan interrupts, and then enters the tower.

Arius Hawkstorm, former Captain-Guard of Jaydemyr, realises that 'boy' was misplaced, and that it was Charan reprimanding him, not the other way around. Who is he? Really, who *is* this man? Hawkstorm cannot begin to answer, but he knows – someday, he will call him 'My Lord'.

Much later that night, Charan stands upon the very same balcony that has played host to the discussion of his plagued dreams. He looks down, perhaps admiring the churned dirt and patches of blackened ground. His fingers toy with a little knife and a piece of paper, both adorned with blood, a measured, careful amount that served only one purpose. Dog-Ears remembers the process so vividly, but until now, it had not actually been done.

The moon and the cross. Jaydemyr. Two names either side. Dhiana on the right, Charas'z on the left. One name at the top. Charan.

He has the strangest feeling it is not finished, but cannot say anything beyond that.

"Can't sleep?" Dhiana asks upon finding him there. He can hear how much she enjoys the banality of the query, but doesn't look away from the troubled world below them.

"Very funny." Hopefully *she* can hear that he approves of her light-hearted mirth.

"It's strange," she says, coming to stand beside him, not so close but not so far either. "I've been listening to you for over a week, and yet I genuinely have no idea what to say to you. Who you really are."

"I'm your son," Charan replies. "Or so this tells me."

He lifts the scrap of paper, holds it towards her.

"I like seeing my name written that way," Dhiana says without touching it.

"I'm not sure about mine," Charan admits. "It seems— I think I've seen something else. Did you ask me about it? I don't remember much of that already."

"I'm sorry," she says, although he cannot tell for what or why. "I didn't. What exactly do you mean?"

"Look." And he places the scrap on the railing, tapping his name with the knife. "Charan. Charan Jaydemyr." Then the name on the left. "Charas'z Jaydemyr." On the right. "Dhiana Jaydemyr. Our family. But where is *she*?"

"Who?" Dhiana answers too quickly. She can see what he cannot when she looks at his name.

"In the dreams, there was always another. She wasn't always Vachaelle. I thought she was you. But, Eph damn it." He stabs the paper, rending his name into gibberish. "I can't see it."

"Stop that, Charan." Dhiana moves to grab his offending wrist, but he's already pulled away.

"Mother. What I do remember, I remember through Vachaelle's control. And she always kept things just out of my sight, until she'd decided it was safe for me to know. Not safe for me, but for her. If you know what I'm talking about, if you can help me, please. Just do so. Don't be like her."

And that decides it. The moment Charan can even casually compare her to the Nightsong, Dhiana knows her nemesis will have won. That she will have been his 'mother' after all.

The Lady takes the piece of paper and holds it on the railing in front of her. Rather than using a knife, she runs a fingernail along the back of the hand securing the scrap. Dark blood wells up, but even as she daubs her nail in the tiny gash, it begins to close over. There is enough, however, for her to scratch a new name into the paper just above where he'd torn his own.

"I cannot read that, Mother."

"Sariana Jaydemyr. Daughter of Charas'z and Dhiana."

Charan sighs, where Dhiana expected a cry or a gasp. "If so much has been uncovered by you sifting through the lives I remember, by extracting my name from that mess, why is she still hidden? Hearing her name does nothing for me."

"Because unlike yours, her concealment was solely Vachaelle's creation. Your sister had no Dog-Ears scenario in which she learned what it was to be humiliated, beaten, downtrodden. That was mine, because I felt it imperative to remove *anything* resembling a lord from your thoughts. Chaelle, of course, had to try her way first, in which you were offered just about anything she could think of short of actual power. Your sister was less of a concern. The Jaydemyr name does not hinge on her survival."

"But my own survival might hinge on hers." Charan thinks about what his mother has said. "Will she be remembering who she is, just as you have? I know that whatever you have done to me now triggered everyone's memories of what happened, but you must have known something before this, to lure me as you did."

"She is your sister. When you first said your name, nine years ago in the Haven. That is when she would have felt something. I can't say anything else. I doubt that her concealment was as thorough as yours. Vachaelle tells me you actually met her last year."

Charan's hooded head bows, and his shoulders tense. Thinking. Always thinking. Then he sags.

"I think I know. She had a pendant. I tried to take it, but—Shit. I remember what happened now. All of it. *Fuck me.*" Then he remembers that, for once, perhaps for the first time, he is not alone with revelation. "Oh. Sorry."

"They are just words, my son. With what you've been through, I'll not punish your tendency to strong language."

"Good, because fuck and fuck again. I *did* meet her. Almost killed her, too. Before I knew it. Then there was her song, you know. And I forgot. No, not forgot. Just remembered something else. Just another routine dispatching of fools serving the Night."

"Somehow I doubt Vachaelle would have allowed you to actually kill her, Charan."

"Who knows? Either way, I have to find her, Mother. I know you're amassing forces here now, that the old allies of Jaydemyr will be rallying here. You probably expect me to lead them. Or at least be some sort of symbol. Is that correct?"

"That's more her plan than mine. I didn't think much further than stopping you from being her weapon. Than freeing you from her grip, once I understood that's what it was. It seemed motivation enough. You know," She stops, takes a largely unnecessary breath, and just says it: "You do know that I love you, don't you?"

Given how many times Vachaelle has abused the word, the declaration, there is every chance he will deny her this, but if he is to leave again, it won't be without him at least hearing those words from her mouth.

"I do," he replies too quickly. "I can't really think of any other reason for you to have done what you have done. Not if you're not going to use me as well. So, I am free to go? Just like that?"

"Right now, freedom is all I can give you, Charan. But I will not lie: we will need you. You are Jaydemyr. I won't threaten any sort of future wherein you do not heed the call, but I will believe that your search for her will show you the way home. I never once expected you to just stay with us, even though you *are* home. That's your choice to make. We will be waiting, but it's very likely our enemies will not."

"A year." Charan nods, to her and to himself. "I will return in a year, with or without her. And that is when I will repay my debt to you. Vachaelle. What about her?"

"She's staying, apparently." Dhiana shrugs, not something a Noble should do but between herself, her son and the cold night sky, she really does not care. "She'll leave you alone."

"So the three of you, waiting. That's, yes, that's her. Mother?"

"Yes, Charan?"

"What colour is Sariana's hair?"

They both know the answer, and neither can explain it. Instead of saying anything, Dhiana reaches out to hold him, but does not do so until his lack of withdrawal makes clear that she may.

Dhiana is surprised at how light he is, how unlike the dead weight she'd borne from Viestrada Forest barely a week ago.

Charan is surprised at how warm she is, how unlike a Noble she can be.

Eventually, she lets him go. Eventually, he lets her.

This is how I conclude his song:

We watch him leave.

Awake at last, Charan Jaydemyr must depart again. But he does so on his own terms, one foot after another, steady and purposeful. He might once have been the tiny, hopeful creature Dog-Ears, or the terrible and hopeless beast Char of Kaifeng, but now by any measure, it is Blackcloak who strides into the unbroken waves of night. He slipped the bonds of not one conjured cage but two, each enough to satisfy any but him. A song promising impotent immortality failed his grasp; he has rejected any reality but his own, and so they are not realities at all. An inadmissible truth.

We watch him leave.

"Are you absolutely sure about this, Chaelle?"

Three of us, relics of a clan that was, icons of a clan that will be. Nightsong, Hawkstorm, Mindwarp. But we are not standing in that order on the balcony. Dhiana, proud in her inferiority, is careful to place herself between Arius and the one woman she cannot seem to best. The slight play of reluctant resentment threatens to restructure her poise. No war-leader she, nor some mythical queen of inscrutable austerity. It is Dhiana, the mother of Charan, who is holding her jealousy for all to see, although she no doubt thinks she is holding it back.

Poor woman.

"Were I not, Arius, I would go with him. You cannot and the Lady Dhiana must not. Besides, you have seen now. He is no worse off alone than with us."

"Does he even know where to go, Vachaelle?" Dhiana asks, gripping the balcony's railing less for support than some inhibited desire to crush something else. There is just so much she wants to ask, but cannot. How can she admit that no matter how well she Delved, she will never understand what really happened in Kaifeng? At least she knows better than to try to Delve me, but if she had tried, I would not hold it against her.

"He knows. We have already been there. Still: he was obsessed with you, Dhiana. He did not know why. You were giving chase but he was the one trapping you. I suppose blood answers blood."

"And spills more blood," Arius notes, eyes locked upon the treetops and the faint filament of light starting to slice the canopy. His weathered old face, the stonework of his resolute cheeks, those pursed lips between chalky bristles no Noble should be able to grow: I have seen that look before.

Sometimes I am convinced that flies are not only aware of the spider's web, they like to see if they can pass between the strands.

"Eventually that will no longer be the case," I say for their benefit, knowing that 'eventually' means when everything has happened, and there will be no blood left to spill.

"We must be ready for the next attack," Dhiana declares, but she is just looking for an excuse. Her eyes find no glamour in the glowing wire about to garrotte the horizon. No, she is all business and survival. Cannot say that I blame her. It must be frustrating, but she will see. In the end, everything I do is for her and hers.

"There probably won't be any more, My Lady." Arius is careful to look at her with this reply: portrait of the Champion as a sycophant. So the morning call is no siren to him yet. Good. "They were after him, but when reports get back with what he can do, Xenides-Ra himself will look into it. Ah, if only I could see the boy face the Fox! And then the other two. And then, who knows?"

I do.

"The sun is coming up. Best if both of you head inside to rest."

I am not ashamed to love how my 'human' self can dismiss two Nobles with nothing more than a reminder of what happens every day.

"We have much to discuss, Chaelle," Arius says by way of parting, and I am not surprised to hear Dhiana slam the door behind her before he has a chance to follow. The second time I hear the door open and close, it is much more subdued.

This is how they are moving now: where the Mindwarp struts in her heels across the frozen lake of my design, the Hawkstorm tries to tip-toe – in full armour. The cracks racing away from their every step spread with viral fervour, each a chasm over which the Scourge shall struggle to stand. I do not have to laugh which is why I do. Everyone's nature is to struggle against their own nature. My sweet Half has taught me nothing if not that.

He turned out so much better than even I expected. I hope he hears me, out there. I hope that my Song has a place in his head if not his heart. I hope— I know she is waiting for him.

"Godspeed, Half," I mumble, afraid and excited, tired but awake. All these years yet to come, he and I. One mistake by him, or me, and I lose. We all lose.

But he is the Scourge; that is my weapon.

There shall be blood answering blood. There shall be blood spilling more blood. There shall be blood everywhere I look.

That shall more than suffice.

Yes, Charan, you give me such hope.

I suppose it is because no matter what befell the night, the sun always rises.

Of course, he is just the sword, just the weapon. She will be the fist who has to hold him, the heart whose hammering to which he will have to dance.

END OF BOOK ONE

W. James Chan

APPENDIX I: Glossary

The abbreviations in parentheses indicates the language from which the term or name originates:

ZC Ziegerian-Common
MF Mifūn-go
CK Chūnko-go
NS Noble Speech
KD Kas'Daenne
JD Jaydemyrian

A.R. (NS): Aen'a Raenta. Actual meaning lost to common usage. The year 0 A.R. saw Afraen's death on the gates of Ruslym. According to The Book, He is expected to return in the year 1000 A.R., but scholars have never agreed upon a date.

Adael (Unknown): According to the AkraVahm, Ephriem's angelic lover.

Aerian (ZC): Air/wind user (noun); pertaining to air/wind elementalism (adjective).

Afraen (NS): The First Night's Own. Also known as 'Angelflay' and 'Ephriem'.

Akra (NS): 'Light'.

AkraVahm (NS): 'LightDark'. Kaef're's bible.

Anata (MF): 'You'. Used either very formally or very intimately.

Arius Hawkstorm: Champion of Dhiana Jaydemyr and Captain-Guard of the Jaydemyrian Eagles.

Attendants: Those who maintain the Respite and assist worshippers.

Ayakawa, Lord (MF): Current human ruler of Chūnko, Tsukamoto by blood or marriage.

Az'hraeth (NS): Holy Keeper of the Burning Gate. A Night's Own responsible for admitting the dead into Heaven Below.

Bitter Lotus: A village in Chūnko. Home of Elder Leung Guan-Pi and Plump Treat.

Blackcloak: One of the titles Char gives himself, and is later given to Dog-Ears by Wu Ming.

Blood Peddlers: World-wide organisation devoted to weeding out the sick and the socially misaligned people of Kaef're and delivering them to the Nobles.

Bloody Shadows: A gang of Kaifeng, often known to harass Rats.

Blossom: A human Blood Peddler of the Malevolent Hand Chapterhouse.

-Chan (MF): Suffix. Can indicate affection, condescension or intimacy.

Chang Tong-Kut (CK): The Knife. A Half Blood Peddler of the Malevolent Hand Chapterhouse.

Char Ah-Ran (CK): A Half member of the Society For Disadvantaged Youth.

Charas'z Jaydemyr (JD): Former Clan Lord of Jaydemyr.

Chūnko (CK): 'The Middle Realm'. A country / province in the Mifūné Empire.

Chūnko-go (CK): Language of the Middle Realm.

Chūnkojin (CK, MF): A native of the Middle Realm.

Commandments, The Twelve: The Rules of God, taught in every school and influencing every law.

Common Altar: The public altar within a Respite always open to worshippers.

Common Hall: the largest building in a typical Chūnko village, used for meetings and feasts.

Curl the Flail: to make the gesture that wards off evil.

-dailoh (CK): 'Big Brother'. One's superior in a gang or informal hierarchy.

Daimyo (MF): Lord.

Dao-chi (CK): Earth energy.

Dao-sha (CK): An earth Elementalist.

Darkbirth: The process of passing under the First Arch.

De'Hrex (NS): Third Talon slain by Charan during the Viestrada Forest incident.

-Desne (NS): Suffix. 'Realm' or 'Land'. Used by humans in many languages, possibly derived from ZC 'demesne'.

Dhiana Jaydemyr (JD): The Clan Lady of Jaydemyr, formerly known as Dhivashes.

Dog-Ears: Derogatory nickname given to Wong Shah-Long in Swimming Carp.

Dohsh'ta no, shisho? (MF): 'What's up, Master?' Note that shisho can also be 'mentor'.

Eph: human curse-word. Abbreviation of 'Ephriem'. Can be used as a noun (Eph!), adjective (Ephing) or verb (Eph off!).

Ephriem (Unknown): Afraen's name when he was under the control of He Who Shines. Also known as The First.

Erotas'z en fhia'rez, Sa'hre. Vahm en. (NS): "Accept the offering, Sa'hre. Unto dark (ness)." In this case, the comma serves as a colon, making Sa'hre (sz) the offering to God.

Fa Shai-Yeh (CK): A serving girl for the Kas'Daen working in the Five-Fold Palace.

Fana'Hrez (NS): Fourth Talon slain by Charan during the Viestrada Forest incident.

Feng-chi (CK): Wind/air energy.

Feng-sha (CK): A wind/air Elementalist.

Feuermacht (ZC): Fire-power, fire-wielder. See also Pyrotic, Huo-chi.

Fha! (NS): A slightly derogatory form of exclamation. Can also be a playful term between close friends or relations.

First Arch: Outermost of three archways in a Respite. Symbolises God's invitation into Her house of worship.

Five-Fold Imperial Palace: The royal compound in the middle of Kaifeng.

Flail, The: Afraen's symbol.

Gaifu (CK): Healing.

Gaikojin (CK, MF): Foreigner, outsider.

Garden: Blood Peddler term for a potential lair or any other concentration of Roses.

God's Mark: The curled f that symbolises Ephriem's Flail.

Goddess of Swords: One of Char's names for Fa Shai-Yeh.

Goong (CK): Grandfather, Gramps.

Half: Somewhat derogatory term for those humans who possess Noble blood.

Happy Apple: Zhang's grand-daughter.

Haven: A tavern or inn that serves as a safe house sanctioned by the Blood Peddlers in which people can take refuge at night.

Havenkeeper: A person responsible for the operation of a Haven.

He Who Shines: Kaef're antithesis to God.

Heaven Below: Home of God, Afraen and all the Heavenly host. Original dwelling place of the Night's Own.

Her Greater Design: Generic term for God's will.

His blood is blue: A human saying that equates to calling someone a coward, impotent or useless.

House of Joyful Leave-Taking, The: A Haven outside of the Capital, Kaifeng.

Hra'Xis Sladaria (Unknown): Clan Lord of Sladaria and Voice of the Sladarian Overclan.

Hua-Shi (CK): A Half thug Wong Shah-Long encounters in Swimming Carp. Also leader of the Kaifeng gang, The Bloody Shadows.

Hunt, The: Generic term for the nights when the Night's Own roam Kae'fre. Always a full moon.

Huo-chi (CK): Fire energy.

Huo-sha (CK): A fire elementalist.

Hydrotheurgy (ZC): Vachaelle's word for Water-wielding; see also Shui-chi.

Imperial Kaifeng Guard: The official watchmen of Kaifeng.

Inahs'z (NS): Second Talon slain by Charan during the Viestrada Forest incident.

Jaku (MF): a bully in Swimming Carp.

Jaydemyr: A Clan of Nobles eradicated in the year 868 A.R.

Jaydemyrian Eagles: The elite warriors of Clan Jaydemyr.

-Jin (MF): Suffix. Person of a certain country.

Jodan-no-kamae (MF): A sword stance, with the sword held at waist height and in front, the blade angled away from the ground at a 45 degree angle.

Kaef're (NS+): The world. This is one of the few Noble Speech words that has found its way to virtually every human language.

Kaifeng (CK): The capital city of Chūnko where Char grew up.

Kashensan (Unknown): A prophet and wise man of the AkraVahm.

Kasuden (CK, MF): Kas'Daen.

Kiend're (KD): 'Child'. Rare case of a Noble dialect being influenced by a human language.

Kind (ZC): 'Child'.

Kono Ama! (MF): 'Bitch!'

Kuraidengeki (MF): Hua-Shi's favourite attack, a jumping kick to the head. A pun. Ku-raiden-geki: 'Nine Lightning God Attack'; Kurai-dengeki: 'Dark Electric Shock'.

Leung Guan-Pi (CK): Elder of Bitter Lotus village. The Godfather of the Society For Disadvantaged Youth. Also known as Goong-sinsan.

Lighting The Lantern: a ritual all patrons of rural Havens must go through before entering.

Lily: A Healer of the Benevolent Hand Haven.

Liquid Night, The: a Priest(ess)hood devoted to divination and social manipulation.

Longstride The Feral: Name given to the sacrificial cat of Viestrada Forest by Vachaelle.

Maliscience (ZC): Mind-reading.

Menu, The: A list drafted by the Thorn containing the names of each month's Weeds and Roses.

Mifūné (MF): 'The Three Boats'. The Empire presided over by the Tsukamoto. Also The Three Isles.

Mifūn-go (MF): Language of the Mifūnjin.

Mifūnjin (MF): People descended from the original occupants of Mifūné.

Mifūné Armed Forces: Specific branch of the Tsukamoto Corps pertaining to recruits from Kaifeng as well as the Three Isles.

Mindwarp: Title used by Dhiana Jaydemyr when she was Dhivashes Kas'Daen.

Miss Master: The schoolteacher of Swimming Carp.

Mo ichido (MF): 'One more time'.

Neh'raz: A Talon.

Night's Own, The: Most common term for the servants of God left to govern Kaef're when Afraen ascended.

Noble Speech, The: The language of the Night's Own.

Noble: Multilingual title for the Night's Own.

Nse'ante (NS): 'humans' or 'people'. Originally meant 'vermin'.

Ocharaya: Site of the last battle between the Night's Own and the fallen Angels of He Who Shines.

Omeh no aite wa oré da! Ik'ze! (MF): 'I'm your opponent! Here I come!'

One-Slash Butterfly: A human Blood Peddler of the Malevolent Hand Chapterhouse.

Oni-Goroshi (MF): 'Demon Slayer'. Name given to Charan's sword.

Orchid Witherheart: A Half Blood Peddler of the Malevolent Hand Chapterhouse.

Overclan, The: A conglomerate of clans including Kas'Daen, Zieger and Tsukamoto, lead by Clan Sladaria.

Perfect Perception: Another term for 'The Window'.

Picking A Rose: Blood Peddler term for capturing a Wild Rose.

Plea, Afraen's: The request made by the Noble Afraen to become the First Night's Own.

Plump Treat: daughter of Leung Guan-Pi.

Prick: Title for a Blood Peddler whose primary role is removing Weeds.

Pulling A Weed: Blood Peddler term for abducting someone whose name is on The Menu.

Pumpkin: Charan Jaydemyr's nickname for his daughter.

Purashena (Unknown): Unconquered land south of the Ziegerian Empire.

Pyrotic: Vachaellee's word for Fire-wielder (noun); Fire-wielding (adjective). See also Huo-chi, Feuermacht.

-Ra (NS): Suffix indicating 'Lord' or 'Lady'.

Ran'za (NS): First Talon killed by Charan Jaydemyr during the Viestrada Forest incident.

Rat: A non-Elder member of the Society For Disadvantaged Youth.

Respite: Multilingual term for God's temple.

Revolutionary: Anyone in Kaifeng who displays discontent with the current society, laws and/or its rulers.

Rika Fas'z (NS) : 'Dull tooth'.

Rose: Short for 'Wild Rose'. Term given to Night's Own that lose their faith and go insane.

Ruslym (unknown): City mentioned in the AkraVahm as an unholy mecca of He Who Shines. The site of Afraen's martyrdom.

Ryusui-Gedan-no-kamae (MF): A sword stance, with the sword held low and to the side, blade facing forward.

Sa'Ha'Khra (NS): Faithwar.

Sa'Hres'z (NS): One of the Jaydemyrian Talons involved in the initial capture of Charan Jaydemyr in Viestrada Forest. The last to die during the foray.

Sariana Jaydemyr: daughter of Charas'z and Dhiana Jaydemyr, sister to Charan.

Saseruka! (MF): 'I won't let you!'

Scourge, The: Title given to (or taken by) Char of Kaifeng and later used by Charan Jaydemyr. See also Blackcloak.

Seiyansi (CK): A bastardisation of the Noble Speech 'nse'ante'.

-Sha (CK): Suffix. One who uses or is adept with the former. Example: Huo-sha: fire-wielder.

Shining Legion, The: The armies of He Who Shines.

Shui-chi (CK): Water energy.

Shui-sha (CK): A water elementalist.

Shynsa, Lady (NS): 'The Ragemother'. Soul mate of Afraen. Second-made.

Sin-san (CK): 'Mister', 'sir'.

Siu-Tsin (CK): A lower class suburb in western Kaifeng.

Slaughter Pit: a large square hole in the Common Hall used for butchering livestock and fowl.

Southern Dissidents: Unknown threat south of Kas'Daen and Mifūné.

Swimming Carp: The village in Chūnko in which Wong Shah-Long grew up.

Sword: Title for a Blood Peddler that wields a sword. Other titles include Knife and Chain.

Swords of Heaven: Unknown group whose name Zhang passes on to Charan.

Talent: An ability that all humans manifest during puberty. Talents include elemental manipulation, healing or mind-reading.

Talon: The name taken by Charan Jaydemyr's daughter.

Talons (JD): The elite vanguard of Dhiana Jaydemyr.

Talonslash: The sword wielded by the Captain-Guard of the Jaydemyrian Eagles.

Tangariel, Lord: A fallen Angel serving He Who Shines. Also known as Bitterspite of Shamain.

Terasawa Jaku (MF): a Mifūn-jin member of the Society For Disadvantaged Youth.

Teriss-Luniir (ZC): Main realm of the Ziegerian Empire.

Teristra (ZC): Capital city of Teriss-Luniir.

The Book: The AkraVahm.

The Moon Never Blinks: human saying signifying the omniscience of God.

The Nest: Common name for the headquarters of the Society For Disadvantage Youth.

The Night Knows My Name: A saying that can be said either in great fortune or despair, depending on the context. Can also indicate vulnerability.

Those Who Hunt: the Night's Own.

Thorn: Title given to a Master of a Blood Peddler Chapterhouse.

Three Beasts, The: Collective term for Lords Kas'Daen (fox), Tsukamoto (snake) and Zieger (wolf).

Tsukamoto Corps: Generic name for the army of Mifūné.

Tsukamoto Genma (MF): A renegade human member of the Tsukamoto Clan, also known as Leung Guan-Pi.

Tsukamoto Imperial Army: Another name for the Tsukamoto Corps.

Tsukamoto Tatsunojo (MF): A high-ranking human official in the Five-Fold Palace, father to Tsukamoto Genma

Tsukamoto: Ruling family of the Mifūné Empire.

Tzara-Min Jaydemyr (JD): The name Charan would have given his daughter.

Vachaelle: The Nightsong.

Vahm (NS): 'Dark'.

Vahm En (NS): 'Unto Dark(ness)'. The phrase uttered after any Prayer to God.

Viestrada Forest (KD): A small woods on the eastern border of Kas'Daen-desne. Location of the last Jaydemyrian stronghold, also referred to only as 'Viestrada' or 'Vizstrahtza' (JD).

Ways of Life: A nickname for Swimming Carp used by the Bloody Shadows.

We Who Hunt: Self-referential term for Night's Own.

When the moon shines round, be asleep, safe and sound: a rhyme taught to children to remind them to stay inside during the full moon.

Window: Wong Shah-Long's term for moments of perfect clarity and perception, typically experienced by the Night's Own during the Hunt.

Wolves: Unknown term used by Vachaelle to indicate an enemy defeated by Ran'za.

Wong Chu-Deng (CK): Father of Wong Shah-Long of Swimming Carp and Village Elder. Elder of the Society For Disadvantaged Youth. Leung Guan-Pi's second in command.

Wong Shah-Long (CK): A villager of Swimming Carp.

Wu Jen-Wah (CK): A girl of Swimming Carp. A Chūnkojin member of the Society For Disadvantaged Youth.

Wu Ming (CK): 'Nameless'. Hua-Shi's name while hiding in the House of Joyful Leave-Taking.

Xenides Kas'Daen: Clan Lord of Kas'daen, also known as The Fox.

Xenides-ra Kas'Daen fha hremor'kha, kien'dre! Sax en sa'ha'khra dah'resz! (NS): "Lord Xenides Kas'Daen has marked you, brat! Thus begins again the Faithwar!" (literally, "Xenides, Lord Kas'Daen is the marker, child! Again the Faithwar will be!")

Zhang (CK): Havenkeeper of the House of Joyful Leave-Taking. Also, Zhang-sinsan.

APPENDIX II: The Hours

(With approximate modern comparisons)

Highmoon – Midnight to 1am
Lethalmoon – 1am to 2am
Lazymoon – 2a to 3am
Lowmoon – 4am to 6am
Bladesun – 6am to 8am
Morningsun – 8am to 10am
Nighsun – 10am to 11am
Highsun – 11am to 1pm
Aftersun – 1pm to 2pm
Lazysun – 2pm to 3pm
Eyesun – 3pm to 4pm
Fallingsun – 4pm to 5pm
Lowsun – 5pm to 6pm
Dyingsun – 6pm to 7.30pm
Awakenmoon – 7.30pm to 8pm
Risingmoon – 8pm to 9pm
Fullmoon – 9pm to 10pm
Eyemoon – 10pm to 11pm
Nighmoon – 11pm to Midnight

W. James Chan

APPENDIX III: The Twelve Commandments

1. God is The Night. There is no God without The Night. Revere and fear The Night and Her Own.

2. Closest to God are Those Who Dwell in the Night. Hearken unto Them, cower from Their wrath and exult in Their benevolence. Those Not of the Night are distanced from God and are not to be worshipped or honoured.

3. The name of God is sacred. Do not invoke the Name of God and Of The Night for any purpose other than praise and worship.

4. Sleep at Night. Do not work while the Moon shines. You may work under the sun for the glory of God, but The Night is for rest, for God and Her Own. The Night is sacred.

5. Honour the way of your parents before yourself. Emulate their lives and perpetuate their beliefs for they are closer to Heaven and to God.

6. Do not kill without the Night's blessing. Life is Given by The Night and only The Night may take it away.

7. Propagate. It is your duty to create children who will serve God and The Night.

8. Do not reach for anything you cannot hold. Ambition is the seed of discontent.

9. Do not hold anything you cannot keep. Blessed are they who know their limits.

10. Do not lie or spread falsehoods to further your own station. The truth is sacred.

11. Do not ask questions if you don't know the answer. Curiosity is a sin beyond Salvation. Thought is the seed of rebellion. The Night provides all you need to know.

12. The word of the Night's Own is holy. They are closest to God and know Her Name and Will. Their command overrides all.

APPENDIX IV: On Pronunciation

1. Noble Speech

The oral / aural component of Noble Speech is actually very easy for humans to master. It is the mental aspect they cannot handle, and this is why humans feel physically sick whenever they hear Noble Speech: the language tries to convey not only what the word means by convention but also what it means to the person saying it. This requires Noble blood to work.

In an attempt to 'write' down what the spoken language looks like, I have used apostrophes rather than the traditional double consonants.

An apostrophe after a consonant indicates a slight pause or elongation of the preceding consonant, not unlike the human language Mifūn-go, which would use a small 'tsu' character for much the same effect. Example: *Raen'ta* = Rah-en-n-ta.

When an apostrophe follows a vowel, the consonant after the apostrophe should be added to that vowel. Example: *Sa'ha'khra* = Sah-hak-khra

When an apostrophe appears between two vowels, the speaker pronounces it as a 'y' sound. Example: *Nse'ante* = Nseyante.

2. Mifūn-go

Some readers may recognise the source of this language, and I wouldn't claim to have made it up. I have attempted to write it as it is spoken, rather than following the traditional romanisation methods. Thus a word which would be written as 'I ku ze; I have scribed as 'Ik'ze' , since the 'u' is all but silent in spoken Mifūn-go.

3. Chūnko-go

Another blend of familiar languages. Where possible I have placed hints in the text as to how this lower-class language is pronounced. One example is 'Hua', which is pronounced 'Wa'. Less easily guessed is the pronunciation of 'eng', which becomes 'oong'. Thus 'Feng', being air or wind, becomes 'foong', with the 'oo' sound from 'foot'.

W. James Chan

Thanks and Acknowledgments

This book is the result of over a decade of work, on and off. I wrote the bulk of it in a very short span, less than a year, but as the saying goes, the devil is in the details. Sometimes I didn't touch it for several months, and sometimes I couldn't stop thinking about it. Ten years is an awfully long time for just about any endeavour let alone a novel, which by professional standards should be done from go to woe within a year or two. Moreover, it's an awfully long time in terms of who you meet, who you talk to, who you spend time with, and I'd be lying if I said that I didn't somehow owe just about every one of them something in regards to the creation and completion of this book.

I think family goes without saying, because without them, there'd be no me, let alone a book. Today I feel blessed that I have two parents and a sibling to whom I talk all the time, who are there for me and I for them. This book is my way of saying 'thanks' to them. For everything.

Beyond family, the task becomes a little tougher. It's been over ten years, guys – if I miss you, just let me know and I'll add it (the joys of epublishing!).

Before anyone else, Peter Carlson deserves credit for getting me into fantasy and sci-fi reading all those years ago. His enthusiasm manifested in a generosity I feel I've never quite reciprocated, but this work is my humble attempt at doing so.

To Peter Kawecki, who not only did the wonderful cover design but also read several versions of this work, leading me to create a version that didn't put him to sleep once. I considered this a major achievement.

Benjamin Drake, whose talents seem almost as endless as his humility and erudition, provided the first representations of the moon and cross symbol, the first real artwork of Charan (and Plump Treat) and the first serious rejection of this book. I cherish that he fully approved and supported the existence of this work without necessarily loving it himself.

The Night's Own would not be the same if not for the conversations between myself and Nicholas Butler, who also read an early draft. I cannot recall how many likely dumb questions I threw at him regarding a race of vampires who had to be more than just afraid of sunlight and crosses. His input affected not only this book but those to come, as I continue to flesh out the Nobles and their traits.

Concerning Charan's origins, thanks must go to Melissa "Sparrow" Murry, who was there when I first conceived of Blackcloak, who supported me through years of my obsession as I tested him as a character in various online contexts. To her I owe the confidence to even undertake this journey. Thanks also to her son David, for whom I was entirely too young, too selfish and too naïve to make a decent father figure.

Three women, whom I shall name only as VAnessa (Misery), MiCHelle (Mystri) and MichAELLE (Eclipse), also had a profound effect on this work its in early days and my life at various times. They were none of them *quite* so bad as my sum of their parts.

I want to thank the #Teristra Crew, who hopefully enjoyed the collective writing exercises and roleplays as much as I enjoyed hosting them. Special mention must go to Michael Howell, for providing such an incredible antithesis to Charan, without whom many core characteristics would not exist. Anyone who bore the title 'Weaver' has my eternal gratitude for sharing in the vision. I could cheat and look up all the names from those times, but you know who you are.

This would be a woefully inadequate list without Siri Ranva Hjelm Jacobsen, who invited me into her world and encouraged me to not only write, but to pursue an academic career with it.

And with my undergrad years at the University of Wollongong, we come to my bitches: Marlee Ward, Tori Thomas, Alex Cullen, Alise Blayney, Sally Clair Evans, Arcadia Lyons, Kristie Davis, Heather Dixon…and Michelle Peterie, honorary bitch due to her wicked Twister skills. It was through our sharing of writing and critique that I came to a much greater understanding of the value of merciless self-editing and how to be critical and constructive.

That leads me to my first and last creative writing teacher at UOW, the inimitable Shady Cosgrove, whose first and thus most enduring lesson to me was that the moon is a horrible cliché. Goodness knows what she'd think of my throwing a cross in there. I later had the honour of critiquing two of her manuscripts, which not only allowed me some slight revenge for years of her ruthless red ink but also showed me first-hand how a great literary author packs meaning into every single word. Always from a place of love, Shady.

Thanks then to my own early readers and providers of critique: Amber McGahey, Andrea Pacione, Richard Jonkman, Jennifer Walker, Elizabeth Roberts, Keith Hutchison and Will Zuidema. You've all said something that changed this book. I am sure I've missed someone at whom I've thrown this thing, in part or whole, whose response critically shifted this bit or that.

It is important that I give a nod to my former employer, Oliver Wady, who may or may not have turned a blind eye when I used various company resources to edit, print and ring-bind drafts of this book.

There were at some point two professional manuscript assessment services I engaged for no small fee whose feedback was in detail not very useful but the shared statement of 'this should be much shorter' has never quite stopped ringing in my ears, and did indeed result in very heavy pruning.

An extra big thank you to Axxon Echysttas, who not only bore through an earlier draft and gave some excellent tips but paid for the experience, thus representing my first true sale.

Finally, words cannot express how grateful I am for my partner and last-minute quality control expert, Kate, to whom I read *an even longer version* of this book out-loud over many Skype sessions, and despite this ordeal she still wanted to spend her life with me. It's 3am as I write this, she's in bed down the hall and, as with many such nights, not once has she demanded I do anything but that which I want, and in this case that which I must. But now it is done, so now I shall rest.

Until tomorrow, when the next blank page calls.

W. James Chan
February 25th, 2015

Preview of Book Two
Gildenhammer: The Beating of her Heart

What Mother Told Me

When it happened, the baby girl who made it all possible suddenly stopped crying. In a village not an hour away from Teristra, the capital of Zieger, the child of a famous singer no longer wailed for her absent mother. Her father, tired from another day in the workshop, caressed her still-soft forehead as she lay silent in her crib, but she was too young to remember the weathered feel of his skilled, gnarled fingers. Years later, she'll be told what he did for a living, but that won't help make the memories any more real. She'll also be told why her mother was never home, and in much more detail.

Like everything else in her mother's world, the newborn girl soon lost importance other than as an idea for the next crowd-pleaser. But that's not what she told her little girl, when the child finally learned how to ask, when it was too late for any answer to matter. Instead she told her daughter how fast it all went, how it seemed like just yesterday. Now crawling, now walking, now talking, now stop asking questions! Mother's delight at her girl's growth was like lightning, and Mother was far more interested in the rain. All that mattered was that the ballad gained new verses as the girl grew. But the girl didn't know any of this, and entered childhood much the same way as other children, knowing she was the centre of her world. It was then that she asked her mother, because she couldn't ask anyone else. How was I born? What was it like? Why do you have to do my ears?

What did you used to sing about?

And Mother, now obliged to stay with her daughter more nights than not, would assume a wistful expression a child mistakes for love, an adult for thoughtfulness. At that point, I was her only audience, and she indulged me by indulging herself. Ignorant to this and almost everything else, I just listened as she told me, although I didn't understand much at first. Like everyone else, I enjoyed her song without really thinking about the words. And after I did, I started to add my own lines, shared with her only in the fury of argument and spite. She wasn't there for me, not even then. Not for Father, either. Out again, soaking up the adulation of strangers. Singing, dancing, whoring. Telling your beloved audience about miracles and happy endings, when you couldn't even. Not even for one night. Eph 'n Shyn, I'm sorry, brother. That's not what she told me. Well, she sang. But it's only the words that I can relate; you'll just have to imagine the music that accompanies them. That's what she told me. Imagine. Close your eyes and—

Imagine a great hall, a dense expanse of flagstone floors, drunken fists thumping wooden tables, and balconies running the walls, tiers upon tiers, each crammed with sweat, laughter and beer. From the middle of the ground floor, a single blaze spread its light and heat; a ring of benches huddled around the pit, and not one was unoccupied. Smoke obeyed an occasional wave of a lazy hand; the fire, although tempted, cowered within the stony circle as one occupant or another gestured for its compliance. Only the gust from the main doors opening and closing affected the flames.

It might have been snowing or raining outside; new arrivals stamped their feet on the doorstep, shook the winter from their shoulders. Some but not all deposited the tools of their trade at the counter near the entrance; all were at least stopped for a moment by the amiable giant not exactly guarding the entrance. After being cleared by a beaming nod of the stocky man's bald head, newcomers headed down the few steps from the landing into the main room proper. The remains of their frosty breath dissipated like doubt in the smiling face of an old friend. A serving girl with curly, bouncy red hair threaded between patrons and chairs; she was saucy and sassy but never salacious. Now and then she got a pat on her passing rump, but the rules of this Haven were the same as any other, and enforced more strictly than at most others: the guards were welcome here in their off-time, and even then they were still guards. For such a large place, the Haven seemed unusually untroubled; all who entered were there for simple, congenial things. There were other places in the city for other desires. Citizens of Teristra came here for food, drink, company. Distractions all, but none rivalled the promise of hearing Chantal sing.

For years, a slight young woman with simple blonde hair in a plain white dress took her place on the large stage at the front of the Haven's main room. She may or may not have carried an instrument, but if she were, it was a comfortable, worn thing, a lute or maybe a lyre, looking out-of-tune, weary. If not, the audience noticed the same qualities in the woman, and they knew her songs had aged her, that while her body might have looked innocent, her voice was rich with experience. There was a small stool upon which she arranged herself, regarding the revellers around and above her 'til they recognised her poise; she would remain seated only until the audience realised she was seated. Surging beats of lyrical wings soon returned her to inspired heights, but first the air had to be cleared. She sat there, inhaling the staleness of the hour, exhaling the immortality of the moment. She waited with the certainty of a historian, a prophet, a visionary. Hers was the patience for the inevitable.

The hush began with those who knew the ritual and lowered their banter to incomplete mumbles. A caught glance here, a flash of lashes there. The louder people, less attuned to the gradual convergence of attention on the stage, found themselves burping at turned heads and chuckling by themselves. The woman might have inclined her own head, not so much curious as amused; she knew none of them, not even the most blustery of boors, would have done as she had done and will do again. With a single suppressed sigh, she made every man in the establishment a beast, announced herself as the maiden who shall lay with the beasts, or at least lull them to sleep. And she was right. Hers was the generosity for the implacable.

When she could hear her own breathing, the woman gave her name. I am Chantal, she said quietly, and masked her appreciation for the unspoken murmurs in the illuminated eyes watching her. *The* Chantal. Even the regulars thought of her that way, although in such a busy city there were always new faces upon which her songs could create a hearty flush or streak effortless tears. What few women occupied the Haven any given night usually reacted poorly to the focus, rolling their eyes or sitting back in resignation. None of the *other* performers in the Haven received such reverence, so why should this one? Look at her (their scornful glances wanted to say), a slip of a thing timid as a rabbit; you can almost see her shivering in fright. She isn't wearing finery, hasn't even gone to the effort to rouge her cheeks – well, her blush is enough there. And of the few ladies present, maybe one or two reserved their disdain for the others, because they knew. They had heard the songs. This is Chantal. Hers is the serenity for the irascible.

Some nights she started by talking, revealing just enough of herself to set the audience at ease. Tonight will not be a gruesome, bawdy, rollicking mess of repetitive rhyme and catchy chorus, but she didn't say that. Chantal would look at the carpenters, the cobblers, the dock workers and the hunters, and tell them about a long-forgotten kingdom made of shining stones and full of happy, hard-working men and women, about a king who loves his subjects so much he moves among them in disguise and helps those who have given themselves selflessly to king and country. And then she sang about a carpenter, or a cobbler, a dock worker or a hunter who received such secret blessing. And by the end of her first song, someone in the audience was ready to go home. He left wordlessly, entranced, driven. Her song had renewed whatever spark of enthusiasm for life itself that life in the bustling, cloying trade-capital of Teristra could often sap. And for everyone remaining, Chantal always had one more song. She could sing them into the dawn, but never did. The next night, there was always at least one returning member of the audience. He thought it was just because he liked her music, or maybe her face, but she knew. He had seen others receive that glow, but he couldn't put it into words. All he could do was listen and hope.

But one night, not long after I was born, a slight young woman with simple blonde hair in a plain white dress does not take the stage in Teristra's largest Haven, just as she hasn't for the past six months. It is a Hunting night; people do not come and go. The doorman looks sullen but alert, waiting for desperate knuckles to pound against the door; the lantern on his counter is cold and dead. Saucy-Sassy is on Healing duty, and no one pats her rump. The balconies are quiet but for hushed conversation, and the firepit crackles low and cautious. The Havenkeeper, a portly man with cheeks good for both grinning and glowering, keeps his sigh in check; it is barely Eyemoon, according to the notched candle melting into its saucer on a shelf behind him. Hours and hours yet. He is polishing the same glass he's been polishing most of the night, and trying not to watch the entrance. Havens outside the city have to keep their doors open, always, but here in the civilised heart of Zieger, the concept of 'Haven' has dwindled, and actual refugees from the Hunt are almost unheard of. It isn't even called a Haven anymore by most of the locals, who have named it after another function, this one neither archaic nor official: The All-Trades Inn.

Other than the woman in a dull ruby dress, rumpled and wrinkled with remnants of radiance, the bar is bare. Behind her slouched back, she can hear only sporadic half-sentences. No crowd blocks the distant fire from prickling warmth against her spine, although it is doing a poor job compared to the drink. She'd always enjoyed a little before a show, a little more after. She liked to brag that her ballads are so intoxicating, just singing them leaves her breath thick and dizzying. I think even my father stopped believing that one eventually.

"Do you know what might be good?" Jerich asks her, still twisting his cloth into the glass. She doesn't look up from her own glass, which is half-empty for the time being. He's asked this before, and when she doesn't answer, he says the same thing each time. "A bit of a song. Cheer things up. Isn't that why you're back?"

But it was more than her hoarse voice that worked whatever charms made her 'The' Chantal. Her smile was never simple, and people always said too much when she let it out to play.

"Well, isn't it?" Jerich presses when she only stared up at him through her scraggly hair, lips wolfish and never far from the glass's rim. "You couldn't stay home even tonight, and you knew it'd be quiet. Not my place to ask, but you've been performing here for years. You know the off-nights. I did say you had open tap for as long as you sing here, least I can do. Why don't you accept just a bit of pay, Chant?" The Havenkeeper tries not to sound smug, but it's difficult to remain humble when you think you're helping someone out of their spiral. "Now there's your baby to think about, carpenters aren't exactly well-paid...and yet you know you can pull the biggest crowds in the city—"

"Shut your fucking mouth," the great songstress Chantal grumbles. "Was never about the money. Just about the song. And just how much of that do you think I can do now? My gut feels like an empty, swollen sac and my breasts throb even when the little bitch isn't sucking them dry. I *have* brought in the crowds for you, Havenkeeper, and all I ask is a night or two to take it easy, to get back into the feel of things. Tell me," she coos, eyes narrowing around a wicked thought. "How's business been for the past six months or so?"

"...Fair enough," Jerich replies, and refills her glass without being asked.

Outside, the wind rises and rattles the few windows of the All-Trades. One of the less-subtle distinctions of the place is that it keeps its own time, ruled only by the ebb and flow of custom. Not even the small gap in the ceiling, several stories directly above the firepit, easily reveals whether it is day or night out there. Despite that, Chantal always sings only at night.

"Thank you." She takes a slow swallow of the beer, sniffs and turns her bleary eyes downward again. "I'll be at it again soon. In no time, I promise. It's just so...hard to think about anything."

"For Eph's sake, Chantal, why don't you just go home and be with your family? Pardon my language."

"I'd expect worse from other people, Havenkeeper," the devout and pious Chantal says. "Trying to show me just how worried you are that the 'Trades might be losing its local celebrity? Pffft. No need to blaspheme for that. God knows I was done with the thing the moment it came out. If only she'd...great, now I'm the one spouting sacrilege. Like I said, I'll be back in form soon enough." She drains the glass to half-way again.

" 'The thing'," Jerich echoes.

Chantal draws a breath, sniffling again. "Has a name, right? Of course she does."

The main doors shudder and before anyone has time to look, the deep boom of impact prompts Jerich's very polished glass to slide from his hands. The doorman grabs his lantern and it flares into life. Armed, he evacuates his post; the Havenkeeper steps back from the shards and catches Saucy-Sassy's eye; the buxom serving girl storms down the stairs, dodges furniture and a few stunned customers.

"It's a good name, too," Chantal breathes into her drink.

Great wooden doors almost fly off their hinges as doorman and Healer wrench them open and the chill rushes in, blasting both of them back. Veterans, they maintain their footing and look down at the body, then at the doors. The doorman steps over the doorway, holding the lantern out. He waves it left, then right, then left again, but the light flame doesn't diminish. He nods; Saucy-Sassy is kneeling beside the body, touching it with a care and attention many of her patrons would pay almost anything to receive. This person has, unfortunately, paid a higher cost than she'd ask of anyone. Her expression, so unlike her fiery hair, waxes ashen as the doorman closes the door and bends to lift the corpse.

"Drained?" the Havenkeeper asks from the bar, pausing mid-sweep.

"Almost," Chantal says, and upends her drink.

"Not you," Jerich snaps.

"Drained," Saucy-Sassy says, shrugging and dragging her feet back towards the stairs. "At least he's at peace now."

"*Vahm en*," Chantal mutters out of habit, and thumps her empty glass on the wooden bar a few times, glaring at Jerich. "*I'm* not dead yet, so keep 'em coming, eh?"

The doorman lumbers into a side room, the body slung over his shoulder like a slab of meat wrapped in rags. Jerich pours Chantal another drink, noticing the clothing of the Hunted is tattered, mismatched. Of course only the poorest Teristrans are out there this night. It doesn't stop him from grimacing, right as Her High-and-Mightiness screeches, "Jerich, stop! It's full!"

But he hasn't filled her glass to overspilling. Occupational instinct pulls his hand and Chantal is forced to drink by leaning over and lapping, slurping. I wish I could have seen that.

The doorman closes the side room off and returns to his post after retrieving the lantern, which once again ignites the moment he lifts it, and flicks out upon its return to the counter. Saucy-Sassy stays out of sight.

"Shit," Chantal says, licking her lips as the liquid's level lowers. "Look at you. The Haven's doing its job and you're all shocked and shaken. Better than the alternative, I say."

"You're not here to *say* things, Chantal," Jerich points out, but what he really wants to say is 'you're not here to drink yourself to death'. What he really wants to do is shake her, hard. He really should have.

"I even gave her a beautiful name," the songstress says, pointedly ignoring Jerich's implication. "Eyes like…I don't know. Green. Sea. Peas. Spinach. Moss. You couldn't call them 'Jade', but I did."

"It is a beautiful name," her number one (and currently only) supporter agrees. "The Adventures of Princess Jade. That could work."

"You want me to sing about a little monster that does nothing but cry and make a mess of herself?"

"Don't think about what she is," Jerich says with that off-handed wisdom that comes to him so easily whenever he isn't really trying, that I so loved about him. "Sing about what she could be."

And I think it was just like the doorman's lantern. The moment something living, warm touches it, it too becomes warm and living. Before me, Mother was vivacious, energetic, frenetic: she was alive with song and dream. With me within her, Chantal's already inflamed heart swelled to capacity as it tried to keep up with her belly. She couldn't perform but she didn't need to; her song was about to be realised. Then I was no longer within her, but she was without me. Not even her famous talent for exaggeration could pretend this fatty little frog, with its head the shape of a bruised melon and its fingers chubby and clumsy, was the gift from God for which she'd waddled, vomited and yet still prayed. There was no song powerful enough to make of me any more than what I was.

And, of course, there were my ears.

"Because she could be anything," Jerich adds, scooping the last of the shattered glass into a pan.

Chantal knew the fat would eventually be filled; the fingers would lengthen and learn. But there was no explanation for those monstrous ears. Daddy couldn't even accuse her of the obvious, because everyone knew that a woman taken by the Fey died in labour. My parents didn't consult any priests, and kept the nature of me naturally out of sight, and likely out of mind as well. But they had to deal with it anyway. Daddy called me a miracle, and said that even if the child wasn't his, at least everyone was alright. Later, I realised this only made Mother even angrier. But at the time, she didn't want to fight. Just wanted to get back to her life. Unfortunately, I had other ideas, and my rejecting her milk was just the permission she needed to drown it all out, night after night. One of the first sounds I can remember is her being sick out back of our cottage. I guess nothing really changed from when I was a lump in her gut: I was making her throw up in the morning again.

"Think about those who aren't as fortunate as you," the Havenkeeper says, and my mother, biting back her sniping ideas of 'fortune', empties the glass and places her hand over the rim. Jerich hasn't reached for the bottle; he's looking past her, at Saucy-Sassy, who is chatting with the doorman, wringing her once-white-now-red hands though a towel the same colour. "Think about—"

And whatever else he says, she doesn't hear it and won't remember it. Chantal just slinks from her stool and steers herself towards a door deeper into the Haven. It's far from her first trip to the Water Room tonight, but it's the first time in many nights that she almost doesn't make it in time. But this time it's not to be sick; if anything, her squatting over the scented Hole is exactly the opposite.

That's how epiphanies work. Just like peeing. You can drink water, beer, wine, even milk, but what comes out is always the same golden stream. And only you know when it's ready to come, when the processes of transformation are done and it's time to release. Pressing, urging, demanding. Also, best to do it in private, because even a trickle of relief can turn into a gush of embarrassment. Even though everyone does it; you die if you don't. I've seen her scribbling frantically, the final step in her mystical, forbidding art. She never looks so vulnerable, so open to everything as when she's bringing it all together and letting it all out for the first time.

And by the time Chantal's finished, when the faint odour of urine stings her nose, the door is almost ready to be opened. She stands, steps away and listens to the silence of the Hole as it takes over her role. You can't drink Holewater, not even from the really expensive, private stalls of the All-Trades, but it's definitely not piss anymore. Even that banal fact feeds into Chantal's current state and will later emerge as an image worthy of poetry.

She exits the Water Room with the same dazed, enthralled expression so common to her audience. She's too dazed and enthralled to enjoy what this means, but she's enjoying being dazed and enthralled.

"Feel better?" Jerich asks neutrally, letting the words play themselves into whatever shape she needs to hear.

"I will," Chantal replies as she retrieves her satchel from under her stool. She holds onto the bar with her left hand even after straightening.

"What are you doing? You can't go home now." The Havenkeeper almost leans into the last word, because he's made it clear he does wish she'd gone home, or just not come in the first place.

"I'm going to need water, Jerich," Chantal says as she looks at him, and then away at a table in the shadows under the multi-tiered walkway. "Water and bread. And that's all."

He's too much the professional to say anything, to do anything more than nod at her back as the faded songbird finds a new nest. You can run a lamp on alcohol if you have to, and you can make alcohol from all sorts of vegetation. But to really keep a fire burning, you have to dig deeper, tap some heavy, primal blood thick with dormant darkness. You can't just boil a few potatoes and use a few tricks when you want to feed the sober, frenzied flame that both schemes and dreams. It demands sacrifice; it is just like the nurturing Night, hungry and holy. So when Chantal takes only bread and water, when she takes her leave, what she's really doing is taking herself apart, apart from everyone, and restructuring all those unrelated ideas, notions and whims, and she's using the only glue that suffices. She might as well be writing each verse with her blood, her spittle, her urine, coating her nails with all the precious ink her body can spare and tear against the paper her reckless, helpless release.

Chantal stayed out until just before dawn, not looking up even once as Saucy-Sassy maintained a steady supply of what the songstress requested. Mother took her leave of the table in the shadows only to use the Water Room, and two of those trips were just to conceal brief outbursts of dangerous overflow; as I grew up, she would occasionally grip my own arm and dig her nails in, all the while keeping her eyes closed as though trying to steady herself. I didn't cry out, not after the first few times. Jerich also knew better than to question the tiny scratches up and down the woman's arms as she stalked back to her table. She wasn't drinking, feeling sorry for herself or exploding at him. She wasn't even really there anymore…which is why he hardly noticed when she left, either.

She came in the door just as Daddy was making breakfast, and I was due to feed. On some whim I'll never understand, Mother took the milk away from Daddy right as he was about to dribble some into my mouth. She even kissed him, licked the milk away from his now-speckled beard and drank the bowl before he could protest. She just smiled at him, tired but full, wordless but complete. And because he was my Daddy, he left for his work as Chantal became my cow. And I accepted this just as readily as Daddy accepted her absences and arrivals, her movement in and out of our world.

Chantal was not seen at the All-Trades for a month. Since she hadn't been performing anyway, no one really missed her, although everyone listening to whoever was singing that night felt some unnameable twinge, some nostalgic tug on the strings of an instrument they owned but didn't know how to play. But no one actively thought about her, because she was not meant to be there. She was at home. She slept soundly every night because for that month, her child did the same. Her husband provided for the tiny family, and for a tiny while, it seemed that Chantal had been rewarded for her decision.

But if it ended there, there'd be no use me telling you. This is what she told me: once she understood who I really was, it was time to tell everyone else. To share the miracle; to teach the lesson.

The Jaydemyr Saga continues in **Gildenhammer: The Beating of her Heart**